I've travelled the world twice over,
Met the famous: saints and sinners,
Poets and artists, kings and queens,
Old stars and hopeful beginners,
I've been where no-one's been before,
Learned secrets from writers and cooks
All with one library ticket
To the wonderful world of books.

© JANICE JAMES.

THE SHAWLMAKERS

In 1870, the Allen family of Kilbarchan, Renfrewshire, are weavers. The young Allens are growing up fast. There is clever, handsome Dougie, for whom the family is scrimping to send to university. There is Meg with her heart set on a local minister, ambitious Elsie, and jealous, flighty Bella; and there is lovely Jessie, who becomes mother to young Lilias when Mrs. Allen grows too ill to manage. It is Jessie who tells of the Allens' joys and tragedies, and their struggle to make ends meet in a fast-changing world.

ISOBEL NEILL

THE SHAWLMAKERS

Complete and Unabridged

ULVERSCROFT
Leicester

First published in Great Britain in 1992 by
HarperCollins Publishers
London

First Large Print Edition
published January 1995
by arrangement with
HarperCollins Publishers
London

British Library CIP Data

Neill, Isobel
    The shawlmakers.—Large print ed.—
    Ulverscroft large print series: general fiction
    I. Title
    823.914 [F]

    ISBN 0–7089–3226–6

Published by
F. A. Thorpe (Publishing) Ltd.
Anstey, Leicestershire

Set by Words & Graphics Ltd.
Anstey, Leicestershire
Printed and bound in Great Britain by
T. J. Press (Padstow) Ltd., Padstow, Cornwall

This book is printed on acid-free paper

Acknowledgements

The author wishes to thank staff at the following: Paisley Reference Library; Paisley Museum; The National Trust Cottage, Kilbarchan; Mitchell Library, Glasgow; Boots, Nottingham; Ashe Consumer Products Ltd; also, Dr Ian Campbell, University of Edinburgh, Barbara Acton and Claire Rayner.

1

IT was Lilias Day, 1870, just after my tenth birthday. Kilbarchan had been astir from early morning. People were out in the village streets putting finishing touches to the floral arches. Crowds of visitors and returning Habbies would walk under them later in the day. It always irked me that I couldn't call myself a Habbie though I was born in Kilbarchan like Dougie, my big brother, and my four big sisters, Jean, Meg, Elsie and Bella. You see, to be a Habbie, you have to be born in Kilbarchan of parents born in Kilbarchan and ours moved to the village after they were married.

The name came from Habbie Simpson, our famous piper and poet. We had been told at school that Robert Burns admired him greatly and adopted the Habbie stanza. Dougie often sang that funny song about Maggie Lauder and I would join in at, 'There's nane in Scotland plays sae weel since we lost

Habbie Simpson.'

Everybody knew that the Renfrewshire weavers were the best in Britain and we knew that the Kilbarchan ones were the best of the lot. At first Faither had rented our lovely wee cottage with its stone weaving shed in the garden. But he had worked away steadily at his loom and in ten years managed to buy the property. Then as each of my sisters left school, he bought another loom. Jean is nearly fifteen years older than me. She married Tam when I was seven and went to live in Johnstone — that's two miles and a bittock from Kilbarchan — but it didn't stop her walking all the way up the hill to Killy every morning to work at the beautiful shawls that she and Meg turned out.

Even at that early hour on Lilias Day, the women were in their braws giving an anxious twitch to the clean net curtains or hanging the canary's cage out in the warm July sun. Mind you, that sun had a lot of competition from the array of polished brass door handles.

I sensed all the hustle. After all, that fair had been the highlight of my year

2

since ever I could remember. The bands and the rest of the procession would line up to march round the village. All the groups would be dressed up to represent the various phases of Kilbarchan's history from as far back as the Druids and the monks of St Barchan who came to oust them.

But Lilias Day 1870 was different. In fact things seemed to have been different for months, especially between Faither and Dougie. Something was wrong but I couldn't tell what. They didn't get into the furious arguments that upset me any more. This was worse. There was a sort of wariness between them. And Dougie, my big brother and hero, would go off whenever he could, taking long walks, coming back without a word and slipping up to his bedroom. We had all been so proud when he came out top at the big school at Johnstone. Dougie was clever, you see, and was going to university in November but when Faither had said, "Well done, lad," Dougie muttered, "Thanks," and turned on his heel. Even Mam seemed to have changed a bit, always sitting

3

down for wee rests instead of bustling about attending to our needs. Sometimes when I got home from school I'd find one of my older sisters at the big wheel in the living room where Mam usually sat winding the pirns for the weaving shed.

Then there had been that whispered conversation I'd heard between Jean, my eldest sister, and Meg, the next in age.

"I warned Tam before we married, I'd go through that for nae belted earl."

"But Mam loves us all," Meg spoke in that gentle way she has.

"Aye, maybe." Jean's voice was always sharp. "But she's 42, she's brought up six o' us and she's too old now for this sort of caper."

They clamped their lips firmly when they saw me and I knew it would be useless to ask questions. Jean could be quick — and not only with her tongue. Many an undeserved slap had come my way for being too near at the wrong time.

But in spite of all that, I had been relieved to see Jean walking up the brae that Lilias Day morning and had run to meet her in sudden tears, crying, "Oh,

Jean, Jean, you don't usually come on a holiday."

"What's wrong? Is it Mam?" Her step had quickened.

"Aye. How did you guess?" I asked, puzzled. "She went to bed early last night because she had a sore head but it's got worse. She keeps making funny wee groans."

Jean was almost running by then and I had a bother keeping up with her as I answered her quick-fire questions.

"What's Faither doing?"

"Mam sent him out to get on with his work but he's just smoking . . . "

"Aye. Men! All right for them. Has he sent for Nurse Duncan?"

"Nurse Duncan?" I asked. "But Mam just usually takes a cup of tea when she has a sore head."

"She'll need more than a cup of tea the day, I'm thinking."

We were in the living-room by then. Jean started issuing her orders while she hung up her shawl and unpinned her bonnet.

"Bella . . . Elsie . . . out to the weaving shed with you. There's mouths to feed.

5

Meg . . . aye, I see you've put the place to rights. You'd better light the range, I think. We'll be needing an awful lot of hot water. You, Jessie, get the sticks for the fire and help Meg. When I've seen Mam, I'll maybe need you to fetch Nurse Duncan."

I had the sticks in my arms and was crossing the passageway when Jean opened the bedroom door. I heard Mam's voice, faint and weary, from the bed, "Oh, Jeanie lass, I'm real glad to see you."

"I didna like the look o' you last night, Mam. Is it time to fetch the nurse?"

"I'm not too sure."

"We'll send for her. She can aye come back if it's too early."

I heard Jean's quick footsteps and darted off to join Meg.

★ ★ ★

Nurse Duncan's knocker winked as brightly as the others in the lane but failed to summon Nurse Duncan. In desperation I tried again and again till my frenzied attack brought two neighbours from their gardens.

6

"Who is it, b' God?"

"Shush, it's wee Jessie Allen. Is it your mother, lass?"

"Aye. She's got an awfully sore head," I said.

The women looked at each other, one of those adult looks that made me uneasy. Were they laughing at me? But, no, their faces were anxious, too. The younger one turned to me. "You try the fleshers', lass. She's got visitors the night. She'll be needing meat. I'll see if she's at old Aggie Shaw's. She dresses her leg for her every day."

As my feet flew over the cobbles my mind worked furiously. Jean had guessed it was Mam before I even told her. But then, Jean had noticed something wrong with Mam the night before. But these women, Mrs Macarthur and Lizzie Forsythe, they hadn't seen Mam and they had guessed. Could it be that Mam had something serious, a dreadful disease that everyone else knew about? Was that why Faither was standing at the back of the weaving shed, puffing his pipe till he made a reek like a bonfire?

I went flying into the fleshers' and

collided with the big stout woman who was talking over her shoulder to someone.

"Here, lassie, can you no' look . . . Oh, it's you, Jessie. Steady there! Is it your Mother?"

"Aye," I gasped. "She had a sore head all night, Nurse Duncan."

"Sore head. Aye, she would have, that's right. Just you help me home with my parcels and I'll pick up my bag. Is your Faither with her?"

"No, he's outside by the weaving shed. Jean sent Elsie and Bella out to work and Meg's kindling the range."

"So, Jean's there! Did your mother send for her?"

"No, but she said she didna like the look of Mam last night."

"Aye. She's a sensible lass, your Jean. A sharp tongue, maybe, but a guid heart. I mind fine the way she used to look after her wee sisters when she was just a wee tot herself. A rare help to your mother, aye." We were at her door by then and she got me to open it. Then she went off to put the meat somewhere cool. In spite of her bulk Nancy Duncan was deft in her movements. I watched her pack her starched white apron and cap, then a big rubber sheet.

"What's that for?" I asked.

"Oh, I need that when . . . " She stuttered and stumbled a bit then came out with a rush, "I might need to give your Mam a nice wash if she's been sweating all night."

There was a gentle rap at the door and Lizzie Forsythe came in. I hopped from one foot to the other while they discussed arrangements for feeding Nurse Duncan's visitors, then we were off, hurrying through the decorated streets.

* * *

In the hubbub of her arrival I was ignored so I wandered out to the weaving shed. At the far end Faither seemed to be concentrating on setting up an elaborate shawl. He had already been working on it for several weeks and I knew the job would not be completed for many more. If he had heard the nurse arrive, he gave no indication. Elsie and Bella were working furiously. I knew by Bella's heightened colour that her excitable nature was roused to fever pitch. Even Elsie, dreamy Elsie, was concentrating as if her life depended on it. If Mam only had a headache, they wouldn't be so upset, I reckoned. But Nurse Duncan would know and she would be in the bedroom with Mam.

Quickly I threaded my way through the aromatic sweet williams and pinks till I was under the open bedroom window. The briar rose was big enough to screen me from the weaving shed if I crouched down.

My arrival scattered a shower of soft white petals round me. I inhaled their scent. Mam and Nurse Duncan were murmuring softly. It seemed to go on for ever but no matter how I strained the sound of their voices could not reach me above the buzz of the bees, busy around me. My knees began to ache but the slightest change of position dislodged a tell-tale shower of petals and caused an angry flurry among the bees. I was thinking of giving up when I heard Nurse Duncan's voice as she walked round the bed.

"It's no wonder you're tired, Bess," she was saying. "I'd like fine to have the doctor to see you. He's down at Johnstone at the hospital this morning. Could Wattie or your Dougie ride down and give him a message?"

"No . . . no . . . I think we should wait and see. Wattie's that upset; I sent him out to get on with his work."

"Well, Dougie?"

"Dougie just disappears these days with a book in his hand. We've hardly had a word out of him since he found out. It's embarrassing for him at his age, you see. Sometimes I see him look at his faither as if he hated him . . . Well . . . he's too young to understand the right way about it, but oh, my heart's sair for Wattie when I see the hurt on his face."

"A kick up the backside is what that lad needs, Bess."

I gasped in disbelief. It was Dougie they were talking about! Dougie who was so clever; who had come out top in nearly all his subjects at his big school at Johstone; who knew Latin and Greek and physics — whatever that was — and mathematics and chemistry. Dougie who had started designing shawls when he was only fourteen and whose designs, Faither said, were as good as any of the ones done by the specialist designers in Paisley. Rich ladies chose the shawls Faither sold to the merchants even though they were very expensive. How could anyone talk about my lovely big brother like that? Dougie was always ready to help when he was needed. He could do any of the jobs in the weaving shed and tell you interesting things about the world while he was doing them, too. Dougie would saddle Rusty and ride down to Johnstone like lightning if he knew Mam needed the doctor. But where was Dougie? There were so many places he could be . . .

I knew what I must do. Hadn't Dougie taught me how to saddle Rusty? Hadn't he let me ride the patient mare round the field when no-one was about? This was an emergency, that's what Dougie would call it. I would slip up to the farm myself and saddle Rusty. Then I would gallop so fast that nobody would see my petticoat and drawers and the doctor would come and Mam would get better.

I lost no time in slipping out of the garden by the back way. Soon I was darting past the outlying cottages and making for the farm. Dougie always hung the harness on the same hook at the back of one of the barns. The hook was high but I could stand on a bucket. Then suddenly I remembered Queenie and a cold fear clutched me while the blood began to pound in my head. Queenie was what the adults called a one-man-dog. The collie would do anything Rab Shaw told her but even Dougie steered a wide berth when Queenie was on her own.

There was no sign of her when I reached the barn. I got down the heavy saddle but as I struggled to hump it across the yard there was a frightening rush and Queenie was snapping at my heels. I suppose my nerves were already stretched to the limit. I found myself screaming uncontrollably till suddenly the kitchen door was flung open and Rab's coarse voice rang out. "Whit the bluidy hell?" Then he rounded the corner.

"Queenie you daft bitch, get oot o' it . . . Heel, you bluidy bitch!" Queenie dodged the quick cuff he aimed at her before he turned to me. "You shouldna scream, Jess. It just excites her. Here, here, whit's wrang? It's no' like you to be sae upset."

I gasped and sobbed, "It's Mam. She needs the doctor and Dougie's no' there. I'm going to gallop to Johnstone."

"The hell you are! Dougie went up the hill no' that long ago. Here, Queenie, earn you keep, you daft bitch. Fetch Dougie . . . Dougie . . . *fetch Dougie!*"

Rab was waving his brawny arm in an arc as he spoke. Queenie, ears cocked, watched him intently then shot off like an arrow.

Rab turned to me. "Now, lass, we'll catch Rusty and saddle her. If there's nae sign o' Dougie by that time, I'll ride doon to Johnstone masel'. It's no' fitting for a wee lass like you. Now, just dry your tears and fetch Rusty to me. She's aye been used to your voice just the way Queenie's used to me."

The russet mare came instantly when I called but jostled and nuzzled me continuously as I led her back to the yard.

14

"She's looking for her carrot," I told Rab. "I forgot to bring her one."

"She'll get it when she gets back," he said. "Steady noo, Rusty . . . Just leave it to me, lass."

I watched Rab's strong work-bitten hands adjusting and securing the straps. Golden hairs stood straight out on his thick arms among the sprinkling of enormous freckles. He had put on a clean muffler and cap while I was up at the field fetching Rusty, so he had meant what he said about riding down to Johnstone himself. Some folk didn't like Rab — said he was coarse and a tink: that he drank too much and had a rough tongue. Mam was never too happy about letting me go up to the farm but Dougie always said that I'd come to no harm. And Dougie knew everything, in my opinion — certainly more than Nurse Duncan. What did she mean that he needed a kick up the backside?

Rab was leading the mare out towards the lane. He turned to me, "We'll see if there's ony sign . . . Aye . . . see . . . there they are; she's found him."

15

I saw Dougie, tiny in the distance, shade his eyes then break into a run at the sight of us. Queenie turned her head and gave one sharp bark before starting on her own way back to Rab. He waited till he saw her streaking across the last field then, handing me the reins, said, "You haud the mare, lassie. I'll get Queenie before she scares the beast." He walked towards the gate the collie was making for and caught her as she hurtled over. "Weel done, lass," he said. "Now, back to the house with you and get a drink . . . Quiet, noo . . . " He was ushering her firmly across the yard as he spoke. I fidgeted with vexation as I waited, torn between pity for Dougie who must be bursting his lungs running so fast in that heat, and poor Mam who needed the doctor. Rab was back by my side by the time the last twist of the hill path brought Dougie into view again.

Rab's coarse laugh rang out as he bellowed, "It's a pity you canna squeeze under the hedges like Queenie."

"What's wrong?" Dougie called painfully. "Is it Mam?"

"Aye, it is. Your wee sister was havering

about galloping to Johnstone hersel'."

Dougie was soon panting beside us. "Johnstone?" he asked. My voice was shaking as I answered him. "I heard the nurse say she would like the doctor to see Mam."

"Did she not ask Faither?"

"She wanted to, but Mam said he was that upset and to wait a wee while. Then the nurse asked about you and Mam didn't know where you were and the doctor is at the hospital in Johnstone so I thought I'd try to go . . . " My voice broke.

Dougie had mounted while I was speaking. He leaned over quickly to pat my head. "You did just fine, Jess. Go back and tell them I'm on my way. Maybe in just over half an hour you could start walking down to meet me and we'll walk Rusty the rest of the way together."

I felt a great surge of relief as Dougie galloped off. Everything would be fine now that he had taken over. I was sure of that. Dougie was so clever. He could speak to anyone. He would tell the doctor that the nurse wanted him to see Mam and the doctor would come just like that! I had dreaded that part of the mission more than meeting Queenie, more than perching astride the old mare with my drawers showing all the way to Johnstone.

There had been that time nearly two years before when my stomach had ached and ached and I vomited. Mam had been that worried she had sent for the doctor. I could just picture his stern red face and greying whiskers as he leaned over me and demanded, "Now, young lady, where's the pain?"

I had been terrified. Not a squeak would come, try as I might. His stubby fingers were poking my stomach while he looked at me so fiercely that I was mesmerized.

"Stealing apples, eh?" he had shot at me and I immediately burst into guilty sobs. The doctor had stood up, snapped his bag shut and been out of the door in an instant with Mam hurrying after him. There was a sort of barking sound before the horse was whipped up, then Mam was back in the room, shaking her head disapprovingly and asking why I hadn't told her instead of wasting the doctor's time like that. My pent-up guilt had burst its bounds then and Mam had rocked me in her arms and said, "There, there, now, we'll talk about it tomorrow."

'Tomorrow' brought a confession from this little sinner and a gentle talk from Mam. Stealing apples from people's gardens was just like taking things from their houses and I would never do that, would I? Shaking my head vehemently I had caught sight of Faither winking at Mam and then I'd seen Mam's mouth go funny as if she would like to laugh but wouldn't.

Nothing more was said about that episode but I vowed there and then that no matter how ill I felt — dying, even — I would never, never let Mam send for that stern red face again.

But now, more than anything, I wanted to see the doctor's gig come up that hill from Johnstone. First I had to tell the family that Dougie was away. How was I going to do that without letting on that I had been eavesdropping? I could pretend that while I was pulling a carrot for Rusty I had just happened to hear the nurse.

But that was lying and Mam was strict about lying. Time was going on. Dougie had said I was to tell them so I had to do it. Perhaps they would be so cheered up they would forget to ask how I knew. The thought quickened my step.

The door of the weaving shed was open. Jean stood before Faither whose voice rose indignantly, "And how did you no' tell me sooner, lass?"

"Well, the·nurse told us on the quiet, like, but Mam didna want to upset you."

"Upset me! God! I'll away for Rusty."

That was Faither. Faither who never took the Lord's name in vain. I opened my mouth. No sound came. I gasped and heard a sort of croaking whisper, "Dougie's away."

The looms stopped as Elsie and Bella joined in staring at me.

"I heard the nurse," I stammered, "and I went up for Rusty. Rab sent Queenie to fetch Dougie from the hill. Rab saddled Rusty and then Dougie came running all the way and he said I was to tell you . . . " The tears which overcame me then were shed in Faither's arms as he stroked my long hair and murmured, "There, there, my bonnie lass."

"I never knew she was about when we were talking," muttered Jean. Then, raising her voice, "Give her threepence, Faither, and she can get a nice bit of neck mutton from the flesher. I'll make a good pot o' soup."

"It's a gey hot day for soup, Jeanie, lass."

"The range is on and we might as well use it. Besides, it'll maybe be gey late and the sun doon when we get to our dinner . . . and Mam might be glad o'a sup . . . "

"Right your are!" He counted the required pence into my hand as Jean hurried back to the house, but before gently closing my fingers over them he slipped in a farthing and with a wink whispered. "Mint humbugs are a very present help in time of trouble."

Jean's recipe in a crisis was work, work and more work. No sooner had I returned with the mutton than I was sent into the garden to pull carrots and pick parsley. In the back kitchen Meg was already chopping turnip into minute squares. It must be nearly time to go to meet Dougie, I reckoned. Jean would probably find another job for me — puddling lentils or washing dried peas. I sighed as I hurried indoors with my load of vegetables.

Meg's smile was understanding. "You want to go and watch for Dougie?" she asked. "All right, pet. Slip out the back way as soon as I've finished scalding the barley here. I'll keep Jean talking a wee while."

Thankfully I skipped down the road to the look-out stone. My jaw bulged satisfactorily over a mint humbug. Mam was still ill but Dougie was fetching the doctor and the doctor would know what to do. Faither had been pleased with me. Rab, too, had been kind in his own way, changing his bonnet and muffler like that. It showed he had a good heart. That's what Nurse Duncan had said about Jean. It just showed, didn't it? I had always dreaded Jean's sharp tongue and the ready slap that accompanied her scoldings. My heart had gone out to Elsie, the dreamy one of the family who could drive Jean mad with her inattention to instructions. Not that Elsie seemed to mind. Even as she apologized, a sweet half-smile would hover round her mouth while her eyes showed she was embarking on her next daydream. Most of the time Faither kept Elsie on the routine weaving — woollen shirtings and things like that — because she could not be trusted with the complicated designs. Yet it was always Elsie who mooned over the beautiful finished shawls, draping them round her and walking with her peculiar grace the length of the weaving shed, a faraway look in her eyes.

"Born to be a lady and not needed," Mam said once, watching her daughter's performance. "It'll no' get the wean bathed or your man's dinner ready, though."

Elsie's face had been bleak as she reluctantly peeled off the soft folds and handed the shawl back to Faither. Where did Elsie's dreams take her, I wondered? Often when we had to ask her things three times, Elsie would say, "Sorry, I was dreaming." But though I asked her time and time again what she had been dreaming about, the answer was always,

"Nothing, nothing, really." You couldn't spend all that time dreaming about just nothing. And just nothing would not bring that soft flush to Elsie's cheeks or the bright light that was almost like tears to her tawny eyes. Whatever they were about, Elsie was not willing to share her dreams with the rest of us. I asked Dougie about it once but he showed no interest. "She's away with the fairies, that one," he'd said.

"She speaks like you, Dougie."

"What d'you mean?"

"Well, she says things the way you do, the way the dominie does and the minister and the doctor an' folk like that. Yet she didn't go to the big school at Johnstone."

"I hadn't noticed. But if you want to get anywhere in life, Jessie, you have to learn to communicate and that means good clear speech that will be understood not just in Kilbarchan or Bridge of Weir . . ."

"Or Paisley," I took up the theme.

"Or among the black savages in Glasgow where I'll be next year, I hope."

That had been before Dougie passed all his exams at the big school. Dougie . . . yes, where was he? I shaded my eyes from the merciless glare of the sun. There was a horse but it couldn't be Rusty because . . . It *was* Rusty . . . but the figure in the saddle wore a top hat and I knew, though I couldn't see them, that grey whiskers would be fanning out below its brim. Where was Dougie? If the doctor had taken Rusty, Dougie would have to walk home in the sizzling heat of the sun. Quickly I slithered down from the rock and ran back to the cottage.

"I don't care if he comes on an elephant," was Jean's response to my news. "I just want that doctor here. Dougie can take care of himself. He's all the man he'll ever be by now, surely to patience. And you be ready to take Rusty to the trough when the doctor dismounts."

I hung about the weaving shed where I'd had a more sympathetic reception till I heard Rusty's hooves on the cobbles outside. Then I slipped out and stood behind Faither as he greeted the doctor. I kept my head down as I reached out silently for the reins. They were held firmly in one hairy hand as the Doctor tilted my chin up. "Taking her for a drink, eh?" he asked. "Good girl! Don't give her green apples, though."

I looked up in terror then saw that the blue eyes which had mesmerized me were twinkling. I heard that barking sound again. He was laughing at me. I gave him a wee smile as I took the reins and turned away.

"Break a few hearts, that one, I'm thinking," I heard him say to Faither as he ducked under the lintel of the front door. Grown-ups were funny, I thought. 'Unpredictable' was the word Dougie would use. And the doctor was the most unpredictable one I had ever met. What did he mean about breaking hearts? Mam usually said I was a good lass; so did Faither. And I was Dougie's favourite though he never said so. It was only Jean who complained and she complained about everybody. Unpredictable, that's what he was — but he would know how to make Mam better?

While Rusty drank her fill I counted the remaining humbugs in my pocket. I would have to keep plenty for Dougie. Jean had said we wouldn't be getting any dinner till night-time. But she had the girdle on the big range beside the soup pot and the big kettles. That meant she was making scones or oatcakes. Everything was different from usual. It was Lilias Day and everyone was on holiday. Yet Elsie and Bella were working in the weaving shed and even poor old Rusty had had to work instead of grazing contentedly in her field. On all the other Lilias Days I could remember, we had been up early to give a last shine to the house; Dougie had helped me to gather a big bowl of strawberries before taking me out to watch the last minute preparations being made for the procession. Then the whole family had sat down to dinner at noon so that we would be in plenty time to join the festivities.

Rusty had drunk her fill. I stood undecided. Should I go up to the farm again and maybe meet Queenie? Rusty would be startled if the collie rushed at her. No. I would lead the mare gently down the hill to meet Dougie and he could ride her to the farm.

I led her under the decorated arches, taking a roundabout way to avoid our house. Jeanie would be sure to find a job for me and I just wanted to be with Dougie; to ask him so many things.

Before I reached the look-out stone he was in sight, walking fast, his face red with exertion. I broke into a run with Rusty trotting beside me.

"What's going on?" he asked anxiously as we met up.

"The doctor's there with Mam."

"Nothing's happened, then?"

"What d'you mean?" I asked. "Mam's got an awfully sore head and Nurse Duncan thinks it's going on too long. That's why she wanted the doctor. And Jean's that bad-tempered . . . She's ordering us all about . . . "

"Jean's there? Who sent for her?"

"Nobody. She didna like the look of Mam last night so she came but she's on the rampage."

"A bit of a termagant, our Jean, but a very present help in time of trouble."

"Oh, I'd forgotten," I said, clutching my pocket and withdrawing the bag of humbugs.

"Started Lilias Day early, haven't you?" Dougie asked.

"Well," I said in a rush, "Jean asked Faither to give me threepence for mutton and he slipped me a farthing and said mint humbugs were a very present help in time of trouble."

Dougie threw back his head and laughed. "Good old Faither," he said. I joined in, happy. Everything was just fine. Mam must have been imagining things when she thought Dougie hated Faither. It would be her sore head that made her think things like that but the doctor would soon put that right. And the doctor wasn't an ogre after all.

We were walking back towards the farm. Dougie had the reins in one hand while the other rested on my shoulder. That meant he was pleased with me. It began to feel like Lilias Day after all.

★ ★ ★

Well, that was how Lilias Day 1870 started and I don't think life was ever quite the same for any of us again. Certainly it was fun eating a picnic lunch in the weaving shed with Dougie on the seat-tree beside me, threatening to tilt me off if I didn't finish my oatcakes and cheese before starting on the scones and raspberry jam. Dougie was going out of his way to keep us all cheery, I noticed, but Faither's smile was wan and Bella looked ready to burst into tears. Meg shuttled quietly between the house and the weaving shed carrying plates of Jean's light scones, jugs of milk and a kettle of tea. Dougie greeted the third visit with,

"My compliments to the cook, and where is she?"

"Seeing to the doctor's lunch."

"And I suppose Whiskers is having his in the parlour?"

"That's right." Meg turned away with a smile while I choked with laughter. Elsie and Bella giggled nervously but I saw that Faither, with hands clasped round his mug, was staring into the distance. The food on his plate was hardly touched.

The sounds of the gathering procession were filling me with restless excitement in spite of the tense atmosphere in the shed. It was gentle Meg who understood my difficulty. "Faither," she said, "don't you think Dougie could be taking the lassies to see the procession, or are you needing them here?"

"Oh . . . no. No . . . I was forgetting. It's Lilias Day . . . Aye . . . you take your sisters, Dougie, and here," he added, "treat them."

Dougie took the handful of coins rather reluctantly but then turned resolutely to me. He pursed his lips and put on Jean's voice. "And you, my lady, will get Dougie to carry a basin of hot water to your room and you'll give yourself a good wash and put on a clean dress and you'll brush that hair till it shines or I'll do it for you and it will hurt."

The processions and the side-shows were as good as ever but people kept stopping us to ask about Mam. Dougie was brusque, almost rude at times, answering them. Bella would keep clutching people's arms and whispering. Then they would turn and look back at me in a funny way I didn't like. Dougie won me a doll at one of the booths but it was a silly-looking thing you couldn't dress yourself and anyway, I was far too big for dolls. I was wondering how to thank him but he saved me any embarrassment. "It's too bairn-like for you," he said, "but maybe you could pass it on to some wee smout."

The crowds were thinning as we turned back home. I noticed that even Dougie's step seemed to slow down when we turned the corner of Shuttle Street — as if he were afraid of what he might find.

Out of habit I glanced into the weaving shed. Jean was sitting limp on a chair. Meg was applying damp cloths to her forehead. I gasped. Meg turned to reassure me. "She fainted but the doctor soon brought her round. He said to keep her in a cool place. Just leave her in peace for a wee while, Jessie. She doesn't feel like speaking. There's a nice surprise for you in the house, pet. Go in and see."

I joined the others in the living-room. Faither was sitting in his usual armchair by the fire but though he smiled at us, his face was grey and stubbly looking. Bella and Elsie were watching me excitedly. Did they know what the surprise was, I wondered? I turned to Dougie. He smiled at me encouragingly. Why? Then I heard a funny noise in the passageway. The door opened and in sailed Nurse Duncan with a squalling bundle.

"Here you are, Jessie," she called above the din. "Your new wee sister. Isn't she lovely?"

I stared in dismay at the red puckered face which seemed to be all mouth. "No, she's horrible," I gasped, "and Mam didna need another bairn."

"Tut-tut . . . what a funny thing to say! What will your Mam think . . . and the doctor. He's just saying goodbye to her now. He brought her the bairn to make her headache better."

Much of what happened in the next few hours is blotted by misery from my memory. I remember running so fast that I dodged even Dougie. Then I got caught up in a group of drunk trippers. I was struggling to get clear of them when I saw one of them holding Dougie. "You'll leave that wee lassie alone or I'll . . . " he was saying.

"She's my sister, you gowk." Dougie gave a heave which landed the man sprawling in the dust. Threatening voices

33

were raised all round us. Dougie elbowed two unsteady would-be attackers aside and, grabbing my hand, yelled, "*Run!*"

It was quite cold sitting by the burn under the birch trees but Dougie held me close, explaining things — some things but not everything I wanted to know. When I asked, "Why did the doctor not just give Mam the bairn when he arrived?" he hesitated.

"I'm not too sure about that. Maybe Jean or Meg could tell you. It's nice that they're calling her Lilias, don't you think?"

"No, who told you that?"

"Faither, when we got in. I think you went to the shed first."

"Aye. Jean was there. Fancy her fainting."

"Some folk can't stand the sight of . . . I mean the heat. Don't you like the name Lilias?"

"No," I said untruthfully. It was a lovely name — far nicer than 'Jessie'.

"Would you rather they had called her Beltane? That was the old name, you know. It was the Beltane Feast in the days when the people of Strathclyde were under the dominance of the Druids. It was changed by Baron William Cunninghame of Craigends in the early eighteenth century. He called it after his daughter Lilias."

I tried the word 'Beltane' and couldn't help giving a wee chuckle. Dougie smiled. "Mind you, I was none too happy when I heard they were going to call you Jessie."

"No, it's awful," I agreed. "I wish I had a nicer name."

Dougie was playing with a birch twig, not looking at me. He spoke as if he hadn't heard. "But now it seems quite a nice name because it means you, you see."

"Really?"

"When somebody says 'Jessie' I think of long golden hair and big eyes, blue as gentians . . . " He paused to make sure of his ground. "And a mouth that's always asking me questions and if we don't hurry back, Jean will have a few questions of her own to ask and I'll be getting the blame, for I'm 'the big yin'."

I laughed as he pulled me to my feet.

"I'll be 'the big yin' compared with Lilias."

"That's right. Only, for pity's sake, don't get bossy like Jean."

The rest of them had started dinner when we got in but Jean wouldn't allow us to take our places. "Mam's been asking for the pair of you so you can just tidy yourselves up and get ben there."

Somehow it was almost like going into church. Mam looked so different, almost a stranger . . . her voice gentle and quiet. I clutched Dougie's hand. Neither of us could find much to say. After a long pause we were glad to tiptoe out and tackle our belated dinner.

Surprisingly, Jean forgot to order me off to bed at the usual time. Half-heartedly I began to wash the latecomers' dishes. As I played with the soap bubbles I tried to puzzle things out. Held up to the window in the late evening sun, each perfect sphere showed enchanting pictures which gave no answer to the problems confronting me. Why were Dougie and Faither so different now? When the other men came into the weaving shed to have a crack with Faither in the early evening,

Dougie was no longer there, joining in the discussions. Nor did they engage in the fierce arguments which had sometimes frightened me; when Dougie would warn Faither that changes were in the air and that the weavers were depending too much on the shawl trade and that could change at the whim of fashion. Faither would say that if you turned out a good article — something better than the next man — it would aye sell.

Dougie's designs were very special. Faither kept them hidden in the sliding drawer under the seat in the bible chair. The bible chair was safe. It had lead weights inside it to stop it toppling over when you laid the big heavy bible on the shelf beside the left arm.

I studied a particularly fine bubble as I reflected. It was funny how people thought out these things. Dougie was good at that. What was he doing in the weaving shed, I wondered. Quickly I wiped the sink surround and skipping through the back door hurried to join him. A strand of honeysuckle brushed my face. Pausing to loop it up, I heard my name. It was wrong to listen, I knew, but nobody could blame me for tidying up the honeysuckle. It always got in a mess at that time of the year. Dougie was talking about me. "Jessie's an intelligent wee lass and it makes her sound a right gowk talking about Mam's headache like that. She asked me why Whiskers didn't give Mam the bairn as soon as he got here. Couldn't one of you enlighten her?"

Jean's voice was sharp with scorn. "And you're that enlightened, I suppose — glowerin' about wi' a face like fizz these last weeks; scarce a civil word to Faither; and Mam breaking her heart o'er the pair o' ye."

"It's all right for you. I've had to face the lads from school and their remarks."

"I hope you shut their foul mouths for them. Their mothers wouldna know them if I had my way."

Dougie snorted, "That's your answer to everything — lash out. Oh, it's hopeless. I see I'll have to talk to her myself."

"You'll do nothing of the kind. We'll keep her an innocent wee lassie as long as we can." Jean was resolute.

"And she'll get it from dirty talk in the playground?" he asked.

"Mair like frae her bible as we got it, eh, Meg?"

Meg's voice was gentle. "Aye, Dougie; best leave her for a wee while longer. A lassie has a lot of things to face."

I stood bewildered, breathing the sweet scent of the honeysuckle which always filled me with vague longings. The front door of the shed closed. There was silence for a few minutes; then I heard Jean's voice. "Was I hard on the boy, Meg?"

"Aye, Jean."

"I don't mean to be. My tongue just rins awa' . . . "

"He kens fine. He's a clever chiel."

"Tam says he's right about warning Faither. His faither minds when the Paisley weavers were the best-paid workers in the whole o' Britain. Then, no' that long after, there was a recession and they could hardly earn a tenth o' what they had had. Things are better noo but it's aye worth mindin', he says."

"Faither's that proud o' his two Jacquard looms," Meg ventured.

"Aye. There's no' mony folk can boast about gaitherin' the gear Faither has got. He's aye spent wisely — his ain looms, then his ain hoose and noo twa Jacquard looms replacing the auld yins."

Meg's voice was thoughtful. "There's no doubt about it. We've a lot to be thankful for. Nurse Duncan was telling me a wee while ago how Mam didna want us to grow up wi' weak legs by being strapped in a cradle or carried about in a shawl and she said you were such a help to Mam, keeping an eye on us so we could crawl about up in the bedroom or in the garden."

"I canna mind the time, Meg, when I didna hae something to dae. Noo, I'd better be getting doon to Tam. No' a word to him about me fainting, mind!" Jean warned.

Quickly I got to the back door and up to the safety of my bedroom. The clue was somewhere in the bible-but where? The box bed was too dark for reading in but if Jean came up to inspect me and found me still with my clothes on . . . The thing to do was to turn down the bed, undress and sit near the window.

Then if I heard Jean's step on the stair, I could dive into the bed and hide my bible under the pillow.

The treacherous sun set on me and Lilias Day ended long before I had reached the end of the 'begats' and I was forced to abandon my search. The bible was a gey long book, I realized, and at this rate it was going to take me ages to find the answer. I would just have to listen hard every time I was near Jean or Meg. Maybe Elsie and Bella knew too but they would be feart to tell me in case Jean got hold of them. And Jean on the warpath was terrifying.

So I became a dedicated eavesdropper. With Nurse Duncan in the house for a good part of the day and always asking me, 'Would you mind, pet?' I was kept too busy to listen in the weaving shed but that proved to be no bad thing. It seemed that an endless procession of women dropped in to bring 'a wee thing I knitted for the bairn'. Before that I had always found the women's gossip in the living room dreary stuff compared with the discussions that Faither and the other men had in the shed and the fascinating things Dougie could tell me. But now as I buttered scones in the back kitchen my ears were flapping. Every morsel of that gossip was treasured and hoarded to be juggled into shape. A deaf visitor was a great help, for then the raised voices carried clearly to me. Why were they warning Mam that she would have to rest a lot? A slow birth like that . . . " I had asked Dougie why the doctor hadn't given Mam the bairn right away. It was no good acting on his advice to ask the girls. Even gentle Meg wouldn't tell me. 'A lassie has a lot of things to face.' What did she mean by that?

Mam's headache was better but she was still in bed. I had asked Nurse Duncan about that. "I never let my patients up till the thirteenth day," was her answer. Then her face flushed and she said quickly, "You see, your Mam needs lots of rest to feed the bairn." Folk fed weans for a long time, I knew. Surely Mam wasn't going to stay in bed for months — or was it years?

That doctor was daft bringing Mam another bairn that we didna need. She just gave us all a lot of work. Surely he could have found some medicine that didna greet at night and land us wi' a big pile of washing every day. I remember humping a basket of snowy hippens out to the garden one morning and thinking that half the day seemed to be spent hanging them out and taking them in. Bairns were gey wet things! I supposed I had been the same. That set me wondering who would have been hanging mine out. Would it be Jean? Probably. Jean would be thirteen when I was born. When I had finished pinning the things out, I sat on the little wall to admire my handiwork blowing in the breeze and my mind wandered. Mam had been a long time recovering. What would she do when school started up again? As it was, Meg had taken over the pirn winding but Faither had nearly finished setting up the next shawl. It wouldn't do to have the expensive Jacquard loom lying idle. Meg would be starting the shawl. Only Faither could do the heavy work of the butchers' aprons and there was a steady demand for them.

So far all I had learned was that a slow birth was a bad thing. It left a woman tired. What did they mean by a slow birth? I'd heard that expression before somewhere — aye, up at the farm. Rob said it once about a calf. Maybe if I listened hard next time we went up for Rusty I would get the answer. It was funny how different the talk could be in places. Faither was always calming down the other men when they got indignant about the rates the wealthy manufacturers paid them. "Make the best of the system, lads," he would say. "Turn out a good article, you'll get a good price. And you've got your independence. You wouldn't have that in a factory, now, would you? I owe a penny to no man. I've got my home, my weaving shed, my looms. I'm blessed wi' a guid wife and bairns. No, I wouldna call the Queen my cousin."

Only with Dougie did he seem to lose patience. "Aye, lad, it would be quicker setting up the shawls if I let the beamers do it but I like my independence."

"You're the only one left, Faither, who doesn't use a beamer."

"Aye. But there's a lot o' restlessness about — grumbling about the Paisley manufacturers no' paying enough."

"They don't."

"Well, we're managing well enough. I'm not tied to any one of them. In this shed we can turn our hands to anything. I don't like all these threats o' strikes an' I'm not going to be caught up in it."

"Shawls won't always be in fashion, Faither."

"There have been shawls as long as I can remember, lad."

"Aye, Faither, but the pace of life is changing. Just look at the new railway, now. Folk have only to walk down to Bridge of Weir and they can get a train to Glasgow or Greenock. Last year at this time they had to get a canal boat from Johnstone to get to Glasgow and if you read back a bit, before the canal was constructed the folk here could live in Kilbarchan all their lives and never even get the length of Paisley."

"By all accounts they were contented — living in a bonnie wee place like this wi' braw gardens. And the things o' the mind have never been neglected. I doubt if many o' your rich mill owners have the fine collection o' books you can find among the weavers."

"I grant you that, Faither, but, you see, that was based on a small community prospering in hand-loom weaving. The fact that it was prospering has increased the numbers here. Because of the new mills in Paisley and elsewhere the prices are bound to drop. Hand-loom weavers will have to work gey hard and long hours to compete. There won't be time for books and philosophical discussions then. It'll be slave labour for the lot of you."

"And what are your fine proposals, my mannie?"

"Maybe the transport business."

"What?"

"Well, you harness the cart once a week and take the finished work to the agents in Paisley don't you?"

"Aye — "

"That isn't economical use of your time, or Rusty. I know at the moment you've plenty of work . . . butchers' aprons, shirtings and muslins. But the factories will soon take these over and compete once they have made some refinements to their looms. I doubt if they'll ever manage the rare shawls but they'll certainly manage a cheaper imitation. And anything that depends on fashion is precarious, anyway. The pace of life is quickening, Faither. Transport is going to be needed more and more."

"Well, son, maybe with all your fine learning you'll be able to set up your transport company. I'm quite content the way I am."

That argument, like many others, had left Dougie frustrated and angry. I had watched him fling himself out of the shed and followed him discreetly for a short distance to find out where he might be heading. It was up the hill to the farm. Aye! I heard something funny that day when I fetched a carrot for Rusty and followed Dougie up to the farm. Rab's voice was echoing round the yard. He was swearing as usual but Dougie had told me never to pay any attention when Rab swore; just to let it in one ear and out the other: farmers seemed to think that was the only language animals understood. So, I had listened to the bellowing voice and filleted out the bad words. "The bluidy day wasted, lad. That bugger o' a bull — broke down the pen! Lucky I had the pitchfork handy. It took me and twa o' the lads to catch him and thell we had nowhere right to put him. And whit a hell o' a mess he had made afore we catched him. It'll take a week to mend it a'. He's mair bluidy bother — "

Dougie interrupted him then, "Come on, Rab, from what I hear you make a wee fortune in fees around about. How many cattle does he service?' Then he had seen me and cried, "Jessie! What are you doing here?"

"I brought a carrot for Rusty. What did you mean about fees? Does Rab teach things?"

Rab's "Oh, Goad" and bellow of derisive laughter had disabused me of that idea.

Dougie was quick. "Rab thinks Thunderer is the worst bull in Christendom so I was suggesting he put him in a circus and charge people fees to look at him."

"Circus!" Rab was off in another fit of laughter. "You're a bit of a turn yourself, Dougie."

The joke seemed to have cured Dougie

of his bad mood and he had answered my questions quite patiently as we climbed. "Why can the beamers set up the shawls more quickly?"

"Because they've got the equipment, Jessie: large cylinders with pegs they can spiral the yarn round. They can make sure each length is exactly right. It makes no difference whatever to the finished work — having it set up by the beamer. I mean. Faither is just being obstinate in measuring it all out himself. Our shawls will always be expensive anyway because of the work involved. Only the rich can afford them now and they won't think it worth waiting for special designs once something nearly as good is being turned out quickly in factories. Anyway, as I see it, with all the changes in transport, women — even the richest — are going to want simpler clothes they can move about it. A wire cage or whatever covered in miles of flimsy material isn't much help when you're climbing into a railway carriage."

"They don't have miles of material," I had protested, and Dougie laughed at me.

"That's right. Put me in my place."
The business of the bull hadn't been
mentioned again.

Mam's voice suddenly jerked me out
of those daydreams. I jumped quickly off
the wee wall by the bee-skeps and ran
indoors with the basket.

"Are you all right, lass? You've been
out there a long time," she asked me.

"I just sort of started dreaming, Mam,"
I said. "I was thinking about who would
be hanging out my hippens when I was
wee . . . and things like that."

"I was blessed wi' Jean," Mam said.
"She was aye a rare helper and she got
the younger ones busy, too. Aye! Jean has
aye been a blessing an' I'm sure you'll be
the same, lass."

It was fine for Mam to praise Jean. She
didn't seem to realize how she bullied
us. I was thoughtful as I set about my
next task. Of course I knew I should
be helping to look after my wee sister
but if Mam didn't get stronger what
would happen when it was time for the
big school at Johnstone? I desperately
wanted to go there to learn all the
wonderful things Dougie had learned;

to join him in the exciting world that opened up far beyond Kilbarchan. That bairn had spoiled everything at home. What if Mam needed me too much? What if . . . The thought was too awful. A wave of foreboding shook me.

2

THE paper-dry leaves were irresistible. My scuffling feet sent them up in showers of yellow, orange and occasional crimson. There were millions of them, never two exactly alike, wonderful! And yet some folk, wielding their angry brooms thought that autumn leaves were just a nuisance. How could they? It was such a pity to burn all that loveliness. But the bonfires could be fun too, especially if Dougie was in charge. Dougie! I dropped the leaf and hurried homeward.

In a few weeks' time Dougie would be starting university. Then he would be leaving early in the morning while it was still dark and not getting home till long after we had finished tea. I had worried about what would happen to him when the cold weather came but he had reassured me, "I'll have my big boots and that muffler you knitted me for Christmas and my warm suit and the jersey Bella knitted me and my great big warm coat. I'll be like a wee steam boiler."

Dougie was doing his best to keep us all cheerful. Mam was still weak and tired but a few weeks earlier, when the August sun was scorching the hillsides, Dougie had arranged a couch for her under the old birch tree in the garden where she could rest during the day. Then he had decorated the whole house, starting with Mam's room. The weather held while the decorating was going on and we had lots of odd meals — 'bunfights' Dougie called them — in the garden. I had performed my chores happily, joining in with Dougie's cheerful snatches of song. "You sing the tune," he would throw at me from a bedroom window, "and I'll harmonize." This was while I was stringing out the never-ending washing.

The large stone boiler on its dais had been a secret terror to me. Firstly, there was the problem of lighting the fire. The fire-well went so far back that your sticks fell off the paper twists and disappeared where you couldn't reach them. You had either to risk stretching over the burning paper with the long iron cleik to claw the sticks back or wait till the paper twists you had made so laboriously burned themselves out. That meant starting the whole business all over again. Dougie had been furious the morning that he found me nursing a scorched wrist and my face smeared with tears.

"They've no right leaving you like this," he had hissed angrily. "I've a good mind to go out to that shed and tell them what I think of them."

"No, you mustn't!" My whisper was desperate. "Mam would see you and guess something was wrong."

That was only half the truth. By common consent in these days the family avoided any arguing which might upset Mam. But there was a more important reason for keeping Dougie out of the weaving shed. Jean and Faither were seizing the opportunity his decorating gave them to work furiously at the two lengths of cloth which would be presented to Dougie on his birthday in September. Then the tailor in Johnstone was going to make them into a suit and a coat for him. It had all been arranged but was to be kept secret. Jean would murder me if I let it out. So it was with relief I had seen his glance turn towards the tree in the garden.

"Right, pet. As quick as we can, let's roll some more twists. Then watch how I balance the sticks — that's the important bit."

Every morning after that Dougie had supervised me as I lit the boiler. He had also taken over the heavy task of wielding the big pole I used to lift the clothes out of the boiler and into the rinsing tubs. Now that I was at school all week I lost all that time with Dougie. I skipped faster till I was almost running. Every moment with Dougie was precious now.

But those precious moments flew by. The short golden days of October ended and one misty morning in November I stood by the look-out stone waving goodbye to Dougie till the last bend freed me to put my handkerchief to another use.

Meg took one look at my red-rimmed eyes. "Here, Jess, come closer to the fire and I'll pour you another cup of tea," she said. "He'll be back tonight, you know."

"But it'll never be the same again — "

"What d'you mean? He'll just be a wee bit longer getting home than he was from school."

"No," my voice was muffled, "it'll be different." How could I explain the desolation that had me in its grip — this feeling that Dougie would never belong to Kilbarchan again? True, he would still live with us but his mind would be soaring far away among all the wonders of Gilmorehill.

Meg's voice was at my elbow, "Come on now, sup up your porridge. Mam's feeding the bairn. You'll be able to nurse her for quite a while before school starts at ten o'clock. She likes to hear your voice. That'll let Mam lie down for a wee rest. She's feeling it too, you know. We're all her bairns."

"And he's her only son. I suppose he's special to her just the way he's special to me — though I love all my sisters," I added hastily.

"Aye, fine I ken." Meg's laugh was reassuring. Then she added more soberly, "I think there's an awful lot of things we don't understand . . . I mean about why we're attracted to some folk and no' to others. Dougie and you have aye had this special kind of love, you aye see the best in each other and I think that's what makes for a happy home — when you get twa folk, man and wife like that together."

"Like Mam and Faither?"

"Aye."

"Will you not get married, Meg?"

"I wouldna say that . . . maybe . . . Here, Jess, you hurry and get yourself dressed for school and then I'll bring the bairn through to you at the fire."

I swayed backwards and forwards, crooning gently to the rosy wee bundle. Gradually her twisting and turning stopped. Her brown eyes opened wide and a big gummy smile of recognition spread over her face. Then, as the song went on, her dark lashes fluttered and fell. I tiptoed gently through to the bedroom and tucked her into the clean wee bed Meg had prepared. Mam smiled appreciatively. "You're a good lass, Jessie," she said. "Mind you're not late for school."

In spite of the need for speed, I was

reflective. No one ever mentioned the big school at Johnstone these days. Certainly there was still time. Mam would get stronger — she was bound to — but even Dougie hadn't said anything about it. Of course, Dougie had a lot of things to think about. He was so thrilled about going to university and, just think, he was going to be one of the very first students in the grand new building they had built at Gilmorehill. I couldn't wait till night-time to hear about it. I broke into a run till I got to the school gate then tried to look dignified.

That first evening the hours dragged in spite of the succession of jobs that always seemed to be waiting for me. Then suddenly Dougie's steps rang on the flagstones and I flew to open the door.

"Here, here, Jessie. I've only been to Glasgow; not to Timbuctoo." He was gently disengaging me.

"Your coat feels cold and damp, Dougie."

"Just outside. See, feel the inside."

I ran my hands over the warm lining. Dougie whipped the big coat round me and called, "Where's Jessie? I thought she would come to meet me."

We were all laughing when he let me go, reassured that he was still mine in spite of the wonders he was encountering in the world outside. And what wonders there were! Lilias fell asleep in my lap, unnoticed, while I listened to Dougie's enthusiastic recital.

"Some day will you take me to see the grand new building, Dougie?" I asked at the end. "It sounds as good as a castle."

"Maybe if you save up your pennies I could take you some Saturday, but meantime I'd better get upstairs and on with the work. I'll see you in the morning."

"Not tonight — for supper?"

"You'll be in bed, Jess, before I've finished."

I had known what the pattern would be but it vexed me just the same to have so little of Dougie's time. Now that I did not have his company to look forward to, it was tempting to linger on the way home from school, joining in the ploys of Patty McPhee and some of the other wilder spirits in my class. But a stubborn sense of duty drove me back every day. I would get a welcoming smile of relief from Meg or whoever was at the pirn winding. Mam's health was still a worry to us all. A persistent cough was adding to her general weakness.

"And the winter's no' right started," I had heard Jean say to Meg. "Faither's wondering about sending for the doctor to her but she hates us to fuss."

Meg had agreed. "Aye, it's no' easy. You see, she's aye been the one at the heart o' things in the house. She's bound to feel she's no' daein' her job. So we've got to be careful how we go about it."

I knew that if I stayed to play with the other lassies nothing would be said, but Mam would be trying to do more of the work herself. And I had seen her with a hot iron in one hand, hanging on to the dresser with the other while that cruel cough shook her till her breath was caught in long gasps, and tears ran down her flushed cheeks. No, Mam needed all her strength just to feed Lilias. And Lilias was no longer the puffy, wrinkled stranger who had horrified me that long-ago summer day and I had secretly hated for weeks afterwards. Lilias was the prettiest bairn that ever was: small-boned with dainty features; silky dark hair that I hoped I might be able to coax into soft curls later; lovely shiny brown eyes and two tiny dimples that showed every time she chuckled when I went near her. Now Elsie was teaching us younger ones how to sew — not the dull useful things they taught you at school, but pretty dainty things that would make our little sister the brawest lass in Kilbarchan. And Elsie was always full of ideas for clothes.

My step quickened. Lilias was usually awake at that time of day, ready to listen to me singing as I wound the pirns. And Mam would be relieved to see me, too. Mam had been coughing all night. The sound had carried all the way upstairs to the bedroom which we girls shared. Bella slept quietly beside me but, in the other bed, Meg and Elsie had murmured, concerned. Then there had been the creak of the living-room door opening and the low rumble of Faither's voice in Mam's bedroom. Next, he was back coaxing the damped-down range into life.

"He's making her a hot drink," I hissed.

"That's right, pet." Meg's voice was kind. "But we'd better get back to sleep. We'll all be needed tomorrow."

It was good to be needed . . . in a way . . . but if I hadn't been needed I would have been looking forward to the big school in Johnstone and nobody ever said a word about that now. I turned the corner of Shuttle Street and stopped dead for an instant. Then my feet flew. The doctor's gig could mean only one thing. Mam was worse — maybe dying.

The weaving shed was empty. That in itself was unusual enough to make my heart race. The handle of the thick door was stiff in my hands. Frustration made me so desperate that I landed on the flagged floor of the passageway. Ignoring my bruised knees I slammed the outer door shut and propelled myself into the living-room. They were all there except Meg, standing in a solemn semi-circle with the doctor in the middle. None of them smiled at me. Jean moved to the range and, lifting the big teapot, poured tea into a cup on the table. "Drink that up, Jess," she ordered. "It'll warm you. Mam's ill. We'll all be needed to help."

My feet refused to move. "What's wrong with her? Is it something awful serious?"

It was the doctor who cleared his throat and answered, "My dear, you know your mother has had a bad cough for some time?" I nodded wordlessly. "Well, it's caused by a severe inflammation which is affecting her lungs badly." He saw my eyes fill with tears and answered my unspoken question. "Don't worry, she won't die if I can help it." His voice was gruff.

It was no use running to Faither for comfort. Beside the rosy-cheeked doctor he stood ashen pale. His cup was shaking in its saucer, spilling the tea he hadn't touched. Meg must be with Mam. And Dougie was so far away. The doctor had said that Mam wouldn't die if he could help it but what if he couldn't help it? If Dougie had been there I could have talked to him, asked him things. Dougie always gave me sensible answers. Well, Jean gave sensible answers too, but her answers were often frightening. Dougie, now, would say, "Let's get things in proportion."

But if Mam died, what would happen to us all? Faither looked so different these last months, worrying about Mam. Maybe he would die of a broken heart. And then maybe Dougie would have to leave university.

My mounting catalogue of fears was interrupted by the doctor's departure. He paused at the door to speak to Faither: "I'll be back this evening, Mr Allen."

"It's awfully good of you, Doctor. We appreciate it."

"Nonsense! It's a pity Nurse Duncan's got such a heavy load just now but I daresay your daughters will turn up trumps. Weaning the child will give you all a few sleepless nights, I'm afraid. If Nurse Duncan could find time to give the child the first bottle and show your daughters the ropes . . ." His voice faded as Faither and he walked out to the gig.

Funnily enough it was Jean who put solid ground under my feet. "If the bairn's to be weaned," she said, "Jessie's the one to dae it. She can quieten it like naebody else."

"But what about school?" Bella croaked with nervous stress.

"She's well forward there, thanks to Dougie. Tomorrow's Friday, then there's the weekend. By next weekend the wee one will be used to the bottle and whoever's at the pirn winding can do it," she said decisively.

"And maybe by that time Mam will be strong enough to handle the bairn herself," Meg was saying. Her words were directed at Jean but I knew fine she meant them to comfort me.

"Aye, maybe." Jean was sceptical.

But Jean, slow to praise, had paid me her highest compliment, confidence in my ability. Knowing I was a necessary part of the team brought an immediate surge of strength. School wasn't all that important. I would work extra hard when I got back.

So I was the one who watched Nurse Duncan hold the squirming bairn firmly in her arms as she struggled to squeeze a few drops of milk into the constantly jerking mouth. "Maybe, if you could sing to her, pet, she would stop struggling," she suggested.

I obliged with the song I had been learning that day at school. "Young Jamie lo'ed me weel and sought me for his bride," but Lilias was not impressed. "Maybe something cheerier, Jessie . . . " Nurse Duncan prompted.

After a wee hesitation I plunged into "March, march, Ettrick and Teviotdale." Nurse Duncan dandled the bairn to the rhythm. Dougie was brushing his boots in the back kitchen so he joined in with his strong baritone. The crying stopped. Nurse Duncan squeezed some milk into the open mouth, tickled the wee tongue with the teat and then the tiny lips fastened fiercely and the jaws worked in earnest. While I watched the busy bairn, fascinated, Nurse Duncan explained all the procedure to me in detail. Then, satisfied that I was safely in charge, she packed her apron and left.

Jean departed too with Tam who had come seeking her, but not before she had issued her orders. "Faither's got to drive to the agents in Paisley tomorrow so he needs a' the sleep he can get.

Meg and Elsie can take turns to sit up wi' Mam tonight. We'll see how things are tomorrow."

I prepared for bed that night on tiptoe. Lilias was sleeping peacefully in the little bed Dougie had carried up to my bedroom. "Right! wee mother," he had said to me, "if you need any help just tap on my door. And if I'm snoring, tickle my toes. That should wake me." That made me chuckle. The slightest sound always alerted Dougie. "Could hear the grass growing, that one," Mam often said. Mam! She wasn't getting much sleep. Her cough wasn't quite so noisy but when I had pointed that out, Jean squashed me with, "She hasna the strength, that's why." The range was being kept aglow all night for Mam needed hot bottles round her and Meg and Elsie would be giving her hot drinks with honey and maybe hot milk with an egg beaten up in it to keep her strength up. There was also a mysterious performance about 'expressing milk' which only Jean and Meg were admitted into. I knew it was no use asking questions.

Elsie was already in the other bed when

I got there. Her eyes were closed and a dreamy look curved her lips but it was impossible to tell if she was sleeping. Bella was still downstairs, soaking the meal for the morning porridge and hanging bedlinen on the lines which had been strung across the living-room. Jean's first dictum when the doctor left had been, "Now, lassies, every bit of linen that goes on Mam's bed has to be toasted by the fire first. The last thing she needs now is a chill."

Dougie had helped Meg unearth the chest of spare linen and carry the heavy bundles down to the warm living-room. While all the bustle went on Faither had been shut in Mam's room, loth to leave her. Gentle Meg was insisting that Dougie should get to his bed, too. "How would Mam feel if your studies were coming to harm because of her?"

This was unanswerable, of course, and Dougie had quietly retreated but I knew by the line of lamplight under his door that he was still studying. I pulled up the patchwork quilt and prepared to pray as I had never prayed in my life before.

In spite of my determination to stay

awake all night and listen for the bairn, I was in a deep sleep when I gradually became aware that Lilias was crying sorely. I leapt out of bed just as the door opened and Dougie appeared, oil lamp in hand. "Ah, you're up. Good!" he said. "I heard the wee one giving the odd whimper a while ago. Meg's got the bottle ready. She thought you might like to come down to the fire. Put a shawl round you and tuck wriggly worm inside. It'll muffle her howling a bit." He crossed to Elsie's bed and shook her none too gently. "Get dressed quickly. It's past time you were down. Meg needs you to help change Mam's bed."

The oil lamp cast our shadows on the whitewashed wall. "You look a right wee fattie," Dougie hissed. I looked, giggled and stumbled. Dougie grabbed me firmly. "Daft of me," he muttered.

In spite of the constant anxiety about Mam, who seemed to show little sign of improving, that week of enforced absence from school gave me a sort of thrill I felt guilty about acknowledging even to myself. There was no question that I was part of a purposeful team and an important part at that. Lilias accepted my attentions happily and rewarded me with smiles and chuckles which I treasured. It was funny to think I hadn't wanted this wee sister whose progress I noted carefully and with pride.

"Don't you see her getting bigger?" I had asked Jean one day when, for once, she seemed to have a minute to sit by the fire and watch the bairn being bathed.

"She's coming on fine, Jess, but she'll never be big, I doubt. She takes after Granny Watson."

"Grannie Watson?" I stared in amazement. I had only once met my maternal grandmother who lived far away in south Ayrshire with her youngest unmarried daughter. Mam and Faither had wakened me early one summer Saturday and we had travelled in the cart with Rusty (a young horse then), a big picnic basket for ourselves and dress-lengths of silk for Grannie and Aunt Polly. I could remember my disappointment when after the thrill of jolting mile after mile along country roads, we had finally arrived at Grannie's cottage.

Half the house, it seemed, was out in the garden. Aunt Polly was spring cleaning. The wrinkled, quavering old lady who was my grandmother seemed to bear no resemblance to Mam at all. Mam was pretty and rosy with shining dark hair; she bustled about looking after folk all the time. I had expected Grannie Watson to be like that only with grey hair, maybe. And Aunt Polly . . . Well, Polly was such a cheery name . . . you'd expect . . .

"If you'd let us ken you were coming . . . " had been Polly's opening remark, delivered without a smile, as she led us through to the little parlour where Grannie Watson sat by the fire. The heat was stifling. The old lady wept with joy as she fondled 'my bonnie Bess' and then me.

"And which o' them is this?" she asked.

"It's Jessie, our youngest."

"She's got Wattie's mother's hair. Is it no' braw! But what a pity we didna ken you were coming. You see, Polly didna get the cleaning done at the right time for I was in bed wi' my chest."

71

Mam bit her lip in vexation at that. I bit my lip too — to stop giggling. I could imagine Dougie saying, "And how could she be in bed without her chest?"

It was Faither who answered, "I'm aye working on a Saturday, Grannie, but I took in the shawl I had just finished yesterday and instead o' starting to set up the next one when the weather was so braw, I thought it would be such a treat for Bess and the bairn . . ."

The old lady did not seem to be listening. "Polly aye makes a steak pie when folk are coming . . . I dinna ken whit we've got in the hoose — "

Mam had broken in desperately, "Mither, listen, will ye? We came here to see you — and Polly, of course — we didna come to be fed. We had a nice picnic on the road and we'll dae the same on the way back. Wattie and I can give Polly a hand to get ony o' the things she wants back in. Maybe we can a' hae a nice cup o' tea and a bit o' cheese."

"Polly will want to dae better than that," Grannie Watson said. And the clatter from the kitchen backed up her words.

72

"I'll gae through and see if she wants anything lifted in," Faither had announced. "Are you coming, Jessie?"

The kitchen could hardly have been described as cool with the range roaring full blast but the door to the garden was wide open and a scented breeze fanned us. Faither's voice had been abrupt — the way it sometimes was to Jean, sort of defensive, you might say. "Just tell me what you want lifted, Polly, and I'll see to it."

Polly had considered, then, "We'll leave the carpets. Give me a hand in wi' the table and chairs and if you, Jessie, could fetch a bit parsley . . . "

There was a lot of Jean in Aunt Polly, I'd decided, then worked it out that it would be the other way round, of course. A seemingly non-stop list of 'if you would justs' had resulted in me setting the table for a meal of tasty broth, cold mutton and salad, enormous helpings of strawberries and cream, washed down by strong tea and huge slabs of fruit cake.

Mam and the old lady had wept at parting and Aunt Polly had nearly torn the corner off her apron, twisting it. My memory of Grannie Watson had been a pathetic, rather ugly one. Where on earth was the resemblance between that grey quivering face and lovely wee Lilias? Jean must be letting her imagination run away with her, I thought. Yet Jean didn't usually do that. Getting old was horrible but it would be a long long time till Lilias was old, ages and ages. I fondled the lovely soft skin of her wee stomach. Lilias chuckled up at me and I was comforted.

3

JEAN'S voice was quite matter-of-fact as she said, "Well, lass, back to school on Monday with you."

"But Lilias maybe won't take her bottle from anyone else," I protested.

"That bairn would take it frae the sweep now. She's got the measure o' it, a' right. But we've got tomorrow and Sunday before you go back. We can a' take turns."

Jean was to sit up that night with Mam. Then she was to take Saturday off and stay at home wi' Tam, Faither had said. Though Mam was still weak and a wee bit fevered at times everyone had relaxed a little, feeling that the crisis was past. Jean chased me to bed early even though I declared I wouldn't be able to sleep.

"You're sleeping on your feet," was her answer, "And the bairn'll be getting you up during the night."

With the patchwork quilt pressed

against my nose I had time to think about Monday morning. It would be queer playing at peevers and skipping ropes when all that work was needing to be done at home. Now I thought about it, it had been a hard week, especially in the early stages, dealing with a fractious bairn and trying to dry the never-ending washing which sometimes came off the line frozen stiff. But though Jean never gave me a word of praise, I knew by a quiet nod now and again that I had her approval. The thought was comforting.

Lilias woke earlier than usual. The air in the bedroom was chill. Luckily there was a bit of moonlight to guide me down the stairs, so I didn't have to waste time lighting the lamp. The living-room door was wide open and the fire roaring merrily but no bottle stood warming on the range. Jean must be in Mam's room, I reckoned. Faither's bed was empty too. Lilias was making such a din; it was difficult for me to think. Rushing to the table where I had laid the things in readiness I poured some milk into the pan and carried it in my free hand to the stove. It wasn't going to be easy dealing with the milk while I held the struggling bairn in the shawl. Somebody else had always done the pouring for me. But the milk began to rise and there was nothing else for it. Gingerly I lifted the bubbling pan just as Lilias kicked out angrily. A fierce jet of steam rose from the hot embers. I cried out but hung on grimly to the handle.

"Lay it on the side hob, lass." Faither's voice came from the doorway. He was extra gentle so as not to startle me. I did what I was bidden. Quickly Faither crossed the room and examined my wrist. "It'll be painful, my lass," he said, "but at least the skin's no' broken so it'll heal clean."

I fought back sobs as he filled the feeding bottle and turned to me anxiously. "Do you think you'll manage wi' your sore hand?"

"Aye. She's awful hungry . . . I'll need to," I said.

"Jeannie's waiting for a basinful of hot water but I'll be right back to feed the bairn," he assured me.

"What's wrong?" It was Dougie's voice.

"Jessie's scalded her wrist. Your Mam's in a terrible fever. I'm taking this to Jean."

"Right, Faither. You stay with Mam. I'll see to Jessie and the bairn. Now, wee Jessie, we'll quieten the bairn first. Come beside me in the big chair and tell me the secret of feeding this little monster."

Through my hiccoughs I issued directions and suddenly it was quiet. In spite of the cheerful crackle of the fire and the comfort of being close to Dougie and him in charge, I kept shuddering. "Have a wee cry, lovie, it might help and the bairn'll never notice," he whispered.

I giggled, gulped and finally released the pent-up sobs. Then Dougie said, "See, she's nearly finished it."

I remembered my responsibilities and started babbling. "Oh dear, I forgot to tell you. You're supposed to sit her up and rub her back half way through."

"Like this?"

"That's right."

Lilias belched loudly. "Good girl," I said automatically.

Dougie pretended to be indignant. "I used to get skelped for that."

I was between laughter and tears as I clutched his arm. Jean bustled into the room. "Whit's a' this?" she demanded. "Your Mam's delirious and you twa are sitting there carrying on like bairns at a pairty."

"Jessie's scalded her wrist trying to manage the bairn and the milkpan at the same time. Delirious — are you sure?"

"D'you think I'm daft?" Jean's voice was biting. "She keeps talking about the black bun and then she tries to mind the receipe and the sweat's lashing off her. If she says 'Jamaica pepper' again, I'll go daft."

Dougie spoke firmly, "Sit down, Jean, or you'll be the next invalid. I'll make you a cup of tea, then I'll be off to fetch the doctor."

"You canna, Dougie," she said wearily. "It's thick fog, and ice on the cobbles — no' fair to ask the doctor. We'll just have to struggle on, trying to keep the fever down. Every time the bedroom door opens there's a cold draught . . . "

"Well maybe I could do something about that tomorrow."

"There's no way we can stop the

draught frae the front door — "

"Lizzie Forsythe has a big heavy draught screen she never uses. I saw it when she called me in to help her move some furniture one day I was passing. It was her mother's and she doesn't like to sell it. She'll be glad to lend it to us."

I hesitated then spoke up. "Faither aye says, 'Neither a borrower nor a lender be — '."

"This is nae time for pride or poetry," said Jean. "If you'll pour three cups, Dougie, I'll take them through to Mam's room. There's some nice cauld buttermilk in the pantry you could be dabbing on Jessie's wrist."

I shivered and squealed when he began his ministrations. "It's freezing," I said.

"Correct me if I'm wrong, madam, but I thought we were trying to cool you down."

"Aye, but . . ." I subsided. After a minute's puzzling I said, "Dougie, I thought Jean wouldn't borrow things under any circumstances."

"Our Jean is pragmatic."

"What does that mean?"

"She'll settle for what's practicable rather than bemoan the ideal." His voice became brisker. "But she'll knock the stuffing out of herself if she goes on like this. If you're feeling better, I think you should wake Meg gently and tell her Jean needs a rest. Then get back into your own wee bed."

"Aren't you coming upstairs?" I asked.

"No. I'll wait. Faither might be glad of a rest, too. I can keep the fire going for Meg. Don't worry. I'll have a wee doze in the chair. Wait! I'll see you up the stair. Wriggly worm upsets your balance."

"She's not wriggling now," I said.

"No. She's a bonnie wee thing."

"Was I a bonnie wee thing?" I waited anxiously for his answer. Dougie spoke gently. "I used to think you were like that picture in our school reader — you know the one: 'Non Angli sed Angeli' — not Angles but Angels."

The ache in my wrist was nothing. Again Dougie had raised me to the heights.

★ ★ ★

81

By early morning Mam's fever had abated and Jean decided that the crisis was past. As soon as breakfast was over Bella and Dougie hurried off to Lizzie Forsythe's and struggled back with the heavy wooden screen which they set down at the foot of Mam's bed. Then Jean turned to the next job in hand and we got our orders. "Now, Jessie, I've been looking out the recipe for black bun. If it's worrying Mam we might as well get it made and be done wi' it."

"Mam usually does it the first week of November," I started.

"Aye, well, we'll get it made the first day we can and that's today."

"That's pragmatic," I said, savouring my new word.

"Is it? I thought it was sense. Now, read this out loud till I see if you've got it right."

I read the long list to Jean's satisfaction and my own growing amazement. "Do you need fifteen different things to make black bun?" I asked.

"Aye! That one's Grannie Allen's recipe."

"I reckon that adds up to nearly eleven

pounds," Dougie broke in. "Jessie will need a hand." He turned to me. "I'll come along and fetch you when I've got the fire going in the weaving shed. The grocer's will be busy on a Saturday and it'll take them a while to weigh that lot out."

Jean took down her bonnet and shawl. "Now mind, the first sign o' fever and Dougie's to fetch the doctor and let me know."

Meg reassured her. "Don't worry, Jean. Faither's watching Mam. I'll see to the black bun and things. Have a good rest. You're needing it. See you Monday."

As I skipped over the slippy cobbles I reflected that every one of us had been delighted to have Jean's support when things seemed black. And yet the weekend without her wary presence would be a relief. Coming back later with Dougie, I tried to put those thoughts into words.

"I know what you mean, Jess," he said. "She's like a coiled spring; always under tension. It's a good thing Tam is such a quiet, steady type. Yet when we were all scared about Mam — even Whiskers looked out of his depth — it was Jean who put backbone into the lot of us."

"That's right," I agreed. "I was feeling awful . . . helpless . . . and just wanted to cry and then Jean said I was to wean Lilias and — I don't know . . . "

"She put smeddum into you and you did a grand job. She's proud of you but never expect her to tell you so." He threw back his head and laughed.

It was unanimously decided that the back kitchen was too cold to work in so Meg spread an oilskin cloth over the big table in the living-room. It seemed almost like a party, I thought as I chopped and stoned the big blue raisins. Dougie had had to fetch down the huge brass jelly pan because the mixing bowl wasn't big enough. Elsie, cutting the large squares of greaseproof paper for the weighed ingredients was giggling at Bella who had managed to get flour on her hair as she struggled to make the thin pastry. The smell of the fruit and spices reminded me of other celebrations — of the big birthday dumplings which hid new-minted threepenny bits wrapped in oiled paper in their rich depths. The fire behind us crackled companionably.

Though Mam was sleeping like a bairn, Faither had refused to leave her bedside and was dozing in the armchair there. The old cradle had been put in the draught-free corner between the fire and Faither's bed so that I could keep an eye on my charge. Dougie was ticking off the ingredients as Meg weighed them. He announced each item in the funny voice of a swell who had come up from England once to support our local candidate. Faither had taken Dougie along though he was really too young to be at the meeting. For a long time afterwards, Faither's cronies would ask Dougie to 'gie us yon English chiel'. Dougie was clever, I told myself, in spite of what Nurse Duncan had said. He could imitate anyone. He could even . . .

"Dougie," I called out, "could you imitate Nurse Duncan?"

"Nurse Duncan? Never thought about it. Let me see . . . "

He puffed out his chest and sketched an imaginary figure round him then put on a high falsetto and rattled quickly, "I always like my patients to have a nice wash. Would you mind, pet, fetching

85

through a basin of water. Your big brother can boil the kettle — he's not much good for anything else . . . and be sure, pet, to put lime water in the bairn's bottle. It breaks up the curd, you see — and, while you're at it, pet, could you just . . . " His voice finally gave out and he doubled up with laughter.

It really was like a party with Dougie involved at every stage of the proceedings, stirring the heavy unwieldy mass in the jelly pan and packing the stiff mixture into the pastry-lined tins. Jean would have insisted on clearing away the mess and washing the dishes as soon as the cakes went into the oven but gentle Meg said, "Now, I think we deserve a nice cup of tea and a lump of cherry cake by the fire. Then Dougie can get back to his books while we clear up the mess."

I enjoyed a delicious mixture of guilt and defiance as I munched my cherry cake in the middle of the debris. What if anyone came in, I wondered?

But folks had stopped dropping in because of Mam. Jean would be 'black affrontet' if she could see us but

Jean wasn't there; only gentle Meg who worked away quietly and yet got everyone to heed her. Meg would make a nice mother. She was pretty, too. Yet nobody ever came courting Meg. And Jean, sharp-tongued Jean, had won the heart of the steady thoughtful Tam. Would they all get married some day, I wondered — even Dougie? But no one could ever be good enough for Dougie, not even the nicest girl I knew. I studied my handsome brother as he twisted round in his chair to call something to Meg. I knew he didn't like his black shiny curls for I'd seen him plastering them down with a wet hairbrush but I thought they were lovely. With his head turned away like that he looked like a picture I'd seen, 'Head of a Roman.' I liked the way his mouth would open suddenly in a wide smile showing his stront even teeth; the way his brown eyes shone when he laughed. Nothing was too heavy for Dougie to lift, I decided, and his hands were so strong they could open anything, no matter how stiff. His legs were long enough to touch the fender when he tipped his chair back like that.

That was why he could run so fast, of course. A cold thought struck me. Surely he wouldn't be silly and fall in love and go away and leave us . . .

Meg was back, starting to clear up. Dougie surrendered his cup, gave a quick wave and was off to his room.

"That's right," Meg said. "He's lost a lot of study time. Now, I'd like Faither to get through here by the fire while I watch Mam. Bella can start the ironing. You can help Elsie with the dishes, Jessie, and laying the table for tea. After that you'll be busy with the bairn."

The delightful smell of the black bun began to tantalize us as we sat at our meal.

"I could deal with a lump of that stuff," said Dougie.

"You can forget that," Bella assured him. "Jean won't let us lay a finger on it till Ne'erday."

"What's Jean got to do with it? Who fetched down the jelly pan, checked the vital list of ingredients, stirred the agglomeration . . ."

"Who made the pastry, though?"

"Who stoned the blue raisins?"

"Who lined the tins?"

Dougie covered his ears against the chorus. "Right, right, lassies. We're daft, you know. We should have made a wee extra one for ourselves. Jean would never have known."

Meg laughed. "It would never taste the same if you ate it before the bells rang out. I must admit the smell is awfully tempting. You know, I was just thinking . . . Mam looked a wee bit better when I took in her tea. Maybe when the cakes come out the oven we could take them through, just to show her."

The triumphal procession was headed by Dougie blowing a mock fanfare. My eye went from the bright spots of colour on Mam's cheeks to her pale freckled hands trembling on the bedspread. Mam had never had pale hands before. In fact, after a cold washday they had usually been red and cracked and I had often seen Faither rubbing them gently with ointment while he asked. "Better, lass?" That was what Meg had meant no doubt about a happy home when you got two like that, man and wife together. I studied Faither as he stood by the bed, his head bent over Mam. What had been a thin patch on top of his head was now shining bald. The silky golden brown hair caught in the lamplight had silver glints in it. He loved Mam so much. He had cared for us all so proudly. Why had Dougie been so disapproving? What was it he 'didna ken the right wey aboot'? Something to do with Lilias. Yet Dougie loved wee Lilias too and he couldn't do enough to help Faither and the rest of us now that Mam was laid up. There were so many things I didn't understand and even Dougie didn't seem to be able to tell me.

We were to have a quiet Hogmanay because, though Mam's fever didn't return, she was still weak and just got up long enough every day to have her bed made. It would be a strange occasion without the normal succession of first foots and the unstinted hospitality which went on till all hours of the morning: the one night in the year when every child in the village was allowed out of bed at midnight. Usually I was sent to bed at the usual time and then someone woke me at eleven o'clock. That gave me time to wash from head to toe and to put on my new dress. I had wondered if we wouldn't be getting new clothes that year — it would be awful to start the year in old clothes — but in the middle of all the work and worry about Mam, Jean had allocated the materials and Elsie had taken command of the dressmaking. My dress was made of red flannel with little grey flowers on it. I had had to hide my disappointment when I first saw the material on the bale but Elsie knew exactly what she wanted to do with it and as the work progressed I grew more and more excited.

Hogmanay was the usual hechle about clearing every speck of dirt from the house. I willingly ran round at Meg's direction that evening, freeing Bella and Elsie to put the finishing touches to their handiwork. Bella's face was scarlet with effort as she stood over the goffering iron, coaxing the frills of her new blouse.

Dougie had appointed himself stoker and odd-job man and would take over Faither's last minute task of removing the ashes from the fire and carrying them out as the old year was ending. Elsie had sent me upstairs to wash, promising that she would bring up my dress in a few minutes.

I was in my clean petticoats and brushing my hair when at last she appeared. I gasped, for though I had watched with growing interest as she worked out some complicated pleats, tucks and gathers, the dress was now completely transformed by a three-tier collar in white crochet with matching cuffs. I had seen Bella crocheting furiously at the lace but assumed it was for one of their new blouses. I shivered with excitement as Elsie started to fasten all the back buttons and gathered each layer of the collar by the black velvet ribbon slotted through it, till three neat bows completed the picture.

"It feels lovely, Elsie," I said, swirling the skirt.

"Just wait. There's something here."

The broad ribbon she picked up from my chair was the same shade of red as my dress and Elsie had edged it with the black velvet ribbon. Now she was carefully parting and gathering my hair till she found the angle she wanted, then she anchored it with a ribbon bow. Stepping back to inspect her work, she looked a little like Jean. It was the first time I had ever seen any resemblance. "Mmmmm . . . just exactly the effect I wanted," she murmured, "well clear of your eyes but soft over the shoulder. Yes, you're a picture. Now run down and see what the others think. I'll carry your basin."

There was a chorus of approval when I showed myself in the living-room. I turned eagerly to Dougie who hadn't said anything. His face was intent. "Jess, don't you dare fall asleep till I've had a chance to draw you in that outfit. It's . . . " He moved to Elsie and gave her a quick hug. "It's a fine piece of work." Elsie looked surprised and gratified. I had never seen Dougie hug her before though we all kissed one another at New Year, of course.

Mam's face flushed with delight when I presented myself at her door. "Oh, Wattie," she said turning to Faither with tears in her eyes, "I'm getting up out o' this bed and I'll see the new year in with my clothes on. Send Meg to help me."

Faither hesitated but I was off to the living-room like a shot.

Meg, bless her, managed it and five minutes before the new year Mam appeared on Faither's arm dressed in her Sunday best dress and shawl. There was a lot of scurrying about for cushions and stools but Mam was safely ensconced in the best chair before the big clock gave its usual clonk and whirred its way to the first stroke of the new year.

As usual we made our round of kissing, but that year more solemnly. I think we had all suffered from a secret dread, one we didn't dare put into words. But there was Mam, thinner of course but with cheeks flushed and eyes sparkling, stretching out for the glass Elsie was offering. Dougie had taken over Faither's job of carving the stiff black bun into manageable cubes while Meg broke the cakes of shortbread into jagged pieces which she criss-crossed carefully on the plate. The sweet strong ginger wine burned my throat in its usual satisfactory fashion. Dougie was staring at me now and then with his eyebrows drawn into a half-frown that meant he was concentrating. Bella teased him about not eating his black bun after all the threats he had made the night it was in the oven. "It'll keep," was all he said. Soon he had nipped up to his room and was back with his sketch pad, coaxing me to leave the wine and cake aside for a few minutes while he made some quick sketches.

"It won't be just a few minutes," I protested. "You always take ages when you start drawing."

"Well, Jean's not here. You can stay up all night stuffing yourself with black bun and shortbread."

"I'd like to remind you that Mam's back in her chair," said Meg with a laugh.

"And happy to be here," Mam said. "But we forgot about the sirens."

"I remembered," said Meg, "but I didn't want you in any draught."

It was only on a very frosty night that we could hear the ships' sirens on the Clyde welcoming the new year.

"It's sharp enough tonight," sid Faither jumping up. "We're late but the sailors sometimes start them up again when they've had a wee bit too much to drink."

He struggled with the window catch while Meg wrapped Mam's shawl more securely round her. Then the icy air hit us. We kept still but the only sound was the homely one of merriment from the neighbouring cottages. Suddenly we heard a far-off voice, wheezy as a foghorn. Then it was joined by a sharp hooter which beat a staccato rhythm high above it. The unholy duet went on for a long while till Mam signalled to Faither to shut the window.

Dougie sketched busily. I longed to return to my feast but was flattered just the same that Dougie was putting all his effort out on me. Mam had retired and Bella had banked up the fire before he said, "There, get back to your bun. I've got enough to work on."

I drew nearer the fire. Everyone looked tired and happy. Mam had been dressed and on her feet again. Everyone had liked my dress. Elsie was clever. So was Bella. She'd done the lace.

Dougie moved quickly. I thought he'd been hit by a spark but his hand was closing round my glass. "You nearly spilled that on your new dress. Would you like me to carry you up to bed?"

"I'm far too big for that," I said indignantly.

"Oooooh . . . " he wiggled his eyebrows at me . . . "isn't our Jess quite the young lady? May I offer you my arm, Miss Allen?"

He knew how to coax me, did Dougie. It would have taken a lot of persuading to make me leave that lovely fire and climb the cold stairs to bed. But Dougie in his Sunday suit was offering me his arm as if I were a real lady. And I felt like a real lady in the dress my sister had designed.

The stately pace we had adopted in the living-room soon changed to a scramble when the cold air of the passageway hit us.

"Don't waste any time," he urged me at my door.

"No. Bella wrapped our nightgowns round the hot pigs when she carried them up."

"Good! Right, Jess, happy 1871."

"You too, Dougie," I croaked sleepily.

4

THE new year seemed to have been a turning point in Mam's illness and she made steady progress — nothing spectacular, just getting dressed mid-day and eating her meals beside us, dandling the bairn at times. Gradually she resumed her duties about the house though we all knew without being told that she would never recover her vigour and any heavy work would be a strain on her heart. Life took on a steady pattern of helping — working to each other's hands, as Faither put it. Meg was always careful to consult Mam. "I was thinking it would be nice to have a cherry cake in the tin now that your cronies are dropping by," she said one night.

"Well, if you're not too tired, Meg."

"No. I'm fine. While the lassies are clearing up I'll weigh out the stuff."

"Don't start mixing till I'm there," I called. If there was anything I loved, it was watching the big cakes being made.

"Well, maybe Elsie and Bella could manage on their own and you could come and line the tin for me," Meg said.

I grabbed at her offer though I had never tried to line a tin before. Of course kind Meg knew this and patiently stood over me as I measured, cut, folded and tried to persuade the paper into its appointed place. "See, pet," she would say, "like this . . . A deeper fold and one will slide into the other without the top turning over."

At the time I did not realize how much I was learning that first year of Lilias's life. There was always so much work waiting to be done and I joined in without noticing that I was learning new skills which were bound to be useful to me later on. Meg was the ideal teacher of domestic subjects, patient, encouraging and thorough; applauding each achievement but gauging my capacity and calling a halt before I was too tired. Our efforts that night produced a real picture of a cherry cake which was never to be forgotten though we didn't know that at the time.

In the first week of the year there was a meeting of the Kilbarchan Literary Association. Nobody had been thinking about going, but Mam was feeling so much better that she chased Faither and the lassies out to it. I was desperately keen to go but was sent to bed at the usual time. I had to bite my tongue not to remind them that they treated me as older when there was work to be done. I muttered my resentment for a long time under my quilt, then I felt guilty, of course. Dougie was too busy at his books to go, but I quizzed Bella when we were dressing in the morning. "What was it like? I wish I could have been there."

"Well, we had tea. There was lots of nice home baking. The tea was a bit stewed . . ."

"But what did you do?"

"Nothing. We just listened. Mr Weir made a speech. He said the aim of the association was 'the enlightenment of the young mind'."

"That's just the same as school, then," I objected.

"Oh, no! There were readings and songs and recitations; no, it wasn't like school. Maybe you'll get to it next year," she added kindly. "But something else happened — no, maybe I shouldn't tell you."

"What was it?" I was desperate to know.

"The minister was at the meeting."

"He's always at these things," I pointed out.

"Aye, but he had a young man with him that's just newly out for a minister only he hasn't got his own church yet. Oh, he's handsome! And he speaks so nicely . . . and you should have seen the way he looked at Meg. He held her hand so long when the minister introduced them and his face went pink and you should have seen Meg's. That was just before we had our tea. Then he was speaking to her just after tea before the concert started and then again at the end. Meg says he's coming to preach one Sunday soon. Elsie and I think they are in love."

"In love — but he doesn't even know our Meg."

"Love at first sight: haven't you heard of that?"

"Yes . . . " I was unsure. I had often thought that Meg would make a nice mother but had failed to consider the preliminaries. I was very curious indeed about the new suitor. Mam still hadn't been back to church because of the cold weather. I hoped fervently that she wouldn't choose to start again the Sunday Duncan Williamson was coming, for then I might be the one chosen to stay at home with Lilias.

Frost patterns on the window pane were a secret relief to me when that Sunday arrived. It was dark, yet I had heard our bedroom door close quietly and steps descending the stairs. Meg was already about her business. Elsie always slept till someone woke her. In a sort of common understanding we all made a special effort that morning. I noticed that Bella was flushed with excitement as we helped each other with buttons; she then woke Elsie to give her a hand. Elsie was the acknowledged expert with hair and, in a good mood, would patiently improve on the others' efforts. She had tut-tutted over Bella's as she swiftly rearranged it. My brushing was approved of and she decided that a low bow beneath the back of my bonnet would look best. Meg had escaped her attentions by being downstairs early but as we all stood by the living-room fire with our bonnets in our hands, Elsie shot at me, "Fetch Meg's comb."

"It's too late," Meg objected.

"One minute — or maybe two . . . " Elsie was quickly removing the hairpins. We all watched, fascinated, as the expert fingers twisted, anchored, crossed and looped Meg's soft hair into a much more becoming style. Then she picked up Meg's bonnet which she had volunteered to re-trim the night before, fixed it carefully and completed the picture by teasing a few soft curls round the temples.

Faither and Dougie had already set off as Faither was a duty elder that Sunday. We had to hurry while trying to look as if we were not in an unseemly rush. As it was, we had no sooner taken our seats than the vestry door opened and the beadle led in the young minister.

He *was* handsome, I thought, but not so handsome as Dougie would be, of course. He was awfully serious, too. I glanced at Meg but she was very busy, smoothing her gloves. The minister was moving his notes from one side of the big bible to the other. His hands were shaking. He was nervous. Fancy a minister being nervous, I thought. Some folk were feart for ministers and here was Mr Williamson feart himself. Was it because Meg was there? Dougie always said that first impressions were very important. Often people were much more influenced by them than they realized themselves.

By the time we reached the sermon, I was a bit wound up myself. At first his voice was very tight. I felt heart sorry for him standing there with his knuckles showing white where he clutched the edge of the pulpit. He started talking about the winter weather, the frost, the snow on the ground and everything being dead. But then, he said, when the snow melted we would find the bonnie wee snowdrops were there all the time waiting to show themselves and that they were just the first of all the many flowers that would bloom fresh and new, making our gardens resplendent. I remember 'resplendent' because I had to ask Dougie about it later. The minister went on for quite a while, quoting texts and telling us that paradise was the Persian word for a garden and gradually he worked it round that what we called death was simply a withering away of the useless body which would renew itself in God's garden.

It seemed to go down well with the congregation. Old Aggie Shaw was blowing her nose noisily. Bella was chewing her lips the way she does when she feels like crying. I thought paradise sounded lovely but I was glad Mam hadn't gone there. She was better sitting under the birch tree in our own bonnie wee garden where we could all see her.

Duncan Williamson stood beside Dr Graham, our own minister, at the door. I watched closely as he shook hands with Meg and pricked up my ears as he stammered, "I understand your mother has been ill. Does she have many visitors?" Meg's voice was very low and I could not make out her reply.

I hurried forward to Dougie and

Faither. "So I suppose you'll want the parlour fire lit?" Dougie was saying.

"Aye. Your mother will surely want that if the minister is bringing the young man along."

"A bit unusual, surely?" said Dougie. "I mean bringing someone with him like that . . . and on the sabbath."

"Aye." Faither was thoughtful. "But I suppose he's showing the young man the ropes — he's a far-out relation — and parish visiting is an important part of a minister's job. I hope it's no' too exciting for your mother but Meg'll watch that."

Dougie turned to me, "And what did you think of the visiting minister, Miss Allen?"

"He was awful nervous," I said. "Maybe it was because Meg was there. Bella says it was love at first sight."

"What's that?" Faither was startled. Dougie started talking quickly, saying that Bella was soft in the head and daft about anything in trousers and thought everyone else was the same. I asked him about 'resplendent' and he explained. Faither didn't say any more.

While we were setting the dinner table, Dougie got on with lighting the parlour fire and carrying in another scuttle of coal for later. As soon as dinner was over, he hurried off to his books. For once I did not mind his absence. As I amused Lilias I was listening to the low murmurings of Mam and Faither by the fire and the occasional snatch of Bella's voice as she and Elsie carried the dishes back through to the dresser. All of them seemed to think the visit was surprising. Meg was working even more diligently than usual, with attractive pink spots shining in her cheeks. When the parlour was judged warm enough Faither started carrying through some chairs and we prepared to leave the familiar living-room for the more formal parlour. Meg refused to sit down, finding small tasks to excuse her restlessness. The cherry cake was cut in luscious cubes in the back kitchen, the best china on a large tray with its snowy lace cloth and the kettle singing on the hob with the best teapot handy.

It was only when Faither rose to

answer the minister's knock that Meg scuttled in beside us. If anything, Duncan Williamson was more nervous than he had been at the start of his sermon. Mam answered his enquiries as to her health with a comforting gentleness. I could see that his unease, whatever its origin, touched her motherly heart. Meg soon rose to fetch the tea. Elsie and Bella went off to help. Lilias was sleeping peacefully so I had nothing to do but study this interesting stranger. Our minister was leading Faither on to talk about the intricacies of the special shawls. "Jean and Meg do the weaving. I set them up."

"I've had the pleasure of meeting Miss Meg but I haven't seen Miss Jean, have I?"

"My eldest daugher is married; lives in Johnstone but she still comes up on weekdays to keep us all in order." Mam and Faither laughed.

"And does she keep you in order, Miss Jessie?" he asked.

"She puts smeddum into us," I said. Dr Graham led the laughter this time, as Bella opened the door for Meg bearing the heavy tray and followed by Elsie with the teapot.

Duncan Williamson looked relaxed and happy now and much younger than the stern fellow who had stood in the pulpit. It was only when Meg held the plate of cherry cake in front of him that I saw a flicker of unease return. Meg had turned away to serve the others when I noticed him picking the cherries out of his cake. But he wasn't taking them out to eat them first as I'd been in trouble for doing. No! He was leaving them on his plate and eating the plain stuff.

"Don't you like cherries, Mr Williamson?" I asked in astonishment. He flushed and stammered, "No, I'm afraid not." Then in desperation, "Would you care to have them?"

I needed no second bidding but moved my stool beside him. Meg was distressed. "I'm sorry, Mr Williamson . . . You should have said . . . there's shortbread here."

"It's a beautiful cake, Miss Meg. I'm enjoying it. It's just that I don't like cherries . . . " his voice tailed off.

"I'm glad you don't like cherries," I

said, relishing my bonus. In the general laughter he relaxed again. Emboldened, I spoke up. "I'll always sit beside you when you're eating cherry cake."

"That is a charming offer." I saw him look at Meg. She went pinker than ever. Bella had slipped out when I was changing places. She came back then with a plate of gingerbread and made straight for the young minister saying, "Meg made this too." Young as I was I sensed that Bella had said something embarrassing. Faither gave a slight frown, Mam plucked at the braid of her dress and Doctor Graham began to ask about Dougie's studies.

Shortly afterwards the two men rose to take their departure. While Doctor Graham was talking to Faither about church matters, Duncan Williamson turned to Meg. I saw Mam watching them. Elsie and Bella were supposed to be gathering up the tea things but they were keeking too. Meg looked so pretty with her rosy cheeks and her hair in the soft style Elsie had fashioned. I got a funny feeling watching them smiling shyly at each other — a sort of mixture, a thrill of shared excitement, fear of being excluded from Meg's world and bewilderment at the change in our lives that were following one another so rapidly.

Soon the letters began to arrive for Meg from Glasgow: letters that invariably brought a heightened flush to her cheeks and a sparkle to her hazel eyes. "He thanks you for your hospitality, Mam," she said after reading the first one. "Would you like to see it?"

"No, no, Meg, it's your letter, lass. Remember us to him when you write back, though."

In one gentle little speech Mam paved the way for Meg's courtship. I watched Meg grow prettier and prettier as the days went by. 'Mr Williamson' changed to 'Duncan' after the first few letters — the name always accompanied by a happy blush. Duncan was having plenty requests for pulpit supply, she told us, but still no sign of a church of his own. Of course it was very good practice and he didn't have enough money to furnish a manse yet anyway.

"But aren't his parents comfortable?" Bella asked.

"Yes, I think so. But they've done a great deal putting him through university and I think they had to help the other brother when he was setting up practice."

"It'll be handy having a doctor in the family when you marry Duncan," I said.

Meg blushed furiously and said nothing. Dougie, who had been downstairs for his meal, asked me to come up to his room and to wear my good dress. He was still working on my portrait. For a long time nothing was said as he carefully mixed colours and made slow delicate strokes. Then, without looking at me, he said, "You've embarrassed Meg, you know."

It was rare for Dougie to find fault with me and I felt it keenly. "I didn't know I was saying anything wrong . . . " My lip trembled.

"No, no, of course not. It's that daft Bella filling your head with ideas."

"Don't you think she'll marry Duncan, then?" I asked.

"Well, for what it's worth, my personal opinion is that she will. They are very well suited apart from the fact that Meg's education has been limited. And that could be put right with a bit of study. She's intelligent enough. No, what I meant was that it's awkward for Meg to have people making remarks like that when she's not betrothed. You see, sometimes people change their minds. Duncan might find someone else and so might Meg."

"I don't think Meg would."

"No. But don't you see, Jess, how much worse that would make her feel? After they're betrothed we can talk about things — when it's a *fait accompli*."

"What's that?" I asked. So Dougie wrote it down for me and explained and quizzed me about the other French words he had taught me till at last my pride was salvaged.

I was very careful after that. Remembering Dougie's words I contented myself with watching Meg go about her work with a radiance that had turned her quiet good looks to beauty. One rather odd thing to me was the way she and Elsie seemed to draw closer. When a letter would arrive for Meg, Elsie lit up with excitement and listened attentively to every scrap of information that Meg passed on about Duncan. One evening she took time off her own sewing to encourage Meg to trim her new serge skirt with braid.

"You're so thin," I heard her saying. "You need a bit of fullness on the skirt to balance you." She brushed Meg's practical objections aside. "Well, if it gets dirty, it won't take long to unpick it, wash it, and put it back on." I had begun to look at Elsie with new eyes. Though she was always dreamy and not much use in the weaving shed, according to Jean, ever since the success of my New Year dress I had begun to see that her blouses were in a different class altogether from the ones that the others wore. Bella was quick at crochet but it was Elsie who worked out new patterns for her to copy. Though she would slip out of the routine work like ironing and peeling potatoes in favour of sewing, she was always good-natured enough about picking up lost stitches for us and correcting patterns that had gone wrong.

Winter eased into spring with Mam continuing to improve and Lilias thriving, though becoming too heavy for Mam to lift. So we were all kept busy in a quiet way. Then one Friday in April there was a diversion. First we heard the clash of cymbals — I couldn't think at first what the noise was — then we heard the voice of the town crier: "A female lecturer — Female Suffrage." The weavers, always daft about politics, jumped off their seat trees and ran to the doors to see what it was all about; then they shouted to one another, "Aye, we'll go, we'll go."

Dougie came home just as Faither was leaving with the lassies for the Parish School. "It's a pity I can't go with you," he said, "but I'll expect a report. Meantime Jessie can tell me who's speaking and what it's all about."

While I busied myself with the bairn by the fire and Mam dished up his meal, I put Dougie in the picture as well as I could. "Well, it's a Miss Taylor. She's going to talk about Female Suffrage — that means votes for women." I saw Dougie give Mam a quick wink and she turned away to the range with her shoulders shaking. "If you're going to laugh at me, I won't tell you anything," I threatened.

"No, no, carry on, Jess. I was just thinking that Mr Boyd won't have far to look when he needs a new infant mistress in ten years' time." I couldn't help grinning at that. Dougie went on, "Don't you think our Jessie will make a good teacher, Mam?" I saw Mam's smile waver. She hesitated before contenting herself with, "Aye, she's a good lass." Dougie's black eyebrows gathered in a quick frown before he turned smiling to me again. "Any more you can tell me? Who thought it up?"

"Well, Mr Fraser of Newfield House is to be in the chair. I don't know if he thought it up. There's a Miss Dick Lauder coming with Miss Taylor and she's the daughter of somebody famous, I think."

"Would it be Sir Thomas Dick Lauder?" Dougie asked eagerly.

"Aye, that's right . . . a reformer or something."

While Dougie tackled his dinner he tried to explain some of the things that the famous man had done but I've

116

forgotten them now. I was in bed, of course, and Dougie at his books before they all got back so it was really the following evening when Dougie was at his dinner that I got some inkling of what it was all about. Bella was particularly enthusiastic. "And she said there was no reason why a woman shouldn't vote just the same as a man."

"And what do you know about foreign trade or economics, Bella?" asked Dougie. Bella gulped and looked around for assistance. Meg, for once, took up the cudgels. "I daresay a lot of the men who vote don't know much about it either, Dougie. Surely we could learn . . ."

"That's exactly the point," said Dougie. "A girl's education should be just as important as a boy's. Take Jessie, she's as intelligent as any boy. She could see the boots off any of them when she gets to Johnstone." I saw Mam and Faither look at each other and Meg watching the two of them. I could guess by their wariness that Dougie had said the wrong thing but he was going on, "Some day in the not-too-distant future girls will go to the university, too."

Faither broke in, "And when they've all had their fine education will they be content to stay at home and wash the hippens? Tell me that, lad."

"Oh, well," said Dougie, "I didn't say they would *all* go to university, just the intelligent ones like Jessie." Again I saw the wary looks and knew that my hopes of getting to big school were slender indeed.

In June we heard that Duncan had got a church. His induction was to be in July and Doctor Graham was to take it. He was travelling by trap and would be happy to take Dougie and Meg with him if they felt they would like to witness the ceremony. Dougie was doubtful. Though he was on holiday from university he still spent most evenings and weekends on his books. During the week he worked alongside Faither at the butchers' aprons.

"It would be meant to keep me company," Meg urged him shyly. Dougie's head jerked up. "Oh, of course, I wasn't thinking. Surely I'll come, Meg, and be your chaperon."

"I could keep Meg company," I offered eagerly, ignoring the new word.

"Is Doctor Graham taking anyone else?" Dougie asked Meg. "She could maybe come with us."

"I don't know," said Meg. "I really wouldn't like to ask . . . "

"I'll take a walk up to the manse later," Dougie said. "There are some books I want to discuss with the minister."

I was awake at dawn and listening for the slightest sound from Dougie's room. He could move about very quietly but there was one very creaky floorboard near his door which he could never avoid. As soon as I heard it, I was up and out like a shot before he had even closed his door. He was startled. "Jessie, what's wrong?"

"What did Doctor Graham say?"

"He'll be delighted to have your support for Duncan." I danced my joy. "But don't let Mam see you with bare feet," he added. "Get back into bed and I'll bring you up a wee cup of tea."

I was careful not to wake Bella as I slipped under the covers. A special cup of tea brought by Dougie was a treat I had no wish to share with anyone.

* * *

My one worry about the great expedition to Glasgow was that the weather would be wet. July was often our wettest month. "You've to pray for a dry day for Meg and Dougie and me," I reminded the family at frequent intervals.

"And Doctor Graham can get as wet as he likes?" Faither teased me. Faither was beginning to recover his confidence now that Mam was on her feet again. Lilias would sit up and play 'peep-bo' with him, loving his gentle deep voice. The tension in the house seemed to relax as we became aware that he was in command again. There were rumblings outside among the weavers that the factories were taking over more and more of the market but though those reached us we were still reasonably secure in our own little world. It seemed to me that these rumours of disaster were just put about by people who liked being miserable.

My birthday was just ten days before Duncan's ordination. Elsie made me a beautiful muslin dress trimmed with blue ribbons. Faither had allowed her time off work in the shed so that I wouldn't see her make it. Jean took me off one Saturday and bought me lovely white slippers — not boots! I had never in my wildest imaginings thought of possessing such wonders. When I gulped my thanks, Jean dismissed them in her usual curt fashion. "You'll no' mak' a fool o' Meg at Duncan's induction." Quiet Tam had winked at me and smiled his pleasure. Everybody in the family had contributed to my outfit. Bella's crochet was evident on the underwear that Elsie and Meg gave me, and on the beautiful lace-edged handkerchief which was her own gift. But Dougie's present was the most amazing of all. I unwrapped the oddly-shaped bundle then gulped. "Open it," he urged. "You've seen a parasol before."

"Me with a parasol . . . " was all I could say.

"The grammar is debatable but I think you understand the situation," Dougie teased me. "Now, for pity's sake, open the thing."

"Don't put it over your head indoors," Mam warned. Dougie laughed at her superstitions but I knew better than to upset her. I twirled the beautiful blue silk round in front of me to gasps of admiration. "Look at the ruching," said Elsie, "it would take ages to make that."

"The colour of scyllas," Faither said. "You'll look a picture under that, my wee lass." Turning to Dougie he added, "Now I know what you did with your half sovereign."

"Oh, Dougie, you didn't spend all your money on me!" I was shocked. Dougie's university chum, Angus, had asked him if he would sing at a rather grand wedding in Glasgow. It was an emergency. The professional they had booked had lost his voice. Dougie was reluctant but Angus said that his sister, Maisie, who was studying music, would give him a run through in the church hall before the ceremony. Everything had gone well and Dougie had been awarded with half a sovereign which he proudly presented to Mam.

"No, Dougie, lad," she had said, "I'll wait for your first pay as a schoolmaster. You give yourself a treat. It's nothing you get but work, in all conscience." Dougie had put the shining coin away. Now I knew where most of it had gone. I felt my eyes filling with tears.

"Oh, well, if you don't want it, I'm sure Pattie McPhee would find something to do with it," he teased. The idea of the hoydenish Patty handling my beautiful parasol was enough to make me close it carefully and clasp it to my chest. I smiled at Dougie through my tears and he was well satisfied.

That was a nice birthday. Mam made a big dumpling for tea. Jean stayed on and helped lift it out the pot. Faither and Dougie were the last to come in from the shed. Dougie sniffed, "Ah, the spices of Arabia. How does it feel to be an Arabian princess, Jessie?"

"I *do* feel like a princess," I said, "with my lovely dress and slippers and parasol and everything. Oh, dear, it's *got* to be a nice day for the induction."

"Don't worry, it will. I feel it in my bones," Dougie said. "And if it isn't, I can always hold Faither's big umbrella over your parasol."

This time Lilias added her happy little chuckle which made us laugh all the more. Yes, it was a good birthday.

5

DOUGIE's bones were right. We got a perfect day for Duncan's induction. I could tell by the slight haze over Bridge of Weir in the morning that we would have a scorcher by mid-day. "Will it be just as warm in Glasgow?" I asked anxiously at breakfast.

"You won't be able to see it for dust," Dougie assured me. "There'll be no need for your parasol except to swat the flies." I looked at him uncertainly and he gave me a solemn wink.

It was still quite cool when the trap drew up at the door but I proudly unfurled my parasol for the family send-off. Dougie waited till we were well clear of the village then suggested I might be able to do without the parasol till the sun got really hot. "Your bonnet has quite a deep brim and your arm will get tired if you hold the thing too long," he said. "Of course, if you really need it, I'll hold it for you."

My shoulder was already aching so I closed the parasol without much persuading but I wouldn't hear of Dougie holding it for me, of course. Anyway, my bonnet was well worth showing now that it was freshly trimmed by Elsie. She had ruched some of the same blue velvet ribbon that trimmed my dress and fixed it at the base of the crown. Then, helped by Bella, she had cut and crimped strips of my dress muslin and formed them into tiny flowers which cascaded in sprays from the velvet down over the brim. Even Faither was impressed. "It's no' just Dougie that's artistic in this family," he said to Elsie when she asked him to view her work. Meg had refused to have her bonnet re-trimmed, saying that it was fine the way it was. She did allow Elsie to arrange her hair, however. At the time I found it difficult to understand how Meg, who obviously shared my pleasure in my lovely outfit, was unwilling to benefit from Elsie's artistic efforts but I understand now, of course. Duncan's church was in a poor district. She had no wish to draw attention to herself as a model of fashion. It certainly would not be expected of a minister's wife in that area. And Meg's faithful heart had been given to Duncan.

We clip-clopped our way through Johnstone and turned on to the Paisley Road. I was just thinking, "It's a pity Jean wasn't able to see me in my braws," when we rounded a bend and there she was with Tam, waiting by the roadside. The minister obligingly drew up to let us have a word. Quickly I raised my parasol and stuck out my slippers for her inspection.

"Aye," was all Jean said to me but she muttered something about having dust in her eye and fished out her handkerchief. I looked back as we drove on and saw Tam tuck her arm tightly in his as they turned for home.

I had never been in any church but our own and found that one strange. It had a different smell — more metallic and dusty though it was obviously cleaned. The brass shone and everything was neat but there were no trees waving near the window and no hedges to trap the dust from the road. Mam had warned me to behave especially well in Duncan's church and not to be tempted to turn round to look because everything was strange. But we were there early. Doctor Graham had escorted us into the church and gone straight through to the vestry where Duncan would be waiting for him. At first I kept my eyes straight ahead but then I noticed that Dougie was quite openly studying the building and Meg was glancing shyly about her. The congregation seemed very thin. Then, about ten minutes before the service was due to begin, there was a bit of a commotion and the Sunday school was herded in by a handful of teachers. It was a revelation to me. In Kilbarchan we all wore our best clothes on Sundays and no girl, however young, would appear in church without a hat. Even Patty McPhee, who could be a picture of disorder on weekdays, always had her hair plaited tightly for Sunday school and a hat squashed firmly down on top. And we all wore gloves even on the hottest of summer days. I tried not to stare at the display of poverty in front of me. At least half the young girls had no hat at all. Pathetic little strings of over-used ribbon tied back hair that had been roughly brushed and insufficiently washed. Girls and boys alike wore heavy boots, some with gaping soles and some obviously too big. For every trim and tidy child there seemed to be two with rents in their clothes or elbows poking out of jerseys. As they passed to their allotted pews they stared at me, a strange child in their midst. All through the early part of the service I suffered from a constant head-turning in my direction. Leaving home that morning I had felt proud of my lovely outfit but now that joy was marred by a feeling of guilt. I had never before thought of myself as either rich or poor. I knew from the attitude of my older sisters that we were lucky; that Faither had worked hard and we always had enough to eat. But I had never met anyone who did not have enough to eat. Starving people lived far away and we sent money to them. We took care of our clothes and made them last but there were always new ones for Ne'erday and other special occasions.

I missed quite a lot of the solemn

ceremony as so many thoughts teased at me. Mam's insistence on being clean and tidy at all times had often irked me, and Jean's peremptory commands in that direction had made me mutter in rebellion. Now I looked at wee lassies who were half-washed, and maybe hungry too and pitied them with all my heart. I glanced at Meg. She was watching Duncan, her cheeks flushed and her lips slightly parted. Her hands were tightly clasped, the nails marking the fair skin. I willed myself to look straight ahead for at least ten seconds then I glanced at Dougie. He was unaware of my scrutiny. Were they not worried at the sight of all these poor children? Meg was so kind-hearted but, of course, she was absorbed in watching Duncan. This was the most important day of his life, after all. And Dougie was maybe used to seeing poor children now that he went to Paisley and Glasgow so often.

Doctor Graham in his address said that their new minister was young and starting a new life in the ministry. This gave them all the opportunity for a fresh start and he appealed for their love and loyalty for their new leader. He pointed out that there were many people round about who found life a struggle and had given up hope but there was hope for all in Christ and it was up to all of us to do our best to make that truth evident by our loving and caring for those less fortunate than ourselves. I felt he was speaking directly to me but I couldn't think what I could do about it. Now, maybe if Meg married Duncan and she knew poor people who couldn't look after their bairns, I could go with her and help them . . . But Dougie had warned me not to think about Meg marrying Duncan till it was a *fait accompli*. *Fait accompli*: I liked learning French words. They began to parade through my mind: *merci . . . non . . . oui . . . quelles jolies fleurs . . . qu'est-ce que c'est . . . un petit morceau*. Somehow they matched my beautiful parasol. But Doctor Graham had ended and we were rising to sing a hymn.

We had shaken hands with both Doctor Graham and Duncan and were lingering uncertainly outside when we were approached by a couple I immediately labelled 'swells'. The man addressed us. "I believe you are friends of Doctor Graham. I am George Williamson, Duncan's father, and this is my wife." Dougie took over and made our introductions, then Mrs Williamson invited us to come to their house with Doctor Graham. "Just a cold lunch," she said, "but we do hope you can join us."

I had a moment of dismay. Dougie had taken precious time off his books to come with us but if Doctor Graham were waiting for lunch, what could we do? I needn't have worried. After one quick glance at Meg, Dougie accepted most readily. I felt so proud of him. He knew exactly what to do and how to speak to strangers. Meg would have been lost without him. Soon it was settled that Meg and I would travel with the Williamsons while Dougie would wait for Doctor Graham and Duncan.

★ ★ ★

The first shock was having the door opened to us by a maid. "I'll take the ladies upstairs, Betty," Mrs Williamson said, "and when you bring the sherries through, bring some nice lemonade for this pretty young lady." The girl smiled shyly at me before she turned to the kitchen. Mrs Williamson showed us into a high-ceilinged bedroom where dark mahogany furniture gleamed against damask curtains and coverings. "I shall be next door in my own room. If there is anything you need, just give me a knock. The bathroom is just a few steps down on the half landing."

"Bathroom!" I whispered to Meg when we were alone.

"Oh, yes, all the new houses in Kilmacolm and Bridge of Weir have them."

"Does Duncan's manse have one?" I asked. We had left the trap in the grounds of the begrimed, rather forbidding house.

"Yes, but I gather the whole place is in a dreadful state. The old minister lived alone with an elderly housekeeper. They did nothing themselves to the house and the congregation are poor and canna be asked to pay for redecorating."

That gave me some food for thought.

All the people who lived in big houses near us were well-to-do with servants and gardeners and coachmen.

The Williamsons' dining-room had big windows that looked on to a lawn like a bowling green. A stained-glass door on the same wall led to a conservatory. The shadow of palm fronds fell on the dappled glass. The oval table was covered in snowy damask and set with silver cutlery, cruets and a high silver dish which all bore tribute to Betty's elbow grease. Dougie explained later that the high dish was called an *épergne*. That gave me another French word to add to my store. The food wasn't much different from what we would have had for a cold Sunday lunch at home but it tasted exotic in those surroundings. Duncan's brother, Grant, had hoped to be at the induction but was tied at home because of a confinement. This puzzled me. Surely if you were tied at home that *was* a confinement. How could you be 'tied because of a confinement'? I decided to ask Dougie later.

★ ★ ★

"And, unlike your mother, I have no lovely daughters," Mrs Williamson said to me. We were sitting in the garden where Betty had brought out coffee. I looked up from my lemonade, surprised. With so many girls about the house I had always thought of Dougie as Mam's prize possession. Yet here was Mrs Williamson, with one son clever enough to be a doctor and another a minister, speaking as if she envied Mam. It was strange. Mr and Mrs Williamson seemed to enjoy talking to me though I could see that their eyes kept straying to Duncan and Meg as they strolled round the garden. They were sizing Meg up but I didn't let that worry me. Nobody could find fault with gentle, sensible Meg. I was sure of that.

I was quite sorry when Doctor Graham said we would have to be setting off on our long journey back. They both hugged me warmly before we stepped into the trap. Mr Williamson said something aside to Dougie and he answered, "I think so too but, of course, I'm prejudiced."

The afternoon sun was still beautifully warm and I fell asleep. Dougie woke me gently when we were climbing the hill from Johnstone. "Right, Jess, put your bonnet straight and get your parasol up while I rub my stiff arm. You're getting to be quite a heavyweight, you know." I needed no second bidding. I'm afraid the poor children I had worried over earlier were quite forgotten as I made my triumphal way home.

When I asked Dougie on the Monday what Mr Williamson had been saying to him when he left Glasgow he wouldn't tell me — just kept putting me off and then said he'd tell me on my wedding day.

"I'm never going to get married," I protested. "I wouldna like to leave you all. But I'll have a bairn."

"God forbid," said Jean sharply and pushed me towards the house. I went slowly and heard Dougie round on her. "Maybe you'll listen to me now. I warned you. We live in the country. It would be easy if only you didn't keep her so sheltered. All the boys in the village know when Thunderer is serving the cattle. She'll hear it the wrong way." Jean's lips were clamped firmly shut.

He turned to Meg but she gave him a half smile and gently shook her head. We were leaving the shed at the time. Faither and the other two had already gone into the house. Jean marched in, collected her bonnet and shawl and with a quick, "See you in the morning," was off. I saw Meg hurry out after her and, sensing something was up, I slipped out the back way in time to see the two of them walk into the shed. I desperately wanted to know what all this mystery about bairns was for it was clear that was what had upset Jean.

As soon as I was within earshot of the open window I started to dead-head some pansies. This was always my job because I was nearer the ground that the rest of them, as Dougie put it.

"I've been trying to get you to masel' a' day," Meg was saying. "Jean, he's asked me — yesterday . . ."

"I canna say I'm surprised," Jean laughed. "And when's it to be?"

"Well, that's what's worrying me. Duncan says the big manse is that miserable and lonely . . . yet he hates to tak' me awa . . . and I feel that I canna be spared. Mam's never going to be that fit again and Jessie should be getting to the big school at Johnstone and then training to be a teacher. And Dougie'll no' be finished for a long time yet . . . So, I've decided to say 'no'. We'll have to wait awhile — "

"See here!" Jean interrupted her. "You've a right to your chance just like everybody else. You're twenty-two years auld and you've worked hard for Faither ever since you left school. It's a' right for Dougie to talk about Jessie getting an education, but he should mind the sacrifices they're makin' for *him*. Many a lad is earning a man's wages at his age."

"But he works hard when he's no' at university."

"Aye . . . aye . . . I ken . . . There's no' a lazy inch in Dougie but he's one o' these idealists and no' aye that practical. Faither's got to keep at the butchers' aprons because that's steady money coming in every week. So that leaves you and me at the fancy shawls. Elsie's awa' wi' the fairies half the time. She's aye dreaming something up and when you're doing the shawls your mind has to be on the business. One mistake she didna notice could leave you wi' nothing worth selling. Bella's a quick worker but that excitable . . . anything in trousers. I'm thinking we'll have to get her married off early or we'll hae a red face."

"Jean, don't say that . . . she would never — "

"There's nae harm in her, Meg, it's just that's she's . . . oh . . . emotional . . . excitable . . . Every chance she gets she's wi' the silliest lassies in the village and they're hingin' round the horse trough, giggling at a' the daft laddies. I'll be glad to see her decently settled. So, if Dougie's to get his chance at university and Mam get help wi' the bairn an' a' that, Jessie will have to learn the weaving. She'll mak' a better job o' it than these two, I'm telling you that. No, Meg, you've got your right to happiness. Duncan's a fine lad and, by whit you tell me, he needs you beside him."

Their voices faded as they walked to the gate. I looked at the miserable bundle

138

of pansies in my hands — withered like my hopes. Quickly I threw them on to the compost heap and ran to the privy where my tears could flow unnoticed. Resentment boiled up in me. Meg had just newly met Duncan. Surely they wouldn't be getting married for a long time; time enough for me to get to big school and then Dougie would be finished at university and I could train as a teacher. Jean didn't care. She was encouraging Meg just because Dougie wanted me to go to the big school. Jean was a bitch. I whispered the bad word: bitch . . . bitch . . . *bitch*.

It was difficult to force my food over the lump in my throat that night. Everyone assumed I was overtired from my trip or had had too much sun, so I was sent to bed as soon as the meal was over. Burrowing under the quilt I stuffed my fist in my mouth and cried till at last relief came. When I calmed down I felt ashamed. Of course Meg must have her chance of happiness. Dear, gentle Meg who was willing to leave our bonnie wee cottage to go and live in that grim big building where most of the windows were uncurtained. Jean seemed to think it was right for Meg to go and, reluctantly, I had to admit that Jean usually knew what was what. If I mentioned the school at Johnstone at all or let Dougie mention it, Jean might say something about Dougie, my lovely Dougie who worked so hard and was such a comfort to me, too. I strung all the French words he had taught me like a litany and fell asleep.

★ ★ ★

Next morning as I dressed beside Bella, I made up my mind how I would behave. I would be noble, a heroine. No one would ever know the despair that lurked in my breast. No one would ever know the hopes I was sacrificing. I would be the best weaver in Kilbarchan before I was finished. Faither would tell people he couldn't do without me in the weaving shed. No, he would say I was 'indispensable'. Mam would say she couldn't do without me in the house and people would look at Lilias and say, "See that bairn? Jessie brought her up. A perfect wee mother."

I fetched and carried all day, amusing Lilias and never showing any signs of tiredness. "It's just been a wee stomach upset you had," Mam said with satisfaction. She had been anxious to hear all the details I could give her about the Williamsons' grand house and I was delighted to oblige. Mam didn't know what an épergne was and I was able to tell her. "And they had these lovely grapes, the kind folk bring you when you are ill. They weren't from their own conservatory but Mr Williamson said they would have their own ready by the end of August. He said it was a pity I didn't live nearer. He would be delighted to give me some. They seemed to like me. It was a good thing I had my parasol and things."

Mam laughed gently the way Meg does. "Judging by Duncan, I would think his folks see beyond braw clothes." It seemed almost like a rebuke yet Mam was smiling fondly at me. Another puzzle. That night Meg wrote a wee letter to Duncan's mother and a much longer one to Duncan. I was getting Lilias ready for bed and had a fine chance to watch her every time I turned round to pick up something I needed for the bairn. Meg's cheeks were flushed as if she was sitting over a hot fire. She had started eagerly, then stopped to chew her pen for a long time. Her eyes looked bright and moist as if she was somewhere between laughing and crying. Then she started scratching away at a furious speed. Gradually she slowed down a bit but I counted five pages before she finished. Then she read the whole thing through twice with a funny sort of half-anxious smile on her face. "She must be saying 'Yes', I thought, "but fancy taking five pages to say it."

Duncan's letter two days later asked if he might call to speak to Faither on Saturday. We all knew what that meant though nobody actually came right out with it. Faither said, "We'll just tak' a holiday, lassies, and you can a' be in your braws." It was arranged that Jean and Tam would come up from Johnstone in the afternoon and supper would be early so that Duncan could have both dinner and supper with us. Meg was walking down to Milliken Park to meet Duncan.

I was surprised and thrilled when she asked me to go with her. Dougie came to me when I was out in the garden picking flowers for the table. "Jessie," he said "you know that you are going with Meg to the station."

"Of course," I said.

"Well, there's a reason," he said. "The others don't bother to explain because they underrate your intelligence. I think it's worth telling you that you are really there as a kind of chaperon."

"What's a chaperon?" I asked.

"Well, it's a sort of guardian, I suppose . . . A French word — another for your collection. I know the idea is strange to you because Meg is so much older but, you see, a young lady — a well-brought up one, that is — doesn't go out alone with a young man. Once they're affianced, then it will be different. Duncan will be responsible for Meg and her reputation."

"You think it's a *fait accompli*, then?" I asked.

Dougie laughed. "Good for you. You learn fast. And, Jessie, mind that Duncan and Meg will be a wee bit shy. Nothing can be said openly till he's spoken to Faither. Yet they'll have a lot of things they want to say to each other. If you could just skip ahead and pick flowers . . . "

"Give them peace to talk?" I asked.

"See! I knew fine you'd get the idea."

Dougie was leaving for Paisley as soon as he had his dinner. This seemed to happen most Saturdays. His chum, Angus, shared some expensive books with him and they met, he said, to discuss problems with their work. If the weather was dry Dougie would walk all the way home. Sometimes he would walk up over the Gleniffer Braes and down by the Brandy Burn. Dougie really walked to save money, I knew, but he could make it sound so fascinating. I'd never met anyone else with his capacity for making life real and exciting.

I would have liked to wear my full rigout again but Meg said folk would stare at us and anyway I could not walk far on the rough road with my slippers. So, it was back to boots for me and my next-best dress. Elsie did my hair for me and I had new pink ribbons so it wasn't too bad. Meg kept dropping things when it was time to leave and I was afraid we would be late. Lilias seemed to sense that something unusual was going on and started to cry when she saw me going out of the door. Bella held her up to the window and I waved but it made no difference.

"I hope she's not going to be fretful all day," Meg said.

"Not a bit of it." My tone was resolute. "She'll forget us as soon as we are out of sight." And I'm afraid I soon forgot my tender charge too, in the thrill of being Meg's chaperon as we waited for the train that was to bring Duncan to her side.

I had wondered what he would say when they met but Duncan, whose face had flushed and paled alternately as he walked towards us, contented himself with shaking hands with each of us. Meg made a stilted enquiry about the journey. He said it had been rather hot. So, we set off up the hill, none of us completely at ease. I felt that this matter-of-fact behaviour was a dreadful anti-climax. Remembering Dougie's words, I moved on ahead of them and pretended to be interested in the dog-roses which shed their petals on our path. 'Of course,' I reasoned with myself, 'a minister couldn't just sweep Meg into his arms and cover her face with kisses the way daft heroes in love stories do.' I glanced over my shoulder. They were walking quite sedately. Meg's arm in his. Then I carefully picked a spray of flowers, half-turning so that I could check a little detail. Yes, they were walking arm-in-arm like any old couple but Meg's hand was clasped firmly in Duncan's. I tossed my head and skipped happily ahead.

Duncan had no sooner given the family courteous greeting than he asked to have a word with Faither and they disappeared into the parlour. Meg hovered smiling but almost in tears near the door. The rest of us were not much better. I played with Lilias and cuddled her close to me to atone for my previous indifference. Then Faither called, "Meg!" and she almost ran to the parlour. Soon the three of them were back. Meg ran to Mam's arms; then Duncan was kissing us all and Mam was weeping happy tears and Dougie was getting out wine glasses and asking Bella to fetch some lemonade for me; and Lilias was standing on my lap and almost strangling me as she joined in the general excitement. She had grabbed a handful of Duncan's hair when he tried to kiss her and I'd had to tickled her to set him free. It was funny to see Duncan looking like a boy with his hair all stuck up in the air. Then he stood with his arm round Meg's waist as Faither proposed their health and gave Duncan a wee word of welcome. Next thing, Dougie was hammering on the table and demanding a speech from Duncan.

Duncan made a few false starts with everyone laughing at him. "Well," he protested, "it is rather strange, you must admit, to acquire four sisters all of a sudden."

"Four!" Dougie said, "you can't count, man. Wait till you meet Jean. She'll sort you out . . . eh, Meg?"

"Don't frighten him, Dougie," said Meg, "or he might run away."

"No need for that," said Dougie. "If you want any advice, Duncan, just apply to me. I've got them all under control. I had to, you know, in self defence. But I must say Meg makes the best cherry cake." After this it was more difficult than ever for Duncan to make a sober speech. He contented himself with thanking Mam and Faither for parting with their pearl — he supposed we all knew that the name 'Margaret' meant 'pearl'. (I certainly didn't and I found out later that Dougie was the only one in the house who did.) Meg had been called after Faither's mother, of course, being the second daughter. Then he said he was sure he would be happy among us all, once Dougie had taught him a few tricks.

After that Mam took over. "You two young folk will have a lot of things to discuss, I'm sure, so off you go to the parlour where it's nice and cool while we get the dinner ready in here." I was sent to the dairy to buy a big jugful of thick cream. Meg had made a trifle the night before but with the weather being so hot we had decided to leave the decorating till the last minute. Elsie was going to do that. Meg had worked terribly hard all

Friday night to get things ready. There was a lovely cold lemon pudding in the pantry that we were to have with our supper.

When I got back from the dairy Bella was scrubbing the tiny Ayrshire potatoes that Mam always boiled with a sprig of mint. Meg had cooked the chicken and the ham which we would be having cold with salad and the wee potatoes. Late at night she had boiled up the chicken stock for the broth we were to have at supper. It would be followed by cheese soufflé and the lemon pudding. It seemed to be all the things I liked that we were having that day.

I really can't remember much about the rest of the celebrations. It's got so mixed up with all the fun of their wedding. And maybe it got swamped, too, by my music lessons. Now, that was something that took my breath away! Dougie came back from Paisley that Saturday night just after Duncan had left and I was beginning to feel the reaction to all the excitement.

"How would you like to have music lessons, Jessie?"

"Me! But how could I — we haven't got a piano and lessons cost a lot of money, don't they?" I stammered.

"Angus's sister, Maisie, is training to be a music teacher and she needs pupils to practise on," Dougie said. "I told her you were a good singer and she said that was all the better. She will be teaching singing, too."

"But the piano?" I said.

"I've thought of that," Dougie said. "Lizzie Forsythe has a piano she never uses. I'm sure if I spoke to her she would let you practise on it. She would probably be glad of your company, living alone like that. I expect the thing is out of tune but Maisie has got me another engagement to sing at a wedding so I'll be able to pay for the tuning with my fee — "

"Just a minute, my mannie," Faither broke in. My heart sank. Was he going to say we had never been beholden to anyone and he was not going to be beholden to Lizzie Forsythe now? If Faither said, 'No,' that would be the end of it. "Haud your horses, laddie," Faither was saying. "If onybody pays for the piano tuning it'll be me. But I'm no' very sure if we should be asking Lizzie Forsythe . . . what do you think, Bess?"

"Well . . . " Mam hesitated. "I think Dougie's right about her enjoying the wee lass's company but I'm thinking she would be putting the fire on in the parlour and that's mair expense for her . . . "

"Aye," Faither spoke ponderously, "and she's proud."

"I know we couldn't offer her money," said Dougie, "but there must be other ways . . . I mean, Mam's black bun is the best in the village. You could give her one at Ne'erday, Mam."

"And Meg and I could make her a cherry cake," I broke in. I hadn't meant to be funny but Faither looked at Dougie and the pair of them exploded, remembering Duncan's dilemma. It lightened the atmosphere, however, and in the end Dougie was given permission to sound out Lizzie Forsythe. "She's to be treated with respect, mind!" Faither warned us. "That good woman had nae life o' her ain — sacrificed everything for her invalid mother."

I was sacrificing everything, wasn't

151

I . . . the big school at Johnstone and the chance to be a teacher? But it wouldn't seem such a sacrifice if I could have music lessons and a trip to Paisley every Saturday with Dougie. I was a good walker and it wouldn't be long before I could walk all the way back, too, maybe over the Gleniffer Braes.

Dougie chose Sunday afternoon to make his call on Lizzie Forsythe. I was mad with impatience and took Lilias out into the garden as soon as she woke from her afternoon rest so that I would see him turning out of Church Street. Though Lilias was small for her age she was getting quite heavy for me to hump about. She would stand on my lap and jump energetically up and down. It seemed time to try her with her bare feet on the grass. Though she crowed with pleasure, curling her toes under her, her wee fingers were digging tightly into my arms. Gradually she got a bit more confident. I stood her a yard away and she moved forward, falling into my arms. Time after time she collapsed laughing, then I started to move her just a few inches further away. The game went on

152

for a long time. We were both absorbed in her efforts and I had just shouted in triumph, "Four steps, clever lass," when the gate creaked and Dougie, with Lizzie Forsythe by his side was standing applauding.

"Well done, the pair of you," he said. "I've brought Miss Forsythe along to have a word with Mam. You'd better come in out of the sun. You look like a pair of lobsters."

I smiled shyly at Lizzie Forsythe. Her presence here surely meant that Dougie had been successful. "So you're going to have music lessons," she said. And my joy was complete. Meg served tea and I played quietly with Lilias while Dougie went back to his books. Lizzie Forsythe was enjoying herself and only made a token protest when Mam said, "You'll stay for a bite o' supper, Lizzie. There's nothing hurrying you and Wattie will be glad to see you and to thank you. He's awa' for a walk wi' some o' his cronies. They'll be sitting by the burn, smoking a pipe and putting the world to rights."

"My faither used to smoke a pipe," said Lizzie, "and he aye looked that happy when he stairted it up and got puffin' — like a bairn wi' a comforter."

I watched them nodding happily at each other. My music lessons were secure. Life was good.

6

AND life stayed good all that autumn. Lilias, having found her feet, started trotting about happily. We had got her off hippens so I didn't have to face hanging out washing when I got home from school. Dougie went off to university again in November but I didn't feel it so badly. Life was opening out for me. And, besides, I always had his company on Saturday afternoons. Sometimes Angus wasn't there at all but Dougie would come in with me and Maisie would run through a song with him. And once, when Dougie had earned a fee, he took Maisie and me out to a tearoom, and a waitress in a starched apron and cap took our orders and brought a three-tier cake stand to our table and a toast rack and things like that, and the lemon with our fish was cut like butterflies. I thought it was all wonderful and I got ready to tell Dougie so but he was gazing at Maisie,

155

his face lit up and kind of shy and she was gazing back at him. It was almost like watching Meg and Duncan. Meg and Duncan! Could my Dougie be falling in love just like Duncan, like other folk? Would Maisie take him away from us all, the way Duncan was going to take Meg? And I had liked her so much, too! Was she giving me music lessons just so that she could see Dougie? I looked at my false friend but she was smiling at me — a real smile.

"Come on, Jessie," she said, "we're expected to eat the lot."

With so much to think about, I found it difficult to eat but Dougie made up for us and sat back in his chair well content.

We walked home but by the direct route as Dougie decided it would take too long to go up over the braes. My thoughts were going round in circles. Dougie had been going to Paisley most Saturdays for a while. Had his stories about meeting Angus just been a blind? Perhaps Angus was starting to go elsewhere and Dougie needed a chaperon for his meetings with Maisie . . .

"You're very quiet today, Miss Allen," Dougie teased. "What are you thinking about?"

"Nothing," I started to say automatically.

"You sound just like Elsie," he said. "Don't tell me a mind like yours idles along thinking of nothing."

I smiled but it was no use. Dougie had always been my confidant. "Dougie," I said, "did you and Maisie need me as a chaperon?"

"What!" Dougie stared at me. His face went red then white. I had my answer but was uncertain how to cope with it.

"Oh dear, oh dear," Dougie said, "I might have known . . . you're too quick by half. How can I put this to you, Jessie? I don't want you to be involved in deceit of any kind . . . ever. It's like this, pet. I am fond of Maisie and I think she is of me, though nothing has been said because nothing could come of it for a long time. You understand that?" I nodded and he went on, "Apart from the fact that I'll be studying for many years yet, I'll have to work for a while after that to make up to Mam and Faither for all their sacrifices. So you see . . . " he paused. I could think of nothing to say. "Between ourselves, Jess, I think Maisie will be the only lass for me. When I first met her she gave me your shy smile and it drew me to her. Then her love of music . . . Well, I hope some day I'll be able to marry her but, of course, that's all in the far distant future."

It sounded so sad put that way. I grasped Dougie's hand. "Look, Jess," he said, "I don't want to lay any burden on you but do you think you could forget what you have guessed and just see Maisie as your music teacher?"

He was looking anxiously at me so I nodded and said, "Of course, Dougie." Anything that would help Dougie was a sacred duty to me.

★ ★ ★

Life got busier than ever as the wedding day drew near. Elsie was making Meg's dress and Meg and Bella were helping with the bridesmaids' dresses. Meg wasn't to put a stitch in her own gown — that would be bad luck. On top of that we had 'Dougie's night school' as it came to be called. It had really started after Duncan's induction. Meg had felt shy and rather awkward at the Williamsons' house. "If I could only speak to people the way you do, Dougie," she had said that night when the three of us were in the back kitchen.

"No reason why you shouldn't," said Dougie. "Once you're sure of your grammar, the rest is simply a matter of reading. If you choose the right books, you can learn almost anything. The foundation of good speech is good grammar and the best way to acquire that is by learning Latin."

"Latin?" Meg was as surprised as I was.

"Yes, I mean it." Dougie was firm. "It gives you the construction of language in a clear-cut way. It's a very disciplined language. Of course, if we had time, it would be worthwhile studying other roots — Anglo-Saxon and Greek — but I think we'll content ourselves with Latin. What d'you say, Meg? While I'm off we could have a little class, say, nine to nine-thirty every night, eh?"

"Can I do it too?" I asked eagerly.

"I don't see why not," Dougie was expansive. "You've no school in the morning and Lilias sleeps pretty well now. In fact, till the nights draw in we could do quite a lot of the basic memorizing in the open air — up the hill."

It started with just Meg and me. Elsie and Bella were always out with their own gang of friends in the light evenings. Bella couldn't pass boys without giggling. I heard Elsie telling her once that she should keep her dignity — it would intrigue the boys more — but restraint was quite beyond Bella. But by September when there was a nip in the night air and we were pursuing our studies at the living-room table, Elsie and Bella would join in chanting declensions and conjugations. Dougie was a born teacher and, though taken aback by the unexpected additions to his class, he was not long in adapting the lessons to suit. When he went back to university in November I feared that would be the end of our studies. But Dougie decided that we should carry on the class on Saturday evenings. By then Meg and I knew enough to be set exercises to do during the week.

Mam was right about Lizzie Forsythe putting a fire on in the parlour for me. She looked forward to my practising almost as much as I did, I think, and would never let me start without sampling one of her homemade candy balls. This lasted through most of my piano practice and sometimes had to be gulped before I could start on a song. For Maisie, true to her word, was giving me singing lessons and was delighted with my progress. I always remembered what Faither said about respecting Lizzie Forsythe and thanked her nicely at the end of each practice. I don't think I'll ever be able to play a scale without remembering the delicious flavour of candy balls.

Dougie had designed Meg's kirking shawl as soon as the engagement was announced. I think he had been trying out sketches even before it was a *fait accompli* but when I asked him he just started to tease me. He promised that his very finest effort would be kept for me. I was tempted to say, "What about Maisie?" but decided against it.

The days began to race and drag alternately. I was desperately keen to be wearing my bridesmaid's dress and the coral velvet tippet we were all to have over them. Meg's dress was to be white velvet because Hogmanay was always cold. Elsie was making a sort of cloak for her in the same velvet so that she wouldn't have to wear a shawl with her veil. I had heard Jean's startled reaction to the proposed dress for Meg. "White! Naebody in Kilbarchan wears white . . . and a veil . . . "

Meg had been hesitating. "Elsie says that's the kind of wedding the well-off people have and Duncan's parents will be used to it."

Jean had looked doubtful but hadn't said any more in my hearing.

We knew that, even if it snowed, Kilbarchan folk would make sure that every scrap of snow would be swept up so that the bride could walk to the church. Bella had crocheted extra petticoats for us in fine Shetland fleece to keep our legs nice and warm. The velvet had to be bought, of course, but Elsie and Bella had woven the ivory silk

for our dresses. It was a shade deeper
than Meg's velvet. Each night I fell asleep
dreaming of cream silk and coral velvet.
They took me right out of the everyday
world — not that the everyday world was
all that bad for a girl who was having
piano lessons . . . and singing lessons
. . . and Latin . . .

It was a wonderful day, crisp and
sunny. Everyone was happy, even though
we were losing Meg. I think Faither
must have gone through even more
agony during Mam's illness than I had
realized. I was standing behind Elsie and
Bella in church, feeling nervous, excited,
thrilled and aware that every woman in
the congregation had melted at the sight
of Meg, serene and happy as she made her
slow way down the aisle to join Duncan at
the communion table. Faither disengaged
his arm, nodded to the minister, then
joined Mam in the front pew. I saw
him take her hand firmly in his and
turn to smile at her in the same way
that Duncan had smiled at Meg as she
drifted towards him. And I remembered
Meg's words to me, "I think that's what
makes for a happy home — when you

get twa folk, man and wife, like that thegither."

As they made their solemn vows there was a hushed stillness which made a tiny shiver go down my spine. I had no doubt of Meg's happiness.

We could hear the horses getting impatient before we left the church. The coaches were to take us in relays to the Buchanan Arms Hotel in Kilmacolm for the reception. Meg had been willing to have a very quiet wedding for the sake of Mam but Mam would have none of it. "Jean got her guid send-off," she said, "and the rest of you will get the same. Faither and I aye planned it that way."

I felt very important taking my place at the top table. We had drunk the toast to the bride and groom as soon as we arrived and Meg and Duncan had cut the cake. I didn't get much icing on my portion, I remember, but Faither slipped me his. Now the smell of hot food was making me ravenous. None of us had eaten much breakfast. One good thing about being at the top table, I felt, was that we were served first. Sipping my lemonade, I watched the others. Meg looked a picture of happiness. She wasn't eating much and though she didn't actually turn and look at Duncan very often, I had the feeling she was seeing him all the time; that the happy din round about was not reaching her. Faither was talking to Duncan's mother — about me, I think, for they turned together to look at me and smiled. Mr Williamson was asking Mam questions and then nodding at her replies. Lilias, in Jean's charge at the top of one of the tables which were set at right angles to ours, was getting restless and trying to crawl over the table to get to me. Jean was saying, "You'll see Jessie later." That didn't do much good so Tam took out his big watch and held it to her ear, then opened the back to let her see the wheels. Jean and Tam were going to take her away before the speeches started and they would spend the night at our house. I had heard Meg thank Jean, "I'll feel easier for Mam if you're there: all the excitement of the wedding, and another daughter leaving the nest . . ."

Mam still had quite a lot of daughters

in her nest, I'd thought at the time; and Duncan bore me out in his speech when he made much of the fact that he had grown up without a sister's refining influence and Meg would have her work cut out: he hadn't got used to the idea of having five sisters but Dougie had promised to show him the ropes. Faither too complained that he had always been outnumbered but now the balance was being redressed and he would soon have a nice curling team of his own.

The guests, now wined and dined, were in a happy mood and ready to laugh at all their sallies but when Dougie started to reply to the toast to the bridesmaids, pandemonium ensued, as they say. I hadn't realized how many funny things had happened in our house. Retold and embellished by Dougie, with all our voices mimicked, they left us all helpless. He worked his way to Duncan's appearance on the scene, then gave his dramatic version of the cherry cake incident. "'This cake is symbolic,' Duncan thought, clasping his hands to his heart. 'I am to know my fate.' So, in trepidation, he removed the cherries one by one. 'She loves me . . . she loves me not . . . she loves me . . . '" Then he went on about the preparations for the wedding and how he was wading through silk and velvet in every corner of the house; and threads stuck to every chair so that his Sunday suit looked as if he had slept in the hayloft. "And, by the way, everyone keeps saying how lovely the bride's sisters are, what about the bride's brother in his new suit?" Of course, that brought a barrage of rude remarks. Faither's old Uncle Mattha suggested they should enter Dougie for Kilbarchan horse fair. Rab Shaw, who'd had more than a few drinks, shouted, "And if you're no' careful, Dougie lad, it'll be the gelding class."

I couldn't understand what was so funny about this but old Uncle Mattha was clutching his stomach and tears were running down his face. I looked at Faither but though he was smiling, he was giving Dougie a look that carried a warning, I could tell. Dougie drew his speech together then and ended on a more serious note by saying that the lovely bridesmaids would miss their lovely sister but her sunny presence would bless the home she made for Duncan just as it had blessed ours. I saw Mam wiping her eyes and Bella looked as if she might cry, too. In fact, I wasn't far off it myself but I knew it would spoil the nice picture we made for Meg on her important day.

And we still made a beautiful picture in our dresses as we prepared to see the new year in. It would have been a scramble to get ready when we got home with only half an hour to spare had it not been for Jean. She had the fires roaring merrily in both the living-room and the parlour where the men might want to take their pipes. The stone pigs were in our beds with our nightgowns wrapped round them. Tam had brought in an ample supply of coal. All Faither had to do was get out the bottles while Dougie performed the ritual of taking out the old year's ashes. There was little time to be aware of the new gap in our numbers. We had no sooner drunk our own healths than we heard sounds of our first-foots arriving.

Elsie and Bella were enjoying themselves mightily, greeting all the newcomers as they arrived and receiving compliments on their dressmaking efforts. Mam looked tired but not ill. My black bun seemed to be lasting for ever. The fire was really hot but I was too lazy to move my chair. The conversation, all about the wedding, seemed to rise and fall in waves round about me. I was glad no one was asking me to speak . . .

I woke up in my own wee bed in the morning. Seemingly Dougie had carried me upstairs, fast asleep, and Elsie had managed to undo the buttons of my dress and ease me out of it without waking me. There I was in my layers of underwear and my big toe caught in one of the holes of my crocheted petticoat. I tiptoed across the cold floor to peep round the curtains. It was cold and misty. Bella was fast asleep. Our wedding finery hung on hooks behind the bedroom door. The ivory silk looked chilly. No one would stir for a while on New Year's morning. The village was dead. Carefully I crept back under the bedclothes.

Meg and Duncan had left shortly after the dancing started. We had given them a cheery send-off. They were going to spend five days in a hotel in Gourock. It sounded lovely. People said you didn't get much frost by the sea and they would be able to walk even though it was winter. Hotels were nice warm places with carpets everywhere. But would Meg and Duncan have two rooms? Married people usually shared a room. But surely Meg couldn't get into the same bed as Duncan! Where would she take her clothes off without him seeing her? Perhaps they would have plenty of bathrooms in hotels . . . I could maybe ask Elsie, or Bella . . . but really, that was the sort of thing I normally asked Meg and she wasn't here and wouldn't be again.

★ ★ ★

Meg's sunny presence was missed as Dougie had forecast it would be. And Dougie, too, was very caught up in his studies. I treasured our trips to Paisley. The weather was too severe for walking back all the way but Dougie took to giving me my Latin lessons on the train. At first I was embarrassed that other travellers might hear us but Dougie asked what there was to be ashamed of. "Supposing we were gossiping about our neighbours," he said, "that would be normal, but would it be better? Get your values straight, Jessie."

We all had to take a turn at the pirn winding now to give Mam a rest from Lilias who rose full of boundless energy from her afternoon sleep. We would try to organize little games which kept her close to us at the wheel. Life was very busy for me — straight to Lizzie Forsythe's from school, then home to do half an hour at the pirn winding, playing a boisterous game with Lilias before her supper, then getting her ready for bed. I loved that part. She would be getting sleepier and sleepier and snuggle in to me as I wrapped her in her warm night clothes. Meg had always carried the tin bath through to the fire for me, then brought a bucket of cold water to pour in before she topped it up with boiling kettles. The first bath-night after Meg's wedding, I tried to bring through the bath myself but Lilias clung to my skirts and wouldn't go to Mam when she called so, after that, Elsie and Bella had to take turns preparing the bath. There was no doubt that I was Lilias's favourite. She refused to go to anyone else when I was around. I think it must have been hurtful to Mam at times, on top of her not feeling fit. I supposed the wee one associated me with food and comfort, and I had had time to play games with her when the others were busy working.

Dougie's term ended in April. It was lovely to know he was near when I came home from school even though he was working hard in the weaving shed. He took over Meg's Jacquard loom. The arguments about employing beamers started up again between Faither and him. Whereas it had worried me terribly before, I took it as a good sign that Faither was recovering his confidence, so badly shaken by Mam's illness. Only now he was shorttempered with it and could not keep calm while arguing his case. Other weavers round about were complaining that the agents no longer wanted shawls — the printed ones were so cheap by comparison — but Faither still found a market for Dougie's special designs. The demand for muslin was declining steadily as the big mills took over. Whenever there was a lull in orders, Faither set Elsie to weave some for Meg who had an enormous number of windows yet uncurtained. "For everyone that sees the inside o' her hoose, there are a thousand see the outside," was his philosophy.

Meg's letters were eagerly read by all the family. They spoke of a life that was far different from ours. In spite of her restricted means, Meg had had to employ a little maid. "It's expected of a minister's wife," she wrote. "I can't be seen scrubbing the doorstep or polishing the door handle. In spite of their own poverty they have a standard for the manse that I must live up to. I chose a shy little girl who had had no experience but seemed willing. She was completely lost at first and over-eager. I had to beg her to stop working and take a rest. I think we will get on very well. She is learning fast and simply loves having a room to herself. I am teaching her patchwork and she is going to make her own quilt."

My Saturday trips now included the

long walk home with Dougie. One week we cut my lesson short and we all went to the wonderful new museum at Paisley. Angus and Maisie had been before but it was new to Dougie and me. We could have stayed for ever but there was the long walk home ahead. In spite of that we went to a tearoom and had tea and cakes. Angus and Maisie were going to walk right over the braes with us and down the Brandy Burn, then they would go back to Paisley along the main road.

When we got clear of the town, Angus started to ask me about the various plants and the birds that were singing and darting around us. I was surprised that he knew so little. There was nothing Dougie did not know about the countryside. Perhaps Angus did not get out of Paisley much. Eagerly I filled the gaps in his knowledge. Then he wanted to know all about Lilias Day, and I described the floral arches and how each street competed for the prize for the best-decorated one and how lots of people came back to Kilbarchan for the day and how strangers came to see the festivities and some people got drunk.

"Perhaps I'll bring Maisie some time," he said. "D'you think she would like it?"

"Oh, yes, and she could have dinner with us and see my wee sister," I said, quite unaware that I was being manoeuvred by a couple of artful young men. I have to laugh now when I remember how I told Mam that I had invited Angus to bring my music teacher to see the Lilias day procession.

I prayed for a fine day so that I could show off my native village and my bonnie wee sister. As usual we were all up at dawn with the rest of the folk. Elsie and Bella had been hard at their needlework. I was pressed into doing some simple hemming myself while I chanted Latin verbs for Dougie. He said I was a quick learner and coaxed me through the dull passages with the most outrageous flattery so that my Latin was proceeding quite well in spite of the limited lessons. I was well ahead of Elsie and Bella. Sometimes I thought, "If only I could go to the big school . . . " but then Lilias would twine her little arms round my neck and nuzzle me, and I felt compensated. That Saturday I kept her in her old clothes till half way through the morning then, talking non-stop to keep her from fidgeting, I began my careful labour of presentation. Elsie had decided on a pale lemon muslin dress for her because of her dark hair and eyes. My hopes of being able to curl her hair had been fulfilled and she showed promise of being as curly as Dougie once her hair toughened up. Carefully I coaxed the silky ringlets round the ribbons, all the time telling her what a bonnie lass she was and how Maisie and Angus would love her. "You'll have the wean's head wasted wi' vanity," Faither said.

"She's far too young for that," I stated firmly.

"Oh, hark at Nurse Allen, Mither." He turned to Mam, laughing.

We were to have dinner at twelve and I was relieved to see Maisie and Angus walk down the street with Dougie before that. Dougie made the introductions to the grown-ups but I eagerly brought forward Lilias myself. Maisie's reaction was all I had hoped for. Picking the wee lass up in her arms, she admired her pretty dress, the sash, and the hair ribbons. But Lilias had taken a fancy to Angus and stretched out her arms to him. He stood, hesitating, obviously unused to young children. "It's all right, Angus," Dougie said, "you can bounce them — they're practically indestructible."

Lilias sat upright in Angus's arms for a moment or two, stroking his cheeks, then she kissed him quickly and buried her face in his collar, chuckling. "I can't get the big lassies to do that," he said. We were all laughing then but I noticed Elsie's eye caught his and a funny look passed between them.

"Elsie would like to kiss him," I thought. Then I looked at Bella. Her cheeks were flushed and her eyes bright. Her tongue flicked round her parted lips while her chest heaved rapidly. "She would like to kiss him too," I thought.

A shiver ran down my spine. This loving business was frightening.

7

LIZZIE FORSYTHE became more talkative than ever at my music practice after Lilias Day. I had hit on the bright idea of suggesting to Mam that we invite her to meet my music teacher. Of course, Mam was delighted. "She'll enjoy the company and getting her dinner made for her," said Mam. I agreed. But though I had thought of giving Lizzie pleasure, there was a more cunning thought underneath my suggestion. It would underline the idea that I saw Maisie as my music teacher and make things safer for Dougie.

It seemed that Lilias Day was no sooner over than I was back at school and the autumn leaves were falling, and November took Dougie back to university. All I had to look forward to was the horse fair on St Barchan's Day, half way through December. I was planning to take Lilias to see all the horses being driven into the town. She loved anything that moved. Then there would be the sweetie stands and the shooting galleries and all the cheery crowds for her to see. Mam said it would depend on the weather: she was too wee to take risks. Actually Lilias was as healthy as they come in spite of being small for her age. I prayed for a good day while I hurried to finish the huge muffler I was knitting for her. Bella, sensing how anxious I was, offered to crochet a miniature version of our Shetland petticoats.

It was as well that we had prepared for the worst because the weather was absolutely miserable and Mam would never have allowed me to take Lilias if we hadn't muffled her up till she looked like a wee Russian doll. Faither always closed the weaving shed on St Barchan's Day. In the old days, we had all gone to the fair together but Mam never risked the cold weather now. Faither said he would just have a look at the horses and have a crack with his cronies, then come back to read by the fire.

I had never enjoyed watching the arrival of the horses so much as I did that day with Lilias squealing and chuckling by my side. Her cheeks, always rosy, grew red as apples. There was no question of her getting cold because she couldn't keep still for a moment. I had my work cut out stopping her from getting trampled underfoot. Mam had said we were to come home for a quick dinner and not to eat a lot of rubbishy sweets. Only the threat of not getting back to the pretty horses made Lilias eat anything at all, so eager she was to return.

It was just about two o'clock when we were startled by the sound of a horn and the Renfrewshire Hunt rode into the village in full cry. I was swept along with the others. Lilias nearly went crazy with delight when she saw the horses with their riders in hunting pink. The fox had gone into a village garden and was trapped. There was an absolute melee of trampling horses, desperate hounds and eager young spectators. I found a hole in the hedge for Lilias and myself. The noise was dreadful — baying hounds, shouting children and then a blood-curdling yelp. The fox was caught, torn to pieces and devoured while children, Patty McPhee and her brothers among them, I noticed, danced like dervishes. Waves of nausea washed over me. I trembled helplessly. 'I mustn't be sick,' I kept thinking. 'I'm looking after Lilias.'

She was standing bewildered, unable to take it all in. "What is it?" she kept asking me. "What the doggies doing?" Then I heard a scrabbling of hooves, a horse neighing and a scream that sounded like Bella. I must have fainted then because I found myself on the ground, leaning against the hedge. Lilias was trying to lift my eyelids and saying, "Wake up, Jessie. Want to see the horses." Crowds of people were passing close by but no one was paying any attention to us. I tried to stand but slithered down again, sweat breaking all over me. Lilias started to cry. I never in my life thought I'd be so pleased to see Patty McPhee but when she stopped and said, "What you doin' there?" I burst into tears.

"Is it your big sister?" she asked. "I don't think she's hurted bad. Nurse Duncan was going after her. Her skirt's torn, though."

"What d'you mean . . . my big sister?" A new terror hit me.

"Your Elsie. Mrs Nisbet-Brown's horse reared and she got knocked into the hedge. It was a near thing. Your Bella squealed like a stuck pig but why are you sitting there?"

"Feeling sick," I said. "Maybe too many sweeties," I added untruthfully. Patty McPhee would never understand my squeamishness if I spent the rest of the day explaining and I had no wish to try.

"Is your wee sister sick?"

"No, I think she's just frightened because I'm no' well."

"Will I take her home to your Mam?"

It was a kind offer coming from a rough diamond like Patty McPhee but Lilias, as I had suspected, refused to budge from my side.

"I'll run and tell your Mammie," Patty said.

"No, don't, you'll upset her," I groaned, but Patty was off. I dragged myself up, getting scratched in the process. I would have to find my way through the crowd. A lot of them were drunk. I mustn't get separated from Lilias. She was clinging to my skirt, looking scared. I remembered the sweets I had been keeping for Dougie and drew them from my pocket. "Sweeties," said Lilias, her sorrows temporarily forgotten.

My legs felt numb. Perhaps if I leaned against the hedge the feeling would come back. Lilias was content for the moment. The hunt had moved off as fast as it came and the crowd was gradually thinning, most of them drifting back towards the booths. There was always a lot of drinking went on at the horse fair: a successful deal or a disappointment — any excuse would do. Lilias was beginning to get restless. I would have to make an effort, if only my stomach would stop heaving. If only I could wash the sound of those hounds out of my ears. If only I could forget the blood and the fur flying and Bella's scream . . . Everything was swimming in front of me. Then I saw Faither. He was running. He elbowed one roisterer aside and raised noisy objections from the man's companions. Then I was in his arms and crying, and Lilias was clinging to my skirts and crying too. Then a big, stout figure moved unsteadily towards us. "Whit's wrang wi' the bairns?" Rab bellowed.

"Jessie's sick, I think," Faither said, "and the wee one's feart."

"Bluidy hell," said Rab, more softly. "You lift the wean. I've got Jessie."

And indeed he had got me in one effortless scoop. "It must be like this in a hammock in a sailing ship," I thought as Rab wove his easy way to the cottage.

Nurse Duncan had stayed on to gossip after tending to Elsie and had just been about to leave when Patty McPhee brought her news. As soon as she saw me she tutted, "What's this I hear? Too many sweeties."

"No! It was the fox," I gasped and started to retch.

Nurse Duncan wasted no time. "Bella, a basin and a towel. Wattie, some brandy. Wrap a shawl tightly round her, Bess, while I hold her head. The bairn's had a fright, I think. All right, Lilias," she added, "Jessie's all right — just a wee bit sick. Stop your crying now and get your dolly ready for bed. She's sleepy."

Miraculously, at Nurse Duncan's words, Lilias gulped her last sob and, fetching her dolly from its miniature cradle, sat down on her own little stool by the fire intent on undressing it.

I gave up being brave and thankfully relaxed into being fussed over by Nurse Duncan. Having refused food or drink I was tucked up in my warm bed and told, "Just have a nice wee rest like Elsie's doing, Jessie, and you'll be fine. Bella's helping your Mam get Lilias to bed so you've nothing to worry about." I passed the next hours alternately crying and dozing and being visited by Bella with offers of food and drink I didn't want. Then I opened my eyes to find Dougie by my side.

"It's not often you're sick, Jess," he said.

"Oh, Dougie, it was awful." I burst into tears.

"Tell me, Jess," he said. "Come on, now . . . it'll help you to get it out."

With sobs and hiccoughs I told my story while Dougie gripped my hands in his and listened attentively. "What I can't understand," I ended, "is why they don't buy bones for their hounds. They've got plenty of money. Why do they have to chase the poor foxes?"

A smile had fleetingly crossed Dougie's face when I mentioned bones for the hounds but he spoke to me seriously enough.

"We've got to keep things in proportion, Jessie. Wild animals are ruled chiefly by instinct and that always guides them to protect their own species. Hounds enjoy chasing foxes and if they're hungry when they set out, their instinct urges them on to kill their prey. Foxes are very cunning and often manage to elude even a well-trained pack of hounds. I wouldn't be too sentimental about the foxes. They enjoy killing — look at the damage they did up the hill a few months ago. When a fox gets into a hen-run he kills a lot more than he could ever eat because his instinct is to chase and kill weaker animals. You see, Jessie, that keeps rats and other vermin down. Nature balances things out. What I find more difficult to understand is how the human hunters enjoy the kill. They say, of course, it's good exercise for the horses and the chase brings out the extra effort in them. That's true, of course. But sometimes I wonder if it's the survival of an old instinct. You know, Jessie, before St Barchan came, the druids practised human sacrifice here. I sometimes wonder if it's atavistic memory that drives people to hunt and kill."

"What's atavistic?" I asked.

"Come downstairs, Jess, and I'll tell you while I eat my dinner. I'm starving."

"Oh, Dougie." I was full of contrition. "I didn't know you hadn't had your dinner."

"Right! Wrap up well. I'll be finished my soup before you're down."

He wasn't. I sat at table and was easily persuaded by Mam to have a 'taste' of soup to keep Dougie company. Of course, after that my appetite returned and I ate heartily. Elsie had chosen to stay in bed, waited on by Bella, rather than show her swollen, scarred face downstairs.

"Nurse Duncan likes to stick all her patients in bed," Dougie assured me. "It keeps the place tidy."

So my misery ended in laughter as Dougie helped me 'get things in proportion'. But one thing was still worrying me and I voiced my fears in whispers to him as we climbed the stairs after supper. On the way home from school one day, Patty McPhee had said to me that we should never have called our bairn 'Lilias'. Her mother had said so because the original Lilias had died at sixteen and Patty said our Lilias would die at sixteen too.

Dougie exploded with indignation. Quickly he pulled me into his room and shut the door behind us. "I've never heard such rubbish," he declared. "What about the minister's little lass —"

"Harriet," I supplied.

"Yes, Harriet. How did she die?"

"She fell out of a railway carriage."

"Yes. She died because she fell out of a railway carriage — not because she was six years old. Don't listen to that stupid Patty McPhee or her daft mother. It's no wonder these brothers are in every stupid bit of vandalism round here with a mother like that. She should see to her menage instead of promoting silly scares."

"What's menage?" I asked.

So I had another word to add to my French collection. I lay in bed stringing them together and tasting the sounds. But Patty had told me something else about Lilias — something I had tried and tried to forget; something so awful that I just couldn't believe it. "It's just like the coo an' the bull," she had said, "only they dae it in bed." Mam and Faither could never do *that*. Why, Mam wouldn't let the lassies iron their drawers when Faither and Dougie were about. 'No modesty' was one of her severest criticisms. And yet . . . there had been that day up at the farm. Rab hadn't noticed me and had addressed Dougie: "I hear your Mam's nae better and yer faither's oot o' his ain bed till she's too auld to be interested, puir bugger." Dougie had flushed and hastily said something about the wean aye crying and Faither needing his sleep. Then Rab had caught sight of me and had agreed heartily with Dougie, "Aye, a man canna work if he disna get his sleep!" But it wasn't true. Lilias didn't cry much at nights at all.

And Faither slept in the box bed in the living-room where Jean had slept before she was married. Mam was all alone in the bedroom except for Lilias who slept in the truckle bed which slipped under Mam's bed during the day. Rab had said, 'Puir bugger'. And Faither had changed a lot since Lilias was born, looking older and not so sure of himself. If it was true what Patty said . . . did a man like doing what the bull did? Would Duncan do that to Meg? The hot blood of shame flooded over me and I buried my face under the blankets. But the thoughts would not go away.

★ ★ ★

It was the Tuesday after the horse fair. Faither had stented and pressed a shawl that Jean had finished on Meg's loom the day before the fair. He aye liked to do the finishing himself though he let Elsie and Bella do the fringing. As usual, Elsie couldn't resist caressing the beautiful shawl then slipping it round her.

She started parading up and down the shed. I laughed with Bella and Faither while admiring the picture she made. 'Our Elsie could be a real lady,' I thought. 'She walks as if she were one, never hurrying too much.' And her tawny hair, tawny eyes and straight dark brows gave her a very distinctive look. There was no-one else in Kilbarchan looked the least bit like Elsie.

I was in the corner beside Jean's loom. She was working away as usual, ignoring 'Elsie's antics' as she termed them, when the door beside me opened and two ladies stood on the threshhold. 'Real ladies' I judged them immediately, by their dress. The others did not notice the strangers as they watched Elsie languidly raise and curve her arms to display the rippling design of the supple shawl. Nor did the strangers see me.

"*Tres charmante, n'est-ce pas?*" said the older woman turning to her companion.

"*La fille est charmante, mais quel ménage! Une rose dans une porcherie,*" the other replied.

"*Garde ta langue,*" snapped Mrs Nisbet-Brown.

Jean's loom stopped as she caught sight of the women. The others turned and Elsie came forward with an eager welcoming smile. "Mrs Nisbet-Brown, how kind of you to call. May I introduce my father . . . " As Elsie did the rounds to the manner born I concentrated on memorizing the sounds of their speech in my head for Dougie's translation later. I knew it was French. 'Quel' and 'menage' were familiar to me but it didn't make sense. Our household was not the least bit like the McPhees' and that was the only connection I had had with *menage*.

Then Mrs Nisbet-Brown was urging Faither to allow Elsie to spend Saturday with them. "We would fetch her and bring her back, of course. It would be such a pleasure to have her . . . "

Faither looked uncertain. Elsie's eyes were glowing so brightly that I expected to see them reflected on his face.

"Come into the house, ladies," he said. "It is for my wife to decide."

Jean started up her loom again, disapproval in every line of her stiff back. Of course Bella and I could not resist following the party indoors. She whispered to me, "Mam will likely make tea. I think we should put a match to the parlour fire and get the good cups out." When we slipped into the parlour, we found the display cupboard open and the good china gone. A quick look in the back kitchen showed us beautifully set trays with scones, gingerbread and shortbread. Mam must have seen the two women arrive and had prepared for any eventuality.

And there was Mam by the living-room fire with its shining kettles, in her everyday dress but tidy as usual, and saying, "You'll have a wee cup of tea to warm you up, ladies. It's a snell day. Bring the cups, lassies." She addressed this to us with a steady look which we understood.

Bella was all for lifting her tray and hurrying back to the living-room. "No, that'll look suspicious," I said. "Check the number of cups — aye, she's allowed one for Jean. See, we've got to give Mam time to mask the tea, anyway. Then we'll walk in as if we always used the good china."

"You're getting like Dougie," she said, "always thinking things out." She couldn't have paid me a finer compliment.

That night I followed Dougie up to his room after dinner. He had been unimpressed by the news of Mrs Nisbet-Brown's visit. "Least she could do after knocking the girl into the hedge. It's sickening to see Elsie ready to lick their feet," had been his comment. I don't know why I didn't ask him to translate the French I had heard as soon as he came in. Perhaps it was because these titbits of learning he passed on were something special between us but I think there was more to it than that: an inner voice, and Mrs Nisbet-Brown's reaction, had warned me the remark delivered unsmilingly was no compliment.

"Dougie, what does this mean?" Carefully I delivered the sounds I had heard. Dougie's face went white with anger.

"Who said that?" he hissed.

"The French lady who was with Mrs Nisbet-Brown — her companion, she called her."

"The bitch!" said Dougie who never, never swore. "Oh, Jessie, I'm sorry. It's nothing to do with you, pet. Forget what I said. But . . . to think that Elsie's ready to grovel for an invitation among that lot!"

"But what did it mean, Dougie?"

"It meant, 'the girl is charming but what a household! A rose in a pigsty'."

"Pigsty!" I was indignant. "We gave them the best china."

Dougie burst out laughing then, throwing his arms around me and rocking me like a baby.

"Oh, Jessie, you're a wee treat. I've been getting things out of proportion but I must tell Faither this. That'll put a stop to Miss Elsie's visits to the 'big hoose'."

"Oh, Dougie," I said, discomfited, "I don't know that you should."

"Why not?"

"It'll cause a lot of trouble, don't you see? Elsie's that set on going and she'll be disappointed and she'll upset Faither and Jean'll probably say something to make it worse and Elsie and Bella will blame me for telling you . . . "

"Stop, stop!" said Dougie. "Let's have a think. What has Bella to do with it?"

"I think she's hoping they'll invite her some day, too."

"It gets worse," said Dougie.

"It's Faither really I'm worried about,

Dougie," I said. "He's changed such a lot since Mam was ill — as if the strength had gone out of him, too. He used to tell us what to do. Now he doesn't . . . or if he does, he loses his temper. He's not the same as he used to be. I think we should be gentle with him."

"You're getting more like Meg every day, Jess," Dougie said.

"That's funny," I laughed. "Bella said I was getting like you." And I told him about the tea party.

"Good for you, lass," he said. "What's the good of a brain if you don't use it?"

Dougie heeded my pleas and kept his own counsel about Elsie's association with the big house. She returned from her first visit full of its wonders and begging Dougie to teach her French. "They asked if I knew it," she said. "I said, 'No but I know Latin'. Neither of them did."

"It's just as well," Dougie said heartlessly. "If they'd tried you out you would have collapsed at the first fence." He relented, however, and agreed to include French in our Saturday night lesson.

The visits to the big house became steadily more frequent. Bella would sit entranced while Elsie described the panelled dining-room with its magnificent silver dishes on side tables. She delighted in giving detailed descriptions of the beautiful outfits the women wore. I could understand Bella's jealousy. But Elsie had obviously no intention of sharing the privileges she was winning for herself at the big house.

Mrs Nisbet-Brown had discovered Elsie's gift for needlework and was glad to make use of her. She insisted on paying generously for the work.

"I don't like it," Dougie said to me on one of our Saturday trips. "If there's anything I hate it is being patronized; yet there's Elsie lapping it all up as if we were serfs."

"But Faither pays the lassies for their work in the weaving shed," I said. "When Elsie's away she doesn't earn so much there. Surely it's just the same thing."

"Maybe you're right. I suppose it's just my pride . . . " Dougie shrugged his shoulders but I could see that he still thought no good would come of Elsie's visits. I sensed that Mam and Faither shared his unease but could think of no way to stop them. Elsie worked harder when present in the weaving shed than she had ever done before. Her dreaminess had changed to a purposeful verve. She spoke like a lady and liked to toss the odd French phrase at Dougie who would respond with a rapid sentence in incomprehensible French which he usually refused to translate even for me. I think it was one way of getting rid of his feelings.

Bella, intent on being invited to the big house, was keen to speak French too, so we did make fair progress. Teaching was a gift Dougie enjoyed exercising and I think Mam and Faither found a certain contentment watching us round the table on Saturday evenings. And, of course, I appreciated it more than anyone. It was almost like getting to the big school at Johnstone.

Meg's visits to Kilbarchan had stopped in September. Mam said the weather was too cold for her to travel alone and Duncan was too busy to bring her. It seemed funny to me. The weather wasn't really that bad and there was Dougie — away early every morning all the way to Glasgow. Elsie went oftener and oftener to Mrs Nisbet-Brown's and raved about the Christmas and New Year parties she had enjoyed there. Bella was getting really jealous and bad-tempered. I heard her accusing Elsie of not trying to get her an invitation. I had the feeling that this was near the truth and said so to Dougie on our way back from Paisley that Saturday.

"I expect you're right," Dougie said. "Elsie has carved a niche for herself there. Bella wouldn't fit in. Couldn't you imagine her opening her mouth and putting her foot in it at a posh dinner party? Elsie is much more intelligent than I had given her credit for. Mind you, I don't like the way she is using that intelligence — but she is getting exactly what she wants out of life and manipulating people nicely."

"D'you think that's what she was always dreaming about, Dougie," I asked. "I mean, being a lady some day."

"Maybe. But dreamers don't usually put it into action. It takes determination and Elsie has more of that than I realized." Dougie relapsed into thought.

It was the Monday morning after that that the postman brought a letter from Duncan to Mam. She gave an anxious look at Faither before opening it. Elsie and Bella were upstairs getting ready and I was brushing Lilias's hair by the fire. I saw Faither move over to Mam's chair to lean over her shoulder. "I thought that might be it," he said.

Mam sat, looking helpless, biting her lip. She looked at the clock. "It's time for Jean. I'll be glad to hear what she thinks." Faither patted her shoulder. They both looked relieved when Jean's heels rang out on the flagstones. I pretended to be busy playing with the bairn while my ears were flapping in a desperate attempt to hear what it was all about. Mam handed the letter to Jean with a low murmur. She read it at a glance.

"Well, there's nae time to be wasted. We'll send Bella. Elsie's had plenty gallivanting! Faither can help her doon to the station wi' her box."

"D'you no' think she's young to be

in the midst o' things?" Mam asked hesitatingly.

"It's time she got a fright . . . stop her going daft every time a lad passes the door. Aye, it's time she got a shake-up to her daft notions."

"Oh, Jean. She's a good lass, surely?" Mam said.

"Nae doot," said Jean, "and Meg'll be the one to keep her that way." Then Jean saw me and chased me off to school.

I had plenty to think about on the way. Meg had not been seen in Kilbarchan since the end of September. We were near the end of January now. Why was she keeping away? Patty McPhee said women got fat when they had bairns in their bellies. Was that why Meg had stayed away? Did she have a bairn in her belly? Last time I had seen her she was thinner than usual and a wee bit pale. But Duncan had explained that. He said that she had been working too hard and he was going to put his foot down. And what was Bella too young to be in the middle of? Why did Jean think it would be good for her to get a fright?

Why did Bella go daft when she saw the lads? Could it be that she wanted them to do what the bull did? I shook my head to eject the wicked thought and started running.

8

I DID a lot of head shaking, I think, at the start of 1873. The New Year celebrations had been more subdued than usual because a lot of people were in mourning as a result of a typhoid outbreak we had had in November. Then there was a lot of worry about the wells in the village. Some experts had declared them polluted; then others had said the reports were exaggerated and we had nothing to worry about. I think the scare we had had with Mam made me more worried about things like that than I would have been. The lassies at school would tell horror stories about the wells and the typhoid one minute, then they'd be laughing and joking the next. I kept thinking what would happen if Mam got ill again . . . or Lilias, my own lovely wee Lilias who ran laughing to hug me as soon as I got home from school and would join in with a high tuneless chant when I was practising my songs. It was

Lilias I cuddled when I was worried about Elsie's frequent trips to the big house and the feeling of alienation these engendered; when Dougie's absence from dark morning to dark evening seemed interminable; when I longed for gentle Meg's comforting presence and sunny smile and now when I woke up each morning without Bella.

I tried tentatively to get some information about Meg and the need for Bella's presence at the manse. After all, she had a wee maid already and it wasn't spring cleaning time. But always Mam and Faither would put up a barrier and turn my questions gently aside. I sensed that Dougie was under some sort of constraint and stopped myself from badgering him. Then a letter came for Dougie from Duncan. This had never happened before and I was consumed with curiosity. Desperately I waited for his step and snatched up the letter, thrusting it in his hand as soon as he entered the living-room. "My, my, the postmen are awfully wee nowadays," Dougie said with a laugh as he slit the envlope open, read the contents and turned to Faither. "I wrote to Duncan asking him if I could bring Jessie to see her big sister on Meal Monday."

"When's that again?" asked Mam.

"The first Monday after the last Friday in January," Dougie and I chanted in unison. It was one of the more intriguing titbits he had passed on about Glasgow University, this holiday designed to help poor students who came from far away to return home to fetch another barrel of meal back to the garret they had rented for the term.

"I'd like fine to go masel'," said Mam. "I miss Meg."

"The weather's too chancy, Bess," Faither said. "We'll go in March and take the bairn. I just hope Dougie's in the right o' it."

"Duncan and Meg seem happy with the arrangement," Dougie said. "I don't think you could look for a better commendation."

"Aye. Aye," said Faither, "time goes on and everything changes. One month they're bairns . . . " He tailed off sadly.

Dougie scooped up Lilias and tossed her about the way she loved. He started asking me about my music practice and the tense moment passed.

I had counted the days till Meal Monday and was awake long before time that morning. A line of light under Dougie's door showed me that he was seizing the opportunity for more study before we set out. It gave me a pang. I had the feeling that this trip had been engineered by Dougie for my benefit and he could have done with a day spent over his books. Why had he written to Duncan? Though Dougie was fond of Meg he didn't miss her the way I did or Mam did. Maybe at last I was going to get an explanation for Meg's absence. Maybe Patty was right; women got fat when they had bairns in their bellies. Cows got fat before they had calves. People usually got bairns when they got married. Did that mean what Patty said was true? It seemed such an awful thing . . . surely Meg and Duncan . . . ? But they would never do anything wrong. Maybe you had to do that awful thing to get a bairn . . . like taking medicine. And maybe you just said, "Well, it's got to be done." But that didn't fit in with what

Rab had said . . . about Faither being out of his own bed. "Puir bugger," he had said.

Quickly I slipped out of bed and started to dress. I would creep downstairs and get the porridge pot over the hob. If I used the poker carefully maybe Dougie wouldn't hear me stir the fire.

It was still quite dark when we faced the cold world on our walk down to the station. Faither had had his arm about Mam as she relayed her messages to Meg and Bella. Lilias was mercifully asleep. She might think I was at school when she woke up. That would sound familiar. And anyway, Elsie would be arriving back late morning. The sight of the coach always made Lilias dance with delight. I sniffed the smoky smell that clung to the station even at this early hour. Dougie kept me walking up and down the platform to make sure I didn't get chilled. Then I felt the ground shudder and I clutched Dougie's hand as I always did when the snorting monster approached us. Once inside, this fear always left me. I felt perfectly safe enclosed in the compartment with

Dougie beside me ... stale smoke, varnish, leather and woollen clothing; the windows tightly closed against the cold landscape now lit by a wintry sun.

The huge station at Glasgow was something I could never have imagined ... the height ... the noise ... hurrying people ... sad departures ... happy arrivals. My emotions were battered as Dougie steered me through the crowded station and out into the thronging streets. We were to take a tramcar to quite near where Meg lived. Then we would walk the rest of the way to warm ourselves up. Dougie carried his leather bag, carefully shielding it against the jostling crowd. Mam felt sure that the eggs Meg got in Glasgow could never be the same as the nice Kilbarchan ones. So I had been sent up to the farm to get a dozen and a half. We had carefully wrapped them in rags. Mam said that with a house that size to clean and polish Meg would go through a lot of rags anyway. Up at the farm I had chatted to Rab while Maggie, the poor misshapen woman who was his housekeeper, went to fetch the eggs. Since the St Barchan Day episode when he had carried me home, I felt quite at ease with Rab and just talked to him the way Dougie did. What did a bit of swearing matter when you knew exactly what to do in an emergency!

"So your Meg will be living in a big braw hoose?" he asked.

"Well, it's big," I answered, "but anything but braw." I explained about Duncan working in a poor district where the folk didn't have the money to do up the manse and Duncan and Meg couldn't afford to furnish it all but Faither had got the lassies to weave enough braw muslin to cover all the windows. It's funny, I would never have told anyone else in the village the things I told Rab that day about Meg's privations trying to run the big manse; about how guilty I had felt seeing all the poor children in church; about the special Sunday evening service that Duncan had started 'For Young Men and Maidens' which gave them somewhere decent to go instead of hanging about the streets. I told him how one of the boys had offered to come and dig the manse garden one night a week and soon some others said they could help with the decorating and Meg had suggested that some of the girls might like to come along and make pancakes for their supper. Meg said that some of the girls had had no chance to learn to cook, living in over-crowded tenement houses. Rab said, 'Bluidy shame.' Encouraged, I went on to tell him how the young folk gobbled up the pancakes, no matter how many she made; and Meg couldn't afford all the butter and jam they needed but when the garden was in order she hoped to grow her own jam fruit. Old Maggie appeared with my basket of eggs. Rab sent her off again. "A nice big lump of your butter, Maggie," he said and, to me, "Juist let me ken whenever you're going to see Meg. I'll never miss a bit butter. Puir weans . . . puir bluidy weans . . . " Of a sudden, I realized that Rab's swear words were sometimes blessings and not the curses that people took them for.

And Meg certainly took our unexpected gift as a blessing from Rab. "Wasn't that kind of him?" she said softly. "Folk are good." I looked at the plump matronly figure that had once been my thin sister and was at a loss for words. Something was certainly happening to Meg. It wasn't overeating that had caused the change because her face and neck were still thin. Maybe Patty McPhee was right. But it wasn't fair. Why should Patty McPhee know more about my sister than I did?

I kept my lips tightly compressed as Meg led us through to Duncan's study for a cup of tea. "It's nice and warm there," she said, "and Duncan has moved in enough chairs." The book-lined room was certainly snug. I watched Bella as she fussed over Meg, lifting her feet on to a footstool and stuffing a pillow down her back. Jinty, the little maid, brought in a huge oak tray with tea and heaped-up scones.

"You can see that Bella has been busy," Meg said, nodding towards the scones.

"Excuse me, Miss Bella . . . " I looked in surprise as Jinty asked Bella for instructions about the oven which seemed to be overheating.

"I'd better have a look at it myself," said Bella seriously and left the room. Dougie saw my expression and gave me a lovely wink but I still did not feel mollified. The hot tea and scones tasted delightful after the long cold journey. The fire crackled merrily while Dougie and Duncan talked about university and I brought Bella and Meg up-to-date on news of home and Lilias. Then Bella bustled off to get on with her cooking. Duncan asked Dougie to give him a hand lifting something that was blocking the attic and I was alone with Meg.

"Bring your chair nearer me, Jess," she said, "and we can have a nice wee talk. There now, that's nice! Well . . . I expect you see a bit of a change in me?" I nodded. "There's a very good reason for it, Jess. As the bible would put it, I'm great with child."

"You've got a bairn in your belly," I paraphrased.

"That's right. You don't seem surprised. Had somebody told you?"

Resentment boiled up. None of the people who should have told me had done it. They'd treated me as if I was daft. I vented my spleen suddenly. "Patty McPhee. She said it was just like the coo an' the bull."

Meg gasped in shock, then, "Oh

dear . . . oh dear . . . " she said slowly.
"Dougie wanted us to tell you a while
ago. He thought you might learn the
lovely truth the wrong way. Oh, Jessie,
I've been stupid. Jean and I wanted you
to stay a wee lassie . . . "

I felt the tears rush to my eyes at her
distress. She stretched out her hands and
drew me towards her. "Oh, Jessie, my
bonnie wee Jessie, the truth is lovely,
believe me. Forget Patty McPhee and
her farmyard talk. Put it right out of
your mind. God made us different from
the animals. I'd better start right at the
beginning and tell you what happens to
you when a lassie becomes a young
woman."

So, gently and in her new authority
as married woman and wife of the
minister Meg told me all I wanted to
know, answering my questions without
any embarrassment. In the end, when I
felt there was nothing more to learn she
added, "It's impossible to understand it
fully, Jessie, till you are older and in love
with someone, loving him more than you
love yourself. Then God puts this longing
in you — that your bodies will mingle and

the child they produce will be the child of your loving and always dear to you. So, forget Patty McPhee — poor lass, with a mother like that — and think of all the loving parents you know. I can assure you that Duncan and I don't compare ourselves with the coo and the bull."

We were both laughing heartily when Duncan came back. "I've left Dougie upstairs measuring that old dresser. He thinks I could split it up and use sections of it for storage." He perched himself on the arm of Meg's chair. "Well, what do you think of our news? Surprised?"

"No, not really," I said shyly. "It's wonderful news. I hope the bairn turns out as nice as Lilias."

"I would say our bairn is going to be about three times the size of Lilias at a rough guess," said Duncan, patting Meg's stomach.

"Fancy a minister doing that," I thought. But of course he had done something much worse or Meg wouldn't be like that. But Meg wouldn't have said that it was much worse. She said God gave you those longings for your bodies to mingle so it couldn't be bad.

Then Meg was speaking to me again. "Bella will be busy with the dinner now, so how would you like to come and see the wee nursery we've got ready for the bairn?" This was another idea for me to take in — my sister with a nursery! Only folk in books had nurseries and, of course, the minister and the doctor. But Duncan was a minister. And Jinty, the maid, had called Bella 'Miss Bella' as if she were a real lady — our Bella! Now, if it had been Elsie . . .

Duncan threw the door open with a flourish. I gasped in delight at the white paintwork and the yellow walls which had little fairytale characters dancing all over them. "Where did you get those?" I asked, moving closer.

"I painted them," said Duncan. "It got me away from my scolding wife for an hour or two." Meg smiled up at him fondly. "When we get tired of them, I'll just paint over them again . . . like the tide coming it. But you haven't admired Meg's handiwork." He directed me to the cradle in the corner, canopied and flounced in yellow sprigged white muslin.

"Oh, it's braw," I said, examining the dainty handiwork. "It must have taken you ages, Meg . . . all these gathers."

"I got quite a lot of help from the girls in the 'pancake club' — that's what Duncan calls them," she added with a laugh. "The cradle was Duncan's when he was a bairn. Mrs Williamson is delighted to see it all draped again."

Dougie came rattling down the bare attic stairs and joined us. "Dougie," I said, "wouldn't Lilias love these wee paintings?"

"Mmm . . . I believe she would, but I don't think they would suit Mam, do you? Tell you what . . . we could kick Bella into Elsie's bed and you could have Lilias beside you."

"Oh, yes," I said, then remembered, "but that would leave Mam all alone." Then I remembered why Mam was all alone and what Rab had said about Faither being out o' his ain bed, puir bugger, and it all got mixed in with what Meg had been telling me and I started blushing and couldn't stop. Dougie was watching me keenly and I saw a blush creep over his face too. I often had the feeling that Dougie could sense what I was thinking. It was very disconcerting.

Meg took my hand and led me round the house showing me what they had managed to achieve with their wedding gifts. "So you see," she said as we ended our tour in her bedroom, "we can manage to put up the visiting minister by giving him our bedroom. We just whisk the clothes out of the press and the chest of drawers and we sleep on these two old couches Mrs Williamson gave us. Of course, it isn't so comfortable." I gazed at the bed which Meg and Duncan found so comfortable. It seemed enormous. In our house and all the other cottages there were hole-in-the-wall beds. I had never realized how cramped they were till I gazed at Meg's free-standing bed. "I'm surprised Bella's spread fitted it," I said.

"What? Oh, the bed," Meg laughed. "It didn't. I added two extra flounces."

It seemed we had no sooner finished the lovely dinner Bella had cooked than Jinty was appearing in the study with our afternoon tea. My resentment had long since melted and I don't think my tongue had stopped as I described Lilias's antics and relayed Elsie's tales of life at the big house.

"Ah, tea!" said Dougie with satisfaction, "there's nothing I like better than a big lump of cherry cake. It should help to keep Jessie quiet, too."

Jinty stood in bewilderment till Meg took pity on her and explained the family joke.

Dougie had said we must leave as soon as tea was over; the weather was cold and he thought we might meet fog before we got home. It worried me, too, because time was so precious to Dougie. It was dark as we made our way to the tram which would take us to the station. Already there were signs of fog. "D'you think it will be bad in Killy?" I asked Dougie.

"Not necessarily. The city is always worse — so many coal fires. Anyway we know our way blindfold from the station, don't we?"

"Aye, but Mam will worry," I said.

"Not when you're with me," said Dougie.

I opened my mouth to tell him that

Mam worried when he was out but clamped it shut again. It would only add to Dougie's burdens if he knew that. And Mam *was* worried that night, long before we reached home, for our train was stuck for the best part of an hour in thick fog outside Paisley while the frozen points on the line were dealt with. Dougie wrapped my huge muffler more tightly round me and told me to keep my mouth as well covered as I could because the air was foul. Then he started entertaining me as only Dougie could with tales of people in some hot country abroad and the queer lives they led; and how they got milk from coconuts instead of from a cow and things like that. Our fellow travellers who had been grumbling and groaning about the miserable wait soon quietened down as they listened with me. I don't think I ever remember Dougie stuck for something to talk about. Though he would spend hours happily alone with a book, he seemed to delight in digesting the information then turning it into a story.

It was as well we knew our way from Milliken Park station blindfold for the fog was as thick as I have ever seen it. Our breath froze in the chill air and Dougie with his arm round my back propelled me home. There were oil lamps in three of the windows, yet we did not see them till we were within a few yards of the house. Faither flung the outside door open and practically dragged us in. Mam was sitting by the fire. I could see she had been crying and she was fevered. Even Elsie looked upset. As soon as I approached Mam she threw her arms round me and sobbed, "I thought I was never going to see you again . . ."

"But you knew she was with me, Mam," Dougie said reasonably.

"Aye . . . aye . . . but . . . " Before Mam could say any more, I jumped in: "Is that soup on the hob? My! I'd like some."

Mam was galvanized. Elsie was ordered to lay places quickly while Mam moved the big pot nearer the flames. Dougie and I were to sit by the fire till everything was ready. We squashed together into the big armchair, Dougie laughing as Elsie trotted backwards and forwards at

Mam's commands. I hadn't really felt hungry, because I was exhausted, but the smell of the soup over the dancing flames and the comfortable feeling of being safe with Dougie in our own bonnie wee house soon changed that and I ate as heartily as anyone when we gathered round the table. Elsie had put two pigs in my bed and she kindly came upstairs with me and helped me undress.

So the embarrassment I had expected to feel when meeting my parents again after all I had learned that day completely disappeared in the little drama of our journey home. Half asleep over my mug of tea I had heard Mam ask Dougie about Meg. "A plump little pigeon now, Mam, and a very happy one at that," he had said, adding, "I see a big difference in Bella: more responsible, calming down under Meg and Duncan's influence."

"Jean'll be glad to hear o' it," she said.

As waves of sleep swept over me I remembered Jean's worries about Bella. "She's too emotional . . . going daft every time a lad passes the door . . . " But Meg had said God put these longings in you for your bodies to mingle. Surely He wouldn't give Bella all these longings . . . not for different ones . . . I just couldn't understand it. But she was safe with Meg. That was sure.

In spite of the adventures of Meal Monday, I was up bright and early next morning, prepared to creep down and get the fire poked up for Dougie. As I tiptoed past his door I heard a rasping cough. Dougie! He never got coughs . . . a bit of a cold sometimes, but never a cough. Then I heard a cough from downstairs. Mam! She was ill again! Quickly I ran down to the living-room but Faither was dressed and had the fire roaring up the chimney. "It's you, Jessie," he said. His voice was anxious. "Your Mam's got a chill again. She would have me open the shutters last night when she was worried about you two being lost. As soon as we decently can, I'll get you to fetch Nurse Duncan. No! I'll go masel', it's thick fog."

"Dougie's coughing," I said.

"Dougie? No' like him to hae a hoast."

"Well, he's got one now . . . and you say it's foggy, Faither?"

"Aye. He would be daft to think o' making for Glasgow the day."

"But he lost a day at his books yesterday . . . " I said unhappily.

"I'm sure he's got plenty he can study at hame."

"I suppose so," I said. "Is Mam bad?"

"She says 'no' but I'd like Nurse Duncan to come, if she can. I'll just go up and see Dougie, lass."

I busied myself with the porridge and the kettles, waiting anxiously for Faither's step on the stair. There was no sound of voices but I heard Faither close Dougie's door and knock on the other one. He must be rousing Elsie. Soon he was back. "The sweat's lashing off the lad and he's lost his voice," he said. "I've wakened Elsie and told her to get a move on. Ah doot you'll be needed for Lilias the day, lass . . . " His voice was unhappy.

"I guessed that," I said, "and if Dougie's in bed I'll be needed to run up with drinks and soup and things to him."

"Jean'll be here, fog or no'. She'll sort things oot."

"Aye!" I said unenthusiastically. Faither

gave a wee chuckle in spite of his worries. I was just imagining Dougie's feelings if Jean tried to 'sort him oot' in his present state.

But for once, Elsie forestalled Jean. "I could see to Mam," she said, "and the cooking, Jessie, if you could keep Lilias happy and carry things up to Dougie. Jean will be busy with the shawl she's doing for Mrs Nisbet-Brown's friend. If things are going well here in the afternoon I could go out and do an hour or two at the shirtings." It was the first time I had heard Elsie take the initiative in a crisis, though this was only a minor crisis to be sure.

When Jean arrived we were already into our routine. Faither had seen Nurse Duncan who promised to look in mid morning. Lilias, dressed and breakfasted, was trotting about with a duster in her little hand 'helping Jessie'. Jean's face softened into a smile as she watched her. "You'll be fine then, Jessie?" she asked. "It's a shame to have an expensive loom lie idle but send for me, mind, if Mam seems ony worse. Faither thinks Dougie's caught a chill but he's young and healthy . . . you'll hae the sense to keep awa' when Faither goes up to attend to him?"

"Of course," I said.

"Aye." She paused. "Dougie'll be glad you're here the day."

She meant 'and not at the school in Johnstone'. That was a thought that had previously caused me pain but now I could accept it quite calmly. Our family seemed to have dwindled so rapidly. Even though there were only two members absent — and one of those would be back — with Mam no longer fit for the heavy tasks and Faither ageing visibly, and the loss of Dougie's virile presence most of the time . . . well . . . There was Lilias, of course, but she was a little doll to us all. There were fewer and fewer people I could lean on so it was as well I could pull my weight. In July I would be thirteen and leaving school to take my place in the weaving shed. Already I could do the woollen shirtings. Elsie had surprisingly become quite interested in teaching me on the odd occasion when we were both free. This meant she had stayed on for an extra half hour in the afternoon sometimes or we had gone out together for a short session after supper and worked by candlelight. Though Dougie still thought it a bad thing that Elsie should be so caught up in the life of the Nisbet-Brown family, he had to admit that there was a pleasing improvement in her attitude to work. Dougie's designs for shawls were always restrained and tasteful, unlike many of the ones that were being churned out for the Paisley manufacturers. Dougie called those 'soup patterns' — too much of everything and all thrown in together, he meant.

Mrs Nisbet-Brown had been so impressed by the shawl Elsie was parading that first day that she had ordered a replica. Elsie with her new-found confidence had explained that the Allen designs were exclusive and that no two shawls were ever identical. This idea had appealed not just to Elsie's patroness but several of her friends, too. So a steady stream of orders had trickled through from the big house. The clients seemed in no way put off by the fact that they had to wait for their desired shawls. Dougie was far too busy to start all these new designs from the beginning. What he did was to make slight alterations to the old ones. I had watched him at work so often that I was able to take over his variations and colour the 'new' design on graph paper. It was a nice job for a Sunday evening when we weren't allowed to knit. I think Faither had a wee bit of a struggle with his conscience over it but I was careful to sing only sacred songs while I was working. As Faither was dealing direct with those clients he made more profit than he would have done going through the agent. But he was as scrupulous over business matters as anything else and saw to it that orders through the agent got priority.

After an initial struggle Dougie accepted the force of Faither's arguments and resigned himself to staying in his room. Nurse Duncan had recommended hot drinks and soups to sweat out the fever. Sometimes when I took up a tray, I would find him fast asleep over the scattered books on his bed. Mam was to be kept propped up all the time and on the second day decided she was as well propped up by the living-room fire as in her lonely bedroom. This was a help because it freed Elsie for the weaving shed most of the day and I could spend some time at the pirn winding when Mam had an eye on Lilias. An idea was forming in my mind. "Mam, don't you think I should write to Angus and tell him what's wrong with Dougie then maybe he would bring the books here on Saturday?" I said. "And Maisie might send me some written work I could be doing." Mam was enthusiastic. Even if Dougie was on his feet, the weather was still cold, though clear again. "Tell him that there'll be a bite o' dinner for him and his sister too if they like to come."

I wasted no time in getting the letter off. Dougie was getting bad-tempered. He kept getting up and putting his clothes on then he would feel so weak and washed out that he was glad to go back to bed. Anxiously I waited for Angus's reply. When it arrived, I ran straight up to Dougie. "Angus is bringing the books to you this Saturday," I said.

"But I'll be up and about by then." Dougie was emphatic.

"Aye, but not fit enough for a trip to Paisley. Maisie is coming too, to give me a theory lesson. Elsie and I will make a specially nice dinner and we'll light the parlour fire where we can be quiet and get on with our studies ... " I gave him the big wink I had been practising in front of my bedroom mirror.

"Jessie, you're a wee champion," he said.

9

I WAS really pleased with myself that Saturday. Everything worked out just as I planned. Though Mam was a bit anxious when Dougie said we were walking down to Milliken Park to see our visitors off, she never could resist Dougie's arguments and Faither was out curling with his cronies so that was that. I was careful to take Maisie's hand and talk to her till we were clear of Killy, then I found an excuse to ask Angus something and skipped ahead of him.

There were only three passengers waiting and none of them known to us. 'So much the better!' I thought. As we walked up and down the platform I stuck to Angus with my exciting plan forming in my mind. And it was Angus's hand I held tightly when the train thundered in, even though Maisie and Dougie had joined us. Then I kissed Maisie who looked rather startled. Angus understood what I was about, I think, and received his kiss enthusiastically. "I never say 'no' to this stuff," he assured me. Out of the corner of my eye I watched Dougie kiss Maisie. Though they were both shy and parted crimson-faced, something told me it was not the first time.

Nothing was said about it on the way home. In fact, Dougie tried to fit in my Latin lesson on the walk since he had lost a lot of time with his illness and would have to spend the evening on the books Angus had brought him. Dougie had not wanted to involve me in any deceit, yet in a funny way I felt we were conspirators and closer together than ever.

It was as well we had the arrival of Meg's bairn to look forward to — Dougie had teased her about the probable date, the first of April — because there wasn't much else to be thrilled about. There was a lot of dissension among the weavers about prices paid to them for Lamma shawls. The Paisley weavers were up in arms and asking the Kilbarchan ones to support them. They were demanding fixed prices but the manufacturers wouldn't sign an agreement. The beamers in our village were being warned not to accept work from the manufacturers who refused to pay the prices they had set out in their table.

Of course our shed wasn't involved because Faither had stubbornly remained independent of both beamers and manufacturers. But Dougie took a keen interest in what was going on though he was never home in time to take part in the discussions among our lot.

In our street we took turns to buy the newspaper and it was passed along from shed to shed. Dougie always tried to get hold of it for a quick read. At this time he found a lot to criticize. There had been a proposal to build a hospital in Kilbarchan and a committee was formed. Dougie was always keen on progress and he was disgusted when one wet blanket after another spoke out against it and grumbled about the expense of building the house, furnishing it, paying for nurses, attendants and doctors. One speaker said it would be a permanent heavy burden and the ratepayers should think once, twice and thrice before adopting it. Dougie nearly went up in a blue light when he read that. "We've got upwards of eight hundred looms working in this village," he fumed. "We're one of the most prosperous districts in the whole of Scotland yet they dither and grumble about the cost of a hospital that any self-respecting community should regard as an essential."

Faither as a matter of long habit always tended to present an opposite side of the question. "Well you see, lad, this has aye been a healthy place till we got the typhoid epidemic. The bad wells are closed now and, as soon as a pure supply is arranged, they'll close the others. Folk will aye look twice at their money when something disna' seem to be needed."

Of course when the trouble about the prices began to increase, Faither took it as a justification for canniness. "See, lad, they feel their living is no' secure and the manufacturers can hold them to ransom."

"And what would the manufacturers do without them, Faither? Tell me that. If they got themselves properly organized, a labour force that size, the manufacturers would be forced to come to terms."

"They would end up at one another's throats, lad, and what sort of life is that in a Christian country?"

Listening to them arguing, I felt again that nothing was safe. Meg away . . . and when the bairn was born I wouldn't even be able to see it very often. Other Kilbarchan girls married weavers in the village — not that I would have had her marry anyone but Duncan. Still, it would have been nice to show off the bairn to my school chums. Bella would be back, of course. She still belonged. Or did she? Would she find being the middle one of an ordinary family rather dull after being Miss Bella of the manse? Elsie didn't really belong to us any more though she worked hard for Faither and was invariably kind to me. I just knew this somehow . . . and it wasn't because her talk was mainly of the big house and the latest wonder there, the distinguished artist who was the nephew of Mademoiselle Blanchard. I wondered how Elsie would feel if she knew that the same Mademoiselle Blanchard had described her as a rose in a pigsty. Perhaps she wouldn't mind.

Dougie seemed to think that Elsie would go all out for what she wanted. Perhaps she would just brush the Frenchwoman aside like a fly off a wall . . .

We were rolling paper twists one day for the boiler when I came on a page with a bit missing. "I wonder what was there," I said. "December twenty-first, 1872. Can you think, Elsie?" I saw she was blushing a little.

"Don't you remember, Jessie? That was the report of the Kilbarchan Horse Fair and the hunt coming — and my accident — the accident that changed my life."

I was stuck for words. "The accident that changed my life," she had said. And Elsie did seem to have found a new purpose, a new resolve . . . I couldn't find the words for it. Gaining entry to the big house meant such a lot to her. Was she hoping to marry someone rich and be the lady of the manor herself?

It was the first time that Elsie had seemed willing to communicate on a personal level about her connection with the big house so I chanced my arm.

"I've never seen a Frenchman, Elsie," I

said. "What does this artist look like?"

"Well, he's quite tall and he has an olive skin and gorgeous dark eyes. He's got a lovely smile too, a sort of slow smile that warms you up." She looked as if she was warming up just picturing him.

"Is he as handsome as Dougie?" I asked.

"Dougie's just a boy," she answered quickly and then, seeing my face, "I mean, Michel is twenty-eight. His mouth is very masterful and he has little lines round his eyes with screwing them up in the strong sun. It gives his face character. Dougie will have that later too," she added for my benefit.

Was Michel the attraction that drew her to the big house, I wondered. But she had been thrilled at her first visit before he ever appeared on the scene. And she did seem truly fond of Mrs Nisbet-Brown who often came in the carriage to fetch her and to have a few kind words with Mam, thanking her for the loan of her lovely daughter. Duncan's mother had said Mam was lucky to have so many lovely daughters. Maybe Mam in her generous thoughtful way was doing

Mrs Nisbet-Brown a kindness in spite of her scruples about Elsie's head being turned. I thought of it as I brushed Lilias's hair and got her dressed early one Saturday morning. She was at the window watching for the coach before the rest of us had finished breakfast. But it was the postman who got her attention first. "Ah, it's Bella's writing," Mam said, opening it quickly. "She usually leaves it to Meg . . . oh! my! no! never!"

Faither grabbed the letter from her. "Meg's had twins," he croaked. "Boys!"

I think we all went a bit daft then. It was Dougie who got us calmed down eventually. Of course Mam wanted to see Meg right away. I could see Faither felt the same. "Don't worry about Jessie and Lilias," Dougie said. "I'll take them to Paisley later when we've got cleared up here and damped down the fires. You've got your things packed, Elsie, I take it. You'd better take an apron in case you have to stay on and help Bella."

"But Mrs Nisbet-Brown is coming — " Elsie started.

"If she comes before you leave for the

station, you can tell her yourself. If not, I'll explain."

I saw the swift cloud on Elsie's face but she did not argue. Long before Mam had gathered all the things she felt she needed to take to Meg, the carriage rolled up to the door. Elsie hurried out to make her explanations. I was surprised to see Mrs Nisbet-Brown continue on her way into the house. For the first time I really appreciated the goodness of the woman when I heard her speak to Mam. "Now, Mrs Allen, you mustn't think of going by train in this cold weather. Dick will take me home now but I'll send him back immediately and the carriage is yours for the rest of the day. Elsie will see that he gets fed and looked after in her sister's kitchen. Won't you, my dear?"

Proud and independent as they are, Mam and Faither could see only good sense in accepting this kind offer to have Mam conveyed in comfort from door to door. With Lilias I watched from the window as Elsie accompanied Mrs Nisbet-Brown to her carriage and saw her being warmly kissed. I had a disloyal thought. What if my beautiful sister was just pretending affection for that fine woman who genuinely cared for her?

Dougie decided that since he had lit a fire in the weaving shed he might as well use it for an hour. Now that both Bella and Elsie were away. Faither would find it difficult to supply the woollen shirtings that his agent expected of him. "It's little enough I can do for him till term ends in April," he said, "but even an hour or two helps."

"I'll soon be learning too," I said, "but the trouble is that Lilias always wants to be with me."

"I can see that," he laughed. "You've got a little shadow there. Maybe in the summer when the shed door is open she'll play in the garden."

"Aye, maybe," I said, "but when the weather's really hot, Faither usually decides to shut the shed and go fishing."

"Aye! I wonder," Dougie said, "how much longer that sort of life can continue."

"What d'you mean?" I was puzzled.

"We're exceptional here, you know," Dougie assured me. "Where people work in factories they have to start when the whistle blows and go home when the whistle tells them. They can't declare a holiday on a fine summer day then make it up in the late evening."

"That means Faither's right about being independent," I said.

Dougie laughed. "I've taught you too much, Miss Jessie, I think!"

Maisie would be expecting me for my lesson, Dougie said. He had the grace to blush a little, knowing that I knew another reason for going to Paisley. We would wrap Lilias up well, he said. She would love the train and would play happily. If Maisie's mother was in, Lilias would probably stay with her. Of course I could not help wondering about Meg's bairns. Fancy two lots of hippens! And how would Meg manage to feed two of them . . . at the same time, one each side, or one after the other? It was no good asking Dougie that but some of my other speculations kept spilling over. Bella's letter had been brief and excited. The bairns were bonny though awfu' wee . . . They could yell blue murder . . . Meg was fine but tired. Bella was making lots of soup for her. Duncan was that proud.

When I said — for the tenth time, probably — "I wonder what their names are," Dougie almost lost patience.

"Look, Jessie," he said, "Mam and Faither will be back tonight. They'll tell you everything there is to be known about the whole affair. I promise you I'll let you stay up by the fire till they get home, no matter how late. Will that do?" Even Dougie had his limits so I kept my speculations to myself after that.

It was Maisie's mother who opened the door to us. "My, my, Jessie. You've brought your wee sister. That's nice. D'you want me to keep her ben the kitchen with me?" I blurted out my news about Meg just as Maisie and Angus opened the parlour door. In the middle of all the excitement Lilias made a bee-line for Angus and was soon burying her face in his neck as she loved to do. "See, Mother," Angus said, "your future daughter-in-law. Can you doubt her love for me?" Lilias kissed him again and chuckled.

"We're hoping she'll grow out of it

now she's an aunt," Dougie said.

"Not too soon, friend, not too soon," said Angus. "I might find it difficult to get a substitute."

I had watched Maisie and Dougie while Lilias was carrying on with Angus and could sense the excitement and longing between them.

Mrs Wilson said, "I don't think any of you will be settling down to your lessons today."

"I was thinking that myself," said Dougie. "What about declaring a holiday as they do in the weaving shed, eh, Angus . . . Maisie?" Finding there was complete agreement on this Mrs Wilson hurried off to the kitchen to get the kettle on. I calculated quickly, then followed her, chatting about Meg while I helped her lay out cups and start to butter scones. Soon Angus came through with Lilias by the hand. "She wants us both, Jessie," he said. "I'm afraid I'm not quite the star of her universe as I had hoped." I talked merrily on, both to him and Mrs Wilson. By the time we carried the trays through to the parlour I reckoned that Dougie and Maisie had had quarter of an hour to themselves and not all of it had been spent on the book of songs they were studying . . . not if their rosy cheeks were anything to go by!

Cold as the February day was, when we said goodbye to Mrs Wilson after her cosy tea party, Angus and Maisie decided they would accompany us on a little walk round the town, then see us off at the station. It would be a treat for Lilias to see all the shops lit up, they said. Angus hoisted Lilias on to his shoulders as soon as we reached the street. I walked beside them, leaving Dougie and Maisie to follow. On the station platform Angus made much of Lilias so that she clung tightly to him when the train came in. I kissed Maisie quickly then turned to prise Lilias out of Angus's arms. In the little struggle that ensued Dougie had his opportunity. I was getting quite clever at engineering things, I decided.

That evening seemed interminable. There was plenty for me to do after I got Lilias to bed but I simply could not settle. I had tried to get Dougie to study downstairs but he had said, "Sorry, Jess, I have to be alone." In a sudden surge of jealousy I wondered if he wanted to sit and think about Maisie. Then I looked at the nice fire he had riddled and stoked; the bucket of coal at the ready and the big heavy kettles he had replenished. Ashamed of my selfishness I started to fill the stone pigs to heat our beds. Thinking about Meg, I remembered her pancake club. That put me in the notion so I set the girdle on the hob and was soon putting my frustrated energy into beating up the pancake batter. Mam and Faither would surely enjoy a nice bite when they came in after their journey. And we could fry up some of them with our ham and eggs in the morning.

When the coach rolled up, I was ready with the table set and the kettle singing. It was just as well! Mam and Faither both looked awfully tired after the double journey and all the excitement in between. Elsie had indeed stayed on to give Bella a hand with the bairns.

"Bella's worst job will be to get Elsie out of her bed in the morning," said Dougie.

"Don't be too hard on the lass,"

Faither said. "When she's here she works weel nowadays."

"Aye," Mam added, "and Bella says she'll be a great help wi' the pancake club, teaching them their sewing, like. Meg disna' want the club to stop."

"Oh, aye . . . the bairns," Mam said. "Well, they're wee because they're early. Twins are aye early," she added. I felt an immediate glow. I was to be spoken to like the others — no more mysteries. "Their names are George Duncan Williamson and Walter Allen Williamson. So that's baith sides happy."

Dougie had told me to sit down at table. He would mask the tea and serve us. I didn't argue, only too glad to shoot questions at Mam till I realized that I wasn't being fair and there was always tomorrow. Tomorrow was Sunday and I could have a long lie in. No, I couldn't! Jean and Tam were coming to church with us because it was their wedding anniversary. Jean was coming early to give me a hand. Tam would follow her in time for church. I determined that in spite of my late night I would be up early and the first to give her the news.

Jean got a fright when she saw me running towards her with a big shawl wrapped round me to keep out the frost. Her step quickened as she called out, "What's wrong?"

"Nothing. Meg's got twins — wee laddies," I shouted breathlessly.

"Oh, my Goad!" Jean stopped still in the middle of the road. "Twins! There's nane in oor family."

"No, nor Duncan's. Dougie says it's got to start somewhere."

"When did — " she started and I broke in to give her a rapid account of the previous day.

"I hope Elsie keeps her mind on her work an' she'll dae fine. Meg'll be real happy to have a help wi' them. Pity is, we've a lot o' woollen shirting to be done. We could be daein' wi' her."

"Dougie did some on Saturday morning before we went to Paisley and he let me have a shot, too. He said I would soon be an expert — it was nice and even. I've watched you all so often," I said. "I could maybe be doing a wee bit even before I leave school in July."

"The trouble is Lilias . . . " she began.

"Auntie Lilias, you mean," I said. Jean started laughing and grabbed my hand — not like Jean at all.

Meg made a good recovery and was walking about her bedroom before a week was up. Handling the babies was no problem to a lassie who had always helped with her younger siblings. Elsie waited on for another ten days after that. She was no sooner back in Killy than she was being whisked off by Mrs Nisbet-Brown who said this artist chiel who was staying with them was desperate to paint Elsie's portrait and she was afraid he would change his mind if they kept him waiting. I couldn't see how he would do that if he was as desperate as she made out. The ways of the gentry seemed weird and wonderful to me.

Bella came home rather reluctantly at the end of the following week. It seemed that Jinty was in her element with all the excitement and had assured her she would manage fine with Mrs Williamson. That wee lassie's idea of time off was to take the babies out in the pram. I think Bella had come to believe that the manse could not do without her. "The doctor congratulated me," she said proudly. "He said it was thanks to me that Meg was able to feed the bairns so peacefully and that I was the ideal person for her to have at the time." I gazed in wonder at Bella whom I had tended to dismiss because of Dougie's attitude. I tackled him about it on the journey to Paisley the next Saturday. "Meg's doctor seems to think a lot more of Bella than you do," I said.

"Aye!" He raised his eyebrows at me. "Did you not think it sounded awfully like Duncan speaking? I suspect he had a wee word with the Doctor beforehand. It's very constructive thinking on Duncan's part, of course. And you may remember that I said she had improved under their influence."

"Aye, you did. You're aye right," I added in Jean's flat tones.

Dougie laughed ruefully, "*Et tu, Brute?*" he said, then had to explain.

I couldn't help being sorry for Bella, remembering what it felt like to be displaced, so that night when we were getting ready for bed, I decided to divulge Elsie's confidences about Michel. I had second thoughts about the wisdom of it when I heard Bella's reaction.

"That's why she's never got me an invitation, the mean besom. She wants to keep him all to herself."

I thought quickly. "I don't think it's just that," I said. "None of us has had an invitation, remember. In fact, I don't think we would enjoy it all that much if we were actually there. It seems to me that it's an artificial sort of world. Elsie's always been away with the fairies. Personally, I much prefer the sort of life you've had at the manse — with really worthwhile superior people."

Bella cheered up immediately and started again to tell me what Meg's doctor had said about her. It was the umpteenth time I had heard it but I listened patiently, for I had brought it on myself after all.

Though it had been tentatively suggested that Dougie could take Lilias and me to see the twins, the cold weather and Dougie's intensive studying ruled this out. We had to content ourselves with waiting for the christening on the first Sunday in April.

Mrs Nisbet-Brown had again offered the use of her carriage to Mam for the day and it was only common sense to take it in case the weather was treacherous. Lilias always wanted to be with me so I would go with them in the coach while Elsie and Dougie went in the trap with Dr Graham. He was performing the ceremony. Bella had said that the congregation were all thrilled about the bairns at the manse. "The girls in the pancake club all love Meg," she said. "They've been knitting wee bootees and I've been teaching them some crochet, too."

My trouble on that long journey was keeping Lilias still. She kept wanting to 'see the horsie' and that meant opening the window and risking a chill for Mam. Bella (who had travelled to Glasgow on the Saturday) and Elsie would be carrying the twins but Lilias and I were to meet them in the vestry before the service and we were to sit beside them in the front row, going out with them when the christening was over. I had spent a lot of time preparing Lilias for this. We always sat very, very quiet in church, I told her. The bairns might cry because they were too wee to understand but Lilias was a big girl and would sit in her nice new clothes beside Jessie. Then we would all go to Meg's big house and play with the bairns.

"She'll be fine if Jessie's beside her," Jean had assured Mam who was afraid that a lively Lilias might spoil the solemn ceremony. Jean and Tam were making their own way from Johnstone so our whole family would be together again — a happy thought for me and, I reckoned, for Mam and Faither too.

Dougie and I had had a secret game we played at christenings in Kilbarchan — counting the handkerchiefs. This had always given us great amusement when we compared notes afterwards and Dougie gave me his impersonations of various members of the congregation. Certainly Lilias's christening had been different. It had been held in the parlour at home with Mam still very weak and only the immediate family there. I was still resentful at being supplanted and also fearful of the change in Mam. The ceremony had been a duty and nothing more to me.

But this was different. First of all, meeting Meg in the vestry — slender as ever and with a poise and beauty that made me catch my breath. Quiet Meg had always had her own kind of charm but this new Meg had an assurance and grace that reminded me of Elsie and in addition an overflowing of deep joy which seemed to light up the air around about her. "Oh, my lovely wee sisters," she said, hugging us. "Isn't this a blessed day!"

Lilias was wide-eyed with wonder at two living dolls who could wave their little arms about and yawn and make funny noises like the pigeons on our roof at home. I had no difficulty in getting her to follow the little party in to its place of honour at the front of the church. She just clutched my hand tightly and gazed about her. Then when the singing started she joined in, happily now in tune.

As I said, a christening had never affected me before. But when I saw first Elsie then Bella hand her little charge to Doctor Graham, a big lump came in my throat. These were my nephews, the next generation. Life went on. We were all part of a great cycle and when our bodies were old and useless we would go to that paradise that Duncan had spoken about with all the bonnie flowers. Doctor Graham gave a lovely address, saying that the wee boys, George and Walter, belong to all of them now and recommended them to the prayerful care of the entire congregation.

Duncan's mother had insisted on being responsible for the food that day so that Meg could enjoy her family. Though I had been shown the dining room and drawing room on my first visit, they looked very different now with cheerful fires blazing and the spring sunshine lighting up the heaped buffet table and the lovely dishes of flowers that Mrs Williamson had arranged in every corner.

"There's plenty more food in the kitchen," Meg called to us, "thanks to Grandma Williamson."

"Oh dear," Mrs Williamson laughed. "I haven't got used to that yet. What about you, Mrs Allen?" She and Mam were happy then, talking about the twins: what a surprise . . . none in our family before . . . and all that sort of thing. Dougie was taking Meg at her word, heaping up his plate and, when Duncan teased him, replying that we were expected to eat twice as much when it was twins we were celebrating. Lilias, of course, got lively when her shyness wore off but everybody loved her and I heard Jean — Jean who seldom uttered a word of praise at home — tell Duncan's brother that I had weaned the bairn when Mam was dangerously ill and that I was so capable: just like a wee mother to her.

We were all reluctant to make for home that night though Mam was tired. "Fancy!" she said when we had settled in to the carriage and on our way. "Duncan's mother spent the whole day there yesterday and brought all that food. Meg never had to lay out a penny. Of course they would know she just couldn't afford it."

"Aye, it's a good thing Duncan doesn't like cherry cake," Faither said.

"Is cherry cake dear, then?" I asked.

"Of course," Mam said. "They have to bring the cherries from far awa'."

I had known that we didn't have cherry cake every day of the week but I thought that was because it was a bother to make — all that measuring and beating. With scones you just stuck the girdle on the hob and they were ready in no time at all. Fancy Meg in her huge house with a bathroom not being able to eat the nice things we had often in our wee cottage with its privy in the garden. It didn't make sense. I would speak to Dougie about it. Then I listened to what Faither was saying to Mam about a conversation he'd had with Duncan's father. It seemed that there was a whole road of fine new sandstone tenements going up near the church. They were to have water closets on every landing and Duncan hoped that a lot of his people would be able to move from their old insanitary houses. And two new engineering works were being built not very far away. That should help to bring prosperity to the district.

"It's all export nowadays," Faither was saying. "These engineering works are making bits and pieces for machines on the other side of the world. It's no' canny. Everything's changing, Bess, lass, and we're being left behind.

"We're doing fine, Wattie, just fine."

Mam patted his hand and smiled over at Lilias tucked into my side and fast asleep.

The morning after the christening brought another change in my life. In spite of all Meg's wise counselling, I was afraid of the strange thing that had suddenly happened to my body and all that it foretold. I didn't want to be a woman. I just wanted to be Jessie, Dougie's wee champion.

10

ELSIE spent an increasing amount of time at the big house as spring wore into summer. I couldn't understand how an expert artist would take so long to paint a portrait. Dougie could have done it in half that time. Now that term had ended he spent the weekdays in the weaving shed but studied on Saturday mornings. The shed seemed deserted then. Jean, of course, was always at home with Tam. Meg was married and far away and less likely than ever to be able even to visit us now she had the twins. Bella made for Glasgow each Saturday morning and Mam and Faither were so glad that Meg was having her help that they let her go willingly. I started spending an hour or two at Bella's loom. Lilias would bring her dolly's cradle and we would sing while I worked. Faither would be setting up the next shawl for Jean or getting on with his aprons. Sometimes Dougie would decide there was nothing more he could do till he saw Angus in the afternoon and he would take over Elsie's loom. Those were the times I liked best. Lilias thought Dougie's deep baritone was so funny and she would try to imitate him till Faither would be wiping tears of laughter from his eyes.

In May we were very thrilled when Dougie graduated MA. He was able to do this a year early because he had taken a special preliminary exam in Latin, Greek and Maths and done well in it. Of course he had expected to leave university as soon as he got his degree and start teaching, but something new had started at Glasgow — a BSc degree. When Faither heard that Dougie could get it for maths and chemistry in two years because of the work he had already done, he said. "You go ahead and take it, lad. You'll be able to pick and choose your job." Jean's lips tightened a bit when she heard that but everyone else was happy for Dougie. He would be a headmaster one day and with two degrees the very best schools would want him.

Now that I knew I was leaving school in July, I began to count the days. It was pleasant in the weaving shed with the door open on to the garden and Lilias toddling out and in. She would enjoy being able to see me all day. Then if it was a real scorcher, Faither always declared a holiday. I would take Lilias lovely walks in the woods and tell her about the birds and the wild flowers the way Dougie had done for me. Her favourite walk would be up to the farm, I knew, to give Rusty her carrot. Queenie wouldn't touch her if Rab was there, big rough, swearing Rab who gave Bella a muckle lump of butter for the pancake club every week.

In June we had a sudden shock in the village when one of the beamers, Michael Dick (who was only forty-two) died. He was an expert flautist — I've never heard anyone to touch him — and popular with everyone for his willingness to play at social gatherings. Faither was particularly upset for Michael was dear to his heart, a philosopher like himself. Sometimes when the discussions were getting a wee bit too heated among the weavers gathered for a crack before supper, Michael would get out his flute.

Soon everyone was calmed down. I used to love it when he was in our shed. It was just like that Orpheus that Dougie had told me about.

Mam was upset because his widow was left with a young family. Faither, of course, was one of the mourners, a big crowd of them, to follow the coffin. Elsie was at the big house but Mam and Jean and Bella would be out in the street to watch it go by. We decided that Lilias was likely to be upset — she was so quick and sensitive — that it would be better if I took her up to the farm to talk to old Rusty. I just hoped we would not meet Queenie. What if Rab was at the funeral too and had left her behind?

Fortunately he wasn't. Though Rab knew Michael by reputation and had once or twice heard him play, their paths had seldom crossed. Come to think of it, it was really only because of Rusty that we knew Rab so well. There was the dairy in the village and plenty of other farms to get a chicken from. It was pleasant standing in the sun while Lilias drooled over Rusty. If I looked down one way, there was the

Gryffe winding its silver path through Bridge of Weir with the far hills above Dumbarton in the background. I just had to turn round and there were the Gleniffer Braes, my favourite walk with Dougie. The scent of hawthorn still drifted up from the nearby woods though it was beginning to go brown and rancid down the lanes in the village. Everywhere was so peaceful. Rab's Ayrshires munched contentedly in his low field while the bleat of sheep carried clearly from the hill above. Kilbarchan was a bonnie place, a place to be happy in. Yet, there was Mrs Dick who'd lost her man . . . and all her wee young bairns who'd be greetin' for their faither. Fancy bedtime with no faither to hug! I thought of the fright we had had when Mam was so ill and we were all afraid we would lose her — so afraid that we didn't dare mention the possibility in case it might happen! Impulsively I picked up Lilias and hugged her. "Stay with Rusty . . . please, Jessie," she begged me, "not go home to Mam yet . . . not dinner time." I laughed at her earnestness then told her my secret. We were going to have a little picnic by the burn in the woods, just the two of us. That almost took her away from Rusty till I assured her we had plenty of time. I can still smell the heat of that day . . . hawthorn and rowan blossom in the woods, meadowsweet by the roadside, the pinks and the wallflowers in our own wee garden when I finally took a tired, happy little Lilias home.

All the windows were wide open and I could see Mam and Jean and Bella sitting beside the big teapot. The sound of one loom clicked in the weaving shed. That would be Dougie. Faither would be with his cronies. Maybe they would be having a dram while they talked about Michael and what a clever flautist he was and a good worker too. And a hat would be going round to help Mrs Dick. And I knew that it wouldn't end there. The weavers would see to it that a basket of groceries found its way to her door early in the morning . . . or a chicken . . . a rabbit . . . a sack o' potatoes . . . no, the bairns wouldn't starve.

It was Lilias who saw the carriage first. "Horsie with Elsie," she screamed in delight. Surprised, we all hurried to the open window to watch the carriage draw up. As Dick descended from the box Bella rushed to open the door. But it wasn't graceful young Elsie that Dick handed down the step. Mrs Nisbet-Brown, looking as old and shaken as Grannie Watson, leaned heavily on his arm. The eyes she raised to ours were full of despair. Mam gave a gasp. "My lassie . . . something's wrang wi' ma lassie."

Jean rushed to her as she swayed. "Here, Jessie," she ordered me, "help me to get her in her chair . . . cold water and a cloth, quick!" I rushed to do her bidding. When I got back, Bella was helping Mrs Nisbet-Brown into a chair. Dick stood behind her twirling his cap, the picture of worry. Jean who was massaging Mam's wrist snapped out, "Speak, wumman, before we a' go daft." Terrified as I was myself, Jean's rudeness shocked me. Lilias was looking around in wonderment, her lip trembling. Quickly I drew her to me and whispered, "Go out the back way. Tell Dougie that Jessie says 'come quick'."

Poor Mrs Nisbet-Brown was speechless, trying to dab her face and open her reticule at the same time. We stood helplessly by. Then she managed to draw out a crumpled piece of notepaper. "Dick, give that . . . " she quavered, indicating Mam. "Read it, Jessie," snapped Jean, never leaving Mam's side.

"It's Elsie's writing," I said, opening the paper out.

Dear Mrs Nisbet-Brown,

I am afraid this will be a shock to you but Michel has begged me to return to France with him. We love each other desperately. I cannot bear to be parted from him. He says I am his inspiration now and his work will suffer so dreadfully if I am not there to model for him. I have tried to write to my parents but find it impossible. There would be so many obstacles if we tried to marry here. Michel says that life is much more free in France. I am so sorry to be leaving you like this after all your kindness. Please tell my parents I never wanted to hurt them but 'amor vincit omnia'.

Love,

Elsie

Dougie came rushing in with Lilias on his arm. "What's all this?" he asked. I handed him the paper and he read it quickly. "Bitch," he whispered.

"Bitch," repeated Lilias, expecting praise for her new word.

Mam started to cry then and Jean snapped at Dougie, "Watch your tongue in front o' the wean." Dougie muttered an apology as he handed Lilias to me. Then he rounded on Mrs Nisbet-Brown. "When did all this happen?"

"They must have left early this morning," she replied shakily. "The maid found it when she took in Elsie's tea."

"And we're just learning about it now!" Dougie was indignant. Dick spoke up, "The mistress has been very ill, sir . . . in a dead faint a gey long while . . . the shock."

Dougie was suddenly contrite. "I'm sorry. I was forgetting my manners. A little brandy wouldn't go amiss, I think. Jessie, two glasses, please." He poured quickly and handed one glass to Mrs Nisbet-Brown and another to Mam.

"Now, first things first," he said. "Does anyone know where exactly they are making for? His aunt, has she any idea?"

"If she has, she didn't tell me," said Mrs Nisbet-Brown.

"Well," said Dougie, "what I propose to do if you are willing, is come back with you just now and question her and the rest of your staff . . . "

"She's gone," said Mrs Nisbet-Brown.

"What! You mean with Elsie and this . . . artist . . . Michel?"

"No . . . on her own. You see, when the maid brought me Elsie's note I hurried to Marie Blanchard's room, thinking we might be in time to stop them . . . "

"And — " Dougie prompted her.

"She said something unforgivable about Elsie . . . said her nephew was throwing himself away . . . I was so indignant I dismissed her instantly. She screamed abuse at me. It was dreadful. My maid helped me back to my room. I fainted then. When I came to, I found that the housekeeper had sent for the doctor. He insisted on sedating me . . . my heart, you see . . . " She looked up pitiably at Dougie.

His voice was gentler. "I still think

266

I'd like to come and question the other members of the staff. Then I'll be after the pair of them as soon as I can." He turned to Bella. "Find Faither. I'll need money. Watch how you break the news."

Jean broke out, "And what good will it do fetching her back? Her reputation's gone and we've got to suffer the red faces. I knew we should have kept her at hame. I'll never forgi'e her for this, never! Mam brought us a' up decent." Mam and the old lady both started to cry at this. Dougie began to look desperate.

"If you could see your mistress to her carriage," he appealed to Dick, "I'll be with you in a moment." He turned to me. "Jessie, I'll scribble a note for Doctor Graham. Take Lilias with you up to the manse."

I was only too glad to get Lilias outside in the flower-scented air. My head was thumping and I was having difficulty keeping Lilias calm. She knew in her quick way that something was wrong. The horsie usually brought Elsie. Did she maybe think Elsie was dead? No, she was too young to know about that. And, anyway, Elsie was as good as dead now from the way Jean spoke. I felt my own lips trembling but Lilias, little trusting Lilias, was depending on me. I started to talk about the lovely flowers in the manse garden.

Luckily the minister was at home. He opened the door to us himself and invited us into his study. The windows were open there to the scents of the flowers and carefree birdsong. Everything seemed so serene, the opposite of the tension and despair we had left. Lilias hurried over to the window to watch a spider weaving its web. I handed over my note and watched Doctor Graham's expression change as he read. He looked up sharply. "You know what's in this, Jessie?"

"Yes . . . It's dreadful, isn't it?" My voice faltered.

"Truly dreadful," he agreed, "but perhaps Dougie will yet manage to bring Elsie home before any permanent damage is done."

"Jean says her reputation is gone and we'll all have red faces," I blurted out.

"Ah, Jean! A fine young woman," he said. "High standards for herself and others. But sometimes, Jessie, my dear, we have to make allowances for our weaker brethren. Meantime we must pray for Elsie and do our best to comfort those who suffer most by her actions. Dougie thinks a letter from me to Duncan would be the kindest way of getting the news to Meg."

"Oh, Meg!" I said. "I'd forgotten Meg. But she's feeding her babies. She mustn't be upset."

"I daresay that's what Dougie was calculating," said Doctor Graham.

"Fancy Dougie thinking about that in the middle of all this."

"Your brother is a remarkable young man, Jessie," Doctor Graham said.

"Oh, I know," I responded and remembered what Dougie had hissed for my ears only as he handed me the note. "Don't worry, Jessie, I'll get her back if I have to drag her by the hair of her head."

★ ★ ★

I gave Lilias an extra walk after we left the manse to tire her out. It didn't take long to get her to bed when I got back and she was fast asleep by the time I had tidied away her things. Jean hadn't gone home, afraid to leave Mam who had reacted in horror to the idea of a visit from the doctor or even Nurse Duncan.

I had just hurried downstairs to see what I could do when Faither came back with Bella. I don't know which of them looked worse. His face was a funny grey colour and obviously he'd been holding himself in check till he got in.

Bella was flushed crimson and breathless. Her eyes, which were filled with tears, darted to Mam and then Jean and then me before she turned fearfully towards Faither again. As soon as the door was slammed behind him he gave great terrible curses . . . Faither, a kirk elder, Faither who had taught us never to swear. I was suddenly as terrified as Bella.

"She'll never darken a decent man's door again," he said, slamming his hand down on the table with a force that made me jump and set all the jugs on the high shelf jingling. "And Dougie's no' going to waste time and money chasing her, it's all one what he finds out at the big house. If we'd listened to Dougie earlier this would never have happened."

Jean stood by Mam's chair. Her lips were tightly compressed and pink shadows had formed under her eyes. She kept glancing at Mam but said not a word. Bella stood transfixed, her eyes on Faither. She reminded me of a rabbit mesmerized by a stoat. Somehow I felt I had to break the spell. I lifted one of the kettles and made for the back kitchen to fill it. Jean hurried out after me. She spoke in a low husky voice.

"I'll stay here the night in case Mam gets a heart attack wi' a' the worry. Faither's in a fair way to end up wi' a stroke. Tam will come seekin' me and we'll sleep in the living room bed."

I was just going to ask her where Faither would sleep but I checked myself. That problem and the knowledge behind it, imparted inadvertently by Rab, still made me feel guilty. The present carried enough hurdles for me to surmount without touching on that one.

It was quite late when Dougie got

back. We gathered round the table while he ate his belated supper. I was expecting to be sent off to bed by Jean any minute but she replenished my cup and warned me to put plenty milk in — the tea was fresh-brewed — without a hint of bedtime.

Dougie had found the visit frustrating at first. One after another of the servants had disclaimed all knowledge of their likely whereabouts. "I had the feeling sometimes they were keeping something from me, but I might be wrong," he said. "It could be they felt their information might hurt me. I gave up eventually and thought I'd make my way home over the fields to clear my head. That meant going through the walled garden to the far gate. I was waylaid by an old fellow who works there from time to time — when he's sober, I suspect. He said he'd heard I wanted to find out where the French bastard had taken my sister." Jean drew her breath in sharply at this but Mam and Faither sat staring at Dougie without a word of reproach for the bad word. He went on, "The old rascal hinted it was thirsty work in the garden all day in the hot sun. It was obvious he'd been drinking before I met him but luckily I had put a half sovereign in my pocket so I walked him down to Bridge of Weir."

"Bridge of Weir?" Bella interrupted.

"Aye! I didn't want half the inn to be listening . . . though I daresay there isn't a man, woman or child in Killy who hasn't heard and chewed over the juiciest scandal to come their way for a long time."

Mam's tears flowed afresh at this. Faither put his arm around her in a fierce protective gesture. An angry scowl made his face almost unrecognizable. Elsie, my beautiful Elsie, had done this. I found the knowledge hard to bear.

"And what did you find out, Dougie?" Tam was asking.

"Nothing conclusive, really, but he's pretty sure that they would make for Paris. Seemingly the painter chiel, when in his cups, kept extolling the joys of Paris . . . the wine and the women."

"He'll be a papist?" Faither broke in.

"If he's anything," Dougie answered. "I think hedonism is his religion if my informant is anything to go by." Bella and I looked at each other. Obviously this was a new word to her too. "He tells me that a certain little dairymaid at the farm the other side of the estate is breaking her heart. She says the French gentleman promised to marry her. My old fellow suspects she's in trouble . . . oh, and something else too, seemingly when the painter was drunk one night he told them that the governess was not his aunt but his mother," he ended.

"And that's what our weel brocht up daughter has chosen," Faither said bitterly.

"She'll change her mind when I get hold of her," said Dougie. "I'll make straight for Paris and hope that that drunkard was right."

I jumped as Faither's hand thumped down on the table, setting the cups rattling. "You'll stay where you are, Dougie, lad," he said. "She's made her bed and she'll lie on it. I'll never forgi'e her for what she's done to your mither. Noo, we'll a' get to our beds." He helped Mam to her feet and they walked slowly out. For a moment there was a stunned silence then Jean spoke sharply. "Right! the rest of you . . . upstairs! Tam an' I'll see to the fire."

I lay quietly beside Lilias trying to digest all the new things I had had to swallow that day. Bella was quiet too for a long time then I heard the even breathing that told me exhaustion had caught up with her. A thread of light under the door showed that Dougie was still awake — poor Dougie who was itching to go to Paris and drag Elsie back by the hair of her head.

I dreaded going to school in the morning, reluctant to face the sympathy of my friends. In my tense state one kind word could make me dissolve into tears. Jean, her face stern, had ladled out the porridge. We ate in silence because the subject that was nearest to all our minds didn't bear speaking about. I gave Lilias an extra hug after I had brushed her hair, and waved with more vigour than usual to the tiny figure at the window as I turned the corner. Dear wee Lilias represented normality in a world that had turned upside down.

Quite a crowd of girls had gathered

at the entrance to the school. It was going to be worse than I feared. I squared my jaw. I mustn't cry; it would embarrass them. But when I got nearer my step faltered as I scanned the faces. *That* wasn't sympathy: curiosity, yes; smothered amusement; smug satisfaction. A voice from the rear of the group spoke, "How about the high and mighty Allens now? Them and their fancy big weddings and white dresses and veils and things." And Patty McPhee jeered. "How does it feel to have a whore for a sister? He'll be painting dirty pictures of her with no clothes on."

I looked round at the girls I had thought were my friends. Many of their faces were screwed into expressions of shock but their eyes betrayed them, lit up with excitement tinged with triumph. They were enjoying my dreadful plight. Why? What had happened to change them? Had their friendliness all these years been a pretence?

I took my place quietly in class, still shocked and puzzled. Automatically I answered when my name was called in the register. The teacher gave me a brief sympathetic smile and I felt the tears well up immediately. 'I mustn't cry. I mustn't cry,' I told myself repeatedly. I could not understand the motives of my erstwhile friends. Betrayal had been the last thing I had expected. I summoned up Dougie. What would he say? 'Stare them out. Keep your dignity.' Yes, that's what Dougie would say. The muscles of my neck tightened. My lips pressed firmly against my teeth and the tears were halted. Looking back, I realize that the teacher, bless her, was probably thinking of me when she set a lengthy arithmetic test. At the time, when others were groaning round about me, I was thinking, "Good! I won't have to speak." And I didn't have to speak all morning. Parsing and analysis followed the arithmetic. Then, before lunch she read to us; a special treat, this! The book was *The Heart of Midlothian* — one of my favourites. With relief I realized it was time to go home for dinner. I had kept my dignity as Dougie would have wished. Unhurriedly I cleaned my slate and prepared to leave.

Again a knot of girls had gathered

round the entrance. I looked neither right or left as I elbowed my way through. It was Patty's voice which started up the chant I'll never forget.

"Elsie Allen, quack, quack, quack,
The Frenchman's got her on her back."

Soon a few of the bolder ones had joined her. My control broke. I took to my heels and ran as if the devil — or Queenie — was after me.

I never went back to school.

11

DOCTOR GRAHAM had not written to Duncan. Instead, he had risen that morning and set off in the trap while, at the manse, the big airy guest room was being prepared.

When I ran sobbing into the house it was not Mam's arms that were first round me but Meg's. I clung to her like a limpet. Dougie's sharp ears had picked up the sound of my flying feet even above the looms and he came hurrying in, closely followed by Jean and Faither. For a while I could not speak. Meg stroked my back gently, telling the others to be patient . . . I'd been upset but I'd soon be better. And of course she was right. Gradually I unwound my story of betrayal and hurt but when I came to the final indignity, I broke down again.

"I'd like to wring that Patty McPhee's neck," Dougie growled.

"Oh, Dougie, Dougie," Meg protested gently, "the poor wee girl has never been taught any different."

Mam started to cry and we all knew she was thinking about Elsie and how she'd always taught her how to behave . . . to be modest. And maybe Patty McPhee was right, I thought, and Elsie was letting that man see her without any clothes on and maybe he would sell pictures like that . . . I started to sob again.

"Now, now, this won't do." Meg's voice was firm. I was aware that it was she who was in command of the situation while Jean clattered the kettles on the hob and prepared to infuse tea, unable to think of any other solution.

"You have found out a sad truth about human nature this morning, Jessie, but it is only a small part of the story. No-one's perfect, after all. There was only one perfect man and not everyone liked Him."

"But I didn't know they hated me. Why should they?" I stumbled over the words.

"Oh, Jessie, my wee love, they don't hate you. They're just a wee bit jealous . . . You've got a mirror, haven't you?"

"You mean they wish they had my hair. Some of the girls have said that but I didn't feel they grudged me it."

"No, no . . . " Meg was reflective. "I don't want to spoil you and make you big-headed but maybe I should tell you what Duncan's father said the first day he met you."

"I was keeping that for her wedding day," Dougie said.

"Oh, well, I shan't spoil it," Meg laughed. "There now, I think you're better, Jessie. Go upstairs and wash your face and stay quiet in your room for a wee while. Then you can walk up to the manse and fetch Bella and Lilias for their dinner. The babies are in the garden and Lilias was itching to see them. The workers can get back to the shed now while Mam and I see to the dinner table."

I waited till school was safely in session before making my solitary way to the manse. There was such a lot to think about: love, hate, betrayal and the sound, loyal people who stuck by you through thick and thin. But Elsie's love was different. It tempted her to do wrong, to run away, leaving a trail of misery behind her. Meg said that God put these longings in you but why did God give Elsie longings that hurt everyone else? And if you read some of the greatest love stories in the world the people seemed to be doing what Elsie and Michel were doing. Michel . . . if Elsie married him I would have a French brother-in-law and if she had a bairn, would it speak French? "*Bébé.*" I said the word out loud and had to laugh at myself.

Meg had it all worked out. Solidarity was the answer. Mam and Faither would find the first Sunday in church difficult so we were going to fill the pew. Jean and Tam would stay on till then. Lilias would play with the babies at the manse with the little maid in charge. That left Bella and me free to go to church.

It worked beautifully. Bella hurried round to the manse as soon as the service was over and before the chatting crowd had dispersed she and the maid were offering the babies for inspection. Meg, sticking close to Mam's side, smiled serenely and answered all the speculations about the difficulty of bringing up twins with unending patience.

"Spiked their guns. Good strategy that, Meg," Dougie said over dinner.

"Ah, you forget, Dougie, that part of my job is keeping the peace at the women's meetings in the church." She gave a wicked chuckle. What could have been a disastrous day of near-mourning and bitterness was saved by Meg's sunny disposition which Dougie had forecast would bless Duncan's home.

Of course Monday brought the reality of everyday life. Jean and Tam had returned home on the Sunday afternoon. Meg packed up as soon as the babies had had a good feed after breakfast. The trap stopped at our cottage for us to say our goodbyes. I overheard Doctor Graham's words to Dougie, "I'll be able to put Duncan in the picture. I doubt if there's any more you can do. See that your own work isn't affected. I'll be proud to have my first MA BSc in the parish."

Nobody had said a word about my going back to school. I think they realized how deep the hurt went. So that Monday morning after Meg left saw me automatically take over Elsie's loom. Lilias was a godsend to us all, I think. She kept asking me to sing and that gave Dougie a cue to join in. It must have been some comfort to Faither in his bitterness. I would send Lilias trotting over to see Mam from time to time and she would come back to tell us, brown eyes sparkling, "Tea's ready. Mam's got scones," or, in important tones, "Just ten minutes till your dinner." Yes, little Lilias was a comfort: She gave us a sense of continuity.

Meg had warned me not to get bitter, that the little girls at school would be sorry for what they had done and would want to be friends again. Her words seemed to me a counsel of perfection. I really felt hard done-by. Hatred would boil up in me and I longed to punch all their mocking faces. Dougie had accused Jean once of just what I wanted to do — lashing out. But then, Dougie himself had said he'd like to wring Patty McPhee's neck. Meg had taught us all her way of disarming the opposition — family solidarity. I had to admit that it made things easier, so I kept pretty closely to the family circle apart from my Saturday trips to Paisley. Maisie was a fully-fledged teacher now but wouldn't dream of taking fees from me — she said I was her wee mascot. Actually I wasn't so wee but shooting up and rounding out very nicely. Meg's words, "You've got a mirror, haven't you?" had stirred something in me. Before that I had looked at myself to make sure I would pass Jean's grim inspection. Now I looked at my reflection with interest, cupping my hands round my budding breasts and tilting my head this way and that. I had hoped to be allowed to put my hair up on my thirteenth birthday or at least on Lilias Day but Mam said New Year would be soon enough.

* * *

Maisie and Angus were coming for Lilias Day as usual and as usual we would have Lizzie Forsythe to dinner. Bella was going to miss Lilias Day. She seemed to prefer to spend her time at Meg's. I began to suspect some other attraction than the babies and did a bit of sly probing while we were getting ready

285

for bed at nights. Did she still meet the pancake club people or did they not come to Duncan's special service? Some had fallen away but others soon took their place and there were always the old faithfuls like Arthur, for example. I noticed that Arthur's name cropped up oftener than the others. "Was he the first boy, the one who offered to dig the garden?" I asked one night.

"Oh, yes," Bella's tone was eager; "and d'you know, he was doing it on top of such a long day! He has to get up before six on a working day because there's no tram the last bit of his journey till half past seven and that's when he starts work in summer. It's a huge house and they have lots of glasshouses and a big walled garden where they grow every kind of fruit and he has to see that there are beautiful flowers for the house all the year round. He's second gardener and he's only twenty. The head gardener has a beautiful cottage with four wee bedrooms. Arthur says he'll have to move if he wants to be head gardener because Mr Millar is only in his forties and gardeners live a long time. But if he gets a head gardener's job it could be far away . . . and he'd miss the pancake club . . . and things . . . "I watched the telling flush sweep over her face. I was getting quite experienced at this.

"Wouldn't he miss his family?" I asked.

"Oh, yes, but he's got lots of wee sisters and it's a bit of a squash in the house. They don't give him much peace. He says it would be lovely to have a cottage in the country with a garden of our own where he could try to grow some of the rare things that only the big house folk grow. And his Mam and Dad could always come out on a Sunday if it wasn't too far away."

She hadn't noticed the tell-tale slip, 'our own'. I smiled quietly to myself and decided to keep my new knowledge quiet even from Dougie. I was growing up.

Since Lilias Day looked like being very subdued without Meg, Elsie and Bella, why shouldn't we invite Angus and Maisie to stay overnight? Then they could enjoy the festivities right to the end and come to church with us on Sunday. I put my idea to Mam and she accepted it eagerly. Then I saw her bite her lip, "There'll be a lot to do . . . I'd like things nice . . . "

"Don't worry about a thing, Mam," I said. "I'll work all Friday night and Dougie will give me a hand, I'm sure. Lilias will be so happy. She's awful fond of Angus. She'll be a wee angel and do just what we tell her, you'll see. And of course Maisie will help. She's a wee bit like our Meg, you know."

"Funny," Mam said, "that's what I thought when I first met her."

I got Dougie on his own to tell him the news because I knew that, clever as he was, he could easily give himself away. He hugged me impulsively. "You're a wee champion, Jessie." he said. "I'm sure they'll come, though Angus has a budding interest elsewhere nowadays."

"Oh . . . you mean he's got a lass?" I said, rather taken aback.

"Let's say he'd like to have a lass like someone else you know." He hugged me again. "Now, we'll have to see that Mam doesn't try to do too much."

"I can do all the cooking," I said.

"Well, you can count on me to see

to the heavy stuff," he said. "I'll get up at dawn on Saturday if you just tell me what's needed."

"Here," I said, "isn't Lilias going to be jealous?"

"Of what?"

"Of whom, you mean. 'Whoe'er she be' — after all, my little sister is Angus's intended."

Dougie was laughing heartily as he set off to write an invitation to Angus. I had a good idea that a note to Maisie would find its way into that envelope too.

The few days before Lilias Day were absolutely hectic ones for me in planning and preparations. I had only to say, "Getting things nice for Angus" to be sure of Lilias's co-operation.

On the actual morning she was beside herself with excitement and up at the window 'watching for Angus' long before we had even finished breakfast. "Postman," she shouted suddenly. "Dougie open door, please." Dougie obligingly opened the door. She proudly fetched the letter and handed it to Dougie. He glanced at it.

"A French stamp . . . Mam, it's for you and Faither, Elsie's writing."

Mam put her hand to her heart while her face drained of colour. Faither hurried to put his arms round her. "Read it, lad," he said tersely.

That letter is a bit of a jumble in my mind now, I'm afraid. We were all so upset and I was so worried about Mam. One sentence I'll never forget. 'There were no liberties, Mam, before we were married. I can assure you of that.' Mam gave a quiet little sigh when Dougie read these words. Her eyebrows straightened and her face grew calm.

"This church she was married in . . . ?" Faither asked Dougie.

"It'll be Catholic, almost certainly," Dougie said.

"Aye." Faither gave a heavy sigh. "But at least she kept herself decent."

"Aye," said Dougie, "you can put that worry aside now. We can all relax a bit and enjoy Lilias Day. We've nothing to be ashamed of."

Mam and Faither smiled slowly at each other.

Dougie took Lilias down to the

station with him because she was getting hysterical with excitement. She came back on Angus's shoulders and brimming over with happiness.

My cooking efforts were blessedly successful and Mam was able to preside over the table as she had done when Meg was at home. Lilias's bubbling laughter helped Dougie and Maisie to avoid any embarrassment. It fell to Dougie, Maisie and me to wash the dishes. Lilias had commandeered Angus to 'play horses'. Faither had taken his pipe and the newspaper out to the shed. Mam and Lizzie were safely ensconced in the big chairs with another pot of tea beside them. I found lots of little ploys which left Maisie and Dougie alone; emptying the tea leaves beside the briar rose; scattering crumbs for the birds on the grass; carrying dishes and cutlery through to the dresser. Oh, yes, they got plenty opportunities that day.

When we went out to join the milling crowds, we were already on top of the world. The news from Elsie had lifted a load from the Allen family. Lilias had her Angus and Dougie had his Maisie and I was instrumental in keeping them all happy. Meg was right about the little girls being sorry! Quite a number of them stopped that day to make a fuss of Lilias and tell me how beautiful she was. It was gratifying. Bella and I had spent many hours on the cream silk dress, embroidered with little yellow posies, which made our little dark-eyed charmer the best-dressed bairn in Kilbarchan, or so we thought! There were many such encounters to surprise me but the most surprising thing of all was the way Dougie steered us towards Nurse Duncan, whom he generally avoided. After introducing 'my friend' and 'my friend's sister' to 'the nurse who brought me into the world' he answered inquiries as to his mother's health with a casual. "Oh, she's doing well — had a letter from Elsie this morning."

When he edged us on our way, Nurse Duncan was still gasping with surprise. Dougie gave a quiet chuckle. "An excellent woman that, my friends. She'll be sure to follow up her inquiries with a professional visit this afternoon.

A bit of a talker, mind you, but a fairly accurate one."

"Dougie Allen, you're a — " I began.

"What am I, little sister? You were going to say 'diplomatist', I think."

But like the others, I was too busy laughing to tell him.

While I got Lilias ready for bed the others cleared away the supper things but nothing would do for that bairn but having Angus tuck her up and sing her a goodnight song.

"She's going to be jealous, Angus," I said softly as we came downstairs together.

"What?" he looked at me in surprise. "Oh, yes, yes, I see Dougie's been talking. Yes, but not so put out as your big brother when it's your turn."

"Surely . . . " I stopped, puzzled. This was an idea that had never occurred to me.

"I'm surprised that Maisie isn't jealous, the way he talks about his clever wee sister. He's angry that you haven't got to the big school at Johnstone, you know; feels you should have had more chance." Nothing more was said as we had reached the living room door but I had something else to chew over in bed that night.

Bedtime was later than any other Lilias Day I had known for the four of us milked the last ounce of pleasure out of the sideshows that went on as long as daylight. Angus and Dougie vied with each other at the shooting gallery and the muscle testing. Maisie and I stood by enjoying every minute of it. Watching Maisie and Dougie I was reminded of Meg that first Sunday when Duncan came to preach at our church. It was only when the number of drunks in the crowd grew to be a nuisance that we headed for home.

Mam had baked a nice batch of scones. Nobody said a word about my bedtime as we sat cosily round the fire drinking cup after cup of tea and sampling, on Dougie's instructions, blackcurrant jam first, then raspberry, then strawberry. "Work your way to the sweetest," he said.

Maisie was surprised to find the jam fruit was all home grown. "I'd love to have a garden," she said.

"You — " Dougie began, then choked on a crumb. Angus obligingly thumped him on the back till Dougie assured him that the cure was worse than the disease.

"You were saying . . . ?" Angus prompted in amusement but Dougie shook his head.

I looked at his flushed face and wondered if he had been about to give himself away, to say to Maisie, "You *shall* have a garden." Was that why Angus was so amused? Funny to think of it; it was talking about a garden that had betrayed Bella's feelings for Arthur to me. I smiled to myself.

Faither noticed. "Fairies in the fire, pet?" he asked. I nodded. "Aye," he said, "I think we'll all sleep well tonight."

Dougie took the hint immediately and started to get our candles ready. "I'll clear up and see to the fire," he said. Nobody argued. I suddenly realized just how tired I was. The things to chew over in bed would have to wait.

It was lovely standing in church singing that morning. Angus took the tenor line and Maisie, who was really a rich soprano, sang contralto under me. I felt thrilled to be part of the quartet. It was obvious from the knowing smiles of the women in the congregation that the news about Elsie had got around. When we left the church, Mam was immediately surrounded. Dougie murmured to Faither, "Could you wait for Mam while the rest of us get ready for Jean?"

"Oh, aye, Jean." Faither nodded agreement.

We eased ourselves out of the crowd as quickly as we decently could. With Jean and Tam coming, things would have to be just so.

"Your sister Jean sounds rather intimidating," Maisie began. "I feel a wee bit scared —"

"Oh, Jean's fine," I assured her. "She just has an abrupt manner but she's a tower of strength to us all."

"I think Dougie's scared of her," Maisie said.

"Dougie, scared?" I was shocked at the idea. "Dougie argues with her and answers her back and mimics her —"

"Aye, but he's still very much wee

brother to her," Maisie continued.

"Jean's curt with everyone," I said. "I used to be scared of her but not now . . . not since I started work."

I saw Maisie smile at this. Of course, to her I was still a child. But already I had distanced myself from school. Perhaps the humiliation of my final day had something to do with it . . . perhaps the vanity that Meg had been reluctant to stir . . .

Jean's reaction to Elsie's letter was one of indignation — indignation that she had not been told sooner. "D'you mean to say you got this yesterday and Dougie couldna run down to tell me?" Her voice was cracking with the outrage of it. Tam spoke up, sharply for him. "Jeannie, you're forgetting the visitors."

"Aye, aye, it's just that I've . . . " Jean fished angrily for her handkerchief.

"You must have been out of your minds with worry," Maisie said gently. Jean gave a grateful nod.

Lilias was demanding a game of 'horses' with Angus but Bella was trying to dissuade her because of her silk dress. "Show it to Jean," I said

297

with happy inspiration. Little coquette that she was — and is — Lilias deserted her beloved Angus to hold her skirts out and pirouette unsteadily before Jean. Seizing the opportunity to atone for her previous outburst, Jean told Maisie (who already knew, of course) that every stitch in that wee dress had been put in by Bella and me. "Elsie," she went on, "is an expert at these things . . . a genius wi' a needle and she taught the younger ones."

As I left for the back kitchen I could hear Maisie chatting easily. She wasn't scared of Jean. But could she be right about Dougie? My ideas kept being upended these days. But one thing was reassuring — we were going to start talking about Elsie again. Jean had ended that particular taboo.

I missed Dougie when he went back to university in November. It seemed so unfortunate that his absence always coincided with the dreariest months but I suppose from his point of view, it was better to be free in the better weather. Not that you could ever describe his life as free, he drove himself so hard. But his was certainly the sort of presence that was missed.

"Wish Dougie was here," Lilias said one morning.

Jean surprised me by answering, "Aye, we all miss Dougie. This shed is a different place when he's no' here but just you get Jessie to sing a nice song and let's hear you join in." I wondered how I could ever have been scared of Jean. Being away from school had quite a lot of compensations. Nobody chased me to bed early now and yet I was getting up at just the same time in the morning. New Year was approaching, though not fast enough. Every night I stood in front of my mirror and practised putting my hair up. We were sewing our new clothes to wear at Hogmanay. Mam was fit now to sit beside us and match our efforts.

Bella confided in me that she would like to bring in the New Year at Meg's. "You can't," I gasped. "How would Mam feel? She's lost Elsie and Meg's married and Jean doesn't come till the bells ring out . . ."

"You said she's lost Elsie," Bella

countered, "but Elsie's married too, her letter said so."

"Yes, but in a Catholic church," I answered, not having the faintest idea what this meant.

"It's still a church," Bella answered. "In some countries everybody is a Catholic."

It was something I had meant to ask Dougie about but had never got round to. However I was not prepared to show my ignorance to Bella so I quickly switched the subject.

"Just imagine," I said, "if Elsie has a baby you'll be 'Tante Belle' and I'll be 'Tante Jeannette'." We had a good giggle then decided our names sounded better in French.

We had all hoped to hear from Elsie at New Year. In her letter from the north of France she had said they would be making for Paris in a short time. But New Year came and went without further news. Neither Mam nor Faither said much but I noticed that Faither seemed to clear his throat oftener now. My hair had duly been put up and admired though Dougie had paused for a bleak second before he added his approval. Faither said, "I just hope Lilias is no' getting daft notions about hers." Mam swallowed the lump in her throat while Dougie said, "That same girl will not be slow in telling you."

Early in the year Meg's babies both went down with heavy colds. They were at the difficult stage — heavy to handle and not quite walking so Bella went through to help. Mercifully Lilias was a lot tougher than her tiny frame might indicate. With care we got Mam and her through the worst of the weather without mishap. Dougie was working very hard for his exams in April but he kept up my lessons and, of course, we still went to Paisley every Saturday.

Spring came and edged into summer but still no word from Elsie. Mam and Faither had a tightness about the lips now. After the first letter we had assumed we would hear from Elsie as soon as she got to Paris and had an address to send us. And, of course, so had the rest of Kilbarchan. I had grown up and felt secure in a tightly-knit community. Now I began to see the drawbacks. The treachery of my erstwhile friends at school — I still thought of it that way — had been a severe shock. Now, the constant awareness I felt all round me was a nagging pain even though I knew that in many cases it was prompted by kindly concern. Dougie grew short-tempered because he was powerless to influence events. Most people gradually stopped asking about Elsie but when Nurse Duncan unwisely broached the subject after church one Sunday Dougie replied with sarcastic patience, "No, Nurse Duncan, we have not heard from Elsie but as soon as we do we will run round and let you know."

"That was unkind," I reproached him as we walked home. "Mam would have been upset if she had heard you."

"Aye," he said, and kicked a stone angrily out of his path.

★ ★ ★

Lilias Day seemed to get bigger and better every year. Of course it was taken for granted that Maisie and Angus would come and stay with us again since the previous year had been such a great success. However there was a shock addition to our numbers in 1874. It was like this. Just a fortnight before Lilias Day a letter from Duncan arrived for Faither. It came on the Saturday when Bella was already off to Glasgow. Faither put on his glasses with hands that trembled, I noticed. Mam leaned anxiously over his shoulder. "Well . . . Well I never . . . " she kept saying while Dougie and I fidgeted with impatience. Faither looked up slowly. I found it difficult to read his expression. While we waited for him to speak, I noticed how his eyebrows were becoming ragged with hard white hairs jutting out among the golden ones. The thin patch on top of his head was spreading and silvery hairs caught the light. Poor Faither, how life had changed for him. I remembered Rab's 'puir bugger' and felt a guilty smile begin to creep over my face.

"Aye, Jessie," Faither said, "you're a working woman now, no' a bairn, so you might as well hear what Duncan has to say."

He passed the letter over to Dougie who held it low for my benefit. I had guessed right about Bella and her Arthur.

I've known Arthur Clark since I first came here and have found him to be a young man of the soundest principles. Meg feels that if he were allowed to pay court, he would have a steadying influence on Bella who has already improved considerably with her responsibilities here. It is possible that they would have to wait some time before Arthur would be in a position to provide a home but Meg feels that once the liaison is acknowledged, Bella will be a loving, loyal fiancée.

Now, I have another surprise for you, Mr Allen. Meg is two months pregnant again. We had meant to allow more time as the boys are a handful, but there it is! And, of course, we will welcome the child (in the singular, I hope) with open arms. Bella is invaluable in the energy she devotes to the children, allowing Meg a much-needed respite.

This brings me to another of Meg's ideas. We have not mentioned it to

Bella and will not do so unless it is your wish. Meg says that work for the hand weavers is dwindling; that only the heavy work of butchers' aprons and the specialist shawl weaving which Bella cannot do are in demand from you. Many of the ladies in the big houses here engage a 'sewing lady' by the day. If Bella lived here, she could do this work (which is well paid in some cases) and see her precious Arthur more frequently. Also she could pick and choose her time and be of assistance to Meg. I know it would be a vexing thought to have another daughter leave home but Jean's intention of teaching Jessie the specialist work might be invidious for Bella. Here she has a certain status she lacks in the middle of your talented family. I leave this for your consideration.

To revert to the first matter, Meg thinks it would be a good idea to invite Arthur along to Lilias Day with Dougie's friends. He could plead his suit (shyly, I'm afraid) and become one of the family. Mrs Allen's warm heart will go out to him, I'm sure.

"What next?" Dougie said when we finished.

"What next?" Faither repeated. "Next, I put on my cap and take this to Jean or I'll get my head in my hands to play with."

12

THOUGH the weather was anything but good that year, Lilias Day was a great success. Bella and Dougie went down to meet the visitors who would all be arriving on the same train. Lilias, of course, went with them to meet her beloved Angus. Mam and I were glad to be free of her while we were working with the heavy pots. Though a biddable bairn, she was so quick that you needed eyes in the back of your head.

I had seen Mam's lips tremble that morning when the postman passed us by. A year without word from her daughter was an agony that I could understand but only share spasmodically for I had my secret moments at that time of delight in my body and an awaking awareness that I was attractive to the boys of the village. I found myself smiling secret smiles as Elsie used to do. Half-formed pictures would arise of a handsome young man kissing my hand; of myself in white dress and veil floating towards a handsome stranger; of a beautiful baby — the most beautiful in the world — who would be mine, just mine. The father of the baby was always nebulous in these pictures. It was my beautiful baby and it smiled at me with intensely blue eyes and I held it close to my naked body, its skin soft against mine. It burrowed closer and I was filled with a longing that sent a burning ache right through my bones.

These dream scenes could build up while I was doing the most ordinary things. Then I would notice that my hands had slowed down and I would break into a song to speed me up again.

I had found it difficult to picture Arthur and, of course, till Duncan's letter arrived I did not know officially of the situation so it was impossible to ask Bella. "What sort of man would find our Bella attractive?" I pondered. Her rosy cheeks and ready laugh might appeal to a boisterous outgoing type but by all accounts Arthur was shy in the extreme. Certainly she had looked her best that morning as she set out for the station in the outfit she had created specially for the occasion. The blue and white striped cotton skirt flounced attractively round her ankles and cinched her tiny waist. Her snowy white blouse had V-shaped frills which also emphasized her neat figure. Black glossy ringlets escaped from her white straw bonnet with its bold blue ribbons dangling down the back. She was almost dancing with delight as she left, hand-in-hand with Lilias. Dougie had a big umbrella ready for the showers which had been on and off all morning.

Faither had checked that we had enough coal for the range, then retired to the shed with his pipe. I looked at Mam, at the lines which had been deepening round her mouth during the last year, and felt a surge of pity. What could I do to distract her? Arthur was the obvious answer. "Duncan seems to think a lot of this Arthur," I began.

"Aye," Mam answered, "it's nice to think *she's* found somebody decent." The emphasis on the 'she' confirmed that Elsie was uppermost in her mind as I had suspected. People talked of a mother who had an only daughter as having 'one ewe lamb' or an only son being 'the apple of his mother's eye'. Yet here was Mam grieving even though she had six of us left. It didn't seem to matter how many children you had, a bit of your heart was torn out when one was lost to you.

We heard Lilias's joyful chuckling long before they reached the house. No sooner had Angus set her down than she ran to me in triumph. "See, Jessie, Arthur made a boat for me." The tiny sailing boat was exquisitely carved. I held it in frank admiration as I turned to meet our visitor. Beside Dougie and Angus who were both tall and thin, Arthur looked quite stocky in spite of the shock of black hair which had shot up into the air when he removed his cap. He blushed to the roots as his rough hand closed over mine. It was the first time I had met with this reaction. The shyest of visitors had never seemed embarrassed about meeting 'little Jessie'. But, of course, I was not 'little Jessie' any more. My hair was up now and frequent peeps in the mirror assured me that I was rounding out satisfactorily. An answering blush began to creep up my neck while I savoured the knowledge of my new-formed power. Quickly I turned to attend to a pot on the range.

It was a blessing Lilias was there. She was the only one Arthur wasn't shy with. Bella kept giggling about nothing and Arthur seemed as scared of her as he was of the rest of us. Even Mam's gentle inquiries about his family seemed to distress him. It was a relief when Faither came in from the shed. 'Now we'll get our dinner,' I thought. 'By the look of that lad he won't be too shy to eat.'

After a few words of greeting I saw Faither look at Mam. I had long been aware of a special sort of communion they have always had between them. There's nothing obvious about it, no winking or twitching; yet they seem to transfer their thoughts. "Gie's a hand through wi' a couple more chairs, Arthur," Faither said in the same tone he would use to Dougie. Not even a 'please' to the visitor! They disappeared towards the parlour. When they came back, Arthur was actually speaking. "I've heard about these Paisley pinks. The weavers are famous for them."

"Aye, lad, you just wouldna believe the variety they can get. I was at their show last year," Faither went on, "and I kept thinking, 'that's the bonniest pink I've ever seen'; and then I'd come on another one wi' even finer markings. The sizes were quite varied, too. There was a biggish one — a kind o' apricot-peach colour wi' deep wine markings. The colours just sang at you. Maybe next year you could get a day off and we'll go thegither."

That was Faither's way of letting Arthur know that his suit was acceptable. It saved poor shy Arthur a lot of sweat. I doubt that he would ever have got round to broaching the question at all.

For the first time, I approached Lilias Day as an adult with my hair up. All thoughts of Elsie were banished from my mind as our happy group joined the crowds. Lilias was perched as usual on Angus's shoulders which meant that I kept close to him. Dougie was protecting Maisie in the crush while Bella clung to

Arthur. The decorations were superb in spite of the weather. The judges had a hard job deciding which of the streets had made the best effort in design and construction, finally awarding it to the New Street arch.

Jean and Tam arrived in time for supper. By that time Arthur had lost quite a lot of his shyness and responded to Tam's unhurried inquiries about his work quite calmly. Jean was going to help Mam see Lilias to bed so Tam came out with us to share part of the evening session. In previous years I had always stood admiring Dougie and Angus's efforts but was surprised to find that at the muscle-testing, Arthur and Tam achieved better scores than they did. And when it got to the rifle range, Arthur outscored them all. Dougie was quite put out, I could see, and Bella didn't help matters by crowing about it. It was Arthur who finally stopped her by a blunt, "Forget it. It's not *that* important."

"Good!" I thought. "He's quiet but he's not going to be soft with her."

It was raining quite hard on the Sunday night when it was time for the visitors to catch their train. Mam urged me to stay at home and just let Dougie and Bella see them off. I hesitated for a second but worked it out that Bella would be too absorbed in her Arthur to notice Dougie and Maisie and, if she weren't, Angus was clever enough to distract her. So I stayed at home, put the hot pigs in our beds and infused another pot of tea as soon as I heard their voices.

Bella disappeared upstairs immediately after her tea — probably wanting to dream about her beloved Arthur. I sat on, listening to Dougie and Faither discussing the events of the day. There was a pause then Faither said, "A fine lass, Maisie. You'll no' find better. I had a wee talk wi' her faither — "

"I didn't know you knew Mr Wilson," Dougie broke in.

"Oh, aye, I bought my hat for the twins' christening there and we got on the talk. That's quite a while ago . . . I gaither you'll be welcome . . . "

Dougie sat there with his mouth open looking quite silly. "You didna think your mither and me were daft, did you?" Faither asked.

A sheepish grin spread over Dougie's face and he blushed crimson. Mam and Faither burst out laughing and so did I, though I couldn't help feeling sorry for Dougie. Suddenly he was laughing too and then he explained that he'd thought it would upset them if they knew how he felt when he still hadn't finished his studying.

That night Dougie was still singing in his room when I crept into my warm bed. 'More changes in the Allen family,' I thought. Dougie would be getting engaged to Maisie and Bella to Arthur. Sooner or later they would be getting married and then there would be only Lilias and me. If Faither accepted Meg's idea, Bella would be away from home even before that. Our family was dwindling.

Bella did indeed go off to Glasgow at the beginning of September and Jean immediately started to teach me the shawl weaving. Of course I had been watching it all for years — Faither setting up the web, then reading off Dougie's design from the squared paper so that Jean could cut the perforated cards.

315

These were threaded together to make a continuous string and that activated the mechanism. Then whoever was doing the weaving would brush the starch paste on to the warp threads to stiffen them. When that was dry, you could start. Aye! I had seen it all hundreds of times but my heart was thumping like a drum the first time I sat there with Jean standing above me and warning me to watch my tension. Tension was a word we heard often in the weaving trade. If an agent in Paisley wanted an eleven foot shawl it had to be within a quarter of an inch of that or he wouldn't accept it. Jean and Meg seemed to manage it every time. No wonder Faither was proud of them and no wonder he was reluctant to let dreamy Elsie or jumpy Bella tackle the valuable work.

I felt my responsibility keenly as I grasped the smooth shuttle and started. Faither and Dougie carried on with their work, leaving me to Jean's tender mercies. At first I reacted strongly every time I heard her sharp intake of breath and her 'ease up a wee' or 'firm it up a bit' but soon the fascination of the work had me in its grip. By late afternoon a small section of the pattern was formed. I felt a rush of delight at my achievement and burst into song. Jean came to examine my work. "No bad, no bad," she said with satisfaction. "Just stop there. You've done enough for your first day." She turned to Faither and Dougie who had come to admire my efforts. "We'll make a weaver o' her yet."

"Aye!" said Faither with satisfaction, "The Allen shawls flow on."

I waited for Dougie. He seemed to take a long time considering his reply. "It's just what I expected," he said, "but oh, what a waste!"

Jean snorted with indignation at that and I could see Faither was hurt. "I like the job, Dougie," I said; "being here in the shed with the rest of you and Lilias toddling out and in. And I'm still learning French and Latin from you, don't forget."

"Mmmm . . . " he stood for a little while, thinking. "Maybe I'll start you on Greek when the dark nights come in."

Jean was quick. "And what do you

think she'll do wi' Greek — swear at the weans in it?"

We were all laughing when Lilias came to summon us for tea and scones.

That September we had a bit of a scare. Two women we knew in Kilbarchan bought tartaric acid to make some sort of drink. Soon after they sampled it they became violently sick. Doctor Campbell was sent for. Luckily he managed to put the women to rights but a portion of the acid was sent off to be analysed. My first thought, of course, was, "What if I had made it for Lilias?" That wee lass grew dearer to me every day. It was impossible to stay dull in her company. She was so full of life, bubbling with happiness most of the time. And even when she was serious, she had such a charming defencelessness I just longed to put my arms round her. When I was getting her ready for bed she would gaze at me with those melting brown eyes and tell me her innermost thoughts. Sometimes it was hard to keep a straight face. Then she would demand a song and I would keep at it till her dark silky lashes lay still. Of course Lilias was the only one whose life remained untouched by Elsie's departure, though she still had memories of a sort. For example, whenever Mrs Nisbet-Brown's carriage drew up she would say hopefully, "Elsie?"

Oh! that's something I forgot to tell you about. I'll have to jump back a bit. That Lilias Day when Elsie's letter arrived we were all so excited we hardly knew what we were doing. Then Maisie and Angus were there and Jean and Tam, and everything was so high-key that we can be excused, I think. It was when Dougie came over from the shed on the Monday afternoon that he said, "Mam, we forgot about Mrs Nisbet-Brown. She's been worried about Elsie, too."

Jean snorted. She had never rid herself of the idea that Mrs Nisbet-Brown was responsible for Elsie's defection, and should have kept a better eye on her. However, Mam and Faither were in agreement with Dougie and it was arranged that I would walk over with him that night to the big house.

I would have found it difficult to recognize Mrs Nisbet-Brown, I think, if I had met her outside. She had always been slender but straight and proud in her bearing. But when we were shown into the drawing-room that night, it was a scraggy little birdlike woman who rose, leaning on a stick, to meet us. I'm afraid the shock must have showed on my face. Even Dougie spoke more hesitantly than usual. Her delight when we gave her the news took the form of racking sobs. Instinctively I hurried forward to put my arm round her.

Dougie said, "Lean on me, Mrs Nisbet-Brown. We'll get you to your chair. Then perhaps I could fetch you some brandy?"

"Please," she said, pointing shakily to a lacquered cabinet. Dougie opened the doors carefully, selected a bottle and poured a measure into a crystal glass. Holding it to her lips as she sipped, he watched intently till her paper-white skin began to show a faint sign of colour. I wondered that I had ever stood in awe of 'big house folk'. Mrs Nisbet-Brown was just like poor old Grannie Watson — worse, because she didn't have Aunt Polly to look after her, only servants. Elsie had told us that Mrs Nisbet-Brown's only daughter was married to some foreign diplomatist whose work took him all over the world; that her two granddaughters attended a convent school in France and had hardly seen their Grannie for years.

Between the effect of the brandy and a constantly-wielded handkerchief the old lady's nose began to shine red like a beacon. I struggled to keep down my nervous giggles. I mustn't, I mustn't . . . Then Mrs Nisbet-Brown said, "Mr Allen, do have some sherry or whisky if you prefer. Your sister is too young. She would like lemonade. I'm sure. If you ring . . ."

"Please don't trouble," I said. I would have loved some lemonade but I felt it wasn't fair to let the servants see her looking like that so I sat there, feeling noble, while Dougie sipped his sherry and shared Mrs Nisbet-Brown's speculations about Elsie's life in France.

It was after ten o'clock when we rose to go but even then she was reluctant to part with us. "Drop in to see Mam any time you're passing," Dougie said. "She's seldom out and always glad of a wee talk."

It wasn't like Dougie to issue invitations like that and I broached the subject as we walked smartly home, having refused the offer of Mrs Nisbet-Brown's coach. "That poor woman's left with nothing, don't you see?" he reasoned. "Mam has so much in the way of human contact."

"But what if she's at the pirn winding and Lilias has her toys scattered all over the floor?" I asked.

"Better that than being stuck in a mausoleum," he answered, then had to explain the word to me. I was still so bemused by the tale of the terrible earthquake at Halicarnassus when we got home that I only half-listened to Dougie as he described our visit to Mam and Faither.

"Poor old soul," Mam said. "She'll aye be welcome."

That gave me something else to think about when I got to bed. Dougie's phrase 'so much in the way of human contact' stuck in my mind. It was true; yet Mam and Faither had changed since Elsie left. Those little lines round Mam's mouth tightened whenever Elsie's name was mentioned. And after that I noticed that every time Mrs Nisbet-Brown's coach drew up and Lilias said "Elsie?" they tightened again.

Dougie had noticed too, I guess. It was his idea that we should all go by train one day early in October to visit Meg. "The weather's still mild, Mam," he said. "Jessie will take care of Lilias; Faither will take care of you and I'll carry the ton of junk I've no doubt you will consider necessary to take to your loving daughter." Mam's resistance yielded to Dougie's coaxing as usual. The weather held.

I had my work cut out keeping Lilias still. Of course she was used to the snorting monster which brought her beloved Angus from Paisley but that didn't stop her squealing at its approach and burying her face in my skirts so fiercely that I staggered and would have fallen if Dougie had not been near to steady me. All the way to Glasgow she kept up a non-stop commentary on the countryside we were passing. When I grew tired of explaining and correcting, Dougie would help me out.

To Lilias the rattling tramcars with

their trotting horses were almost as thrilling as the train. Mam smiled contentedly at her toddler's antics while Faither, I noticed, had an anxious eye on Mam whenever she wasn't looking his way. The last bit of the journey would be the most difficult for her, the walk from the tramcar to the house. Dougie had said we would take it slowly.

"Duncan!" Lilias shrieked over my shoulder. I turned my head and there, by the tramstop, was Duncan waiting for us. After the greetings were over he suggested that Dougie and I might like to go ahead with Lilias while the others followed more slowly. This suited us fine. Lilias almost ran by my side in her eagerness to play with 'Meg's babies'. Dougie never liked walking slowly anyway.

I knew that people saw me differently now. It wasn't just Arthur's blush; no, there were countless other instances. For example, when I took Rusty to the trough it was no time at all till there would be a group of young weavers 'out for a breather', teasing one another as they lit their pipes or indulging in threats about dooking someone in the trough. Two of Patty's brothers were often among these groups. Big Will, who bore a strong resemblance to his sister in his gipsy darkness, also shared her bold impertinence. His younger brother, Harry, was his admiring acolyte, giggling in nervous admiration at Will's boastful threats.

Instinct and my new awareness told me that the show was put on for my benefit and I was ashamed to find myself pleased at this knowledge of my power, especially since I knew that not one of them could hold a candle to my big brother. Vanity made me careless, I'm afraid, and I let myself smile at their antics, though I knew they needed little encouragement.

One day my complacency was shattered. Will was in one of his most outrageous moods. His talk got wilder and wilder. As usual he was threatening to dook somebody in the trough; then he turned to me. "How would you like a swim, Jessie? Your sister Bella's nearly been in there a few times. You know what Jimmie Gibson calls her, 'Bella, Bella, Chase-a-Fella'. The laughter of the other boys quietened down to an odd snigger.

Harry, far from amused, looked horrified but Will went on with a bold laugh, "It would be a shame to spoil your pretty dress. I could help you off with it. Your sister Elsie doesn't think twice about taking hers off, does she? And think of all the folk that see her when that French chiel paints her. Pity about the wee lass he left at Craigneuk farm wi' her belly bursting."

The freckles stood out on Harry's white face as he leapt at my tormentor. For a moment Will looked surprised as he staggered backwards. Then an evil look came over his face and he began systematically to pound his fist into poor Harry's face. A few of the lads made uneasy remarks. "That's enough, Will, he's only wee . . . " Suddenly my control broke and I screamed. "Stop it you big bully. He's your brother!"

At that, one of the older weavers from a nearby shed came out. "What's this?" he bellowed. "Aye, ye might be sure. If there's trouble the McPhees are sure to be in it. It's time Jo McPhee took his belt to the lot o' ye. Fightin' in front o' a decent lassie, tae . . . you should be ashamed o' yersel's."

The group melted away. Soberly I led Rusty home. What if news of this reached Dougie's ears; or the weaver mentioned it to Faither? I had brought the trouble on myself but they would never believe that and I wouldn't have the courage to tell them. For days I went shivering in my shoes for fear that word would get round to the family's ears but nothing happened. I decided that Lilias was old enough to walk beside me when I led Rusty to the trough. She would be my chaperone. Obviously the new power which I found so thrilling carried its own responsibilities. I was no longer an appendage of my parents.

That was reinforced when Jinty opened the manse door and saw me for the first time with my hair up. "Oh, Miss Jessie," she said, "you've got your hair up. You look so old — I mean different," she floundered.

Lilias piped up, "It all falls down at night." We burst out laughing, ending Jinty's embarrassment. Meg came hurrying out of the study. Suddenly I felt shy. It's difficult to explain. It was something about her being pregnant so soon again and these longings she said God gave you. But Meg seemed unaware of my dilemma as she hugged first Lilias, then me, and then stood back to study her 'grown-up sister' as she named me. "You'll be fighting off the village boys I can see, Dougie," she said laughingly.

"Let them dare," he said, laughing too. But there was a touch of 'half fun, whole earnest' in his tone? I could not be sure. Guilt about the encounter by the trough made me blush. I saw Meg give me a keen glance before she suggested that we might like to go out to the garden.

"Bella probably hasn't heard you. She's playing with the boys in the pancake club's latest creation. Go out and see . . . just past the currant bushes. I'll wait here for Mam, then tea in ten minutes after that."

"With cherry cake, I hope," said Dougie wickedly.

Lilias swung on our hands, getting a free ride as we hurried through the garden towards the sound of Bella and the twins. "Oh, you wee rascals, what next?" she was squealing.

"Tell them Uncle Dougie's coming to sort them out," Dougie called as we turned into the path beyond the fruit garden. There on a stretch of level grass was the pancake club's invention.

"Ah, a pig pen," said Dougie. "A luxury pig pen but a pig pen none-the-less."

"Well, they do behave like pigs sometimes," said Bella laughing.

The pen was a conglomeration of old doors set on their sides, strong stakes and woven ropes — the whole thing painted bright yellow. Two rag rugs in the centre of the arena were supposed to be the resting place for little bottoms — but you know what boys are! George and Walter were putting a sturdy wooden horse to good use — gouging a hole in the grass. And George had just managed to find a wriggly worm.

"He was going to eat it," Bella assured us.

"Ah, many a worm you swallowed at that age, I remember," said Dougie, stepping over the fence with Lilias in his arms.

"I didn't!" Bella was aghast. Dougie

pretended to arrange a lock of Lilias's hair as he winked at me.

"Worms are poison. You die if you eat them," Lilias assured us earnestly.

"And Bella is still alive." Dougie's voice was as serious as hers. "Ergo, she didn't eat worms," he concluded. "We may have a logician here or perhaps she is just repeating someone's words . . . ?"

"Mea culpa," I admitted and we all had a good laugh.

After a wee while Dougie carried the twins, one under each arm, into the house. Mam had been crying, I could see. Meg's hand rested on top of hers on the arm of the chair. I guessed they had been talking about Elsie. Tea was a bit of a struggle till Dougie and Duncan appointed themselves 'retrievers of twins' and announced that they would have a 'decent tea' in the kitchen after the others had had peace to theirs. So Mam and Faither were able to enjoy chatting to Meg over their cups while watching the antics of their grandsons on the rug with Dougie and Duncan. Bella, too, had quite a lot to say about the houses she had already worked at and the odd little ways of the occupants.

Mam and Faither were as reluctant as I was to leave when the time came and only the thought of the train journey could prise Lilias away from crooning over the sleeping babies. It had been an inspiration on Dougie's part, that visit. Seeing Mam so happy and fulfilled in Meg's company, Faither had relaxed and had started to engage Duncan in discussion of working conditions in his parish. Of course Dougie had joined in and in no time at all they were out in the garden, Faither's pipe reeking as he and Dougie took opposite sides in the argument with Duncan holding the balance very competently. It seemed funny then to think that it had worried me when I was younger to hear Faither and Dougie going at it hammer and tongs. Now I welcomed it as a sign that Faither was triumphing over his anxieties, recovering his power.

★ ★ ★

The cold weather soon had us in its grip. Dougie was off early in the morning and studying late into the night. Mam and I made the black bun and started sewing the clothes we would welcome the New Year in. Mrs Nisbet-Brown dropped in quite often — when the mausoleum got too much for her, I guessed. Jean would send me over to join her and Mam in a tea party. Though she stayed resolutely in the shed I think Jean's attitude had softened to the old lady when Dougie gave her an account of our visit.

Mam reigned calmly supreme, queen of her kitchen but, looking back, I realize that I did most of the talking. Mrs Nisbet-Brown seemed to delight in drawing me out about my studies with Dougie, the clothes I was making for Lilias and my progress in music. Maisie had taught me the German words of some of my songs. It turned out that Mrs Nisbet-Brown had learned a lot of lieder when she was young. Often she would ask me to sing one to her. Of course they never sounded the same without the piano but she understood that perfectly well and sometimes we would hum the missing bits together. One day she announced that a childhood friend was coming to live with her.

"We used to be inseparable at school," she said. "Alice was always leading me into mischief, she was such fun. She was widowed in India a number of years ago and her friends have moved away one by one. It seems silly to have two lonely old women . . . the servants — some of them, that is — take a rise out of me, I think. Alice will help me there; give me support . . . "

"Put some smeddum into you," I supplied.

"Exactly, my dear," she said. "You have hit the nail on the head."

As she prepared to leave she asked Mam, "Will it be all right if I bring my friend to meet you?"

"Of course, you will always be welcome," Mam said. We walked out to her carriage where Lilias was already feeding the horse titbits under Dick's careful eye. The cold air prevented any lingering. We hurried into the weaving shed as soon as the horse clipclopped round the bend.

"Fancy her wanting to bring her friend to meet you," I said when Mam had recounted the visit to Jean and Faither.

"I wouldna' depend on it," Jean said flatly. "That's probably the last you'll see o' her once she gets her ain kind."

"We'll see," said Mam calmly.

13

NEW YEAR was bound to be a difficult time for Mam, and I prayed that there would be some news from Elsie to cheer her up. Hogmanay was the usual fiendish round of housework and food preparation. I guessed it was kinder to let Mam tire herself out rather than have her sitting around, remembering. Jean stayed at home, of course, on Hogmanay, getting her own house ready but the previous morning she had spoken to me quietly in the shed. "I was hoping against hope that Mam would have a letter before New Year. Does she say anything to you?"

"No, but I see these wee lines deepen round her mouth when the postman comes."

"Aye." Jean was downcast.

"Dougie says that Elsie is probably caught up in the gay life of Paris and keeps meaning to write — ."

"Dougie's daft," Jean interrupted me.

"If Elsie was happy she'd be writing to Mam to tell her a' about it. There's something wrang. I feel it . . . "

I looked at Jean, at her tiny triangular face which never had much colour; the nostrils pinched with stress were causing a pink flush round her eyes which were bright with unshed tears.

'She loves Elsie,' I thought, 'just the way I love Lilias. She loves her bonny wee sister who's "a genius with a needle".'

I wondered what to say to comfort Jean . . . Jean who was so strict with us all . . . Jean who had complained bitterly about Elsie's inattention at work, who had deplored the trips to the big house which might turn Elsie's head . . . Jean who was looking lost and sadly in need of comfort.

"Why don't you get Tam to take you to visit Meg the day after New Year?" I asked. "Meg would love to see you and you could have a nice wee talk and play with the bairns . . . "

"Well . . . " Jean was undecided . . . "you'd be here wi' Mam . . . and Dougie would be at hame . . . aye, maybe I'll dae just that." She squared her shoulders and was soon hard at work.

In spite of the sadness engendered by Elsie's absence I felt the old rush of excitement as the magic hour approached. Dougie was singing as he stoked the range and fetched and carried for Mam and me. It had taken a long time to get Lilias settled. She wanted to 'see the New Year'. I could sympathize, remembering my own feelings when people had talked about 'seeing the New Year in' and I had felt I was missing something wonderful. Then the first time I had managed to stay awake long enough and Dougie, barely twelve, had carried me down to the living room saying, "She was awake." I had kept saying, "Where is it . . . the New Year?" and they had all laughed at me.

Bella had come home rather reluctantly as it meant being far from her beloved Arthur but, as she confided in me, "Meg says it will probably be my last New Year on my own and Mam is feeling bad enough without Elsie. Anyway, Arthur said we should be with our folks at New Year. There'll be plenty time later, he said."

Meg obviously expected Bella to marry

in 1875 and Dougie would be graduating in May if all went well. And Maisie and he were so unashamedly in love, they probably would be getting married too. It was all going round my head as I slipped into the new dress I had made — blue flannel with a high collar, a tight tucked bodice which showed my shape very satisfactorily and lots of heavy braid on the flounced skirt. What if no-one came to first-foot us? Bella was losing touch with her covey of friends and Elsie's wouldn't come. Nor Meg's. Dougie's former school friends were scattered, many of them married. Of course there would be the old faithfuls among the neighbours but they weren't worth dressing up for, I thought disloyally. Still, a new dress always made me feel good and Dougie would appreciate it.

As we waited for the warning rattle of the big clock, I looked at Mam. She had had a wee cry in the bedroom, I could tell, but she was determinedly bright as she sat in the big chair with her best shawl round her shoulders. Faither, balding now, rested his elbow on the back of her chair. Bella was no longer the coltish young girl. Her spell at the manse had given her a little of the poise she had always lacked. Of course we had all changed — even Dougie. He was still handsome — nobody in Kilbarchan to touch him — but there was a difference: the boyish look had gone, except when he laughed; little frown lines had formed between his eyes and these deepened when he was working something out or getting angry. And I saw them deepen suddenly about half an hour after the New Year began.

The usual crowd of neighbours had drifted in not long after we had finished our family greetings. Soon they were augmented by an unexpected group, headed by Patty McPhee. Of course everyone was made welcome at New Year but I could sense Mam's surprise. Patty had certainly not been one of my closest friends and her group did not include any of those but it did include Harry and some other weavers. At first I was too relieved that the bold Will was not in her group to think any further. Patty shook hands first with Faither then with Mam and asked if 'Bonnie wee Lilias' was in bed. Then she advanced on Bella and me and kissed us. The other girls in the group did the same, giggling the while. Why had Patty put them up to this? My question was soon answered when Harry quickly followed his sister's example, blushing crimson through his freckles. The other boys contented themselves with shaking my hand and smirking. As usual in any perplexity I instinctively turned to Dougie. The frown lines had never been deeper. I remembered his words to Meg: 'Let them dare.' Just then the bold Patty approached him. Holding her hand firmly at arm's length, he wished her a grim "Happy New Year." Even the unquenchable Patty looked scared. I turned hurriedly to poke the fire, pretending that the ash was making me cough.

A long lie in was traditional on New Year's morning but it was difficult to explain this to Lilias. She was jumping around the bed when I was still drugged with sleep. Then Dougie came in with a lovely hot cup of tea for me. "Faither's got the fire roaring and the porridge going," he said. "I'll wrap this wee monkey in a shawl and take her down to the big chair. Just you stay as long as you like."

With my quilt up to my chin and the pillows banked round me I dreamily sipped the tea. 1875 . . . What would it bring? Mam would be hoping for word from Elsie. Meg and Duncan would be thinking about their new baby — not that Meg had much time to think at all with her lively sons demanding constant attention. Bella of course had scarce another thought in her head but Arthur — no, that wasn't fair . . . Duncan said she was invaluable in the help she gave Meg. But if she married in the coming year she would soon be having babies too. But Arthur was so shy . . . how would he ever . . . ?

Quickly I put my cup on the bedside table and snuggled down with my eyes shut and the warm flush stealing over my body. The thoughts wouldn't go away. I cupped my breasts in my hands, loving the firm, warm flesh. If you were in bed with your man would he touch them too . . . as well as . . . ? Suddenly I threw off the quilt and jumped onto the cold floor. The water in the ewer felt icy cold but I would wash in it to get rid of those shameful thoughts.

★ ★ ★

January was always a pretty dull month. Of course if it was frosty the weavers took time off and went curling. That year the only diversion I can remember was the St John's Day parade when the brethren in their insignia marched behind their band through the town carrying torches. Lilias loved it of course and went round for days beating an imaginary drum and singing her impression of the tune she had heard. In February there was grumbling all round us. The ratepayers were objecting to the high cost of the proposed new school. Dougie was furious at their 'unenlightened attitude'. I tried not to get drawn in to the grumbling sessions I encountered but to concentrate on looking forward to Meg's baby.

And Grant Douglas — all bouncing eight pounds of him — duly arrived on the first of March, named after Duncan's brother and Dougie. Mam had been hoping for a wee lassie because she thought boys were such a handful. Jean clucked her tongue and wished she were nearer to give Meg a hand, but a letter from Duncan with the news assured us that Meg was well, Bella was competently in charge and a good woman from the church was now cleaning for them every day since the congregation had raised his stipend. This meant that Jinty could help Bella more.

"I believe it's one of the fastest growing congregations in the west of Glasgow," Faither said. "They should be able to pay a decent stipend."

Dougie's final exams were to start on the seventeenth of April. I suffered for him as I watched the tension build up and his face whiten from long hours of study. Even our treasured trip to Paisley had to be forgone on the last two Saturdays. I wondered if this was wise. It seemed to me that he needed the solace of Maisie's love but it was a difficult thing for me to express and I doubt if Dougie would have listened to me anyway. When he got into that determined mood he would drive himself on regardless. Nothing had come of the Greek lessons. With Dougie spending so much time bent over his own books I had suggested that we limit his work with me to question and answer sessions. This meant he didn't have to take time off as he could quiz me in the weaving shed on Saturday mornings. Sometimes Lilias would try to join in, giving us all a good laugh. Dougie was patient even with her, born teacher that he was, and she was such a good mimic that she had a lovely French accent even when she got the words sadly confused.

Mrs Nisbet-Brown *did* bring her friend, Alice — Alice Newton. I liked her immediately. Lilias was in one of her most entertaining moods and sent the new guest into gales of laughter. You simply never knew what that child would say next and she floored Mrs Newton when she sometimes answered with a French phrase. It seemed funny to me that the gulf between us and the folk at the big house, once so formidable, had been bridged so easily. There was nothing patronizing in Alice Newton's questions about my brother at university, my sister with the twins, the other sister who lived with her and so on. I found myself chatting quite easily about Bella who was so talkative and Arthur who was so shy but such a clever gardener and so strong on the muscle machine and how he hoped to be head gardener some day but that wouldn't be for a long time because the head gardener was quite young.

"Not like yours, Jane," she said to Mrs Nisbet-Brown, "He looks like Methuselah's uncle."

Yes, I liked Mrs Newton and she certainly seemed to have made life brighter at the big house.

Dougie sweated his way through his final exam and, of course, was successful as we all knew he would be. The expensive black silk gown he was to wear at his graduation was ordered. When I told Jean she said, "I thought he had a gown."

"He has a red gown, a student's gown," I told her. "That's what he wore for his first graduation but now that he's an MA he has to wear a black silk gown for his second ceremony."

Next morning I heard Jean arguing with Faither, "But Tam and I would like to . . ."

"Naw, naw, lass," Faither said, "I'll be proud as a peacock to lay out the money for that daft gown. The first MA, BSc in Kilbarchan . . . just think o' it."

"Aye," said Jean and blew her nose.

Maisie and Dougie got officially engaged on the day of his graduation and the Wilsons gave a lovely party. Mam was given pride of place in their parlour and was waited on hand and foot. Lilias's bedtime was completely ignored as she showed off to her beloved Angus.

There was a reaction of course the next day. We were all a bit sluggish and Lilias was still fast asleep when we went out to start work. The morning wore on and I began to long for a cup of tea. "I think I'll go and see if Lilias is awake," I said, rising from my loom, just as Lilias herself rushed in, dress unfastened and feet bare.

"Mam says Jean's to come," she said. We all ran then, Dougie with Lilias scooped up under one arm.

Mam was crouched in the big chair,

her face grey and taut with pain. Jean swung the big kettle onto the fire as she issued her orders. "Brandy, Faither! Dougie, fetch Nurse Duncan. She'll ken whaur the doctor is. Jessie, dress the wean and take her up to feed Rusty."

In a way I resented being dismissed from the scene but my common sense told me that Jean was right. The wee one could only be a burden in the present crisis. And Lilias's troubled questions as I brushed her hair convinced me that she was sorely in need of distraction. In the back kitchen I spread a scone thickly with jam for her to eat on the way up the hill. Then I grabbed a few carrots for Rusty, stuck them in a basket, and we were off:

For once I was glad not to encounter Rab. I wanted peace to think. Long practice had enabled me to answer Lilias on one level while I was thinking on another. If Mam was having another heart attack, it could be worse than the first . . . and just when we were beginning to breathe more easily because she seemed so much better. This would spoil Dougie's joy in his new degree.

But Dougie had Maisie. He would be all right. Poor Faither! He had never been the same, really, since Lilias was born but he had been picking up. Now this! It was a good thing Jean was here. Meg was busy in her own little kingdom and would be for years to come. Elsie! Elsie knew nothing about this. Had she stopped caring? Were things going badly with her as Jean feared? It was a good thing I could look after Lilias. I kissed her flushed cheek as I hoisted her up on the fence to feed Rusty. She was adorable, this little sister I had not wanted. Meantime the best thing I could do would be to keep her happy. "Will we go up to the high woods," I asked, "and see if there are any primroses left?"

"Yes, we could take some to Mam," said Lilias eagerly. "That would make her better, wouldn't it?"

Time dragged for me as I answered her incessant questions. I wished I could find answers to my own.

We were making our way to the low woods in the hope of adding some bluebells to our primroses when Dougie found us. Lilias rushed to him, nearly upending my basket in the process. He swung her up in the air and, rocking her in his arms, started singing in French to me, "Keep a smile on your face: we don't want to worry the little one. Luckily I found the doctor at Barrhill."

"What does he say?" I sang and Lilias tried to join in.

"Another heart attack. He's surprised because she had seemed so much better but, of course, it is always a danger." He smiled at Lilias who was doing her best to imitate him.

"What will happen now?" I sang.

"He can't say. Careful nursing again. Luckily I'll be at home now though I had hoped to take on some tutoring . . . " Suddenly we realized what Lilias was singing: "Ça ne fait rien."

"Do you think she's trying to tell us something?" Dougie asked. "Something like 'It'll all be the same in a hundred years'."

We settled into a methodical routine. I spent most of my time in the house because Jean had an important order on hand. Dougie worked steadily at the routine heavy stuff. This let Faither come

349

in to sit with Mam for hours at a time. Lilias was quite a smart wee helper, fetching and carrying with a cheerful tune on her lips.

On the Friday after Mam's heart attack a young child in the village fell into a pot of boiling water and died on the Saturday afternoon. Though we didn't really know the family, I took the affair badly. Maybe it was because I was upset about Mam but I found myself hugging Lilias at every opportunity and thanking my lucky stars I hadn't left her to go to the big school.

Meg and Duncan had arranged the christening for the last Sunday in May with Doctor Graham performing the ceremony. Mam had been looking forward to it and Faither said he would ask them to postpone it for a week or two. I passed this on to Jean when I had slipped out to the shed.

"Oh, no," said Jean. "I don't care if that wean never gets christened. Mam's staying whaur she's safest — in her ain hoose — and no' for just a week or two."

"Don't say anything meantime," said

Dougie. "I'll have a word with Doctor Graham tonight; warn him that young Grant Douglas is a sturdy wee villain and quite likely to punch him on the nose come summer." Jean laughed in spite of herself.

Doctor Graham when approached by Faither regretted that it would be almost impossible to get a substitute with the holiday time coming on etc., but promised to come in on the Monday and give them a full account of his address on the occasion. I think in a way Mam was relieved to have the decision taken out of her hands. Faither stayed at home with her so it was left to Dougie, Lilias and me to represent Kilbarchan.

I had assumed that Jean and Tam would be making their way to Glasgow too but as Jean left on Friday night I heard her speak to Dougie. "See here, I'm no' too happy about the christening . . . so far away. I'll see how I feel about it on Sunday but I think I'd be happier to take a wee walk up here in the afternoon. She'll be feeling it . . . brings back Elsie, you ken . . . " she tailed off.

"Right, if that's how you feel, Meg will

understand." Dougie's voice was gentler than usual with Jean.

Lilias, of course, was enraptured with the 'wee baby' and the 'big babies', so Dougie and I were free to answer Meg's anxious questions about Mam.

"Jean must be worried or she would have come . . ." she said.

"Och, you know Jean," said Dougie. "Never thinks any of us can do anything right. Mind you, I always feel safer leaving Mam in her charge."

"You're right of course," said Meg. "I'm glad she's there." This was exactly how Dougie wanted her to feel. Clever devil, that brother of mine!

Meg was looking very thin this time but well and happy, I was glad to see. "She and Bella have been burning the midnight oil," Duncan said to us as he prepared to leave for the church, "but you'll see for yourselves," he added mysteriously. The mystery was solved when Bella and Jinty appeared carrying the twins. The lovely white velvet cloak Elsie had made for Meg's wedding had been carefully unpicked and turned into neat coats for two mischievous cherubs who were already struggling to reach the floor. "Oh, no, you don't," Bella said firmly, "not after all our work! You'll go *in* to that church clean, at least."

Duncan had arranged to have the christening early in the service. "The Sunday-school children know it's going to happen," he said. "They'll be restless till it's all over anyway. And Doctor Graham can base his children's address on it while it's still fresh in their minds."

Because Elsie and Bella had carried the twins, I was to have the honour this time. Lilias, of course, was past being any trouble and knew she was to sit with Dougie. It was as well I was used to handling a baby, for Grant Douglas was no light weight and restless with it. I had learned a few tricks with Lilias and during the opening prayer gave him the knuckle of my little finger to suck. He squawked a bit when Doctor Graham took him in his arms but when the water was sprinkled on his forehead he gulped into a shocked silence. I had been too busy with my duties to feel touched by the occasion but when Grant was safely in Meg's arms and the congregation started to sing 'The Lord bless thee and keep thee' and I heard Lilias pipe up clearly, a sudden rush of emotion stopped me from joining in. The family was growing, though scattered. I was surrounded by love. It was love that made Jean miss this beautiful ceremony. Her love was expressed in a dogged sense of duty. There were so many kinds of love: Mam and Faither in their gentle protective caring; Meg and Duncan, happy and fulfilled in their busy family life; Dougie and Maisie . . . shy . . . passionate . . . unfulfilled . . . And it was love that had taken Elsie from us, a different kind of love, one that had possessed her to the exclusion of all else. Where was Elsie . . . what was she doing?"

And that was the question that was troubling Mam late that night. With Lilias safely in bed and Dougie hunched over a book I had sat up late with Mam and Faither describing our day in minutest detail.

"Aye, it sounds a lovely day," she said at the end. "Meg's blessed wi' so many good folk round her. She'll need their help wi' three wild boys and a busy parish. It's the life she was cut out for, of course. I just wish I knew how Elsie's faring . . . " her voice faded. I could offer no comfort. I had come round to Jean's point of view on that subject. Something was wrong.

Faither rose and patted Mam's hand. "Bed! lass. Fretting will no' help. We've done our best . . . aye, we've done our best. We'll have to leave it there."

14

MAM held her own through the summer and we breathed more easily. Dougie had managed to fit in a few pupils, mainly boys who were going to university in November. He worked hard in the weaving shed, too, keeping up my lessons as best as he could. Sometimes on a very hot day Faither would declare a holiday and Dougie and I would pack a picnic and take Lilias off to the hills. I could see the pattern of my childhood being repeated as Dougie taught her which birds would have their nests where and made her stop to listen carefully to each bird call.

"That's a panic call, Dougie."

"Yes, but whose? Listen . . . Listen, Lilias!"

Patiently he answered her questions with only the occasional wink at me when they were far-fetched.

"She's quick, isn't she?" I said once.

"No quicker than you were, Jessie,"

he answered. Again I felt that wonderful glow that only Dougie could bring to my heart. I knew he wasn't given to paying idle compliments, so praise from Dougie was worth treasuring.

September soon came and he went off to teach at the John Neilson Educational Institute in Paisley. The shed felt quiet without him, nor did he get home as early as I had hoped, either. Sometimes he had staff meetings and sometimes he went to the Wilsons' house and corrected homework till Maisie was free of her pupils and could join him in a cup of tea. Gradually he got later and later as he stayed on for an evening meal with her. I began to feel sorry I had encouraged that particular romance. While Dougie was studying for his degree I had at least known he was upstairs and in his own room. Now the days seemed long, even with Lilias's chatter.

She still acted as my unknowing chaperone and I'm not being vain when I tell you I needed her. I suppose I was looking my best at that time for it seemed that half the boys in Kilbarchan wanted to walk out with me. But though at times

I was tempted by the half-formed idea that it would spite Dougie for what I saw as his neglect of me, something held me back, some instinct that told me 'Not yet'.

As the demand for Paisley shawls dwindled, quite a lot of Kilbarchan weavers were moving elsewhere. We became used to hearing that this one or that one was going; but we were not prepared for the shock that this brought to our family. Mrs Nisbet-Brown told us one day that among the departing Habbies was the daughter of her gardener and it seemed she was insisting on taking her father with her.

"I say it's not before time," Alice Newton broke in. "He still works hard himself but he never seems to be able to control his so-called helpers. I believe it has been difficult to get young men because they could earn more as weavers. That may change now, of course, but he's been depending on casual labourers and one at least of them is a drunken lout. I've seen him being unpleasant to the young kitchen maid. But do go on, my dear." She turned to Mrs Nisbet-Brown. "Tell Mrs Allen what you were thinking of."

I had noticed Mrs Nisbet-Brown edge forward impatiently in her chair while her friend was speaking, but now she did not seem to know how to begin. "Well, remember Jessie was talking about her sister's young man: Bella . . . Arthur, I think you said. He is a keen gardener, and strong, you said. It's a good cottage . . . would need some painting . . . but young people could soon cope with that. I'm sorry, I'm rambling. Do you think that this young man, Arthur, would care to be my head gardener?"

Mam and I were too stunned to speak for a moment. Then Mam said hesitantly, "He's awfu' shy, but a grand worker . . . It's managing the men . . . "

"He can be firm," I broke in, remembering Lilias Day and the shooting gallery. "He knows just how far to let things go. And he wants to be a head gardener," I added. "He must feel he could handle the job."

"Aye, you're right, Jess." Mam was making hasty amends. "My son-in-law, the minister, thinks a lot o' him."

Alice Newton was speaking. "We thought it would be nice for you to have a married daughter so near, Mrs Allen . . . with your daughter Meg and her children just out of reach."

They did not mention Elsie but I guessed that Mrs Nisbet-Brown still blamed herself to a certain extent for that disaster. Bella and Arthur within easy distance was to be her recompense to Mam.

Once the ball was set rolling, things moved at a frightening pace. Arthur came on the Sunday and Dougie, Bella and I walked over to the big house with him. There was no formal interview. We all had tea in a wee room downstairs that Alice Newton called 'The Snug'. "Much cosier here," she said, "and near the kitchen too." Arthur and Dougie went off with Mrs Nisbet-Brown to see the glasshouses while Bella and I chatted to Mrs Newton. Soon Mrs Nisbet-Brown was back. "Dougie has taken Mr Clark round the grounds," she said. "So kind of him in this cold weather. Ring the bell, Jessie, dear, and I'll see that there's more hot tea when they get back."

"Fancy," said Bella to Arthur on the way home, "she called you 'Mr Clark' when she was talking to us."

"Well, if Arthur's to be head gardener, she will have to give him his place," Dougie said. "You may find some of your helpers difficult, Arthur. I think that things have slipped badly recently."

"Aye, I can see that." Arthur's voice was very thoughtful. "There's a lot to be done. Unless you like the work you're no use at it but there's bound to be a lad or two that's keen. It could be a grand garden." From Arthur, that was a long speech. Bella was babbling on about the cottage as she jangled the keys proudly in her bag.

"I'll get Maisie and Angus recruited," Dougie said, "then we'll all give you a hand on Saturdays." Arthur was to take up his new duties at the New Year and paint would take a long time to dry in the cold weather.

Mam and Faither listened attentively to Bella's description of the cottage, "Just think! Four bedrooms with good presses. And the parlour's big and it's got two fancy presses to show the china and things. Of course, Arthur's got nothing like that . . . he'll just be living in the kitchen meantime . . . " She looked at Arthur with such naked longing that he blushed furiously. I found myself reddening too. Emotions that I was only too aware of these days were surfacing again. After Bella and Arthur left for Glasgow I was glad to retreat to bed where I could explore those dangerous thoughts further.

Our surprises were not at an end. Late Monday morning brought Duncan. Even Jean left her loom, knowing his visit meant important news. He waited only till Jean and I had quickly prepared some tea and scones before telling us what was in his mind.

"Last night when Bella and Arthur got back, they had a great deal to talk about, as you may guess. In the end I had to chase Meg to bed: she was sleeping on her feet. But Arthur and Bella were so wound up that I felt it would not have been kind . . . I'll come to the point. They would like to get married. That's no surprise, of course, but I mean they would like to get married before Arthur takes up his new duties."

"But that's New Year," Mam said, "and this is — "

"Quite! It must be a bit of a shock, Mrs Allen, but if you think of it, well, really, they are so well suited to each other and the little cottage is there waiting. If Arthur is working hard all day, it will be nice for him to find a hot meal waiting when he comes in."

This was a clever move, guaranteed to appeal to Mam's motherly heart. "Well . . . well . . . " Mam looked at Faither for help but Duncan pressed on. "You know how painfully shy Arthur is. The ceremony is a problem. What Meg and I thought, over breakfast this morning, was that they could be married very quietly in our manse the last Saturday of the year with just a few of the family present; then they could come here and have a little tea with you before going on to their cottage. At this time of year they would rather not be away . . . I'm sure someone would see to it that the cottage was well heated — "

"Tam would see to that," Jean broke in.

"No need, I'm sure," Dougie spoke up. "Mrs Nisbet-Brown has got a couple of her people cleaning it thoroughly at the moment, ready for us to start. I'd be surprised if she couldn't get someone to heat it."

"Well, Mrs Allen, it's a bit of a shock, I'm sure but, all things considered, don't you think it might work out very well for all concerned? Except us, of course," he added with a rueful laugh. "Bella has been a wonderful support to Meg and I think you will agree is turning out a fine, independent young woman. She'll make an excellent wife for Arthur."

Well, that was that. From then on it was all hands to the pump. The old cottage looked pretty as a picture when everything was finished and we had hung up the curtains. I quite envied Bella her little domain. Mrs Nisbet-Brown's coach took Dougie, Lilias and me to Glasgow and brought us back squashed in with Bella and Arthur. I mean *we* were squashed. Bella was still wearing her wedding dress for Mam to see. Some of the girls in the pancake club had made it under Meg's supervision and made a lovely job of it, too!

It was a quiet wedding; an odd wedding by most standards but the ripples of love it generated spread out surprisingly far. All the pancake club knew Bella and Arthur and through that connection a great many members of the congregation had come to know them, too. Meg was overwhelmed with the avalanche of presents which arrived at the manse for her little sister. And, of course, we at Kilbarchan being very much a part of the community, had the same delightful disorganization to deal with. Jean would say, "What a hubble!" and start to clear up; then even she would be wooed by the charms of someone's gift and, handling it, add, "I hope that lassie kens hoo lucky she is."

That was the last excitement we had till Lilias Day came round again. In 1876 it was bigger than ever. Of course Maisie and Angus came and stayed the night. Bella and Arthur joined us for a short time in the evening when the crowds had thinned out. She was very noticeably pregnant and we had to stand quite a lot of embarrassing remarks from Lilias about Bella eating too much now she lived with Arthur. I could remember Dougie's arguments with Meg and Jean about enlightening me on the subject but now that I was older, it was difficult to decide which of them had been right. Dougie was all for getting the true facts known but now I knew that there was a lot more to it than that. A girl is different. That's a daft thing to say but what I mean is her approach to her body is different and that's difficult for a man to understand.

Now that Dougie was earning a salary he was determined to give Mam and Faither a treat: they were to have a holiday in a cottage near Dunoon where Mam could sit and watch the boats go by. Before mentioning it at home he had spoken to the doctor, who assured him that the journey should do Mam no harm. Her strength had been building up steadily since spring and she was looking forward eagerly to Bella's baby due at the beginning of October.

Lilias was almost sick with excitement

at the thought of going on a big boat. I had my work cut out, first of all calming her enough to get dressed for the journey and then stopping her from slipping over the side of the boat. She just wouldn't sit still. Dougie wasn't much help. He was too busy pointing out the landmarks of the Firth to Maisie who was to spend the fortnight with us. The salt breeze tore at my hair as I ran after Lilias. Strands fell over my eyes and I knew my cheeks must be crimson with the exertion. It was quite a relief when three young men, who had been standing beside a pile of camping gear, joined in the chase. One who was obviously used to children hoisted her on to his shoulder. Lilias was very small for her age and he probably thought she was younger. "I've got a wee sister like this one," he announced. "You'll have to chain a barrel to her." Lilias was soon chatting to them like old friends. "And are you going to introduce me to your auntie?" one of them asked.

"Which auntie?" Lilias asked, puzzled. "Do you mean Jessie? She's my big sister."

"Big sister, is she?" he asked, grinning.

"How would you like a big brother?"

His chums chortled when Lilias piped up innocently, "I've got a big brother. Dougie. He's bigger than you."

"That'll sort you out, Bill," one of them said; and turning to me, "He's not worth blushing for, Miss: just can't help himself."

I did my best to steer Lilias away towards Mam and Faither but she was intrigued by the three lads and wanted to know all about the tent poles and the little house they would build in a field. "Can I come to see it?" she asked.

"Sure! Get your big sister to bring you. We'll give you some ginger beer," Bill said.

"Do you make scones?"

"Not when I'm away from home," he said solemnly.

One of his friends muttered, "O Goad," and exploded in laughter. Lilias looked from one to the other. "Jessie will make scones," she said, "and we'll bring them."

Luckily I caught sight of Dougie and Maisie just then and was able to steer her away.

Maisie laughed merrily when Lilias recounted her version of the incident. Dougie caught the blush I was trying to hide and I saw the quick frown which seemed to come readily to his face these days.

"And Jessie's going to make scones and we'll take them to their wee house in the field," Lilias continued.

"Who's idea was that?" asked Dougie.

"Bill's," she said. "He doesn't make scones when he's away from home."

Maisie looked at me and burst out laughing again. I joined in gratefully, trying to chase the frown from Dougie's face.

"It was only a piece of devilment, Dougie," I said. "They're decent lads, I'm sure."

"Aye," said Dougie flatly.

It was the first time Mam and Faither had ever had a proper holiday. We were so lucky with the weather, too. There was a seat by the front wall of the cottage that had an arch of roses right over it and they could sit there for hours just watching the boats and the changing patterns of the lights on the hills. Dougie, Maisie and

I would set out together with Lilias for the sand. We tried out our strategy the first morning and it worked. Just when Lilias had reached the most engrossing stage of decorating her castle with shells and wild flowers, Dougie would decide he wanted to stretch his legs. Maisie would wander off with him. I would murmur, "See you later," pretending to be absorbed in the task on hand. Of course when the complicated castle was finished Lilias was always desperate to show it to Dougie and Maisie but by then it would be time for a paddle which she adored, and after that time for lemonade. So the young lovers got many opportunities for being alone.

Towards the end of the first week we woke to a terrible thunderstorm. It was fascinating to watch but the din was terrific as the thunder rolled round the Cowal hills. Lilias clung to me in terror but, "Look! isn't it beautiful?" I would say as a fork of blue lightning lit up the sea and the hills for miles around. It took a little while for me to realize that Maisie was as afraid as Lilias. She stood, chalk-white, clutching her shawl and trembling beside her bed and winced as if struck every time there was a flash. Dougie's bedroom was next to ours. I urged Lilias to tap on his wall during a lull. "Just for fun," I whispered. Dougie was a light sleeper, I knew, and was probably at his window enjoying the spectacle. In no time he tapped on our door and I opened it. He looked odd with trousers and jacket pulled over his nightshirt. I stared at him over Lilias's head, moving my eyes in Maisie's direction. He patted Lilias, then quickly crossed to Maisie.

"You look cold," he said for Lilias's benefit. "Here, let me rub your hands." His arm went round her, holding her close while he rubbed the tensed fingers. I took Lilias to the window again. From the corner of my eye I saw Dougie turning to shield Maisie from the light. Soon they were in a close embrace. Mercifully, all Lilias's attention was given to watching for the next flash.

As the storm petered out I began to feel the weight on my arms. "Time for bed, love," I said. "it's all over. Just rain now . . . nothing but rain."

"Sure, Jessie?"

"Yes, sure."

She allowed herself to be tucked up quite happily. I was aware of Maisie and Dougie. Nothing was being said yet I could feel the agony of their separation. They moved slowly to the door. As Dougie stepped out I got a glimpse of his face — swollen somehow, distorted and almost ugly. Maisie slipped into bed without saying a word. I blew the lamp out and pulled the quilt over my head but not before I had heard her first stifled sob. Young and inexperienced I might be but somehow I could share their agony. I knew without doubt that Dougie had longed with all his heart to take Maisie back to his own bed . . . to crush her to him and . . . Then Jean's stern little face came before me and I heard her say. "The sooner that pair are married the better." "Amen," I said out loud to no-one in particular.

★ ★ ★

It was the first Sunday in September and we were sitting at our dinner. Mam was worried because Arthur had not appeared at church. Of course Bella had stayed away as soon as her condition became obvious.

"Don't worry Mam," Dougie was saying. He gave a warning glance in Lilias's direction. "You know Bella hasn't been sleeping well recently. Maybe she kept Arthur awake and then he slept in this morning. As soon as dinner is finished I'll take a walk over to the cottage."

It was then that Lilias squealed, "Arthur!" and ran to open the door. His white face was enough to tell us that things had started early. "Where's Nurse Duncan's cottage?" he asked without wasting a word on greetings. But Faither was already lifting his cap from the hook. "I'll see to the nurse," he said. "You get back to your wife, Arthur." Arthur turned immediately to the door but Mam detained him, "Take a cup o' tea, Arthur, while Jessie packs her things."

I was startled but pleased that my services were to be taken for granted. My own first reaction had been. "Jean's not here. Trust Bella to start on a Sunday!"

Dougie announced that he was coming too and ran upstairs after me. I turned, surprised, on the landing. "What could you do, Dougie?" I asked.

"Keep Arthur sane." He spoke rapidly. "You know Bella. She'll squeal like a stuck pig."

"That's unkind," I said, shivering at the thought.

"Wasn't meant to be. Basically she's excitable and in a crisis it'll come out."

"Pity Jean's not here," I murmured.

"Good thing she isn't. She faints at the sight of blood."

I was taken aback.

"Don't you remember the day Lilias was born?" he asked.

"I thought that was the heat," I said. Dougie shook his head as he turned towards his own room. "That's why she hasn't had a family herself."

Quickly I gathered a few things and stuck them in a bag. Word would soon go round the village once we were seen carrying those on the sabbath.

It was as well I was used to walking fast with Dougie, for Arthur had only one thought — to get back to Bella. Dougie kept his hand under my elbow and glanced at me from time to time. Arthur broke into a run as we neared the cottage. "Take your time," Dougie said quietly to me. "A first bairn is never *that* quick."

"What do you know about it?" I asked.

"Observation," he said dryly. "Will you be all right, Jessie?"

"To be honest, I'm a wee bit scared." I admitted.

"Aye," he said. "Just take it calmly. When Nurse Duncan comes she'll maybe want Doctor Campbell fetched. If so, I'll run. But I'll be straight back and you'll know I'm near."

"Aye, Dougie," I said gratefully.

Bella was tossing and turning on the bed. Arthur stood helplessly by. "I was hoping Jean would come," was her greeting. "I forgot it was Sunday. Oh . . . " she gave a painful groan.

"Well, I'm here," I said, trying to sound confident, "and Dougie is downstairs ready to fetch Doctor Campbell if Nurse Duncan wants him. Lilias would have come too, if I'd let her. She said she could wash your dishes — "

Bella managed a faint smile so I went on, "She's going to be real proud tomorrow, though she doesn't know it . . . an auntie again!"

"*Oh* . . . " said Bella. I saw the sweat on her brow and got busy pouring water into the basin and dabbing her with a soft cloth. I ordered Arthur off to toast some bed linen by the fire while I looked out a fresh night-gown for Bella. It took a long time for me to get her sponged down and dressed afresh. My ministrations were constantly interrupted by her restless groaning struggles. It was a great relief when Nurse Duncan bustled breathlessly in. "Now, now," her voice started outside the door. "We'll see how we're getting on . . . and you're in charge Jessie, isn't that grand! If you just do things as I tell you, we'll soon see your sister wi' a bonnie bairn." I made a mental note to tell Dougie of the lovely contradiction in her spiel. He would enjoy it.

Nancy Duncan was no time in tying on her starched apron and scrubbing her hands in the nice hot water Dougie had thoughtfully got going, remembering a previous occasion. I stood by the window admiring the unspoilt view over the gardens which were already responding to Arthur's care. Quiet and shy as Arthur was, he had showed no compunction in dismissing useless workers, reckoning they were a bad example to the apprentices. Now that so many of the handweavers were out of work he was having no difficulty in finding casual workers. Some of the keener ones were likely to become permanent once he got the glasshouses in order again.

Nurse Duncan finished her examination. "Yes, fine, fine, you've started early, aye, but you've got a wee bit to go, Bella, before the real pains start."

"Oh, no!" Bella groaned in despair. "I've been in pain all night."

"The first one's aye slower," Nurse Duncan assured her. "You're widening out, you see. Have you had anything to eat today?"

"I couldna manage my porridge," Bella said.

"No, no, but maybe a wee bit of toast and a nice big cup of hot tea with a spoonful of whisky in it . . . and we'll

377

try to get you settled down for a nice wee sleep," she suggested.

Well, that was my first experience of attending a birth. It was a long, long day. At times I felt I was dropping on my feet, yet I could never nod off in a chair the way Nurse Duncan did when Bella had one of her quiet spells. One of the times I slipped downstairs in the late evening to get myself something to eat. I found Duncan and Dougie both fast asleep by the fire. I kept wondering when Nurse Duncan would send for the doctor but she always said she would wait till nearer the time. Then just after two in the morning Bella, who had been dozing, startled us with a terrible cry. I nearly hit the roof. Nancy Duncan gave a wee laugh, smoothed her apron and said, "That sounds like business. Now, let's see . . . " After a quick inspection she turned to me. "Tell Arthur to fetch the doctor and Dougie to get the kettles boiled up again."

"Don't you mean the other way round?" I asked.

"No. Arthur's better out o' the way," I ran to do her bidding, nearly falling down the last few steps as another loud scream split the air. After that I had no time to feel tired. Nurse Duncan kept me busy with, "Jessie, could you . . . " while she tried to calm and control Bella. "Listen to me, lass, your bairn's nearly home. Take a deep breath . . . now, *push*."

Mam's first wee granddaughter was born just a few minutes before Arthur rushed in, white-faced, with the doctor. I found tears of relief running down my face as Nurse Duncan handed me the wee mite to clean up while she attended to Bella. When Doctor Campbell pronounced himself pleased with the two of them, I joined him by the fire where Dougie had tea ready. I think that was the most welcome cup of tea I'd ever had in my life. Dougie went off with the doctor and Arthur volunteered to sit with the now-sleeping Bella. Nurse Duncan and I were soon ensconced in the big chairs by the fire. In no time she was snoring gently. I felt a sudden reaction. I was only sixteen after all and had been at full stretch for twelve hours and Dougie wasn't there any more. The last thought brought the ready tears.

15

IT was a good thing we had the happy excitement of the new wee bairn, Lizbet, and her christening that autumn. We needed it and the memories of that holiday which had been such a wonderful gift to Mam and Faither. As the autumn wore on things got worse in the weaving trade. The handweavers in particular were having a pretty desperate time of it and many in our parish were destitute.

We were lucky in that Faither still had plenty of the routine stuff to do. The fact that he had never let the agent down through labour disputes and the like stood to his credit now. The demand for special shawls was dwindling. While Faither was setting up the only order we had, Jean spent her time at Bella's, cleaning like a mad thing, of course, but giving Bella a fine chance to put her feet up and play with wee Lizbet. She was back in the shed, though, working on the shawl and I was at the flannel shirting when Mrs Nisbet-Brown called one day.

"Is Mrs Newton not with you?" I asked, surprised.

"No, my dear," she said, "Mrs Newton is tied to her writing desk these days. We have decided to go off for a long holiday in the spring and she is writing to lots of old friends we wish to visit. She complains that I interrupt her and was happy to see me depart. Now I am interrupting you busy people."

"You're always welcome, you know that," Mam said with her warm smile.

Now that I was growing up I had begun to appreciate Mam more and more. A simple weaver's wife she might be but she had her values straight. Mrs Nisbet-Brown's life with her big house and all her servants was far removed from our livingroom, cluttered as it had to be for the pirn winding and with hanks of yarn hanging from the beams. I don't think any of the other cottages had visits from the gentry; but there was Mam, just being herself, kind and friendly, ready to stop work and offer a cup of tea. There was one concession, I noticed. Our best china had always been kept in the cupboard in the parlour but after Mrs Nisbet-Brown became a regular visitor, some of it was installed in the corner cupboard in the living-room. The special Kilbarchan betrothal jugs which they replaced ended up on the high shelf beside the jelly pans.

"We shall be spending quite some time in France, Mrs Allen," she was saying, "and I don't have to tell you that I shall make every effort to find out anything I can about Elsie."

"Aye . . . aye . . . " Mam could not say any more. I noticed that her hand shook and I hurried to take over the teapot. I was so busy worrying about Mam and trying not to show it that I missed a lot of what Mrs Nisbet-Brown was saying. It seemed to me that as time went on and the rest of us adapted to Elsie's absence, Mam got more and more upset about it though she kept her thoughts to herself. Maybe she talked to Faither . . . With an effort I tried to concentrate on Mrs Nisbet-Brown.

"It seemed to me that if the Queen

could see fit to set such an example and wear her Paisley shawls that Alice and I could do the same — be ambassadors as it were. *Pour encourager les autres*, as your brother would say," she added, turning to me. "So we thought that if you could manage to make two of your lovely shawls for us by Easter . . . I mean just before that, really, because we hope to spend Easter in Paris . . . do you think Mr Allen would find that possible?"

"I'm sure he will," I said eagerly. "There's one loom free just now and Dougie would help at the weekends."

"Perhaps your brother and you could bring some designs over on Sunday," she said, "and we can show you our plans for our journey."

I assured her that Dougie would like that. "He would like to travel some day when he can afford it," I added impulsively.

"I'm certain that a clever young man like your brother will make his way in the world," she said as she rose to go.

Back at my loom I thought about her words. Dougie was clever, hard-working and ambitious. Of course he would make his way in the world but Dougie's chief ambition these days was to marry Maisie. I had seen the burning desire on his face that night of the thunderstorm; noticed the quick frown and the sharp words that Maisie sometimes encountered. That had never happened in the early days of their courtship. At first I had thought he was losing his notion for her but then I would see the heightened flush as he made to escort her to the station. I could feel his desperation to have Maisie all to himself, away from other eyes.

And then he had suddenly unburdened himself to me late one Saturday night. We seemed to have had visitors straggling in all that day and when the last of them departed, Faither ordered Mam to bed. Dougie urged him to join her, declaring that he and I would see to everything. It had taken some time to set everything to rights. I had concentrated on the cooking for the Sabbath while Dougie washed dishes, saw to the range and generally cleared up.

"I think we deserve an extra cup of tea, don't you?" he suggested when we called a halt.

"Mmmmmm . . . I'm hungry too with all that work . . . and the smell of soup," I said.

"Look! You infuse the tea and I'll make us some toast," he offered.

It was heaven sitting there in front of the range with a big cup of tea and Dougie, bent forward with the old toasting fork, beside me. It was not tea as laid out for Mrs Nisbet-Brown by any means. Dougie had fetched a tray with the loaf, bread knife, a huge lump of butter and a pot of strawberry jam. He stuck these on the end of the table and shuttled between the fire and his supplies, asking me, "What would Madam like this time?" I forgot all my aches and pains and though I was sleepy had no wish to go to bed.

"Isn't it quiet without Lilias?" I said.

"And the others . . . " Dougie paused, staring into the fire. "Married, one by one . . . "

"What about you, Dougie?" I prompted. "Aren't you thinking about it?"

"*Thinking* about it! Oh, Jessie, Jessie, I'm desperate. You've no idea."

He was wrong there but I didn't say

so, just asked him, "Well, what's keeping you? Is Maisie not keen?"

He snorted at that. "Maisie is as desperate as I am, Jess — for your ears only, of course. But you can see how trade is dwindling. There's no saying how long Faither will be able to earn a living. He's better off than most, but it can't last. The writing is on the wall. I've seen this coming for a long time; tried to get Faither to diversify but he wouldn't listen. I was just a young hothead . . . "

"But Dougie — I mean — " I was stammering. "You can't stay a bachelor for ever."

"That's what Maisie says." He spoke bitterly. "She doesn't seem to understand the sacrifices Mam and Faither made to give me my education. She says all good parents do that and we'll probably — " He stopped in embarrassment. I knew what Maisie had said: that they would do the same for their children.

"But Mam and Faither would understand. They like Maisie. They'll expect you to get married soon," I urged.

"Oh, aye," Dougie spat at me, "and

could you imagine them accepting money from me once I'm in my own house?"

I knew that they wouldn't; but that wasn't the point. Somehow I couldn't find the words to argue with him. It seemed to me that Dougie's idea of what was right took him too far at times.

"Faither has saved up all these years when we were doing well," I said. "The house is ours, and the looms, too."

"Our expensive Jacquard looms are going to be worthless before very long," he said. "Already the draw looms are fetching next to nothing. Oh, aye, there'll be the odd wifie here and there who'll want a lovely shawl like her mother's but that will not keep Mam and Faither in their old age or bring up Lilias. And what about you, Jess — eh? I suppose you'll be able to give music lessons. Plenty of lads will be after you."

"I'm not interested," I interrupted.

"No?" he said. "No, not yet but you *will* be and, by God, he'd better be a good one. He'll have me to deal with."

I was shocked. Dougie never, never swore. But he didn't apologize or look embarrassed; he just started to damp down the fire for the night. We had not mentioned the matter again.

Of course I told Dougie about Mrs Nisbet-Brown's invitation as soon as he got home. "Does Faither think you can do it?"

"Well, he didn't seem so sure," I said, "and he asked Jean but she said work was scarce and we couldn't afford to lose orders."

"Quite right! As soon as the table is cleared we'll get out the designs," Dougie said. "You say there's only one loom available at the moment. What I suggest is that you alter one of the existing patterns a little and put it forward as your choice to Mrs Newton. I've a notion to do something quite different for Mrs Nisbet-Brown. Her skin is becoming quite papery. I think something in soft colours . . . gold going into green and then soft blue and mauve . . . I'd like to think about it. If I could get something down on paper before we see her on Sunday then she might trust me the rest of the way."

And, of course, she did. Alice Newton had been delighted with all the designs but when I showed her my choice for her, she was especially pleased to think that no-one else would have one exactly the same. On the Monday after our visit Faither started to set up the loom ready for me to start the first shawl. Dougie not only worked far into the night to complete his new design but insisted on going out to work at the draw loom some evenings by candlelight so that Faither could concentrate on the setting up. No wonder Maisie was in despair!

Mrs Nisbet-Brown got her shawls but it was a close thing and we were all pretty tired. Faither said that he was closing the weaving shed for three days and, as for Dougie, there was to be no more working in the shed at all. He had a responsible job and needed what free time he had to court his lass.

"Hear, hear!" I said loudly. Dougie for once was stuck for an answer. He flushed. I couldn't be sure what he was thinking but he laughed anyway. I spent my three days with Meg — not really a rest you might say, but a lovely change.

While we had been clacking away at the shawls we had perforce to ignore all the excitement that started up in the village that March. After a false start the year before and a lot of wrangling a new site had been chosen for a school and at last it was well under way. Lilias heard all the rumours and gossip from her schoolmates and invariably came straight to the weaving shed to pass on her news to us.

"Not before time," was Dougie's opinion. He had been exasperated by the short-sightedness of those who grudged the money for this long overdue development. Doctor Graham, of course, was very involved with education and he and Dougie found common ground in their discussions of the subject.

The first morning back in the shed after our holiday seemed dreadfully dull to me. The impetus to work had gone with the successful completion of the shawls. Faither was setting up Jean's loom again for a special order that had come in. She worked away steadily on some muslin in her usual fashion. Weaving and breathing were nearly the same word to Jean. I was back on the flannel shirting, though without any sense of urgency. Dougie had managed to build up quite a stock of it during the time we were slogging away at the shawls. He knew as we all did that Faither would be shattered if he could not fulfil any order.

Our shed was right at the corner and folk passed the window beside me all day long. Many a time Elsie, whose loom it was, had been reprimanded by Jean for noticing folk. "Keep your mind on your work," she would say. "Folks don't expect you to be smilin' at them when you're weaving." I had always found it easy to ignore the passers-by. Though I could talk to Dougie, I had never dared take my eyes off my loom, knowing how easily disaster could strike and long hours of work be ruined.

But that morning I was restless; and when a shadow which had fallen across my work did not move away I paused at the end of the row and looked out. It was Sandy — though I didn't know his name then, of course. I just saw a young man, tall but not so tall as Dougie. His light brown hair curling round his cap had golden glints where the sun caught it and when I turned a blush ran over his fair skin. He gave me a nice shy smile, tipped his cap quickly and was off. I pretended I was feeling cramped, stood up and stretched my arms, moving nearer to the window. He was well down the street, taking long easy strides like someone used to hill walking. Who was he, I wondered? I knew most folk in Kilbarchan though it was more of a town than a village, really. He looked older than Dougie — maybe twenty-two or twenty-three, so if he came from Kilbarchan I would surely have seen him. A farmer? That easy walk . . . he certainly didn't have the look of a weaver. Neither did Dougie, of course, and he had done plenty of it. Where could he have come from? The new school, of course. That *must* be the answer. Lilias had told us about all the horses and carts that kept cluttering up New Street.

Next day was Saturday. Jean didn't come on a Saturday. I would wait till morning then ask Faither if he really needed me or could I take Lilias out. Having formed this strategy I set to work with a will to turn out a good supply of shirting.

Faither was quite happy to let us go and of course Lilias was delighted to drag me along to see the new school which rose higher and higher every day, she assured me. "It would be queer if it got lower and lower now, wouldn't it?" I asked. Lilias responded with her lovely infectious laugh. I clutched her hand and we started running, just for fun. The morning was fresh and sparkling. Earlier we had wrapped our shawls round us as we walked Dougie to the look-out stone. He was going to the library in Paisley, then spending the rest of the day with Maisie. I had asked to be excused my music lesson, pointing out that I had had little time with Lilias all these weeks when we were struggling with the shawls. I think Dougie was none too sorry to have Maisie all to himself. And as for me . . . well, it's difficult to describe how I felt even though the day is still vividly with me — the fresh sharp, spring scents, the bright daffodils and primroses in the cottage gardens, the general business as we got near the site, the incessant ringing of hammer and chisel a background to the chatter of those who had come, like Lilias and me, out of curiosity.

I saw him almost immediately and felt a fierce blush flood my entire body. Till then I had not admitted to myself why I wanted Saturday morning off; why I was so keen to let my wee sister show me the new school. There had been very reasonable excuses which I had used to other people and to myself as well, I now realized. This departure from my usual behaviour threw me into a tizzy. Who was I? What was I? What was I becoming? Certainly not the little Jessie Allen who gave a straight answer to everything without hesitation. I trembled all over as wave after wave of emotion swept over me. He had his back to me most of the time as he helped a man and boy unload lengths of piping from a cart. He was calling instructions as they moved away; a clear voice; a kind voice; a calm voice. Voices were important; if you married someone, you had to listen to his voice for the rest of your days.

The thought behind that thought made me blush even more fiercely. I was 'away with the fairies'. That was what Dougie had said about Elsie. Elsie! Look what had happened to Elsie with her obsessive love. It was frightening how it had sent waves of trouble out in such a wide circle: Mam's life marred by sadness for ever; Mrs Nisbet-Brown aged and unsure of herself, desperately keen to make amends for what she considered her share of the catastrophe; Jean embittered and tortured by a caring kind of love that was different from other folks' but real nonetheless. Dougie seemed to have been able to put it behind him. He could detach himself quite deliberately from some things. He said the people round about would forget about Elsie as soon as the next scandal cropped up.

To a certain extent he was right. Most of the girls who had made my last day at school a never-to-be-forgotten disaster had tried to get on a friendly footing with me soon after. I had numbly rejected their efforts though Meg had tried to show me the right way to go about things. Of course, my pain had eased. When I was being honest with myself I knew that hurt pride had a great deal to do with it. I had thought myself one of the most popular girls in the school and it seemed to me that some were only too eager to grind me down when misfortune struck the family. Then as I became more sure of myself as a person, a valuable member of the Allen household, substitute mother to Lilias and, later on competent weaver and sought after by the young lads of the village, I had been able to take a more balanced view of things. Though Dougie with his high standards regretted my missed opportunities, I reckoned myself luckier than most girls.

Above the noise of the chisels I heard a call. "Je . . . ssie". Three of the girls I had just been thinking about were waving me over. Lilias held my hand as we worked our way over the rutted ground, skirting heaps of builders' materials. They were clustered round a man who was showing them a rough sketch of the new school. He obligingly lowered it to Lilias's level. "See the big windows, there and there," he said. "Lots of sunlight."

"They'll need big steps to clean them,"

Lilias pointed out.

"My! Isn't she a wee smarter?" The site foreman looked impressed. Because she was so tiny, folk didn't expect too much of Lilias. As the girls round about me eagerly joined in praising her, I was surer than ever that Dougie was wrong in thinking folk had forgotten about Elsie. I had been aware that Lilias was used as a means of getting into my good graces soon after the Elsie affair, and as long as they were doing that, they hadn't forgotten the cause of all the trouble.

Now some of the young weavers 'out for a pipe' wandered over. I had seen the cause of all my blushes pass twice while we stood talking but had carefully kept my head turned slightly away. But as time went on I felt an irresistible desire to see him again. Nobody in the group seemed to notice my inner turmoil. They were chatting happily. I risked a glance round. He was only a few yards from me on his way back to the cart and was looking my way. He stopped in his tracks for a moment, blushing. I smiled with a pleasure I could not hide. He raised his cap. Lilias piped up in her most grown-up voice, "It's a fine day, isn't it?" I told you she was a marvellous mimic. The girls hugged each other for support while the foreman called out, "Here, Sandy, come and meet a wee smarter. She's pointed out a drawback in our fine new school."

"And what's that, my wee lass?" the newcomer asked, getting down to Lilias's level.

"They'll need awful big steps to wash the windows."

"Aye, you're right. Maybe we'll have to leave one of these fine big ladders for the janitor. Would that do?"

Lilias considered. "Aye, it might," she said. "Your hair's got different colours in it. Don't put your cap on again, Sandy."

"Lilias!" I said shocked. "You mustn't call Mr . . . er . . . Mr"

"Forbes," he said, rising and offering his hand. I was dreadfully embarrassed. Would he think I had been fishing for an introduction? Could he be a married man? The group around us had gone quiet. It was Lilias, bless her, who broke the silence. "I'm Lilias Allen. You just call me Lilias and you can call my big sister, Jessie."

The weavers made a few interjections at that and I was glad of the excuse to laugh with the rest.

The foreman turned to the newcomer. "I suppose a lucky young bachelor like you will be going to this 'Daunerin' Club' thing on the May holiday?"

"Daunerin' Club?" he said. "I've read about it in the Gazette." He turned to me questioningly. I was in a bit of a fix. Ever since I had been old enough to go on the annual wander they spoke of, there had been the business of Elsie to put me off and Dougie had always been too busy, finishing exams or working his keep in the shed.

"Can I come with you, Mr Forbes?" Lilias asked.

"No, no, it's too far for your wee legs, pet," I said hastily. If I could manage to find an excuse to go that year — if Sandy was going, that was . . . Dreams were forming in my head, lovely dreams scented with hawthorn, the hot sun scorching my skin through the thin muslin of my new dress and

Sandy smiling at me with that lovely wide gentle smile of his while his eyes . . . What colour were his eyes? I looked. Immediately the colour rose again in his face. Of course I flushed up too and started to chatter in desperation to the girls. "Dougie's always too busy but if you were going, Nancy . . . maybe I could . . ."

"We're all going, Jessie." Nancy was not shy. "You must come, Sandy," she insisted. "It's always a rare laugh. Somebody always gets stuck in the brambles, or loses a shoe . . ."

"Or gets captured by Red Indians," one of the weavers added.

"I couldn't miss that," Sandy assured him.

It took me all my time not to skip on my way home. He was coming! The 'dauner' lasted for hours. That was another reason why Dougie never went on it. "I like to stretch my legs," he had said to me, "and I like to explore on my own." Well, I agreed with him on the first one but, for the second . . . There was a lot to be said for meeting folk even if it meant strolling instead of striding. And I wanted to meet Sandy Forbes in a way I had never wanted to meet anyone before. The strength of that longing frightened me. Lots of young men had made it plain either by their shy blushes or their more bold approaches that they found me attractive. I was vain enough to be pleased but usually there was a kind of pity mixed up in my pleasure. None of them was ever a patch on my big brother. Why then did I feel this way about Sandy? He wasn't so tall or so handsome as Dougie. Yet there was something so clean about him in spite of the dust of the building site; something so honourable, so dependable; a quiet strength; a sense of humour. Maybe it was those longings that Meg spoke about that made me see him the way I did. Maybe there was nothing out of the ordinary about him, and it was just me.

But I *did* have those feelings, those longings! When I escaped to my room 'to tidy my hair' I gazed long and hard in the mirror. My eyes were bright and bluer than I had ever seen them. My hair had fluffed up in a sort of untidy halo round my head. My lips were parted in eager joy. I cupped my hands over my tight hard breasts then slowly explored the throbbing flesh of my stomach, then down . . . Was this pain in my loins something God gave you? I had only just met Sandy. But Meg had said God gave you those feelings for the man you married. Or was that quite what she had said? It was difficult to remember with my throbbing body and trembling hands. Was this how Elsie had felt about Michel? Her desire had brought shame and disgrace to the whole family. I would never do that, of course. Dougie felt this way about Maisie. I knew that now for certain. But they had known each other a long time. I had just newly met Sandy.

Quickly I sponged my face, then gave my hair a ruthless brushing. If Dougie could make himself suffer such a terrible deprivation for the sake of doing the right thing by Mam and Faither, surely I could, too. I would go to the Daunerin' Club outing but I would think hard about Mam and Faither and be a credit to them. Perhaps when I got to know Sandy Forbes better I would find he was quite ordinary. Certainly he wouldn't have been to university like Dougie. That thought which was meant to strengthen my resolve only served to depress me.

"What's this?" Faither asked, laughing, when I came downstairs. "The wee one says you might get captured by Red Indians but it's all good fun."

"Oh, one of the weavers was teasing us. It's the Daunerin' Club's outing he was talking about. I think I'll go this year. Nancy Stevenson and Mary Maxwell are coming to meet me. They said everyone is going."

"Aye! It's nice for you to be out with the other young ones." Mam looked approving. It had worried her, I knew, that I had ended school so sadly. And so I was free to think about my outfit. I would have to wear sensible boots, of course, but my dress could be . . . And I drifted off into dreams. It was lucky for me — though I didn't see it that way at the time — that Jean, far from sharing my enthusiasm, saw fit to throw a warning. "Take care you're weel wrapped up. It's a gey lang day if it's raining and nae shelter."

It wouldn't rain: it couldn't rain, I told myself — not on my first outing with Sandy. But then I reflected how often Jean's unwelcome advice had proved wise. Supposing it should rain or even just be cool? I had my lovely new umbrella. That was a start. It matched my blue flannel dress. But a shawl and an umbrella could be awkward to manage on a country ramble. There was some saxe blue woollen cloth on the store shelves in the shed. I'd ask Faither!

Faither, bless him, said, "Aye"; and I cut out a cape that night. It would be handy come winter, I told myself, but if I had it finished in time and the day turned out damp and cold . . . then Jean would have nothing to grumble about and Sandy would see me in a nice new mantle. But in bed at night with those now familiar disturbing feelings washing over me I knew that I wanted Sandy to see me in my thin muslin with its low frilled neck, my arms bare and my tight little breasts accentuated by the narrow sash at my waist. Only under the sheets could I admit what would seem shameful in the morning light, that

I wanted Sandy Forbes to want me the way Dougie wanted Maisie.

It was as well that Mam had helped, stitching away while I was out in the shed, because the morning of the outing dawned cold and misty. Nancy and Mary were fulsome in their compliments on my new cape. "You're lucky with those blue eyes and the fair hair," Nancy said. "I always envied you at school." I was taken aback. That had been Dougie's theory, of course, when they had turned on me after Elsie's defection. Human nature took a bit of understanding. But here they were, prepared to be friendly, giving me the opportunity to meet Sandy and show off my new clothes. What did the weather matter!

16

AS the three of us made our way to the gathering place a fresh worry hit me. Sandy had to come from Paisley. What if he looked at the sky and thought it wasn't worth the bother of trailing to Kilbarchan to wander about a wet hillside? What if he thought the whole thing might be cancelled? But my eager eyes picked him out among the knot already gathered. Nancy said, "There's Sandy. He came after all . . . oh, and there's Jean Lyle and Jim Torrance . . . " Her voice went on while I studied Sandy, spruce and clean in his Lovat tweeds, a sturdy umbrella by his side. I found it difficult to look at anyone else yet it was impossible to hide my blushes as he came towards me, taking off his cap and smiling shyly. Nancy's voice rattled on, introducing Sandy in a haphazard manner. All the time he responded politely I knew that he was as aware of me as I was of him.

Shy he might be but Sandy was not long in managing to manoeuvre things so that we were walking and talking together. We had been still in an untidy group when we stopped to taste the waters of Meg's well, in spite of all the stishie there had been about it and the threats of closure because it wasn't considered pure. Sandy made it an excuse for getting on the talk with me. I told him all I knew about the legal proceedings, but fine I knew his mind wasn't on it any more than mine was. The air between us tingled. All the stories I had read about falling in love had not prepared me for this magic awareness that took over my entire being. When we stopped for a breather at Pennel Brae, Sandy stayed firmly by my side. I saw Nancy whispering with Jean Lyle. They looked at me and giggled. Nancy gave me a knowing little wave. I hesitated for a second then waved back. I was no longer Jessie, unattached little sister of Dougie. Dougie! What would Dougie think of Sandy, I wondered. We were trying to pick out Ben Lomond and could only guess at it by little streaks of silver snow on its sides. Everyone was saying what a pity it was the day was so dull but every time Sandy turned towards me and his face lit up, I knew it didn't matter a jot that we couldn't see the Ben or that the ridges of Mistylaw were like an inkline on the horizon. Our awareness of each other seemed to give a new life to every simple thing around us, the rich redness of the earth, the steady horses pulling and the patient men guiding the ploughs: the workers engaged in the back-breaking work of planting the potatoes. In our closeness to each other we were close to them too.

We made our way down to Bridge of Weir station, noticing that the stacks in the cotton mills were not smoking. Someone said, 'New lairds make new laws,' but I was feeling too content with Sandy to join in any controversy. While we were waiting on the platform we got on the talk with the Bridge of Weir minister and his wife. When he heard we were going to Duchall Old Place, he informed us that the name was Gaelic for 'two waters'. Sandy said nothing at the time but later when we were crossing the Gryffe he said, "I don't think yon minister was right about his Gaelic."

"Do you know Gaelic, then?" I asked.

"No, not really, but my father was a speaker."

"He's dead . . . ?" I said.

"Aye, an accident in the shipyards when I was ten. He was badly crippled, lingered on for a couple of years in pain most of the time." Sandy stopped speaking for a wee while. I kept quiet, then he went on, "He got gey heavy to handle and I was at school and Jenny, my sister, was at work . . . mother damaged her heart though we didn't know it at the time . . . Six months after Father we lost Mother . . . "

My hand had crept into his without my realizing it. He held on to me firmly, then suddenly gave a quick glance round and released me. People must be watching us, I knew, so I quickly got on to the safer ground of the Gaelic place name. "What did you think was wrong with the minister's definition?" I asked.

"Well . . . 'dubh' means dark or black. Two would be 'da'. Of course place names get so corrupted. My father used to snort about it sometimes."

"Did your mother understand it too?" I asked him.

"No. She had this funny attitude . . . I suppose most lowland folk do . . . that it was something to be ashamed of. It was only after Pa was injured and had a lot of time to talk to me that I realized how interesting it could be. It gave me a new outlook on things . . .

"My brother Dougie loves languages," I said. "And he's taught me quite a bit of French and Latin." I was launched on the subject of Dougie. I expect Sandy was fair scunnered at his name before I was finished but he let me go on and on.

Kilmacolm was changing rapidly. We were all surprised at the rows of handsome three-storey houses. The railway had made such a difference. Grand folk could travel to their businesses in Glasgow and Paisley, coming back to the bonnie surroundings of Kilmacolm at night. While we had a rest in the Buchanan Arms — that grand new hotel built in time for Meg's wedding — everyone was reminiscing about the old places that had been pulled down to make way for these handsome new dwellings. "Mind you, they'll take a lot of heating," I remarked to Sandy. "My sister that married the minister, she has a big manse and can only keep two or three rooms warm enough."

"Aye, there's that," said Sandy. "But these folk can afford servants to run round wi' the coal scuttles. Coal's cheap enough except for the poor devils that have to crawl on their bellies underground."

"I suppose we tend to forget that," I said.

"I remember them every time I stick a lump of coal on the fire," Sandy said. Then he gave me a quick smile and added, "Mind you, when I've connected up a gas pipe I don't stop to think it was coal that made the gas that is going through it."

Our walk took us by way of Green Farm which was set at the bottom of a sort of basin. We stopped on the stone bridge that crossed the Green Water. I could have stayed there for ever with Sandy close to me and the sound of the gurgling water in my ears. Then we started climbing the ravine. Sandy had an excuse to take my hand then and wasn't slow about it. The banks were wooded on both sides and covered in primroses. Their fresh yellow seemed to sing to me. When I slipped on a muddy patch Sandy's arms were round me immediately and stayed a second or two longer than was necessary. Our glances met as we separated again. I knew that his ready flush had nothing to do with exertion. If the others had not been there, would he have kept me in his arms . . . would he have kissed me? Not a word was spoken as we toiled upwards and I went on pursuing my daydream. There was a tremor in his grip now that had not been there before and a little pulse beating beside his eye. Had he felt me tremble in his arms? I remembered my resolution of the night before to be a credit to Mam and Faither. People were oohing and aahing now at the site of the Old Place, formerly fortress home of the Barons Lyle. One of the young weavers was teasing Jean Lyle about 'grannie's hoose' and did Granpa kick the walls down when he was drunk? It was all daft, bairn-like stuff but I was glad to laugh away the tension and embarrassment that had been building up between Sandy and me.

Duchall Old Place was quite impressive, perched on its lonely rock. The land round it had been washed away by the Green and Black Waters leaving it isolated. The leader of the walk pointed out its commanding strategic position and told us that at one time it had been stormed and taken by James IV who was to die at Flodden. I'm afraid I missed a lot of the information. It was impossible to be calm and receptive with Sandy within touching distance. And when one of the young lads muttered, "O Goad! Look at this fine herd," I found it difficult to keep my face straight as a party of lady botanists passed us with trowels and baskets, intent on the business on hand. Luckily for me that day, the daunerers were less seriously inclined!

It was lucky too that Lilias invariably wanted to go and look at the new school as soon as she had drunk her afternoon milk; lucky that Faither usually said,

"When Jessie's finished her cup of tea, she'll tidy you up and take you," even though his words brought home the fact that work was slack and Dougie's prophecies were being fulfilled.

The day after our outing Sandy was nowhere to be seen at the school. I chatted away to my fellow onlookers while my spirits sank lower and lower. Other children were beginning to leave the site and Lilias would soon want to move on with them. And anyway I should really be home helping Mam with the heavy pots for the evening meal. But then a cart rolled up to the site. Sandy tossed the reins to the young lad who was sitting beside him, jumped down throwing instructions over his shoulder and came straight towards me, still looking shy but not caring who saw him.

"We thought you weren't here today," Lilias informed him.

He crouched down, obviously used to children, and spoke quite seriously. "I was here when you were eating your porridge, Miss Lilias, but I had to go back to Paisley in the afternoon to get some stuff that wasn't ready for us in the morning."

"Did you get your dinner all right?" Lilias asked in her most grown-up voice.

Sandy straightened up, laughing. "I had something," he said and quickly changed the subject. "What did you do at school today?"

"I learned a new song. Would you like to hear it?" she asked.

"Mr Forbes is too busy . . . " I started. Sandy looked round to where his apprentice and an older man were struggling to unload the cart.

"Aye . . . well . . . I'd really like to, but could you come back tomorrow, Lilias, and let me hear it?"

"Aye, that I will," promised Lilias and he hurried off.

The rest of the day passed in a dream. I looked forward to being in bed where I could abandon all pretence and admit that seeing Sandy had been the highlight of my day. Lilias, now she had committed herself, would insist on another meeting on the morrow.

All the next day I hummed and sang to myself as I worked. "You're cheery,"

Jean remarked, "and your best blouse tae, I see."

"It was such a glorious morning," I said, "and anyway my new blouse will be ready for Sunday so I might as well wear this now." Inside I was saying, "I hope Sandy likes it." My one dread was that someone would gossip to Mam. Our pairing up at the Daunerin' Club outing had undoubtedly attracted attention and there was more than one regular onlooker at the school site.

The blouse was a success — or maybe it was nothing to do with the blouse — but Sandy came towards me with his face aglow. He listened attentively to Lilias's song and applauded heartily at the end. "You sing like a wee lintie," he said and, turning to me, "She's lovely; perfectly in pitch."

"Jessie's a lovely singer too," Lilias piped. "She's going to be in the Glen Concert this year."

"So am I," he said. We gazed at each other. He was as excited as I was. Another excuse for a meeting! I knew I should be letting him get back to his work but I was powerless to break the spell. Then one of the apprentices came towards Sandy. He stopped awkwardly a few yards from us, scuffing the rubble with his studded boots. Suddenly Sandy became aware of him. He bade Lilias 'Goodbye' and, giving me a conscious smile, turned away.

That night Lilias as usual was entertaining Dougie over our evening meal. "And I sang the new song that you liked to Sandy — I mean Mr Forbes."

"Who is Sandy, Mr Forbes?" Dougie inquired.

"He's Jessie's friend at the new school and I told him Jessie was singing in the Glen Concert and he's singing there too."

Dougie's eyes were on me and I could feel the colour rising and rising on my face. A frown appeared between his eyes. "That's a new name to me . . . " His eyebrows were raised the way he did when he was teaching me something.

I answered the unspoken question, "He's got the plumbing contract for the new school; he's trying to build up his own business and this is his first biggish contract; he attends the

Government School of Design in Paisley to learn all about building construction. He's got ambition . . . " I tailed away, realizing I had said too much.

"You seem to know a surprising amount about this man." His voice was accusing.

I tried to sound casual, "Oh, we got on the talk at the Daunerin' Club outing."

"Had you met before that?" Dougie was not giving in easily.

"I'd seen him about," I said. "Nancy knows him."

Dougie was not going to be put off like that either. He continued to stare. It was Mam who came to my rescue. "And did Mr Forbes like your song, Lilias?"

"Aye, Mam, he clapped his hands and said I sang like a wee lintie. He's braw, wi' different colours in his hair and he gets down on his hunkers, friendlylike, when he's speaking to me."

"What sort of age would he be?" Mam asked me gently.

"Twenty-five," I said, aware of Dougie's eyes and what they were making of this revelation of intimacy.

"He's a talkative fellow, then?" Faither asked.

"Oh, no, he's shy and quiet," I said

Dougie spoke in an even voice, "He's shy and quiet but he's told you his age, details of his business, his ambitions, his hobbies — all this in a few casual encounters on a building site and one mass walk with . . . what . . . thirty to forty people. I don't suppose you found out if he was married by any chance?"

"Oh, no, he isn't," I said quickly. "He lives with his sister."

Dougie went on staring. I felt myself trembling. For the first time in my life I found myself resenting his interest in my affairs.

"What's wrong?" I asked. Dougie just went on staring.

"Is he an orphan, then?" Mam asked. I nodded my head.

"A twenty-five-year-old orphan," Dougie said. I could stand it no longer. I rose and started gathering up the dishes.

For the next few weeks I felt I was living on a seesaw. There was the delight of meetings with Sandy, and at the other end of the scale, a first-time-ever constraint between Dougie and myself. In between, there was the more normal pleasure of taking Lilias to Bella's on a Sunday afternoon. There never was a prouder father than Arthur. In his own home his shyness disappeared. Bella, with all the experience of Meg's babies behind her, handled her first-born with confident pleasure. Sensing the happy atmosphere of their home made me begin to doubt some of the standards I had acquired from Dougie. Bella had been regarded by us as excitable and silly. She had had little interest in learning for learning's sake but under Elsie's direction she had become an excellent sempstress: so much so that Lizbet was likely to follow Lilias's footsteps in being the best-dressed bairn in Kilbarchan. Under Meg and Duncan's guidance she had learned the essence of homemaking. Arthur could be sure of having a happy and cared-for home. There was not much wrong with Bella!

I looked forward to the rehearsal for the concert. A few snatched words on the building site were only tantalizing now. At the rehearsal we would surely get the chance of more! Of course Dougie would be there. But with Maisie to distract him . . . surely. As I sat at my loom the possibilities floated through my mind. Sandy and Dougie were bound to meet some time. It mattered so much that they should like each other. Sandy had seemed interested when I talked about Dougie, so why should Dougie display this antagonism . . . that was the only word for it! All my dreams for the future now included Sandy. Did he go home at night and dream the same? Was the difference in our ages too much? I would be seventeen before Lilias Day. If only I could invite him to join us! Angus would be missing for the first time. He had left university a year before Dougie and started teaching. It didn't take long for him to find that he was not cut out for the job. Then he had gone to a shipping company in Glasgow. Fortunately this was much more to his taste and after a few promotions he had been moved to London and was hoping to go next to their agency in the West Indies. Lilias still talked about him and asked Dougie to show her the place on the map where Angus lived, but I could visualize Sandy filling his place in her life.

The morning of the rehearsal dawned grey and ominous. Dougie was depressing. "It's not the rehearsal I'm worrying about," he said. "That can take place indoors. But they've sold twelve thousand tickets — think of it! I suppose it could be postponed. It'll be disappointing for a lot of folk." I heartily agreed. There would be no-one more disappointed than myself. The Glen Concert had figured vividly in my new dreams — the lovely setting in Paisley Glen with its two lochs and sparkling linn, cupped in the Gleniffer Braes. Thousands of happy folk sitting on the grass or perched on tree stumps listening to the familiar sweet songs of the Paisley poet, Tannahill, and the famous Robert Burns. The braes round about would be gold with the whins. The hawthorn would still be blooming at that height. And Sandy would be there in that happy informal setting! Surely Dougie's disapproval would break down when he actually met him. I resolved to pray every spare minute of that day.

Dougie came home at tea-time and reported that the rehearsal was to take place in the John Neilson Institution. "I'll be able to show you my classroom," he said to me. "Maisie's mother wants us to come across to their house for supper afterwards so we'll probably be late. I'll tell Mam."

As I climbed the West Brae that night in pouring rain my heart was thumping. Dougie would of course gravitate towards Maisie but, remembering his inquisition that night when Lilias had given away my secret, I dreaded the almost inevitable meeting between Sandy and himself. We busied ourselves hanging up oilskins and shaking out umbrellas before Dougie started searching for Maisie. She had been watching for us, so it didn't take long. I had seen no sign of Sandy. Could he be missing the rehearsal? Of course, with nearly two hundred and fifty singers milling about it was difficult. And though Dougie was busy talking to Maisie I knew that it was unlikely he had forgotten Sandy's presence in the choir and would be watching my behaviour. Carefully I kept my eyes on Maisie's face. We had drawn into a corner by a classroom entrance and my back was turned to the crowd so Sandy was by my side before I noticed. Maisie looked a wee bit surprised. I didn't dare look at Dougie. Sandy, flushed and clean-looking, had a sort of shy composure about him. "I knew you by your hair, Jessie," he said "Are you going to introduce me?"

My thoughts were racing as I stumbled over the names. Not only had the initiative been taken out of my hands but out of Dougie's too. It was Maisie that Sandy was addressing himself to, saying that his choirmaster knew her well as a fellow teacher. Dougie, the wind taken out of his sails, stood silently by till we were summoned to form up for rehearsal.

The noise which floated up to the cupola was loud and joyful. I think the music was a release from the depressing grey of the day. During an interval the organizer said there would be a committee meeting on the Saturday morning to decide if postponement would be necessary. Posters would be put up at the railway station. He also gave a much more welcome announcement to the effect that some members had suggested a summer outing to the Land o' Burns country. The poor man couldn't get finishing for the cheers that went up. We were still laughing about it later when we went to get our outer clothes. "I've invited Sandy and Mr Ballantyne to come for supper," Maisie said. My mouth dropped open. "That's his choirmaster," she added, misinterpreting my stupor. Or maybe she was just making things easy for me. Dougie looked anything but pleased.

Mrs Wilson was delighted to lay two extra places at the supper table, saying how quiet the house was without Angus. Mr Ballantyne brought up the subject of the Government School of Design which Sandy attended two nights a week.

"You're the first young man I've met who goes there," said Maisie's father. "It's nice to think that Paisley is so go-ahead."

"Well, I'm hoping it will be more go-ahead yet," said Sandy. "I know that some of the staff would like to offer a wider range of technical subjects. Unfortunately that old building is in a bad state. They'll need to find the money for repairs before they can do anything else. I'm sure it will be a success once the men realize what an opportunity it gives. Some are feart that it's too much like university." I glanced at Dougie but he stayed quietly frowning. "Once they try it and find just how fascinating the subjects are, word will go round. The more pupils, the more fees; the more fees, the more courses; the more courses, the more opportunities."

"Your generation are certainly getting more o' these than we got," said Mr Wilson. "I just wish some of the opportunities werena' so far from home." This reference to Angus quietened us all down. Mr Ballantyne said he would have to be getting home. Maisie and Dougie saw him to the door, then disappeared into the parlour to say their 'goodnights'. I had expected Sandy to leave with Mr Ballantyne but he lingered on chatting by the fire with Mr Wilson while I helped clear the table. A little well of joy bubbled up inside of me. Sandy didn't want to leave me a minute before he had to: I was sure of it!

17

LILIAS continued her enthusiastic trips 'to see Sandy' and nobody did anything to stop us. One hot afternoon near the end of June, Faither decided to shut the shed. This wasn't unusual these days when work was so scarce. What was unusual was that Faither spruced himself up and announced that he would take a dauner up to the school with Lilias and me. My hand shook as I tied the bow in her hair. Faither would be bound to meet Sandy. What would he think of him? "O God," I prayed; "let Faither like my lovely Sandy."

There was no sign of Sandy's cart on the site and no sign of Sandy or any of his men. I pretended to be interested in a general way and pointed out various things to Faither while Lilias wondered loudly and persistently where Sandy was. I had worried about their meeting. Now I was sick with disappointment and Lilias's repeated references were beginning to be embarrassing. What would Faither think? Then she shouted, "There he is!" and dashed across the rubble-strewn site to meet Sandy who was emerging from what would be the main entrance. He signed to her to keep back while he buffed down his messy overalls. Then her hand was in his and she drew him eagerly towards us. A red mist swam in front of my eyes as I made the introductions. Faither *had* to like him, he just *had* to!

Though Sandy's fair skin flushed up as it did so easily, his voice was calm as he answered Faither's questions about the progress of the building. "We didn't see your cart," Lilias said in the first pause.

"No," Sandy said. "We got an emergency job in Paisley. I saw the rest of them started and then came on. There's plenty I can do on my own now."

"You won't have the cart to take you home for your tea," she said.

"I've brought pieces," he assured her. "I'll just work on and get a train home before bedtime."

"What about coming over and having a bite wi' us?" Faither asked. "We sit doon just afore six."

"I'm not dressed — " Sandy began.

"Nonsense!" Faither said. "You can clean up in the back kitchen. You'll be welcome."

For once I was eager to hurry Lilias home. Mam would need to be warned and I would need to help her. Because Dougie was away all day, our tea was really a dinner.

The smell of rhubarb pie met me as I hurried in the back door. Mam was clearing up her baking top and took my announcement of an extra mouth to feed very calmly.

"That's fine," she said. "The flesher had such a nice leg o' lamb the day. Maist folk canna afford it noo. I could see he was anxious to sell it so I thought it would be a nice treat for Dougie. Lilias can fetch in some turnips and carrots . . . aye, and mint. If you would just dae a baked custard, Jessie, we can re-heat the pie and he'll hae a nice pudding."

As the preparations proceeded, my suspicions were aroused. Mam was always tidy, of course, but she had on a specially nice blouse. She had washed her hair after her afternoon rest. It was soft and shiny. And, the night before, when Dougie and I had taken Lilias a walk over to Bella's, Mam had been busy putting a cherry cake in the oven before we got back. This invitation to Sandy was no spur-of-the-moment affair.

Dougie was none too pleased to see the surprise guest but greeted him politely enough. I hoped that Lilias's bright chatter and Mam's gentle inquiries about his family would cover up any deficiency. The smell of the food had made me ravenous but now that I was actually sitting opposite Sandy, my appetite deserted me. He ate steadily, I noticed, anything that was put in front of him. I blessed Lilias for her non-stop prattling. Dougie excused himself after the pudding, saying he was going up to the manse to discuss something with Doctor Graham. This wasn't all that unusual but in my sensitive state I took it as a rebuff to Sandy and was hurt.

It was while we were at the tea and cherry cake stage that Faither brought up the subject of Lilias Day.

"I've heard of it, of course," Sandy said. "A lot o' Paisley folk traipse in for the day. I've aye been working."

"You'll no' be working this year," Faither said.

"Angus used to come with Maisie," Lilias informed him, "and they stayed the night and came to church with us in the morning and the singing was grand. You'll be able to come and stay with us this year, Sandy."

I held my breath, looking down at my cup. Mam slipped in smoothly, "Aye, I think you should try, Sandy. There are two beds in Dougie's room. The young folk aye enjoy Lilias Day."

Sandy was hesitant. "If you're sure . . ." he began. I looked up at him and immediately he said, "I'd love to. It's very kind of you . . . but won't Dougie mind?"

"Oh, no," Lilias assured him. "Angus always slept there so it's just the same thing."

I knew that it was far from being the same thing but told myself defiantly that Dougie would just have to thole it.

The idea of being under the same roof as Sandy was enough to put everything else out of my mind for the next few days. Then the blow fell. Lilias Day was to be abandoned. There seemed to be no precise reason — just a general apathy which reflected the crumbling of the prosperous weaving trade. The holiday time had been changed: lots of excursions down the coast were being arranged for the Paisley holiday-makers and many people from Kilbarchan intended joining them. Also, a number of young girls from the village had taken advantage of the free passages to Queensland which were being offered to young domestic servants. Patty McPhee had been among the first to volunteer though she had announced loudly to all and sundry that she had no intention of remaining a servant. It seemed unbelievable to me that Lilias Day, which had gone from strength to strength each year of my childhood, could be cast aside so indifferently. Sandy, too, was disappointed.

"I don't suppose — " he began. "No! It's too soon . . . your folks wouldn't let you come with me on an excursion instead . . . ?"

Hope sprang up suddenly. It wouldn't be the accepted thing for me to go away with Sandy on my own but if I could persuade Dougie . . . No, Dougie was difficult these days.

"Tell you what, Sandy," I said. "I'll speak to Maisie on Saturday. If she could persuade Dougie to make up a foursome . . . " Sandy agreed eagerly.

Maisie, too, picked up the idea. "I'll say that my parents wouldn't be too keen to let me go all day alone with Dougie; neither they would, I think, knowing how much I love him . . . Oh, Jessie!" We hugged each other in understanding.

It all fell out as we hoped and a trip to Rothesay was booked. Sandy and Maisie were coming in early on Saturday morning so that we could all set off together. They were leaving their overnight bags because we expected to be late home. Sandy would be under my roof after all!

The train to Gourock was packed with happy trippers. It was a relief suddenly to get away from Kilbarchan with its empty weaving sheds and signs of poverty and despair that had never existed in my childhood. A fresh breeze met us as we walked along Gourock pier. Dougie's arm went round Maisie and immediately Sandy took me under his wing. It was to be that sort of day, our love acknowledged, unalloyed bliss — or so I thought.

It was a joy to find that Sandy had a lovely quiet sense of humour — the perfect foil for Dougie. As we sailed up towards the Kyles of Bute with the blue peaks of Arran always tantalizingly in the background, I thought I had never seen anything so beautiful: the deep blue waters of the firth, chopped with white horses; the paler blue of the sky, flocked with white clouds. And, of course, Sandy beside me to share in all that beauty.

Like most of the passengers, we started by walking along the seafront at Rothesay, first in one direction to the furthest limit and then in the other. "Let's climb and see the view," Dougie said. The wooded slopes on the edge of the town were certainly tempting. In no time we were off the roadway and walking in dappled sunshine through peaceful glades. The sound of the sea and the pierside traffic drifted up faintly. Everything smelled green and warm. Sandy was surprised that I knew the names of all the wild flowers. I suppose having been at a country school I had the advantage there. Somehow we got separated from Dougie and Maisie. I was not too sorry about that. Our footsteps would pause now and again under a tree and Sandy would take me in his arms.

It was just after one of these little halts that we came on a perfect cameo. Two beech trees framed a circle of vivid green grass, fringed with whin bushes. The centre of the picture was open to the blue sea far below. "Let's sit down a wee while," Sandy said.

"What about Dougie?" I began.

"They'll be doing the same if I'm not mistaken." He smiled knowingly as he spread his jacket for me. I felt a dreadful shyness sweep over me. Sitting down with Sandy in this secluded spot was almost like sharing a bed with him. The hot colour flushed my cheeks. "Oh, Jessie, Jessie," he murmured softly, "you're sae bonny. I've never seen a lass like you.

Never fear," he reassured me, "I'd never hurt a hair o' your head." His arms went round me and I raised my face happily for his kiss. We just couldn't keep apart. One kiss led to another ... then we gradually slid down till we were lying in each other's arms. I felt I could happily have stayed there for ever. It was Sandy who reluctantly suggested that we had better try to catch up with the others. "Not too quickly," I said. He laughed happily as we set off again, keeping the sea on our right. Of course, as I said, we *were* trying to catch up with Dougie and Maisie but I was just as keen to pause for a kiss as Sandy was.

Then Dougie's voice came through the trees, sharp and impatient. Sandy called back, "Coming," while I quickly tidied my hair. Dougie would be bound to guess we had been up to something. I found myself blushing guiltily. Then Dougie came striding towards us. One look at my face brought his brows together. He turned angrily to Sandy while Maisie stood biting her lip in the background. "What do you think you are playing at?" he asked furiously. "Mam and Faither think Jessie is in my care. You've a nerve slipping off like that!"

Sandy was white with anger but he spoke quietly. "I understood Jessie was in my care and I can assure you she is as safe with me as she would be with you." They stood glaring at each other. I shivered. At that moment I felt afraid of Sandy. Quiet anger was something beyond my experience.

Normally I slept in the same bed as Lilias but that night Maisie and I shared the bed that had once housed Meg and Elsie. Though the bairn was dead to the world we kept our voices low, for the things we were discussing were the sort you can only deal with in the dark when thoughts which are repressed during the day can be aired. Having been assured that Maisie thought Sandy was just lovely, a grand man and set on winning me, I gradually worked round to the subject of Dougie.

"He's jealous, of course," she said.

"What do you mean?" I asked.

"He's always been your big hero. Now he sees Sandy looming large in your life."

"But Dougie's got you," I protested.

"Aye, he's got me," she said, "but will he take me? There comes a time, Jessie, when you *should* be married. Your body — " She burst into sobs.

"I know, I know," I tried to comfort her but I don't expect she believed me. We kept quiet after that and eventually fell asleep. During the night I woke up. Maisie's arms were almost strangling me and she was moaning miserably in her sleep. Love could be cruel, I thought; or maybe it was the denial of it that was cruel.

We all went to church on the Sunday. It was heaven for me standing beside Sandy. I knew the stir his presence would be causing in the village. Nancy Stevenson gave me a warm smile and wiggled her eyebrows in the fashion of a fellow conspirator. I felt a rush of love for her. She had been instrumental in getting Sandy and me together. What did a wee thing that had happened when we were bairns at school matter? I was a woman now with the man I loved singing tenor beside me. Lilias was not the only 'wee lintie' in church that morning.

Jean and Tam walked up from Johnstone after church and joined us in our Sunday dinner. I wasn't sure if Sandy realized that this was a seal of approval. I busied myself with Jean, clearing up, while Dougie and Maisie went off for a walk on their own — a walk from which I was sure Maisie would return with her lip trembling. I was tempted to confide in Jean about Dougie's stubborness and what it was doing to Maisie and himself. She knew as well as I did that Mam and Faither would never stand in their way. But Dougie had always resented any instruction or criticism from Jean. If he sensed that any words from Mam and Faither were prompted by Jean's well-meant interference he would dig his heels in even harder. At the back of my mind was the idea that Dougie had some fixed target, a sum he proposed to repay to Mam and Faither. Once that amount was reached he would be immediately stirred into action over wedding plans. And, knowing Dougie, nothing would be allowed to stand in his way.

It was while I was carrying piles of dishes through to Jean, that I glanced out to the garden to see how Sandy was getting on. Tam was crouched over something in the path at the far end. Faither had stepped inside the weaving shed to light his pipe. I saw Sandy follow him. Jean started yelling at me to shake myself and I had to hurry. On my next journey through, I watched eagerly, but they were still in the shed. Was that a good sign? Or was Faither saying I was still too young to have a regular lad? But Bella hadn't been much older. Of course, hers was a different case. Jean had always worried about Bella that way, saying the sooner she was married, the better; and Elsie's affair had left a legacy of anxiety.

It was Faither who suggested that Lilias might like to take Sandy to see Rusty. The poor old mare was pensioned off now. Instead, Faither got a carter to call for him every week. I set off happily, knowing that Lilias would skip ahead in her eagerness on the way up the hill and would be intent on picking wild flowers for Mam on the way back. As soon as we were out of sight of the cottages, Sandy offered me his arm and clasped my hand firmly in his. "I spoke to your father just now," he said. "I've got permission to come courting. You'd like that, I think . . . ?" I could just say, "Aye, Sandy." My heart was too full.

Sure enough, having fed Rusty her carrots, Lilias started her usual ploy of picking flowers for Mam. It was just when we got to a big oak tree that Sandy stopped to fiddle with his bootlace. Glancing carefully, he waited till Lilias was engrossed in a clump of hedge roses, then he pulled me quickly round the other side of the tree. My heart was fluttering again as his arms came round me and his lips met mine, gently at first and then with assurance. The most wonderful feeling of peace came over me. Sandy loved me and everyone knew it. I would be safe for ever in these arms. It was a long time before we broke apart to stand smiling tremulously at each other. Then suddenly we were together again. This time I was crushed hungrily to him in an embrace that was painful but brought a response from me that I had dreaded in my moments of self revelation. My body was seeking his as eagerly as he sought me. It was Lilias's call that wrenched us apart. Sandy hastily grabbed some gowans growing beside us while I smoothed my dress and pinned up my hair. We stepped out to greet her as nonchalantly as we could, the bunch of gowans our alibi. Later, when the train which would take Sandy and Maisie to Paisley thundered in, Sandy was not slow to copy their example. This time his kiss was calm and sure. I don't think I said a word to Dougie on the way home. Now that my relationship with Sandy was acknowledged he was probably trying to come to terms with it. Or maybe he was just longing for Maisie.

The time flew after that. Sandy missed no opportunity to see me in spite of his hard work and long hours. Mam and Faither obviously liked him. Sandy took me home to meet Jenny and her husband, Jim. I saw her first anxious look at me smooth out as the visit proceeded. She treasured her brother the way I treasured Dougie! The small flat was overcrowded with two young children underfoot. I could see what a hard job she had to keep it clean and tidy. Sandy had been considering moving into digs on his own, but now he urged me to think about getting married soon. In vain I cited Dougie and his sacrifice. "Judging by the way your folks have welcomed me," he said, "I don't think they would stand in Dougie's way."

"Oh, no, they wouldn't," I said, "but Dougie wants to pay them back — "

"There are different ways of rewarding people," Sandy said. "Dougie has brought academic honour to the house; he's worked hard at the weavin'. I know all that but he's got Maisie to think about now. She's a bonnie, decent lass that many a man would be proud o'. He's kept her waiting far too long. 'Hope deferred maketh the heart sick', you know." Though I stuck up for Dougie as a matter of habit, Sandy's words were really confirming my own opinion. And Sandy could be persuasive — none better! His wooing was so persistent and our partings so reluctant that he seemed to be spending more time at our house than with Jenny. Of course, Mam had often said that about Dougie and the Wilsons.

Sandy's work in the school ended in September. I missed those daily meetings. It made the ones we *did* contrive more deeply felt, I think. We got engaged at Hogmanay and I proudly showed my ring to Nancy and the other first-foots. Sandy urged a spring wedding. Of course, I was as eager as he was but I felt it wasn't fair to Mam and Faither or to Dougie and Maisie. Sandy didn't waste time arguing. While I was washing dishes in the back kitchen on New Year's night, he put his case to Mam and Faither. Of course they thought I was too young; maybe next New Year would be soon enough . . . Sandy explained that Jenny's house was too small and he would have to move away. In no time he had them persuaded. Dougie accepted the inevitable with good grace, telling Sandy he was one lucky fellow.

It was as well that I was working on plain flannel shirting the next few days for as fast as the shuttle flew, so did my thoughts. Jean was busy on a special order. It was the most gorgeous design Dougie had ever done. He had brought it to me for my opinion. With its lovely creamy background, all the blues you could think of and a little lilac colour worked in, 'ethereal' was the word that came to my mind. It took me floating back to that wonderful day in Duncan's church with my first parasol from Dougie.

"It's a kirkin' shawl, then," I said.

"Aye. Do you think she'll like it?" he asked.

"She'll be the bonniest lass in the kirk," I said and Dougie was satisfied. Now that my own wedding was racing towards me at an alarming rate, I was in a quandary. What about *my* shawl? Jean was busy and even if Faither started to set up another shawl the very next morning I would never get it finished in time. There would be my wedding dress, curtains and things . . . and, of course, we hadn't even started to look for a house. Some folk said it was unlucky to make your own kirkin' shawl. Doctor Graham said that Christians shouldn't be superstitious, knowing that their lives were safe in God's hands. He was right, of course, but still . . .

Dougie said he would start another

design immediately. When I told Bella she said, "It'll be ready for the christening," and laughed uproariously at my blushes. Meg wrote to say that she would like to make my dress with the help of the pancake club. Could I start thinking about patterns and maybe come on Saturday afternoon? She could cut it out using an old sheet to get the fit exact. Meantime, maybe, I could start weaving some silk if that was what I would like. I relayed all this to Jean in the weaving shed. "Faither," she called, "we could gi'e Jessie six or seven yards o' that white muslin for her wedding dress, could we no'?"

"Muslin for a wedding dress? There's nae heat — "

Jean cut him short. "Meg's getting the pancake club onto the job. They'll cut it out o' muslin and fit it on Jessie before they put their scissors near the guid silk." Her tone said, "Men never think!" Faither agreed hurriedly that that would be fine.

"It's quite a waste of muslin," I said.

"Meg'll get them making things for the kirk bazaar out o' it, never fear. That's no' our bother." Jean could be a comfort. I knew that, like the other members of the family, she thought I was too young but Sandy met with her approval and I think too that she worried more than most about the decline in the weaving. With the rest of us settled, there would only be Lilias to provide for.

I found it very hard to show the right reaction when Dougie brought the design for my shawl. It was lovely, of course — all his designs were — but much more vivid than I would have chosen. Against the traditional creamy background there was a lot of bright red, soft green and the occasional sharp blue and yellow. It was beautiful and I told him so but the colours would really have been better for someone with darker colouring. Still, it had been done in love and I would remember that. Jean urged me to get on with weaving the white silk I had chosen. "There's no harm in bein' ahead o' things," she said. And Meg agreed with her, I found. One of the young girls was very good at quilting. Meg thought it would be a nice idea to have a quilted hem and perhaps some quilting on the full upper sleeve. "It would make it a wee bit different," she said.

"It sounds the sort of thing Elsie would have suggested — " I started.

Meg broke in, "That's funny, Jessie. That's exactly what I thought when the idea came to me." We were both silent for a wee while. Then Meg reassured me, "There are a lot of lovely things in our memories of Elsie, pet. Perhaps some day she'll be restored to us."

★ ★ ★

Every day was filled from then on. I hurried ahead with the silk while Faither was setting up the next shawl. Bella wanted me to make the bridesmaids' dresses at her house where she could help me. Mrs Nisbet-Brown had given Bella a sewing machine which she said was seldom used in the house. Yet when Bella in gratitude had offered to repair household linen, Mrs Nisbet-Brown had insisted on paying her for the work. The setting which had been so disastrous for Elsie seemed to be conferring nothing but benefit on Bella. I thought of it in bed that night. Only Jean seemed to be unchanged by the years. Quiet, shy, home-loving Meg had become the lady of the manse, a blessing to all who came under her influence. Elsie had disappeared in a cloud of defiance and shame. Fun-loving, eager, boyish Dougie had become intent and serious, wearing a permanent frown. Bella, whom we had written off as a scatterbrain, was happy as a queen in her little domain. Would I change? It was bound to be different living in a tenement flat in Paisley. No more stepping into the garden to pull a carrot for Rusty; or gathering at the trough on a summer evening, greeting everyone in the street as an acquaintance. You could live all your life in Paisley, they said, and not know the folk up the next close. But Sandy would be there. I hugged myself at the joyful thought. Nothing else mattered.

The early weeks of 1878 flew. I made the silk for my gown. Jean finished the special order she was working on, carefully trimmed all the loose threads from the back of it and performed the laborious knotting and fringing with her usual expertise. Then Faither did the stenting on the big frame and finally Mam did the steam pressing to give it a nice sheen.

We all stopped work to have a cup of tea and admire the exquisite piece of work. Then Mam said, "It's dry now, Jessie, slip it on and let's be seein' it the right way." I had been longing to do just that but, remembering Elsie and her proud parades, had kept my notion to myself. Now I draped it round me with a funny rush of shyness. Only married women wore kirkin' shawls! It felt warm and soft. I walked slowly round the living room, remembering Elsie's graceful movements and trying to match them. Faither blew his nose; Mam dabbed her eyes. I looked to Jean for a verdict. Her face was pinched, her nostrils distended and the pink area under her eyes showed me how she was struggling with her feelings. "Aye, aye . . . " was all she said. "They're all thinking of Elsie," I thought.

Suddenly Jean rose. "Well, Faither, we'd better get on wi' a big silk shawl for Bella if she's to look decent at the wedding." Bella's second baby was due just five weeks after my wedding. We hoped she would be able to come to church even if she had to miss the reception. Lizbet, a lively toddler now, was to be left at the big house where two of the young housemaids would look after her. Jean turned to me, "You'll have to show the shawl to Dougie and Lilias the nicht but then wrap it away carefully. Sandy is no' to see it."

"But it's not mine — " I stammered.

"Is it no'!" Jean laughed heartily. "Dougie saw the way the wind was blowing an' we baith thought it was a guid idea to get crackin'."

"But I thought that was mine I was — " I started.

"That's Maisie's. Which shows that our wee Dougie's no' going to keep the lassie waitin' much longer."

I laughed happily with her. Of course the colours I had thought too vivid for me were just right for Maisie with her chestnut hair and hazel eyes. And Dougie must surely be seeing an end to his self-denial if he had got to the length of having Maisie's shawl started. Next

451

thing was to pray for a nice day for the wedding as Lilias earnestly reminded me every night. I did tentatively suggest to her that it wouldn't matter too much as we would be indoors most of the time but she would have none of that. According to Lilias, every girl in the school was coming to see her walk round to the church in her finery.

18

MAISIE'S mother had kindly gone round all the house factors in Paisley and got the keys of several houses. Then she had done a preliminary survey for us to save our time and whittled the likely ones down to five. Not being used to tenement stairs I had rather dreaded tramping up and down on my own. What did you do if you met a man there? Did you say, 'Good morning', or would that seem forward? With Sandy by my side I would feel safe.

It was the third one we saw. Sandy immediately said, "This is it." Certainly it was the highest rent of all the ones on the list and a wee bit over the figure we had given Mrs Wilson but when we stood in the big sunny kitchen with its two bed recesses and a good-sized scullery off, Sandy said, "I don't think we'll do better for the money. Look, it's got a good range. Replacing that would be expensive. I hate to sound grudging, love, but I want to put every penny into the business just now. Let's have a look at the parlour and see if it's up to the same standard."

We stood and admired the view from the oriel windows. "Well, there you are," Sandy said, "the Gleniffer Braes and you can see that wee hump like a desert island from Kilbarchan, so you won't feel too far away. The kitchen faces east so you'll get the sun in the morning while you're working and then it'll stream in here when you're playing the piano."

I grabbed Sandy's arm. "Wasn't it nice of Lizzie to give us it?"

"Aye," he said. "Mind you, Dougie said he thought she would. It was never used before you started practising."

"But to insist like that . . . "

"Aye," Sandy said, "you'll get a lot of presents, they tell me, enough to furnish the whole house easily. These are lovely mahogany doors on the bed recess here. Let's have a look at the lobby presses."

One turned out to be a deep coal cupboard, then there was a walk-in cupboard for clothes and a shallow one with shelves all the way up. Sandy drew me into the clothes cupboard and pulled the door gently behind us. In the dark we sought each other eagerly. "Oh, Jessie," he said, "I wish it was Easter."

There was a key hanging behind the door. "This'll be for the W.C.," he said. I hesitated. This was one thing I dreaded — sharing a lavatory.

"Come on," he said, "it's a flush W.C., not a cludgie."

The tiny room in question was spotlessly clean, smelling faintly of bleach. Pipe clay whorls round the base spoke of energetic scrubbing. "It's nice and clean," I said.

Sandy spoke softly, "I think the neighbours are very particular. Both their doors are nicely varnished."

"And the brasses clean," I whispered.

We had just locked the lavatory door and were turning up the stairs to the house when a woman appeared from a lower landing. Her ample figure was extended by a number of bulky bags. Sandy quickly ran down towards her. "Let me."

"Oh, bless you ... bless you ... " she said. "Even though the dishes are empty . . . . I take stuff to the mission, you see, it's still a struggle at the last stair. Have you been looking at the house?" she asked in a friendly manner.

"Yes," I said shyly.

"You're not married yet?" She looked at the pair of us.

"Easter," I said.

"Oh, I see," Mrs McFarlane smiled. "Well, it's tiring work so when you've finished looking just come in and have a cup of tea."

"We've two more to look at," Sandy said.

"Aye, well, it's up to you but it'll no' take long . . . "

"A cup of tea would be nice," I said.

"Good!" she beamed.

We didn't bother to look at the other two houses. After a friendly chat with Mrs McFarlane who revealed that the occupant of the middle flat on the landing was a Miss Thomson, a maiden lady, very correct spoken, who read a lot and was pleasant but shy, we decided we had hit on a lucky choice.

From then on I didn't have a moment to spare. Maisie and Dougie both came and helped us at the house in the evening. Faither said I was to concentrate on the cloth I needed for myself. Jean took over the weaving of Maisie's shawl. I longed to tell Maisie about it — to give her some hope — but Dougie was so stubbornly loyal himself that I felt I couldn't betray him. While they were working hard alongside us there didn't seem to be the same strain anyway, but I longed to see Maisie in the same joyful state as I was, looking forward eagerly to her wedding. Yet there were times when I felt a moment of dread. For example, when we were deciding which of the bed recesses in the kitchen we were going to sleep in. One was nearer the scullery. I thought it would be best to site my dresser there so that I would not have to walk too far with dishes but Sandy wanted the other one for the dresser — so that we could be nearer the fire. "Just imagine, Jessie," he said, "on a cold night we clear up the scullery, then we back up the fire, then we take our things off and lie in our little nest the long, long night, just you and me and the firelight glinting on the ceiling." I was in his arms and he was nibbling my ear delightfully, but suddenly I felt cold. "We take our things off," he had said. Did he mean all of them? I didn't know what a man looked like without his clothes. Mam had always been so strict. And, of course, Faither and Dougie had never seen me in anything revealing. Would Sandy expect me to undress in front of him . . . and what would he look like? I shuddered suddenly. "Here, here, lass, I'd better get you home," Sandy said. "It's none too warm in here, but I'll see to all that once we're wed."

In bed that night I thought of his words, "I'll see to all that." Of course he could just be talking about the wonderful gas fittings he had installed. Nobody else I knew had gas jets in the oven of their range. But Sandy had got hold of some American piping, not long on the market, and I would be able to roast and bake on the hot summer days without lighting the fire. I was to have a gas ring in the scullery too. Yes, Sandy knew all about these things but had he meant more? Would the restrained passion I felt in his kisses, and which excited me so, prove to be something else? I whispered the word softly to myself, "Lust." Then I shook myself clear of it. Sandy was decent and loving. Look how patient and gentle he was with Lilias. I just wished I knew what being married would actually be like . . . I couldn't ask Meg to tell me any more about it . . . or Bella. Somehow I had the feeling that Bella would be happy to tell me but that it wouldn't help at all. And the moment of revelation was rushing relentlessly towards me.

★ ★ ★

It was Lilias who woke me importantly with a cup of tea. "It's your wedding day, Jessie, eight o'clock and we've a lot to do. Dougie was out for the milk and he met Rab and Rab says you're going to get a fine dry day, a wee bit of a breeze, mind." Having delivered her spiel she climbed up onto the bed beside me, nearly knocking over my cup. I had been sent to bed early the night before but sleep refused to come for many hours. I kept thinking of that bed in Paisley, decked with Bella's handiwork. The crochet flounced lace of

459

the valance was slotted with blue ribbons, "to match your eyes," she said, "though I don't suppose he'll be looking at your eyes." She had nudged me in a conspiratorial fashion and I had tried to smile back. My last night in my own bed at home; the last night my body would be my own! I had spread my hands and moved them caressingly. What would my wedding night bring? A few nights before while Sandy had been unpacking wedding presents at the flat, I had made up our bed. When the last frill had been tweaked into place I had stood back to admire it. Then the thought came to me. The sacrificial lamb. I would be sacrificed on that bed; I would bleed and I would never be pure again. Then Sandy had joined me from the scullery, crushed me in his arms, murmuring, "Oh, Jessie, I can hardly wait. This is torture." Held tightly like that there was no way I could reply, which was just as well.

Well, tonight I would sleep in that bed in Paisley under the snowy cover, my head on the lace-edged pillow with Sandy by my side. There was no help for it. Lilias jumped down chattering,

"While you were still sleeping I laid out all my things on the other bed beside Maisie's. If you get up I'll make your bed and we can spread your things there. Mam says you're to come down to breakfast in your shawl, then Dougie will carry up cans of hot water for us. Dougie was up early. He's been singing."

Of course Dougie would be singing and Maisie too, for Dougie had sprung the most wonderful surprise on us all. Only Sandy had been in on the secret. It was like this. There was an old cottage in Oakshaw Street near the John Neilson School which had been empty for two years. The factor was offering it at quite a low rent but though a lot of people, including Dougie, it seems, had looked at it they had backed off when they found what a dreadful state of disrepair it was in. Well, Dougie had mentioned this to Sandy who suggested that he and Dougie should go and have another look at it together. Sandy poked and prodded and took notes while Dougie waited patiently. Then at the end Sandy said, "This is what I make of it, Dougie. If you brought in a firm of builders, these are the figures on that side."

"But it's rented property," Dougie said.

"Hear me out," Sandy said slowly. (He can be maddening at times.)

"If we did it ourselves," resumed Sandy, "bringing in a bit of help and taking a long time, of course, we could do it for that. A big difference in price, is it no'? I suggest you go to this factor, tell him to inform his client that you are willing to take this derelict property off his hands for thirty-five pounds. He'll maybe beat you up to fifty. I think it would be worth it. With all that ground you could build a bigger house later." Dougie had taken his advice and their wedding was now planned for Hogmanay.

The thought of Dougie and Maisie lifted my spirits. The other brides in the family had looked happy in their new state, I told myself. It couldn't be so awful. Everyone fussed round me that morning as if I were the lady of the manor who wasn't to soil her dainty fingers. Dougie brought Maisie up from the station and in no time at all we had to start the elaborate business of dressing. Maisie was invaluable — happy and excited but controlled; firm enough, too, to put Lilias in her place when excitement started going to her head.

"I hope Nancy is in time," Lilias said. "We're nearly ready."

"Don't worry," Maisie's voice was calm, "her mother will make sure of that."

"I hope Bella gets Sandy up in time." Lilias was taking her responsibilities seriously.

"If Bella doesn't, your little niece will," Maisie assured her. Turning to me she said, "This is one morning I think Sandy will be eager to get up." I blushed at her knowing wink.

Nancy arrived in plenty time and as the bell started we formed our procession to brave the good wishes of those who were not already in the church before us. As usual at a local wedding every pew was crammed. The organ started, Faither blew his nose, I swallowed the lump in my throat and then we were walking slowly down the aisle. I heard the soft whispers, the murmured oohs and aahs, but I kept my eyes on the two figures who stood, very still facing the communion table. The sun glinted on Sandy's hair. Dougie had tried to flatten his, but a few rebellious curls were curving at the back of his ears. The silk of my dress swished excitingly. It was a long walk and must have seemed longer to Sandy but he waited till I was only a few yards away before turning. I'll never forget the look in his eyes, near to worship; something to treasure for the rest of my days.

Faither gave us a wee bow, then took his place beside Mam in the front pew. Lilias moved round, as Doctor Graham had suggested, to where she could see us both. "It's a pity for her not to see you take your vows," he said. I was aware of her dark wondering eyes as Sandy took my trembling hand in his big, firm grasp. Our voices seemed to come from very far away in the hushed stillness; then we were signing the register; then out in the sunshine again with hundreds of people milling about, intent on giving me their good wishes.

Dougie gave a lovely speech at my

wedding. I've never heard a finer. It's impossible now to tell you just how he put things but just when he had us all nearly in tears he would work in something funny and have us all laughing again. He made a lot of Lilias, of course, how she was an auntie now and he had to treat her with respect. Then he told her a story she had never heard before, of my jealousy when she was born and how it had soon melted and how I had been like a little mother to her. He teased her about all the things he had had to do for her but of course ended up telling her what a treasure she had proved to be to us all and praising her for the part she had played in the wedding.

When the dancing started Sandy and I danced the first waltz alone for a little while with everyone applauding before they joined in. As it ended Dougie said he had an announcement to make. It was traditional for the bride to go off and remove her headdress after the first waltz, he said, but if Jessie would just sit down for a moment where everyone could see her, she would hear something to her advantage. Sandy muttered something to him and they both laughed. Then Maisie made her way to the piano. Tears sprang to my eyes as soon as they started to sing Tannahill's lovely words, 'Jessie, the Flower o' Dunblane.' Maisie had made a special arrangement of it for them. Her soprano, Sandy's tenor and Dougie's baritone had never seemed so lovely to me as in that tribute. Of course everyone applauded madly at the end though there were a few hankies out. You know, I can still hear it, note for note, and it always makes me cry. I think it will, now, till the end of my days.

Maisie whisked me away to get my headdress off and tidy my hair. After that the dancing really got under way. The drink was flowing of course and some of the solos rendered unexpectedly were not quite what we would have requested but it was a perfect wedding — perfect, that is, but for Elsie. We were waved off at eight o'clock. Of course Sandy found a few tricks had been played on him — but apart from a missing collar stud which made his neck rather uncomfortable he was not grumbling. We climbed the stairs slowly. I found myself counting the pipe clay markings as we got nearer our 'wee nest' and wishing I was safely back in Kilbarchan with Lilias's warm little body waiting for me instead of . . . what?

We were surprised to find a fire burning brightly in the range, a dish of flowers on the table and a note from Mrs McFarlane,

Welcome to your own wee home. I got the messages you asked for. They are all in the scullery with a wee scone or two I baked. It was getting chilly so I lit the fire. All the joy in the world and blessings on the pair of you.

Jean McFarlane

I drew thankfully towards the fire while Sandy, without saying a word, went to the scullery and put on a kettle.

"You would like a cup of tea?" he asked.

"Aye," was all I could manage.

"You've no' to worry, Jessie, my love. I'll be gentle with you."

"Aye, Sandy." I shivered in spite of the lovely fire. He made to put his arm round me then withdrew to the scullery door, cracking his knuckles till the kettle boiled. The marriage I had looked forward to so eagerly was now a trap. I was Mrs Sandy Forbes; we were to be one flesh — it said so in the Bible — and all I wanted to be was Dougie's wee sister.

On a fine May morning about three weeks later I woke early to the croo-croo of the pigeons on the scullery window sill. A soft deep breathing told me Sandy was still asleep. I turned carefully towards him and studied his marble face. One eyebrow ruffled by the pillow, stood up like a coxcomb, giving an incongruous air of surprise to his calm wide brow. I longed to trace the outline of his curving mouth which, even in sleep, seemed ready to break into the smile which melted my heart. My heart, Yes! — but not my body. Sandy was hurt and disappointed at my inability to surrender. During these three weeks he had wooed me gently and caressingly, coaxing my body to respond to his mounting ardour but I always tensed up with pain and he desisted. The strain was telling on him,

I knew. The night before, instead of his gentle kiss and 'never mind, lass', he had pushed me away, muttering, "It's hopeless." Turning his back on me he pummelled his pillow till we were both coughing. Later when I was letting my tears drop unheeded I felt a movement beside me. The bed was shaking steadily. I was horrified. Sandy was doing *that*.

A hot flush of shame spread over me. Sandy was a fine man — as good as any going. It was the strain of my refusals that had brought him to . . . I could not finish the thought. "I'm your husband," he'd said to me time and time again when I'd hidden behind the big chair to undress. "We're supposed to be one flesh, yet I've never seen you uncovered. I'd be gentle, my wee love, you know that.

And, of course, he had been, I told myself as I edged quietly out of bed, opened the heavy kitchen curtains and made my way to the scullery. Two pigeons rose fluttering as I held the kettle under the tap but they settled down reassured as I turned to place it on the gas ring. I stepped out of the scullery and stood watching the pair from just inside the kitchen. The cock bird strutted the length of the sill and back several times while the female uttered her soft croo-croo but turned her head away at his approach. 'Just like me,' I thought. 'He's getting nowhere.' The kettle began to sing and I made to reach it, but stopped in my tracks at the mad flutter of wings as the two birds joined.

With water hissing and spitting all over me I belatedly filled the teapot. Something had happened to me as I watched the mating, a quivering, an awareness, a desire that overruled all Mam's injunctions on modesty. I wanted Sandy to want me and be triumphant like the pigeon. I jerked my head, swinging my gold plaits impatiently. Things would be different, he'd see! With trembling hands I lifted the tray and entered the kitchen. Sandy greeted me, propped up on one elbow.

"I've been admiring the scenery."

"Scenery?" I turned to the lace curtains and the speckled view of the tenements behind us.

"The sun was shining through your nightgown."

I flushed crimson. Then quickly laying the tray on the table I whipped off the snowy cotton and let it drift to the floor.

★ ★ ★

I was half awake. Sandy was nuzzling my shoulder as I lay cradled in his lap. Drowsily I listened to the far-off sound of a church bell. A church bell! I groaned, "We're late for the kirk, Sandy."

"Aye, they'll have to manage without us this morning."

"What will folks say?" My voice still dragged with sleep.

"They say. What say they? Let them say." Sandy was perfectly calm.

"You don't care, do you?" I murmured.

"Not too much."

I wriggled and settled myself more comfortably. "What if someone steps by after the service to see why we weren't there. What will we say?"

"We'll not be here. I've got a grand idea. I'm going to bring you tea, my

471

lady; then we'll get ourselves dressed, we'll pull up the bed, make up some pieces with cheese and we'll walk all the way up over the Braes to Kilbarchan."

"But I'd need to wear my old boots for that . . . on a Sunday," I protested.

"Who's going to see them? The guid folk are all in the kirk. Your family have seen you in old boots afore." Sandy's arms were tightening round me, his body pressing against mine. "Come on," he said, "a wee kiss afore I mask the tea."

My body reminded me vividly of that morning's work, but it was not a tremulous girl who turned towards him, not any longer. Now I was a fulfilled woman, happily resigned to the fact that 'a wee kiss' was unlikely to end at that!

19

THE week that followed was the finest gift I could wish for any lass; a joy that seeped through every task no matter how dull; the longing that made me listen for the jangling of his keys as he ran upstairs two at a time in his eagerness to get home. It had been arranged that I would move to Bella's the following Saturday just in case the baby arrived early. In the first few weeks of marriage I had guiltily begun to look on this as an escape, a chance to be myself again. Every time I thought of it now, I clung fiercely to Sandy. He comforted me in his lovely calm way and then threw in a bit of teasing. "If you couldn't do with a rest, I could!" — a statement he disproved very satisfactorily soon afterwards.

Arthur and Bella were glad to see me. I heard Arthur thanking Sandy for sparing me. "I'll slip over as often as I can," Sandy said.

"Aye, do that," Arthur clapped him on

the shoulder. I saw their shared look of understanding and felt my body tingle.

Lizbet was delighted to have Auntie Jessie to play with. She was such an easy child to manage that I was able to order Bella to put her feet up and leave everything to me. Jean came over to inspect us on the Monday morning bearing a large bundle of towels.

"You'll be needing extra," she said. "You'll manage fine, Jessie, then?"

"Aye, I'll be fine, Jean," I assured her, "Maybe afterwards when I'm busy wi' the bairn . . . "

"Aye, aye," she agreed eagerly. "I'll gi'e ye a haun'."

When Bella and I were sharing a cup of tea later she said, "D'you know, I'm surprised that Jean didn't insist on coming. Faither could spare her. Things are that quiet."

"She can't stand the sight of blood," I said. "She fainted the day Lilias was born."

"I never knew that!" Bella was amazed. "Fancy Jean being afraid of anything."

"That's why she's never had a bairn. It was Dougie told me. Then I asked

Meg about it later. Seemingly it was when you were born — Jean would be eight then. She had been around the house, remember, at quite a few births by that time and knew that the babies mysteriously appeared. She had noticed the washings, the sheets in pink water and things like that. It so happened that Faither had been sharpening the big steel knife on the stone that morning and had put it on the shelf above the sink when he was finished. He must have been called away or something because he usually kept it in its slotted box. Anyway, Jean had hurried into the kitchen to fetch something and there was Nurse Duncan getting ready to deal with the afterbirth, her hands covered in blood and the big knife on the shelf. She thought Nancy Duncan had had to do something awful to Mam to get the baby and she went off in a dead faint. Poor Nurse had quite a time, trying to get herself cleaned up, attend to Jean and get Meg to look after Elsie and Dougie so Mam wouldn't hear anything. Of course she learned the right way o' things later but the damage had been done. After that she could never bear the sight of blood."

"Funny I've never heard anything about it," said Bella.

"Never say a word," I warned her. "Jean will come over and work like a fiend once the blood-stained sheets and towels are out of the way. Then you and I will put our feet up."

"I won't be sorry to get rid of this lump," Bella said. "The wee deil's been kicking me all day and I canna sit comfy no matter how I turn."

"Well, you've less than a week to go," I said.

At midnight that night I found just how much less. I woke with Bella groaning, then I heard Arthur's voice. He would not be dressed so I couldn't go through. Lizbet was in her little bed beside mine, as Lilias once had been, and sleeping peacefully. The groans were getting louder. I lit my candle and dressed quickly. My hair was still in plaits when I heard their door open and Arthur's steps approaching my room. He was startled when I opened up before his knock.

"I'm not sure," he started quietly. "She says she thinks it's quicker this time but she's maybe just getting excited."

"Stir up the fire and get the kettles on," I said. "I'll see whether we need the nurse."

I remembered Dougie's words, "She'll squeal like a stuck pig." Lizbet's birth had been quick for a first baby, or so Nurse Duncan had said though it seemed ages to me. A second baby could be quicker. Arthur thought Bella might be getting excited; if he went for the nurse I would be alone with her, and she could get hysterical and frighten Lizbet. How could I cope with a birth if a terrified toddler was screaming? I would have to control Bella: how could I best do that? Only a stranger's voice would do, when she was in that state. I would imitate Nurse Duncan. I was going to have to call on my memories of Nurse Duncan anyway. It was a good thing she was such a bletherer. During Lizbet's birth I had had a running commentary. At the time I had been glad of it, only because it stopped my sick trembling. Over our cups of tea later I had ventured to ask what would happen if the baby arrived quickly before the nurse or doctor. "Well, a quick birth's usually an easy birth," she had said, "and it's best not to interfere. You'll have sent for help, of course. You heard me warning Bella not to sit up till the afterbirth was well clear. That cord must not be severed. You would put the afterbirth higher than the bairn, on the mother's belly; see that its wee throat is clear for breathing and wipe its wee eyes. Keep the room warm, of course, and lay some warm flannel over the baby. Of course, in a dire emergency with no help coming . . . "

She had gone on to explain the more advanced procedures but I did not choose to think of that as I started to calm Bella. I had realized immediately I saw her that things *were* happening quickly. Arthur had run off to ring Dick's bell and then hurry on to Nurse Duncan's. Dick would dress and get the coach out and follow. With a bit of luck Nurse Duncan would be ready to leave by then. She said she left her bag packed every night, just in case . . . It could be done in thirty-five minutes, we had reckoned. Those thirty-five minutes were going to be the longest in my life.

"I've shut both doors," I said, "but if you could just keep a wee bit quieter for Lizbet's sake . . . We don't want to wake her."

"Oh, Jessie, you don't know what you're talking about," she groaned.

"Oh, yes I do, m'lady." My voice was a pretty firm imitation of Nurse Duncan's. "You're well on now, doing fine. You will listen to me and do exactly as I tell you. Nurse Duncan explained everything to me . . . right!"

Wiping her forehead and murmuring soothingly I managed to achieve a few moments of calm for her between the racking pains. But the moments became fewer as the mighty contractions tore at her; then she gave an agonized scream and I was staring at an avalanche of blood and tissue from which emerged a hesitant, then an indignant cry.

"Now, lie back, Bella," I warned. "It's a wee girl and her lungs are nearly as good as yours. I'll be lifting her carefully with the afterbirth, see . . . I'll clean her up as well as I can, then I'll see to you."

The outside door banged open and

footsteps sounded on the stair. "It's Arthur," Bella said with relief.

"He can't come in till I've cleaned you up," I said firmly. Opening the door a crack I told him Bella was fine, he had another lovely wee daughter and would he make us a nice big pot of tea. Soon we heard the carriage wheels and a few minutes later Nurse Duncan was on the landing, talking as usual.

"My, my, my, Mrs Clark was in a hurry this morning."

It was only then that my hands started shaking. While Bella, all smiles, was listening to Nancy Duncan's congratulations as she cut the cord and mopped up the baby I was biting my lip hard to stop bursting into tears, the frightened tears of the childhood. What if the baby had been born dead. What if something awful had happened to Bella? What if Lizbet had wakened, frightened by the screams? What if . . . ? It was a relief when the nurse announced that mother and child were fit to receive visitors.

"Tell Arthur to bring his wife up a nice big cup of tea with a spoonful of whisky in it. We'll have ours downstairs by the fire."

My hands were still trembling as I crouched, suddenly cold, by the fire and tried to lift the heavy cup. "Here, here, lass." Nancy Duncan was all concern. "You've had a fright — I didna' think . . . You looked that calm. Did she make a lot o' noise?" I nodded. "You've no' to worry about that. Most o' them shout when they're feart o' the pain. Then by the next day they're quite jocose. You would think they had never made a murmur. Bella's excitable but she's a real good wee mother, kens just what a bairn needs — food, love and a wee bit o' fun. Now what you need is a nice drop of whisky and then you could maybe make a wee bit of toast . . . I expect Arthur and Bella could do with a bite."

It was the first time I had noticed any similarity between Nurse Duncan and Jean. A few words in Jean's sharp tongue sent us scurrying in a crisis. Nurse Duncan's formula was wrapped up in gentle encouragements but it came to the same in the end: 'Keep her too busy to think'. The toast tasted good.

Arthur and Bella munched theirs like weans at a Sunday school party. It was warm work by the fire and when I sat back, replete, in Arthur's big chair, my hands had stopped trembling.

"Well, I'll be getting along now," Nancy Duncan said. "Dick said he would sit up and be ready to take me back. Just you have a nice wee doze by the fire while Arthur sits up there, then you could put a pig in your bed and sleep till Lizbet gets you up. Bella has the cradle right beside her and kens what to dae."

Early the next morning she relayed word of the new arrival to Mam and Faither before Dougie left for Paisley. He told the Wilsons at lunch time. Mrs Wilson made a point of finding out where Sandy was working and passed on the news to him. And so that night I was in his arms. "Mrs Wilson said the bairn arrived when you were all by yourself," he said.

"Aye, I'm a midwife now," I murmured.

"Was it awful, love?"

"Aye." My lips were pressed into his neck. "She squealed like a stuck pig an' I was feart Lizbet would wake . . . " Tears overcame me. Sandy rocked me in his arms, making the bed creak.

"Sandy," I said, "They'll be thinking . . . "

"Aye, so they will," he said, kissing me gently. "Oh, my wee love, I canna bear to think of you going through that yet. We'll have to take care . . . Maybe we'll have been lucky . . . "

Reflecting on the previous week's work, I knew we would have to be gey lucky indeed. The sleep of sheer exhaustion soon overcame me but a few hours later I woke gradually. Sandy seemed half asleep, too, but our bodies were moulded as one and a gentle creaking had begun in the bedsprings. By morning I knew that it was unlikely that my luck could last through all that provocation.

I soon knew that I was pregnant. Sandy groaned when I confirmed his suspicions. "I had hoped to give you a year to yourself," he said, "but, oh, Jessie, I never knew how difficult it would be . . . "

"Nor how wonderful," I whispered into his ear.

Before I got too bulky we wandered up every night to the cottage in Oakshaw

Street where we were sure to find Dougie and Maisie. Sometimes some of Dougie's senior pupils were there. Clearing Mr Allen's garden had become quite a useful way of getting together in a group for some fun. Sandy, of course, was invaluable in the help he gave. Arthur, too, would tear himself away from his own cottage on a Saturday evening to direct the gardeners and give a hand with any heavy labouring. Once I got too heavy, I would stay at home and make a nice meal for them all.

That particular Saturday towards the end of September showed how the nights were drawing in. There was quite a nip in the air by five o'clock. The soup was simmering nicely; the stew was ready; so was the apple tart. I mashed the potatoes and put the tureen at the side of the hob to keep warm. Daylight was going. I heard steps on the stairs and ran to open the door. It was Sandy and Maisie. "Where's Dougie?" I asked.

"He's coming; another ten minutes," Sandy said. "One of his pupils is giving him back a book he had on loan. Dougie's picking it up in Moss Street."

So we waited and waited. Six o'clock struck; the potatoes were dried and grey. The soup had been thinned five times and the stew was like leather. Then we heard hurried steps on the stairs.

"That'll be him," said Maisie, hurrying to the door.

"No, no . . . it's not his step," I said.

Sandy gave me quick look, then hurried to overtake Maisie. I listened carefully to the breathless young voice but could not make out the words. Sandy's reply was inaudible too but somehow I knew something was wrong even before Maisie started screaming. The boy who helped Sandy support her was chalk-white and gabbling furiously, "I just knew it was Causeyside Street but that was all, then my faither said, 'Ask in all the shops round about for Mr Forbes, the plumber'. Faither was going to the hospital with Mr Allen but the doctor said it was too late. The wee boy had tackety boots. Mr Allen was struck on the temple. They would take him straight to the mortuary."

The boy started sobbing. I tried to scream but not a sound would come. Sandy looked helplessly at us all. Then a terrible pain tore me. I doubled up shouting, "No, not Dougie, no, no, *no!*" Sandy left Maisie to put his arm round me. He spoke almost cruelly to the terrified lad, "Knock on the doors on the landing."

It was Mrs McFarlane who led the three. "Dear me, it's no' your time, Jessie, is it?" she said anxiously.

Sandy spoke quickly, "Jessie's brother has been killed saving a wean that fell from a window."

"Greater love," said Mrs McFarlane automatically, then turning to Miss Thomson said, "Get wee Jim from downstairs to fetch the doctor. Jessie shouldna' be getting this."

"Jessie, Jessie, Jessie," Maisie shouted savagely. "It's always Jessie. She comes first in everything. We have to wait for years but Jessie can get everything she wants. She's got her man and her bairn . . ."

Mrs McFarlane hurried towards her. "Willie, give me a hand through wi' her to oor hoose."

The McFarlanes disappeared with Maisie still shouting and laughing raucously. Silent sobs were pulling me apart. Then I heard my voice through the sobs. "Not Dougie — he's strong — he's getting married at Hogmanay — not Dougie . . . not tackety boots, just a pair of tackety boots . . . no . . . *no*"

Through my tears I could see that Sandy's face had gone green. Sweat was dripping from his forehead as he lifted me up to the bed. So it must be true. Dougie was gone. My lovely Dougie who called me his wee champion — and all because of tackety boots. Dougie who was so clever, the first MA, BSc in Kilbarchan, killed by a silly pair of tackety boots.

Sandy was trying to calm me, patting my hand and wiping my forehead. "Jessie, Jessie," was all he could say as I sobbed on.

Then the doctor was there. He tried to speak to me. I can't remember what he said. I kept thinking of these tackety boots and what they had done to Dougie. Then he was asking Sandy to help hold me steady while he gave me an injection. I hardly noticed what they were doing. Their voices retreated. They were over by the scullery, talking. Then the doctor came back and took my pulse again. I shut my eyes. I didn't want to see anybody but Dougie. I heard him say to Sandy, "That should keep her quiet for a few hours. I daren't give her any more because of the bairn. If she could just calm down a wee bit . . . see what you can do because if this goes on, she'll lose the bairn." I didn't want the bairn I just wanted Dougie. Clouds of merciful sleep overcame me then.

Before I was properly awake I was crying though I didn't know why. Then memory returned and I cried out. Sandy was in the big chair with a blanket round him and the fire going. He staggered as he rose. "What is it, Jessie?"

"What is it?" I repeated despairingly. "I've lost Dougie, my lovely Dougie."

"But you've the bairn to think of, Jessie. You've got to keep calm for its sake."

"It's Dougie I want, no' the bairn," I said.

"Now, now, lass, what would Dougie have said if he heard you say that?"

I can remember feeling angry then.

How dared Sandy tell me what Dougie would say. He didn't understand how special our relationship was, how he had taught me all the birds' songs and showed me where they made their nests . . . the walks he had taken me those long summer days when I was wee . . .

Pain and indignation had me in their grip. I cast aside his hand and cried bitterly. Then suddenly I shouted as a cramping pain hit me. It seemed to tear right through from my back to my stomach, leaving me sick and helpless.

"Lassie, what's wrong?" Sandy was desperate.

"It was a pain," I gasped.

"I'll fetch Mrs McFarlane," he said.

"No, don't leave me." I was suddenly terrified of being alone. I lay spent and shivering with fever while the tears ran unheeded. Sandy started talking softly, assuring me that Mrs McFarlane had told him just to ring her bell if he was at all worried and Willie would fetch the doctor. "You'll be all right, lass," he kept saying. "We'll all look after you."

I got a little warning the second time and grabbed Sandy's hand as I cried

TS17

out. I could see he looked terrible. It was all a nightmare. Sandy waited till I was quiet again, then slipped away quickly. He was soon back, leaving the door open for Mrs McFarlane. In a few minutes I heard footsteps hurrying down the stairs. That would be Willie. Then I groaned as the pain tore at me again. Sandy gripped my hand tight just as Mrs McFarlane hurried in.

"I doot . . . I doot," she said as she saw me. "We'll have a cup of tea anyway."

I didn't want tea. I just wanted peace, a long long peace. But Jean McFarlane coaxed me to sip the hot sweet tea and munch a little bit of sponge cake, just to keep my strength up. I had no sooner finished than I was doubled up in pain, terrible pain that I knew must mean the baby was on its way. Then the doctor was there. The pain was unbearable. I screamed and wanted to shout but I hadn't the strength. It just went on and on till I was in darkness. Sometimes it was the doctor's face that swam into view; sometimes it was Sandy, his face white and half its size.

I lost the bairn, and seemingly I was

so ill that the doctor shook his head over me, too. I can remember Sandy raising me up in the bed and putting his arms round me. "Oh, Jessie," he said, "last week at this time I was preparing to lose you." I had no idea of the time. Daylight came and went. Mrs McFarlane would be coaxing me to 'try a wee scone'. Jean would appear, her nostrils pinched the way they do. She cleaned and cleaned that range till I was surprised there was any of it left. And Nancy Stevenson was with me a lot. I asked her once, "Should you not be at work?" and she said, "There's nae work, Jessie, and Jean said it would be a kindness if I could bide wi' you while Sandy is at work."

"I just can't believe it, Nancy," I said, "how Kilbarchan has changed. Remember what it was like when we were young — everybody busy and the lovely wee gardens and the young apprentices meeting round the trough for a bit of nonsense . . ."

"Aye, and threatening to throw a lass in if they thought they could frighten her. And remember when they were building the school and you used to bring Lilias, the wee pet? We used to watch you and Sandy, how the pair of you blushed. It was funny. And now you're an old married woman and we hardly ever see you in Kilbarchan."

"Well, we've all been so busy with — " I stopped, thinking of the cottage in Oakshaw Street. Then I went on, "Anyway, I find it depressing now when I go back, Nancy. Everything has happened so quickly ... All these houses empty and poverty everywhere."

"Well, with the weaving trade, the whole family is thrown out of work, Jessie. In Paisley you might find that one son is an engineer, another a coalman, a daughter working in the thread mills and another in a shop. Kilbarchan just depended on the weaving entirely. Folks saved up for their looms and their houses and now nobody will buy them ... Everything's gone."

"Dougie used to warn Faither," I said. "They were aye fightin' about it. Dougie said the shawl trade couldna' last. It vexed me to hear them quarrelling."

"But your Faither was proud of the way Dougie argued with him."

"Who told you that?" I was flabber-gasted.

"All the weavers knew. Sometimes that fellow wi' the flute . . . "

"Michael Dick."

"Aye, that's him. Well, he liked a good argument. The men would see him wink at your Faither before he set Dougie off. My Faither said the young lad could keep his end up. But you're right, Jessie, everything's changed. There's six o' our school chums away to Australia . . . I wouldn't like that, would you?"

"Too many snakes."

Nancy looked at me in horror. "I never knew they had snakes there."

"I wouldn't worry," I said. "Patty McPhee will put the fear of death in them."

We both laughed and suddenly I realized it was the first time I'd laughed since Dougie died.

"I wonder what kind of houses they'll live in," Nancy said. "You've such a braw hoose, Jessie. Would you no' like to get dressed for Sandy gettin' in?"

"I'm too tired," I said.

"I would help you," Nancy urged.

"Something nice and warm. It's November tomorrow, mind."

"November?" I said. It didn't make sense.

"You've been ill, Jessie, but you're getting better. It would be nice for Sandy to see you up and dressed. He's that worried . . . "

"Dougie's gone, Nancy . . . my lovely big brother . . . "

"Aye, but you've still got your lovely man, Jessie, and there'll be other bairns. He's that gentle and kind. Jessie you're a lucky lass."

Even in my dull state I detected a wee note of envy in her voice. I think it was that more than anything else that made me take the first step to what was a slow recovery. My legs were like spindles. Nancy said it would be daft putting on corsets when I had nothing to hold in. She coaxed and cajoled me till I was dressed then took my first trembling steps and was seated in the big chair by the fire when Sandy came in. His face lit up when he saw me out of bed.

"I bullied her," Nancy said.

"Good for you," he said, laying his hand on her shoulder. I am ashamed to say I resented that. I was to be the only one in the world for Sandy. Isn't that awful? I had been surrounded by kindness and had accepted it without gratitude. All I wanted was Dougie and Dougie would never look proudly at his wee sister again. I'm ashamed of myself but that's the way it was. Resentment got me on my feet. Sandy said it was grand to taste my cooking again and, on the surface, things seemed to ease gradually back to normal.

But underneath there were dark areas. I could not speak of the baby I had lost and dreaded the thought of Sandy bringing the subject up. Maisie's hatred was another thing I could not come to terms with. We had seemed in some ways closer than sisters. I had aided and abetted them in their early meetings and felt myself loved by both of them. And then . . . I had missed Dougie's funeral . . . my Dougie, and I was not with him to the end! The tears would overcome me whenever I got to this stage in my thinking. Often it would happen in bed and Sandy would take me in his arms to comfort me but any gentle attempts at lovemaking left me unmoved. Sandy thought it was because my body had suffered so much with the miscarriage but it was a numbness of the spirit, not a tenderness of the body that held me back.

Sandy had lost weight and was looking older. I knew this was because of me but could not help myself. Hogmanay was approaching. Hogmanay that would have been the culmination of all Dougie and Maisie's hopes; Hogmanay that we had all looked forward to so eagerly. As I dragged myself round the automatic routine of housework I tried to forget Maisie's angry screams and accusations. I had not seen her since that dreadful night nor had anyone lifted her name.

It was the last week of the year. We had finished our dinner and were sitting in the big chairs beside the fire with our cups of tea. I had seen Sandy make as if to speak to me several times but change his mind. Finally he laid his cup down in the hearth and leaned forward. "What do you want to do on Hogmanay, lass?"

"Go to Dougie's wedding," I cried. The floodgates opened and I wept loudly for Dougie who was gone, for Maisie who hated me, for the wee bairn I had lost and didn't dare think about and for the sweet summer of our love that had vanished. Sandy crossed quickly and took me into his arms. I sobbed on his comfortable shoulder. He rocked me gently, patting my back and murmuring endearments. "This'll do you good, you know, the shock has made you bottle things up . . . Get rid of it, lass . . ."

"Maisie hates me," I gulped.

"Never, never, lass. Never think that. Maisie loved you like a sister. Dougie kept her waitin' too long . . . till it was too late. She's lost everything, lass. Pity her."

"I've never seen her since . . ."

"No. She lost everything, lass, including her reason. She wouldna' eat and then she wouldna' wash and one morning Mrs Wilson found her crawling about the floor like a crab. After that the doctor said there was nothing else for it: she would have to go to the asylum. The papers were signed when Mrs Wilson's cousin turned up from somewhere away up in the north. Mrs Wilson had written telling her there would be no wedding and what a sad state Maisie was in. Seemingly the old wife's kind of eccentric. She was a schoolmistress but when she retired she bought a wee croft. She's daft on animals, takes in injured birds and mends them, that sort of thing. I think she sees Maisie as just that, an injured animal. She got the man on the next croft to look after her crew, then she got lifts from one carter to another and finally got herself to Paisley. She only stayed one night; got them to bundle up some clothes for Maisie and took her off. She said the animals would mend her."

"Have they heard . . . ?" I asked.

"They got to the croft safely and I think that was all that was worrying her parents. Mrs Wilson is exhausted."

"So Maisie never got to his funeral either?" I asked.

"No, lass."

"You were there, Sandy?" I asked.

"Aye, of course I was there. But I was desperate to get back to you."

"Tell me about it, Sandy," I pressed.

Sandy was very reluctant. "It would only upset you, lass," he said hesitantly. "I've got to know, Sandy, even if it does upset me." Sandy looked at me doubtfully before he began. "Well, it was the usual wee service in the house. Everybody was greetin'. Even Doctor Graham was feeling it. He kept clearing his throat. The only one that never moved a muscle was your Jean. It was kind of chilling to watch her — her face smaller than ever, chalk white except for a bit pink under the eyes. The undertaker's men had put a trestle out at the gate. They carried the coffin out ready for us to lift for the walk round to the kirk yaird. The street was packed. A bairn started to greet and its mother hushed it. Your mother and the lassies came to the door. Their heads were bowed and their hankies up. Only Jean stood among them, stiff as a stooky, not a tear on her face. Tam and your faither had the first lift. I was right behind Tam. We had just lifted the box off the trestle when there was the most awful sound. Oh, Jessie, I canna' describe it right but it made my blood run cold . . . It came again and again, something between a scream and a bark, like a fox caught in a trap. It was your Jean. Her body jerked every time this sound tore out o' her. Tam turned, looking near demented. Then that big coarse farmer — "

"Rab?" I asked.

"Aye, that's it, Rab. He just shouldered Tam out of the way and said, 'See to your wife, man. I'll see to Dougie.' Tam looked at the minister. He nodded and we all stepped out. I heard someone saying, 'Let Nurse Duncan through'."

All of a sudden I started to laugh. Sandy was upset. "I should never have told you, lass," he said.

I tried to speak. "Don't you think Dougie would have la — ha — ha — ghed? Big coarse Rab shoving Tam out of the way . . . ?" I laughed uncontrollably. Sandy was not sure whether to join me or to stop me.

"What happened to Jean?" I asked when I quietened down.

"Nurse Duncan said it was a case for the doctor. He came and gave her something to make her sleep. D'you know, Tam told me when we came back to the house that Jean doted on Dougie — nobody ever had a wee brother like hers."

"But she was always getting on to him," I started.

"Aye. I know that. It seems she was feart he would get cocky. Big Rab spoke then. He said, 'Aye, there's plenty used to say he was cocky but I aye tellt them, That lad's got plenty to be cocky aboot, no' like some bluidy fools I ken. That aye shut them up."

Sandy had given a fair imitation of Rab's voice. I found myself smiling, though the thought of Dougie being cocky was an alien one to me. "He was only a few feet away from the minister at the time," Sandy added.

"And Jean . . . " I prompted. "What happened then?"

"She was in bed at the cottage for three days."

"Poor Mam," I said.

"Aye, poor Mam," he agreed. "She was worried enough about you. Meg had to get back to her bairns and Bella, too, had her hands full most of the time. And to see Jean of all people laid up . . . I gather Jean had seldom had a day's illness in her life. But it's amazing how your Mam managed. Lilias stayed off school and was a great wee help. The neighbours were kind, of course. Maybe being needed was the best thing for her at that time."

"Oh, Sandy, she's lost her only son. She'll never get over that." I threw myself into his arms at the thought. Sandy just said, "Aye," and patted me gently. A sudden hunger came over me. I clung to him fiercely, pressing myself against him. "Love me, Sandy," I cried.

"Are you sure?" He was bewildered by my suddenness.

"Aye, sure, sure," I urged him.

There was little loving, only a mad hunger in the demands I made on him time and time again that night. The morning found us both exhausted but the crisis was over. The dark submerged thoughts had been brought to the surface and dissolved in the light.

We went to Kilbarchan on Hogmanay and slept in the room that had been Dougie's. New Year is always a bitter-sweet time, I suppose: remembering what's gone by in the year that's awa' always brings some sadness. Luckily there's usually something to hope for too. Bella was pregnant yet again and seemed to find nothing but amusement in the thought. I was a few days late and confided my hopes in Mam that I too was expecting. "The best cure for a sair heart, lass," she assured me. "Sandy's a fine man. He'll be guid to you."

And of course he was, kind and loving, listening to my 'what might have beens' about Dougie with never the slightest impatience.

Our wee son was born on the first day of September, hale and hearty and with lungs fit for an Italian tenor, as Sandy put it. When I first put him to the breast and felt my body nourishing his, I knew a wonder, a peace and joy that I could never have imagined. All my experience of caring for Lilias came back to me day by day and somehow the repetitiveness of the simple tasks carried its own salve. I found myself singing the songs I had sung to Lilias and realized that singing had disappeared from my life ever since Dougie's death; singing that had been almost as natural as breathing to me.

Meg has managed in twice to see me since the bairn was born. She was kind and encouraging as ever. We've been to Kilbarchan twice and introduced the wee chap to Bella's three — Lizbet, Annie and Jeannie. I don't know when that girl will stop. Sandy teased her and she just said, "The more the merrier," Arthur who has lost a lot of his shyness said, "It's all quite legal, Sandy."

We fixed the christening for today, the first Sunday in October, to get it over while the weather is still mild. Duncan landed on my doorstep on Tuesday morning. I was vexed that he wouldn't see Sandy because he was out on a job till night-time.

"Don't worry about that, Jessie," he said. "Meg saw him on a recent visit. She assures me he is bearing up well in the trials of fatherhood."

"He's happy as a king — " I started, then on honest reflection felt unable to continue. There were times when Sandy looked almost unhappy . . . reflective . . . defeated.

"He's been under a lot of strain, of

course," Duncan said. "And what about Douglas Allen, he looks a sturdy wee chap."

"He's that all right and with lungs to match," I assured him.

"We were particularly happy about the name," he went on.

"That was Sandy's idea," I said. "He should have been after Sandy's father, of course. I didn't want it at first. There will never be another Dougie for me but Sandy said we could call him Allen. It would be a tribute to Dougie and maybe a comfort to Mam and Faither."

"Your Sandy is a fine man, Jessie," he said, "and because of that I shall venture to say something that I hope you won't take amiss, knowing how much Meg and I love you and care about your happiness." I waited for him to go on, having no idea what was coming. "The relationship between you and Dougie was a very special one, a lovely one. When you were born he was at an age when manly protectiveness was stirring in him. You were a beautiful child he could be proud of. You were quick to learn just as he was eager to teach — a born teacher.

You grew up together in happy times when your own father and those round about were prospering. Your childhood was happy and secure and Dougie, your hero, was very much a part of it. Maisie, too, loved you and fostered your music while you were an eager conspirator in the early days of their courtship. All this you know, of course. But perhaps it is difficult for you to see what Sandy had to compete with when he came a-courting. I've used the word 'compete' advisedly. Every man wants the woman he loves to admire him above all others. It is a fact of life, Jessie. Sandy could see what he was up against — your hero-worship of a man who was difficult to fault. The fact that you were so young gave Dougie an excuse to resent Sandy. There was quite a bit of mutual jealousy there."

"But Dougie got over it," I broke in. "He gave Sandy my portrait, framed, as a special present the night before our wedding."

"I know, my dear. Meg says it was his favourite piece of work. You were only ten, I believe. Yes . . . Now I come to the difficult bit. Dougie had grown to respect Sandy and trusted him to care for his precious little sister. Sandy had affection and respect for Dougie. Had Dougie lived, you would have built your respective nests. You would have been happily engrossed with your own young. Affection and understanding would have remained but the dependency would have gone. You would naturally have turned to Sandy more and more. I am venturing now where angels fear to tread. I think Sandy feels that Dougie will always be enshrined in your heart in a way that partly excludes him — young, handsome and perfect for ever. You talk about Dougie a lot, you know. It is understandable but it leaves Sandy helpless. No-one can compete with the dead. Now, Jessie, don't feel I am forbidding you to talk about Dougie — far from it.

"What I feel is that you should try to get it out of your system in a cathartic way. (I expect Dougie taught you the word 'catharsis': a purging.) If you could imagine someone friendly and understanding, a little bit like Meg but a complete stranger to the family;

someone to whom you could confide your innermost thoughts, daft, shameful or maybe downright wicked; someone to whom you could relate everything you remember about Dougie. Perhaps it would be easiest just to tell them piecemeal while you are going about your household tasks. But it might not be a bad idea to start at a given point and put in all the detail you can remember.

"There, now! That's the sermon over. Believe me, Jessie, we want the two of you to be as happy as you deserve. We feel we have been richly blessed ourselves with a love that grows day by day. Will you give my daft idea a try?"

"Aye, Duncan," I said, suddenly shy.

Well, that was Tuesday and I've done a lot of thinking since then. In fact, Duncan's wee sermon has made me take a good hard look at myself and see that I had been so busy thinking of my own heartbreak that I had nothing to spare for Sandy. And, after all, Sandy is the man I chose, the man I vowed to cherish all my days; who's put up with my immature attitudes, waiting patiently for the gift of my body. And now that our happiness should be complete with the birth of our fine healthy son, I've been marring that happiness by my constant talk of what might have been.

Duncan is wise — none more so — and I've made an effort to put his 'wee sermon' into practice. I tried a few times in the next few days but I just kept getting mixed up. The family all came back here today after the christening. Mrs McFarlane had lent me her table to add to mine. Sandy took some bearers out of the kitchen bed and stretched them between two chairs for extra seating. They're all through there, still talking and laughing. I can hear Lilias having a wild time. As soon as the meal was over, Jean chased me through to the parlour bed for a rest. I started to feed Allen and he fell asleep so I put him down and lay back on the pillows myself, trying out Duncan's idea of starting from a fixed point. I've been reliving all my wonderful moments with Sandy, too, and realizing what a lucky lass I am with a man like that. I expect Duncan is right that Dougie would gradually have taken a less important place in my life though it's difficult to imagine that at this stage. But I'll see to it that Sandy knows he's the dearest man in the world to me.

I expect I've missed out a lot of things, but Duncan is right — it does seem to help. And a wee talk I had with Mrs McFarlane one day has helped in a kind of way, too. I had been telling her about Elsie. I can trust her not to gossip. I told her about all the uncertainty, how we don't know whether she is alive or dead. She said, "But, my dear, your sister is in God's hands whether she is in this world or the next. And that goes for your lovely brother, too. So don't fret yourself, lass. Leave things in higher hands."

Twice Sandy has been through but I've pretended I was sleeping. Allen got restless a few minutes ago so I lifted him and started his feed before he could cry and bring Sandy. Dougie has been awfully close to me in all those memories, catching at me in the old way.

But now I'll have to pull myself together. It would never do for Sandy to see me with his ain bonnie bairn at my breast and the slow tears falling for Dougie: Dougie who should be here.

Glossary

Ben	through in (another room)
Braw	fine
Chiel	fellow
Cleik	long iron hook
Cludgie	dry lavatory
Gey	rather (French 'assez')
Gowk	cuckoo
Greet	weep
Hechle	uphill struggle
Hoast	cough
Hippen	baby's napkin
Jocose	cheerful
Keek	peep
Mask	infuse (tea)
Ne'erday	New Year's Day
Peevers	hopscotch
Pig	stone hot-water bottle
Pirn	cone on which yarn is wound
Stent	stretch
Smeddum	courage, spirit
Smout	(smolt) small child
Snell	sharp, keen (weather)

Spiel	a voluble flow of incon-sequential speech
Stishie	disturbance
Tackety	studded
Thole	endure
Wean	weaned child

THE LISTERDALE MYSTERY
Agatha Christie

Twelve short stories ranging from the light-hearted to the macabre, diverse mysteries ingeniously and plausibly contrived and convincingly unravelled.

TO BE LOVED
Lynne Collins

Andrew married the woman he had always loved despite the knowledge that Sarah married him for reasons of her own. So much heartache could have been avoided if only he had known how vital it was to be loved.

ACCUSED NURSE
Jane Converse

Paula found herself accused of a crime which could cost her her job, her nurse's reputation, and even the man she loved, unless the truth came to light.

CLOUD OVER MALVERTON
Nancy Buckingham

Dulcie soon realises that something is seriously wrong at Malverton, and when violence strikes she is horrified to find herself under suspicion of murder.

AFTER THOUGHTS
Max Bygraves

The Cockney entertainer tells stories of his East End childhood, of his RAF days, and his post-war showbusiness successes and friendships with fellow comedians.

MOONLIGHT
AND MARCH ROSES
D. Y. Cameron

Lynn's search to trace a missing girl takes her to Spain, where she meets Clive Hendon. While untangling the situation, she untangles her emotions and decides on her own future.

TIGER TIGER
Frank Ryan

A young man involved in drugs is found murdered. This is the first event which will draw Detective Inspector Sandy Woodings into a whirlpool of murder and deceit.

CAROLINE MINUSCULE
Andrew Taylor

Caroline Minuscule, a medieval script, is the first clue to the whereabouts of a cache of diamonds. The search becomes a deadly kind of fairy story in which several murders have an other-worldly quality.

LONG CHAIN OF DEATH
Sarah Wolf

During the Second World War four American teenagers from the same town join the Army together. Forty-two years later, the son of one of the soldiers realises that someone is systematically wiping out the families of the four men.

THE WILDERNESS WALK
Sheila Bishop

Stifling unpleasant memories of a misbegotten romance in Cleave with Lord Francis Aubrey, Lavinia goes on holiday there with her sister. The two women are thrust into a romantic intrigue involving none other than Lord Francis.

THE RELUCTANT GUEST
Rosalind Brett

Ann Calvert went to spend a month on a South African farm with Theo Borland and his sister. They both proved to be different from her first idea of them, and there was Storr Peterson — the most disturbing man she had ever met.

ONE ENCHANTED SUMMER
Anne Tedlock Brooks

A tale of mystery and romance and a girl who found both during one enchanted summer.

BUTTERFLY MONTANE
Dorothy Cork

Parma had come to New Guinea to marry Alec Rivers, but she found him completely disinterested and that overbearing Pierce Adams getting entirely the wrong idea about her.

HONOURABLE FRIENDS
Janet Daley

Priscilla Burford is happily married when she meets Junior Environment Minister Alistair Thurston. Inevitably, sexual obsession and political necessity collide.

WANDERING MINSTRELS
Mary Delorme

Stella Wade's career as a concert pianist might have been ruined by the rudeness of a famous conductor, so it seemed to her agent and benefactor. Even Sir Nicholas fails to see the possibilities when John Tallis falls deeply in love with Stella.

NURSE ALICE IN LOVE
Theresa Charles

Accepting the post of nurse to little Fernie Sherrod, Alice Everton could not guess at the romance, suspense and danger which lay ahead at the Sherrod's isolated estate.

POIROT INVESTIGATES
Agatha Christie

Two things bind these eleven stories together — the brilliance and uncanny skill of the diminutive Belgian detective, and the stupidity of his Watson-like partner, Captain Hastings.

LET LOOSE THE TIGERS
Josephine Cox

Queenie promised to find the long-lost son of the frail, elderly murderess, Hannah Jason. But her enquiries threatened to unlock the cage where crucial secrets had long been held captive.

THE TWILIGHT MAN
Frank Gruber

Jim Rand lives alone in the California desert awaiting death. Into his hermit existence comes a teenage girl who blows both his past and his brief future wide open.

DOG IN THE DARK
Gerald Hammond

Jim Cunningham breeds and trains gun dogs, and his antagonism towards the devotees of show spaniels earns him many enemies. So when one of them is found murdered, the police are on his doorstep within hours.

THE RED KNIGHT
Geoffrey Moxon

When he finds himself a pawn on the chessboard of international espionage with his family in constant danger, Guy Trent becomes embroiled in moves and countermoves which may mean life or death for Western scientists.